This book should be returned to any branch of the

SKELMERSDALE

09 MAR 2015

FICTION RESERVE STOCK

KNAVE OF
SWORDS

◆ ◆ ◆ ◆ ◆

Nicolas Carter

ORION

Copyright © Nicholas Carter 1998

The right of Nicholas Carter to be identified as the author
of this work has been asserted by him in accordance
with the Copyright, Designs and Patents Act 1988.

First published in Great Britain in 1998 by
Orion
An imprint of Orion Books Ltd
Orion House, 5 Upper St Martin's Lane, London WC2H 9EA

A CIP catalogue record for this book is available
from the British Library.

ISBN 0 75281 009 X

Typeset at The Spartan Press Ltd,
Lymington, Hants
Printed in Great Britain by
Butler & Tanner Ltd
Frome and London

PROLOGUE

*Immaculate
Conceptions*

◆ ◆ ◆ ◆ ◆

Via della Gozzoviglia, Novara, Northern Italy, March, 1519

Fabrizio had made the trap using cheesewire, as fine as a frosted web and as remorseless as a razor. Works of art compared with the rusty mantraps the local hunters left strewn over the hills. It was a wonder of the world their lobster-pot abominations ever caught as much as a one-eyed house sparrow, let alone a sweetly-flavoured lark.

The youth held the featherweight device between his thumb and forefinger, admiring the way the sunlight bathed the raw steel filaments. He carefully inserted his forefinger, watched the wires bend and swell as they caught the light.

A trap fit for an Empress — or a Cardinal, come to that, Fabrizio thought lewdly. He might spark a whole new fashion craze for deadly but ornamental jewellery, he might be commissioned to . . .

'Favio! Fafio!'

The youth started, cautiously removed his forefinger from the trap. He placed it on the cluttered table, pooled with last night's wine and various mice-chewed hunks of bread.

'FABIO!'

The drunken sloth wasn't dead then. Another miracle.

'I'm coming, hold your water!' He stood up, watching his footing amongst the discarded crusts and clutter his master had left behind. Fabrizio bent down and retrieved the berlingozza. It was stale, but it might do for breakfast at a pinch.

'Favio, where are you?' He'd altered his tone this time. Guttural yet pitiful, the sure sign of an old man only too aware his time with a younger one was running critically short.

'I heard you!' Fabrizio called, opening the shutters.

His master was where he had left him, half sprawled over the broken-down couch. It had seated senators and caesars; now it was a broken prop, speckled with Scaralatchi's remarkably vivid vomit. He had spewed over the faded velvet, yawned over the gold leaf ribs, retched over the floor and balcony. The whitewashed wall beneath had also been liberally splattered and was stuck with knots of feeding flies – the bougainvillea pollinated with specks of flying bread, egg and anchovy.

'Favio, a little wine, to clear my head.'

'You drank the lot.' He busied himself lifting any jug or bottle that hadn't been broken from the clutter on the floor.

'Ah, devil take it! The vinegar piss they serve here splits a man's brain in two!'

'Then it is a miracle your brain, *padrone*, is functioning at all.'

Scaralatchi opened one eye and glared at the handsome youth, standing a short way off with his discarded clothing flung over his arm.

'We have a woman for that.'

'You didn't pay her, she left.'

'Then fuck her, and you too, *mia bella giovane*.'

'You tried, once, remember?' Fabrizio replied archly. 'You got down to her drawers and changed your mind.'

Scaralatchi barked and coughed, a grinding, liquid sound somewhere between laughter and vomiting. He threw out his pale legs and slapped his thighs.

'The one with no back to her gown? She was a picture from the rear Favio, but the moustache! I swear on God's books it was bushier than a Bishop's arse!' Fabrizio allowed himself a small smile, threw the gathered clothes onto the couch his master had just vacated.

'Why so early anyway, we're going nowhere?'

4

'You told me you would rise at dawn, and finish it.'

'Pah! I am not a watchmaker! You don't write music at set times like some wretched Venetian mathematician!'

'*Padrone*, you don't write music at all. So we eat slops, drink piss and dismiss the serving woman!'

Scaralatchi waved his chubby arm at his young protégé, slumped back on the couch with a grunt.

'Remind me once more why I share what I have with you,' he growled.

Fabrizio paused, bent down to his shins and lifted the hem of his robe over his smooth brown belly, smiling like the cheapest whore in the street below.

'Enough,' Scaralatchi whimpered. 'Like always, Favio, you make your point . . . admirably well.' The youth abruptly dropped his hem and waved the old man's prying hand away.

'Up and at it. Today you finish the whole work,' he ordered briskly.

'I cannot finish it. How can you write an end without a middle?'

'You over-complicate, as I have told you enough! Everybody knows the popes these days are slower than Germans! You must give them one melody, here,' he trilled a scale, his voice as crystal clear as it had been when he was the leading chorister in the elite Papal Choir. 'You give them bash and bluster and chorus on top of chorus. It is too much for their thick ears!'

Scaralatchi stared at the olive orchard across the road from the run-down pension, digesting the youth's criticisms in sullen silence.

He ran his palm over his tender scalp, still stuck here and there with patches of the stiff black hair which had been the pride of his lost youth. The boy was right, of course. He over-elaborated every work, striving for a perfection beyond the limit of man's comprehension. He closed his eyes, pictured dotted and dashed notes flickering over his eyelids. Silent voices carried the burning notes to the heavens, only for them to fall back to earth like burnt-out matches, forever failing to light up the sky as he hoped.

Cesar Alessandro Scaralatchi, reduced to eking out an existence in this turbulent shit pit! It was enough to make a man weep – every single salt tear a bitter note in his unfinished masterpiece.

He had been lucky, at first. Back when his hair lay as thick as corpses in a plague pit. His dim-witted parents had realised their son showed extraordinary musical ability and had delivered him into the cloying care of the church before he was six years old.

His simple, straightforward arrangements were easy on the ear and had delighted Bishops and Cardinals, moved generals and gentlemen alike. It had been no surprise when he had been called before His Holiness himself, and asked to compose a piece for the sublime Papal Choir.

A commission from the Vatican should have secured his career, made his name for all eternity. But the fabulous promise had been shattered by fortune, his miraculous talents soured by . . . what?

What spirit had invaded his brain, commandeered his heart and driven him to such unnecessary complexities? He had expected the impossible from the tortured boys who attempted to unravel his compositions, worked them until their throats were raw, flayed the notes from their red mouths.

And then he had fallen in love with Fabrizio. The leader of the choir, gifted and tough, energetic and determined, eyes as bold as an eagle in his virgin cassock.

And then . . . and then the rumours.

The breathless, ever more malicious gossip about the unhappy composer and the handsome choirboy. The gossip which drowned out what little music he made, drowned him in a swamp of jealous accusation and gleeful lie. Finally, three years before, Scaralatchi had been denounced as a pederast, humbled and humiliated before a pop-eyed court of pederasts and jesters. The powerful Cardinal Runcini, secretly devoted to Scaralatchi's stunning protégé Fabrizio, had headed the inquiry.

Inquiry? Pah!

Scaralatchi still found it difficult to comprehend how Runcini – one of the most notorious keepers of catamites in the whole of Italy – had dared to order his banishment, this living death of shame and penniless exile. Scaralatchi gazed at the olive orchard opposite, the rich green crowns blowing in the breeze, shimmering silver on their twisted trunks.

'Favio, Favvy . . .'

Where was that damned boy? Out chatting to his new cronies along the street, or perhaps he had taken himself off to the fountain, seen about finding a new patron. He grasped the warm brickwork, held himself steady as his eyes adjusted to the cruel, pounding light.

And then he heard the mockingbird.

The delightful birdsong drifted across from the orchard, a burbling, babbling stream of perfect notes. If only that damned choir could have held such perfect pitch! How could a few lengths of twisted gristle shape such beautiful song? A handful of feathers with jewel eye and jabbing beak, and yet possessed of musical gifts he hadn't dared dream of! Mocking him.

Scaralatchi sobbed, grabbing a bottle from the litter on the floor. He hurled the empty vessel across the road towards the shimmering trees. '*Pestilenza!* Get out of it, you verminous carrion!' he bawled, tears fading into the faded velvet.

The bird in the orchard sang on. A silken cascade climbing and falling.

'You mock me,' he growled, prising himself upright. He lifted a fluted glass from the floor and flung it with all his might towards the olive trees. The singing stopped for a moment, and then broke out anew, fresher, more urgent, more perfect than ever. Damn that bird! Why didn't it fly off? . . . Scaralatchi grinned, filled with a warm satisfaction which clogged his vitals. The wretched thing was caught – trapped in the tree! Fabrizio's doing, no doubt, he was always fiddling with his wires or tying off some noose. The boy had trapped the mockingbird and this was its death song!

As he listened he became aware of a second bird, adding its own voice to the trapped creature's dying song. He leaned over the balcony and spotted it, sitting on a hanging basket two doors down, its yellow, speckled throat stretched taut as it poured a new stream of notes into the superheated afternoon air. Scaralatchi sat back on the couch, listened as the original bird responded to the newcomer. Its own song became more urgent, more plaintive still. Scaralatchi stopped smiling. Listened.

The new bird seemed to be challenging its trapped rival, singing ever more complex melodies in fierce triumph over its doomed cousin. The two birds competed, their song mingling, their urgent melodies forming ever more complex counterpoints.

And Scaralatchi smiled then, because, in one sublime supernova of revelation, he realised he had found the perfect vehicle for his troubled genius. He prised himself up from the couch and staggered into the vulgar room.

'FAVIO!!! Fetch the score, the bloody, bastard score! Fetch my pens, my ink! Favio, where are you boy?'

PART ONE

The Malice of Fortune

◆ ◆ ◆ ◆ ◆

'The Prince who does not detect evils the moment they occur is lacking in wisdom.'

Machiavelli, *The Prince*

Beside Candlewood Keep
in Teviotdale, Scotland

Sandy Kerr's rain-sodden reivers were huddled over their Highland garrons, drenched plaids draped about their shoulders. They were alert enough despite the driving downpour, craning their necks to peer through the squalls, squint at every shadow. The rain had tracked them north, followed them home from the Truce Day down on the border.

Not far now, and they would be back at the tower, warming themselves before a fire and toasting Auld Sandy for cocking a snook at the perfidious Sassenachs.

The reivers emerged at last from the glen, spurred their mounts onto the barren moor beyond. The waste was grey with rain, the cold rocks slick with running water and studded with slowly forming pools. The sparse turf which still managed to cling to the fractured bedrock was swollen with floodwater and turning more treacherous by the moment, hissing and sucking as the Highland ponies followed their noses home across the broad moss.

The slanting showers obscured the few features there were: A gibbet swinging and creaking by the crossroads; a frost-fractured hillside capped with a stand of ancient firs.

Another few miles would see them safe.

Kerr peered ahead, allowed himself a subdued sigh of relief as he made out their slim black tower standing out starkly amidst a girdle of rain-cloaked trees, high on its lonely hill. The road would take them past the crossroads and up around the terraced slopes, the switchbacked silver ribbon cut into the slopes like some crude tattoo.

They had ridden the last ten miles in virtual silence, keeping as keen a watch on their own turf as they had done down on the English Middle March. Kerr had sensed something amiss, sniffed some mischief in the moisture-laden air – and his followers knew better than to question his almost supernatural insights. He had never paid such close attention to the uplands he had made his own, the chattering burns and basilisk outcrops which marked out his hard-won territory. A wilderness of hurt on which humanity had made very little impression.

Auld Sandy rubbed the base of his spine, looked back over his shoulder to make sure the rear markers hadn't dropped their watch, slumped over their saddlebows like tipsy tinkers.

And that was when he caught the sudden movement in the mist, saw the band of grey-clad riders slip out of the glen behind them.

The reiver chief was electrified by the apparition, the shocking speed with which the pursuing horsemen closed in on his weary company. His harsh voice stuck in his throat for a moment before he managed to bawl the alarm.

'Ambuscade! Have a care to your rear!' Kerr yanked his garron around, reaching over his shoulder for the great sword he had slung over his back. He watched his startled rearguard peer over their shoulders at the sudden commotion, fumbling for their weapons as the swiftly moving English swept around them in a slick, grey net.

English?

A moment later Kerr heard the familiar whine of their arrows, fired flat and true from the strewn rocks to their right. A steel-bonneted reiver on a shaggy bay threw up his lance and slumped over his saddle, the startled beast accelerating away with its rider skewered to his rank blanket roll. The six-inch bodkin point had pierced his long leather riding boots, the muscles of his thigh and cut his femoral artery in two before jamming against his mildewed bedding.

The reiver cursed, pressing his fingers about the killing wound as he veered away from his friends.

Another rider was knocked clean off his mount, a goose-feathered flight bristling under his chin. The man fell back into the wet moss, back arched and gurgling as he bled to death.

A third arrow caught one of the Highland garrons in the flanks, dropping the beast to its knees and hurling its screaming rider into one of the moorland pools.

Kerr squealed with fury, astounded by the appalling, unlawful attack. Springing an ambush on a Truce Day . . . breaking the one taboo which bound the Border folk together. God damn the English, to even think . . . But he hadn't time to reckon the rights and wrongs of the case now.

The nimble reiver ducked over his pony's mane, holding his buckler above his head for protection against the lethal arrow storm. He realised with alarm the grey riders had already swept closer, their cloaks blowing as they whooped and bawled.

The renegades were on bigger, sleeker horses – fresher and faster than the bog trotters which had already carried the Scotsmen sixty miles in forty-eight hours. The leader had already drawn parallel with the panic-stricken warband, his long black locks streaming in the wind. He looked more like a damned Tartar, clutching a short, curved bow in his lap.

Eldritch!

The captain was lying about his horse's shoulders, the bow held flat, a black-barbed arrow nocked as he squinted at the fleeing reiver. Before Kerr could blink the arrow had whistled into the highland nag's rear, tumbling the beast into an unseen gully. Kerr threw out his arms and dived away from the rocks, sprawling with a spine-jarring crash. The punishing fall knocked the breath from his body. Blood bubbled into his eyes, misting his vision.

He ignored the shockwaves hammering through his system, prised himself to his knees as a terrified pony clattered past, razor chips flying from its hooves. The beast caught him a glancing blow, spinning him on his knees. He yelled in fear, felt lancing agonies skewer his shoulder, kidneys and ribs. Kerr crouched in the gully, frantic and furious as he peered out over his ridge, watched the horsemen hurtle by.

The grey-clad English had circled around the bog, a chain of mounted archers driving their horses with their legs while they mastered their deadly little Tartar bows. Only an Englishman would have crossed the Border with such a filthy weapon. He groped for his latch, realised the leather strap which attached it to his wrist had snapped.

He cursed in the Gaelic, peering around for the lost crossbow.

The Ride had slowed down now, intent on surrounding the bulk of the reiver band rather than trying to outrun the lucky few who had slipped the net and galloped hard for the brooding safety of Candlewood.

Kerr scrambled down the gully, retrieved his buckler in time to deflect a well-aimed arrow. His great sword was lying in three silver pieces, broken on the rocks. Another arrow skewered his shield, the point jutting against his bleeding cheek. Another inch and he would have lost an eye for sure. The shocking impact jarred his senses, knocked him back on his heels. He hurled the useless buckler aside and hobbled for the open moor.

The reivers were falling on all sides, the rest scattering like a flock of birds across the harsh wilderness. James Eldritch whooped with exultation, spurring his sleek horse after the fugitives.

He had led a dozen of his horsemen over the Border, hard on the heels of the canny but cocksure Scots. They had ignored Kerr's dozing rear markers, leaving them to the murderous attentions of Jeremiah Hobby. The giant sergeant had taken five of the best archers and hidden up in the outcrops at the head of the valley. Not even veterans like Hobby could manage their six-foot longbows while riding a horse. They were trained to ride to battle and fight on foot, and could be relied on to skewer a target at anything up to three hundred yards.

The reivers at the back wouldn't stand a dog's chance. Hobby's hawkeyes would do the real killing while they stampeded the rest, using their lighter, composite bows to speed their panic-stricken flight. The short weapons lacked the penetrating power of the longbow, but only the most superbly trained and iron-willed horse soldier could face their bitter sleet.

Eldritch had spurred past the doomed reivers, thrashing and kicking in desperation as they tried to whip their garrons out of range. They gaped over at him in terrorised resentment even as the first of Hobby's well-aimed arrows found their backs.

The rest of the band had veered away towards the right, the open moss into which they had fled so many times in the past. If they rode hard enough they would come to the Jed Water, follow its course into the more populous glens where they would no doubt rouse up their friends.

The tall captain swung his head, took in the sudden carnage in a blink. He had spotted the reiver chief struggling with his massive two-handed sword, but the heavy weapon would be no use on horseback. And in any case, he had never had any intention of closing in to trade blows with a well-armoured enemy. Eldritch had lain flat over his horse, taken steady aim as the notorious reiver stared back at him, outraged by his insolent attack.

Truce Day or no, he'd stamp out Sandy Kerr's hellfire for good.

Eldritch knew it was a trying shot, holding a steady bead on a plunging target while his own horse was at canter over broken ground, but he hadn't doubted he would hit his mark. Kerr's snorting bog trotter – half a yard of mud-caked hindquarters – had reared into his vision. The garron loomed as large as a barn door beyond the bobbing arrow point.

He wanted Kerr alive. Dead would do but alive would be sweetest.

His first shot skewerd the pony's haunches, tumbling the beast and its drumbstruck rider into a ditch. Eldritch grinned evilly, clenched his thighs to turn the sleek charger away after the fleeing reivers.

A wild fellow in a blowing plaid peered back at him, yelling oaths in Gaelic as the Englishman's stronger horse easily outpaced his pony. The youth appeared to be daubed in green and blue splotches, his red hair shorn into diseased clumps about his protruding ears. His pitiful belongings – small coin and shiny trinkets lifted from some careless peddlar – flew out of his rags as if he was sowing cheap seeds over the moss. The frantic boy fished under his cloak and threw a knife, an awkward back-hander which sent the jagged blade slicing over Eldritch's ducked head. He leaned lower over his wheezing pony as if he could coax another few yards out of the beast. But he had no chance now. The captain drew alongside the hoarsely panting reiver, ducked under his sword swing and leaned over to flick his dirk across the reiver's saddle girth. The pricked beast plunged aside, rearing and kicking, leaving the scrawny boy flying through the rain like a corn crow.

He crashed into a mossy bank and lay still.

Eldritch checked his rouncy, the wild-hearted horse blowing hard after the gallop. He peered about as the last of the reiver band broke up, each man intent on saving himself.

Two more had been shot out of their saddles; another pair had been hit but had managed to cling on, skewered by arrows. The captain turned his horse and spurred back the way he had come, spotted one of the downed reivers trying to stagger away on foot. It was Kerr, the man himself, bloody and muddy in his outlandish Highland garb, zig-zagging towards the sanctuary of the moss in the feeble hope of outrunning the cordon of riders.

'It's Kerr! I want the whore's spawn alive!' he yelled, nocking a new arrow and watching the reiver crouch like a trapped wolf, at bay before a ring of enemies.

Eldritch came to a halt, levelled a horse arrow at the fugitive. From that range the cruelly curved butcher barb would cut through his dirty mantle, shatter his ribs and cut his heart clean in half. The horse arrow was the final insult, a barbarous weapon only used in direst peril when facing advancing cavalry.

But Eldritch wouldn't hesitate to use it on the shrunken-chested reiver, and the shrunken-chested reiver knew it. Kerr was bleeding from half a dozen wounds, but his fierce eyes blazed with loathing.

'I can skewer you now or take you back,' Eldritch said out of the side of his mouth. 'Your choice, but make it quick, I'm not intending to tarry here any longer than strictly necessary.'

Kerr raised himself to his full height, ignoring his hurts.

'Ye broke the Truce Day, your own master said . . .'

Eldritch ignored the rogue's outraged accusations, turned to his nervously-grinning soldiers.

'All right, don't sit there gaping. Grab the loose ponies and strap any of the bastards that are still alive on 'em. Be sure you shake the buggers out, they've more blades than a slow dog's got ticks.'

'Eldritch ye damned clootie,' Kerr snarled, reaching out towards the captain's bridle. Eldritch tugged the reins out of his reach, glared down at his furious prisoner.

The bewildered reiver was seized from behind, tough English troopers yanking his arms so hard his shoulders nearly burst from their bruised joints. Kerr gritted his teeth, refusing to yell despite the massive, smothering pain which washed over him.

He turned his baleful gaze on their captain, but the English oath-breaker had already looked away, keen to gather up his trophies and return to the questionable safety of the hills. They had been devilish quick off the mark, but they were still twenty miles inside Scotland.

A long way to ride and a dark night ahead of them.

'Where's that bastard scout of mine? Hacker! Come here man!'

Kerr cursed, kicking out at his captors with his long boots, thrashing against their pitiless strength. Two of them had pinned his fractured arms behind his back, pressed his elbows together.

'That's it Jock, you kick a bit. But ye'll piss when you can't whistle when they stretch your neck outside New-castle Jail, mark me now!'

Tears of frustrated rage ran down the Scot's cheeks. His head lolled on his shoulders as he shrieked in despair.

Sandy Kerr the reiver was a prisoner of the English.

The sardonic captain ignored his ranting, took a long look at the eerily-lit tower away on the hill. The alarm would have been raised by now, the posse gathered and the hounds slipped.

Eldritch yanked the rouncy around, electrified by his own audacity. In one bold stroke the merchant's boy had solved a thorny problem which had confounded his Lord-ship the Warden for twelve years. He felt the sour thrill of his achievement course through his frame. He had simultaneously established and ruined his reputation; made a name for himself and cursed it for generations to come.

But he didn't give a fig for their foolish truces and prec-ious Border code. The doggerel honour of thieves and cutthroats? Hadn't Alexander won everlasting fame and glory by simply cutting the Gordian knot in two?

Eldritch allowed himself a small smile of satisfaction.

It had been a long, eventful day.

Beside Carter Bar, Redesdale, upon the Scots Border

It had begun, fittingly enough, in the witching hours before dawn. Two rival bands, separated by race and by a long tradition of animosity, riding out beneath a harvest moon.

They rode in extended order, one band heading south the other north, their chosen paths taking them within a long bowshot of one another. Glimpsing them and yet hearing nothing, a night-watching dalesman might have wondered whether they were ghost riders doomed to wander the moss, or worse, bloody-handed reivers busy about their thieving business.

The war-torn borderland between the Scots and English marches was the wildest region in all Britain. Not even the remote peat bogs of Ireland could claim such a desperate population of cutthroats and rider-gangs. Raiding – reiving – ran in their blood like an intoxicating liquor, stealing men's senses and hardening their hearts to their chosen life of banditry, murder and mayhem. Ancient feuds and doubtful alliances extended on either side of the Border, warring English heidmen often marrying their troublesome sons off to a bonny Scots lass to cement some all too temporary truce.

The bleak borderlands ran from the Solway Firth in the west to the desolate mouth of the Tweed at Berwick, mile after mile of cold, debatable lands which roving bands could criss-cross with virtual impunity in pursuit of cattle, corn or easily transportable loot – known locally as insight.

Isolated settlers had long since learnt to protect themselves in sturdy blockhouse 'bastles', the English separated from their Scots neighbours by a meandering line on the map or a turbulent mountain stream. The borderlands were ruled – according to royal warrant at any rate – by the marcher wardens. These grim keepers had been charged with stamping out the ruinous forays, intercepting the raiders whenever they could. But the wardens, isolated in their lonely towers, short of cash and crippled by desertions, had little choice but to join in the dangerous game, looting and stealing in order to pay their homesick warbands. In a bid to impose some kind of order on this dangerous chaos, they were empowered to call Truce Days, special open-air courts where grievances could be aired and the worst of the wrongs put to rights. The deadly fairs brought the wild folk down from the hills, the strict Border code protecting even the most notorious robber from justice, punishment or blind revenge.

Shedding blood during a Truce Day would unite Englishman and Scot, set barefoot lowne and marcher earl riding beneath the same red banner in a sworn quest for bloody vengeance.

But not all men played by the old rules – James Eldritch for one. He refused to be bound by their bucolic traditions, scorning the ancient protocols which had ensnared the Border folk in centuries of chaotic bloodletting.

He was captain of horse to Lord Howath – the warden of the English Middle March – and didn't give pish for their precious codes. He had been an outsider most of his life and his exile on the Border hadn't sweetened his already notorious temper. He was a soldier of fortune and friendless pariah, a black-hearted Sassenach out of the far west. He didn't care for their poxed Truce Days, for any reiver's rights or his kinfolk's bloodily-vowed revenge.

Eldritch had been on the Border three miserable, ballockscratching years, and by Christ that was long enough. He'd make his name and earn a place back at Court or he'd sell his soul trying. The brooding hotspur had led the Ride from their base at Crow Hole just after midnight, brought them by devious paths to the lower slopes of Bladderdown hill — one of the bonfire beacons which dotted the frontier like buboes on a dead man's arm. He meant to cross the border and run a foray of his own, spring an ambuscade where his rival Sandy Kerr would least expect it — safe on his home turf.

An oath-shattering coup which would take the self-satisfied smirk from the reiver's hellishly-scarred face for good — and curse the name of Eldritch till kingdom come, no doubt.

He brought the Ride to a halt a hundred paces from the summit, the lightly-armed horsemen taking cover in a gorse-choked gully. Eldritch dismounted, handed his reins to his sergeant and drew his dirk. He went without a word, ducking down beneath swirling tentacles of mist and bog-bred vapours to climb the furze-studded slope. The jittery sentinel had hoisted his torch and was scurrying from one end of his lonely platform to the other, trailing his spluttering comet and jabbing his spear at the surrounding night as if he was about to be swallowed up by a faery host.

The barefoot lowne must have heard something. Eldritch watched him back towards his carefully-stacked bonfire, eager to raise the alarm and summon the Trod but reluctant to detonate the laboriously-prepared beacon without due cause.

Woe betide the guard who cried wolf in these wastes.

As well as consuming his precious store of firewood and dragging the troopers from their tower for nothing, the bright glow might attract as many arrows as moths — if the wildmen from over the Border *were* running a foray.

Eldritch stole closer. Perhaps the watchman had caught the dim jingle of their harness, the impatient whinny of a horse? The intruder worked his way around the bonfire, crouching down as the nervous guard stumbled away from the witchbrew of night-noises – straight onto the cruel point of his dirk.

'You'll stay quiet, you slow dog, or I'll slit your gizzard for you.'

The foot lowne froze. But surely to God if he'd been ambushed by reivers he'd have been lying in the dirt with his lifeblood coursing between his fingers by now.

'Warden?' he croaked.

'Aye, fortunately for you.' The foot lowne risked a cautious peek over his shoulder. The shadow-shod fiend with the dagger in his back was taller by a head, his gaunt features set somewhere between sardonic amusement and latent savagery. His eyes, black as sea coal on the shoreline, were at once everywhere and nowhere. Howath's man all right. Elderberry? Eldritch.

'I think . . . that is . . . I heard, a band of 'em sir, two score of 'em going sou'east!' the guard reported, jabbing his spear after the long-vanished reivers in the forlorn hope the intruder might overlook his criminal lack of vigilance.

'To Crow Hole, aye. The warden's called a Truce Day.'

The guard hadn't heard anything about the eagerly-anticipated fair.

'But if my Lord the warden knew how idly his sentinels served him I wager he'd never sleep another night, not in his deepest dungeons.'

'It won't happen again sir!' the guard swore. 'Cruel tired, I was sir, cruel tired,' he insisted, his mouth dry. Maybe this long-shanked rogue would like to spend ten hours ploughing the northern tundra before he went gallivanting about the wee hours of the night?

'You're right on that score. You are relieved of your duties forthwith.'

The guard smiled weakly, wondering what hell was coming next.

'I need a good guide. How well do you know Reidswire, the Jed Water, Teviotdale?'

'Well enough to know they're over the Border sir,' the

guard replied smartly, desperate to deflect the dire punishments the brute was obviously brooding over.

'Fool. How far have you forayed?'

'Far as Hawick sir. With the Trod that is, burning turf on a . . .'

'Tullymallock? Candlewood?'

'Christ Jesu, no sir! Tullymallock sir? That's . . .'

'I know whose manor it is,' the captain snapped. 'And if you don't know it by now, on my faith you will by this time tomorrow!'

Eldritch noticed the fireguard's hairy jaw sag in dismay. Tullymallock? Sandy Kerr's territory? Who would dare ride over that hound's barren acres?

James Eldritch, that's who.

He watched as the rest of the Ride urged their horses up the slope, reining in about the eerily-lit bonfire and its bedraggled custodian. The silent company had learned to dread Eldritch's night rides. They might have given the Jocks a few nasty surprises, but his mischief had cost blood – and lives.

'I mean to cross the Border this night and hide up on their turf until Kerr's folk return from the Truce Day,' the captain announced, striding towards his disgruntled men. 'What d'you make of that, sergeant?' he inquired, collecting his horse's reins from the heavyset rider. Jeremiah Hobby had been serving with the young devil long enough to know when to hold his tongue.

'Well?' Eldritch growled, giving the jumpy horse a sharp tug on the reins.

'Well. The Truce captain,' Sergeant Hobby mumbled, desperately trying to avoid the captain's bristling stare. 'We cassn't touch 'em, not on Truce Days.'

The fireguard nodded in agreement. Eldritch sucked in his breath, turning his predatory gaze on the ring of riders.

'I say damn their Truce Day. Kerr's nothing but a bastard's whelp of a Scotsman, not some rosewater-wearing chevalier!'

A few of the riders chuckled at the captain's caustic wit.

They didn't like the sound of it much more than old Hobby. It was the Ride's honour – and their lives – he was risking. Eldritch studied their vacant expressions, sensing their fickle mood.

'This man's a damned murdering bandit, long overdue for the noose!' he insisted.

The riders sat silent, breathing plumes of vapour into the chill air. If they succeeded, they might even win a pardon for Old Gully, the crotchety commander they had followed north. Rumour had it the old man had been guilty of some minor misdemeanour back at court. Some of the men maintained he'd made a pass at one of King Harry's bed-warmers, others that he had beaten him at cards or tennis once too often for his own good. Either way, Howath and his retinue of billmen and archers had found themselves assigned to the forgotten outpost of Crow Hole – and they had been there ever since.

'We've tried fair means and now we'll try foul. Kerr's coming in; he'll be watching for trouble at the fair. What he won't expect is us, on his doorstep when he comes crowing home.'

Hobby pulled at his carbuncled nose.

'But he'll be covered by the Truce, Lord Howath's word, all the way to his hearth,' Hobby said stubbornly.

'A pox on his word!' Eldritch barked. 'We'll go lightly, no armour, just our short bows. We'll be in and out before he can draw dirk!' he vowed.

The fireguard raised his eyebrows at this doubtful strata-gem.

'Do you have something to add?' Eldritch narrowed his eyes, peered right through the hillman's ashen features.

'Ah, but beggin' your pardon sir, they'll be runnin' home with anything that's not nailed down, back warming their arses in Tullymallock before ye can blink sir! Pardon me for saying as I shouldn't, but it's always been a failin' of mine. Sir.'

'You seem a ready fellow . . . ?'

'Hacker sir. William Hacker of Redesdale.'

24

'You're not a local man, Hacker.' The hillman pushed his ancient morion helmet back off his forehead, grinned good-naturedly.

'No indeed sir. St Albans born and bred, that's me. An articled clerk, in former times.'

'Then it was this or a prison, I guess?'

The captain had guessed right. Hacker had been caught altering his master's household accounts and paid the price. Sold into the virtual slavery of field service on the war-torn Borders. In addition to his crippling labours, he was bound to stand guard at the bonfire five nights a week, and be ready with boar spear, dagger and sack of provisions if the Trod came his way.

'St Albans.' The captain sighed. 'You're a long way from home Hacker. Just like Kerr's reivers, eh?'

Sandy Kerr was one of the most feared men on either side of the border. A bloody braggadocio with a dozen killings and countless forays to his name. And this damned fool was planning to raid his Tullymallock manor? God save them all.

'My Lord of Howath has vouched for his security. He'll think himself safe,' the captain confirmed with a peculiar, sideways sneer. Hacker studied the newcomer's dimly-lit features. A challenging stare and a long, tapering nose – well used to being poked into other folk's business, no doubt. Hacker could sense the ache of ambition beneath the captain's carefully-buttoned doublet, a bursting sore stuffed with hot blood. He looked as if he had stepped from his lady's bed – and left all his ironmongery behind him. Where did he think he was going, dressed up in all his finery? Hacker wouldn't have dreamt of setting foot out of doors without his trusted jack. The thick, quilted coat with its carefully sewn steel plates would, with God's grace, turn blade and barb. He slept with more knives under his bed than His Majesty had whores!

Eldritch sheathed his dirk. As well as the dagger he bore a long stabbing sword and a small buckler. His short bow, an unusual weapon for an officer, was carefully wrapped against the weather and slung over his back. The captain turned his weird gaze back upon the inquisitive spearman.

'There'll be no Trod this night, no torches, no burning turf. And no poxed Truce. You'd best get your gear and fall in with my men.'

Before the astonished guard could protest, the tall captain had stalked back to his patiently-waiting horse, steaming quietly beside the cold lumber pile.

Beside Crow Hole,
on the River Rede

The first foot soldiers of dawn yawned and stretched over the bare moor, lit the tumbledown ridge of stones which marked the head of the valley. Grey and olive monoliths surrounded by covens of broken boulders, the serrated ridges were carpeted in rich beds of moss and lichens. The old stones leaned on one another, the largest shouldering their way towards the slowly-advancing light. A stranger on the Border might have ridden straight past the stronghold, mistaking the squat structure for another outcrop. But these stones had been shaped by hardy men as well as brutal nature. The keep clung to the moor like a crouching mastiff, its arrow-slit eyes no more than an archer's palm wide, its towers like great erect ears with their crudely-chewed battlements.

Crow Hole seemed to have sunk in a collar of bare earth and shivered scree, piled remains of the excavations the long-dead builders had left behind them. The rampart shielded the deeply-dug foundations, trapped several feet of peaty water. The only way in to the clumsily hewn structure was by a causeway which ran up against the iron-bound door. The exposed approach was covered by a profusion of lancets as well as gunports, the well-trampled walkway shadowed by the grim watch towers. A red banner blew in the dawn wind, the seams long since torn and shredded by the weather.

The fading motif – a golden hind – had been reduced to a

27

pale shadow of its former self. It danced and writhed in the breeze like a red rag to a bull.

Which is precisely what it was.

Dawn came with a cock-crow and an ear-shattering creak of oak on stone as the drowsy gatekeepers shouldered the vast, studded door open. A foot soldier in a quilted coat stepped out onto the walkway and stamped in the rime which the night had left behind. The guard leaned his spear against the wall and fished under his coat, easing his padded shoulders back as he relieved himself into the ditch below. Another foot soldier wandered out, made a brief reconnaissance towards the river and squatted at his ablutions. A couple of herdboys followed, flicking switches at a lowing gang of red cattle. They drove the hungry beasts out of the nighttime safety of the keep and into the meadow which sloped down towards the Rede. The basement floor was little more than a menagerie, with stalls for the cattle and horses, pens for the goats and dropping-speckled posts for the warden's goshawks, falcons and merlins. The herdboys who kept this fortified zoo would have slept among the manure, a filthy blanket pulled over their bodies to keep out the rats, mice and cockroaches which came with the night. The second floor of the keep served as kitchen, dormitory and dining room for the garrison, while the third floor was reserved for the warden's household.

The lone reiver who had crawled ahead to spy on their outlandish preparations shook his head at these wondrous English, these land-grabbers who came all this way and still tried to behave as if they were safe and warm at home in the south.

The sun peeked above the keep, its thawing fingers reaching for him over the cold stone. The plaid-wrapped reiver scrambled away on his belly, paused for a moment to rub some warmth into his aching limbs and then set off up the rock-strewn dale towards the waiting warband.

The scout made his report, brief and to the point, the way

his chief Sandy Kerr liked it. Crow Hole had been quiet all night – save for a small hunting party which had sallied out shortly after midnight, lightly armed in their long grey cloaks.

'These pock puddings must have boiled their brains, riding about in Saracen gear in this weather,' the chief growled, one side of his mouth permanently stretched into a death's-head grimace by an old wound. 'Mebbe they've taken riggish, gone a-whoring at Berwick?' he wondered aloud, stroking his heavily-stubbled jaw. He traced the old scar with his dirty forefinger. Young Davey the scout was still shivering – the band hadn't dared light a fire this far over the Border, Truce Day or no.

They carried a wide assortment of weapons: long axes, keen swords, and as many ornate daggers as their broad leather belts would allow. Sandy Kerr had hung his great sword over his back and carried a pair of handier knives on his belt. His father had worn his mail shirt at Flodden, and it still bore the rent where an English billman had lopped Auld Andrew Kerr's arm off at the shoulder.

'They've wh . . . wh . . . whores enough at Crow Hole,' the scout stuttered, clutching his thin shoulders. 'These looked like fancy squires off hawking, only they had no haw . . . haw . . . hawks,' he added.

The reiver chief lifted his mail shirt from his bruised shoulder, settled the garment back as comfortably as he was able.

'No hawks, no plate and no lances,' he mused. The scout nodded. Auld Sandy sighed.

'Well they're not gan bother man nor beast wi'out, eh?'

'I said a'right, Sandy,' the scout maintained, wondering if the band suspected he had mistaken himself. 'Flowing robes like a maiden's shift, and wee bows,' he elaborated.

Bows? Were the fools out after a stag? Auld Sandy peered around the isolated outcrop where they had concealed themselves, watched the first of the hill folk making their way down to the remote keep. A Truce Day was a chance to talk and drink, to meet and plan matches. To trade and barter and steal and lift. Howath had given his word he'd not be harmed, neither him nor his people.

Scores would be settled and stolen cattle and goods exchanged. In many cases the robbing English would be buying back their own horses with goods they had lifted from the Scots!

It was a wicked mad business, but it was all they knew.

'Aye, well. They're no worry to us now,' he concluded. Let's see what that de'il spawned warden's in mind.'

John Gulliver had wrapped himself in his bearskin to watch the reivers ride in on their small, shaggy garrons. Bog trotters, the English called them, turning their noses up at their remarkably unkempt appearance. But their bog trotters would outlast the finest Arab, on those wastes. He stood in the chill winds on the gatehouse tower, watched the silent crowd part like pilgrims as the gaudy little host trotted through the flea-bitten congregation.

Northumberlander and Scot, they were much the same to Howath. A race apart, a breed of clay-men bred on the miserable vapours of this frozen swamp. Their one pleasure in life was to steal.

Why, they would gleefully run away with the steam off a man's piss. They would gut a grandmother to lift her bootlaces.

He detested the Borders and longed for the simple pleasures of home. A fire which didn't stink like a marl-pit. A bedchamber without bats. A scullery without its reiving army of foot-long rats.

'Father! Look!' Miranda leaned over the crudely-mortared battlement, pointed out the steel-bonneted raiders as they cautiously dismounted by the pie stalls, keeping a wary eye on the furtive settlers. His daughter's beautiful face flushed with excitement. Had the girl no idea what they were about?

'The Scotchmen are here! I thought they'd come, with all the food and games and everything!' Howath showed his teeth. Her mother had died in bringing her into the world. Sadly, she had taken all the child's wits with her.

'They came to talk, girl. Talk truce and treaties.'

'Well I should think so too! There's precious few treats up here father, life's hard, trying hard for all of them, why it's trying hard for us!' she added brightly.

Exile on the miserable Scots border didn't seem to have dampened the poor girl's spirits. She had been a tiny, rosebud child of four when he had left for the north. He could have placed her with the nuns at Wells, but she was all he had left of her poor mother. Now she stood in her plain mantle, the perfect image of her. Gulliver didn't have the heart to scold her, so he did what he always did when his flesh and blood annoyed him — turned on her saucy maid instead.

'Will ye not bring warmed wine for us? It's cold enough to freeze the ballocks off a mammoth!'

The quick-eyed maid flashed the giant warden a look, but at once modified her expression and curtsied daintily. Merron Eldritch was as bad as her elder brother, more used to giving orders than taking them. He wondered for a moment what had become of the damned captain — off gallivanting on a Truce Day!

He could have done with Eldritch here — and his damned riders.

'Oh, and a venison pasty too, my sweet,' Miranda added, reaching out to squeeze the girl's arm.

The old warrior tugged his bearskin tighter around his scored and scarred frame, watched his retainers busy tugging open the mouldy pavilions they had erected along the meadow's edge. The canvas was mottled and stained, variously shaded by damp and mildew, but would give the warden some small degree of shelter when it turned wet. Liveried retainers had dragged out a large table and a set of matching chairs, thrown a heavy brocaded cloth over the dagger-scarred surface. His clerk Edward Nailer, a tubby little gnome with a pointed beard, was already busy arranging his papers, sorting the charge sheets, indictments and petitions which would be discussed, digested and decided upon that day.

Before they got down to the real reason for the Scotsman's visit, Howath thought ruefully.

The guards stood back, black-lacquered bills tucked into their shoulders as The Lord Howath, King's Warden of Middle March, strode out to greet his unlikely guests.

A dozen billmen in Howath's red and gold livery followed him down the narrow path, out of the keep towards the sacking-clad throng waiting in the meadow. After the billmen came two dozen of Howath's feared archers. Gangly young men mostly, in lighter leather jerkins.

Howath strode down the well-cut meadow towards his unwanted guests, his bodyguard closing in behind him. The crowd tensed, holding their breath as the great adversaries met at last. Howath studied Kerr's scarred features for a moment, bowed his head in greeting.

'Right welcome ye are, Alexander Kerr, Laird of Tullymallock.'

The title was an ancient irrelevance. This man was a damned cutthroat and knave, Howath thought hotly. He disguised his contempt behind a thin smile.

'Right welcome on this Truce Day to answer all charges brought against you and yours.'

Kerr's scarred mouth opened, a terrible grimace intended as a smile.

'And to make counter-charges, aye, agin' ye and yours,' the Scot replied.

Howath motioned to the table, where Nailer was busy sorting through his documents and petitions. The clerk unstoppered a pot of ink and sat ready for their worst. The crowd closed in about the ring of lightly-armed men, eager not to miss a word of the debates to follow. Howath took his seat, holding his dress dagger in his broad lap. Kerr copied him, sitting in the stiff-backed chair opposite looking lost without a ragged pony between his thighs.

'Bring sweetmeats and drinks for our Scots guests,'

Howath ordered. 'Now then Nailer, let's make a start shall we, this weather doesn't look too promising.'

Kerr fidgeted in his seat, glared at the sea of grubby faces washed up on the meadow around him. None of them dared hold his eye too long for fear of some supernatural reprisal. The warden's clerk rambled through a series of questionable affidavits, cross–referring the written testimony to the bewildered peasants he called forth. Howath sat with his knees spread, his great sausage fingers drumming on his ornamental hanger. The reiver watched him closely, but the warden seemed as bored and distracted by the lacklustre proceedings as he was. Noon, and the agitated raider was ready to give himself up to their brainnumbing jurisprudence. He had finally agreed to pay Duncan of Bray three shillings and ninepence as compensation for half a herd of wall-eyed ewes he had lifted the previous Autumn. It was no real loss to the canny Borderer – he had sold the very same herd to one of Bray's neighbours last Martinmas.

Howath, apparently as eager to get the ridiculous proceedings over and done with as quickly as possible, had agreed to buy up Kerr's small herd of Highland cattle – to salt and barrel for the winter ahead. Kerr had allowed his men to celebrate, giving each a palmful of coin to spend at the fair. The excited swordsmen had hurried off to spend their pennies, pressing together as if they were come to play murder ball with their rather demoralised hosts. Kerr watched them mingle with the filth–caked crowd, turned his quick eyes back towards the warden as he finished briefing the clerk. Howath straightened up, gave the reiver a brisk smile. He stepped closer, lowered his voice.

'Perhaps ye'd care for a turn along the river there, before we share a flagon or two?' Howath invited, his creased features betraying his acute agitation. Kerr tensed. The warden strode past the alerted Scot, tugging his cloak about him against the fine rain which had begun to fall.

'I called you away from the rest,' the warden began,

nodding his head over the Scotsman's shoulders. 'To get down to the real business of the day.'

Kerr raised his black eyebrow. Aye, he'd thought as much. The Truce Day had been a pretence all the while. That might explain the hunting party riding out the night before, he reasoned. Kerr had been wondering where that hound Eldritch had hidden himself. Kerr realised he had missed the warden's preamble.

'The long and short of it is this: I have lately been recalled to the south with all my retinue, to join the army His Majesty is preparing to embark for France.' Howath glanced at the reiver, annoyed by his suddenly blank expression.

'Don't pretend you hadn't heard he's off over the water again.' Kerr stretched his scarred mouth in a lopsided smile. 'Aye well, no matter. The fact is I'm cruel short of horse. That rapscallion Cholmley's been badgering the Earl to command all his Borderers. If he gets a foot in the door I'll be finished. There's no love lost 'tween him and I.'

Kerr gaped, then bayed like a wolf at the warden's unlikely dilemma. He'd heard their quarrel went back to Flodden. Did Howath think he'd be interested in a falling out between two Englishmen?

Howath ignored his ironic laughter.

'I'll need at least five score foot soldiers and upwards of three score horse if I'm to hold any influence over my Lord the Earl. I don't need to tell you sir, that I've not counted a tail as strong since . . . since . . .' Kerr fixed the awkwardly-frowning warden with his keen blue eye.

'I'll tell ye when, warden, since Flodden! Is your memory failing in your dotage, that you forget that bluddy day?'

Howath bristled, clutched his cloak as it billowed in the wind.

The reiver slapped his mailed chest. 'I well remember who it was wore this shirt, and who it was began the day with a white banner and ended with a red!'

Howath was stung by the Scotsman's sudden fury, his nostrils flaring amidst his rook's nest of a beard. The reiver was right. Howath had climbed the hill carrying his white device before him. By the time he had reached the summit the shredded tatters were saturated in Scots blood. And it had stayed blood red ever since.

'There's no gain for anyone stirring that pot again Kerr!' Howath snapped. 'Flodden's seven years since! I've come here to make you an offer, come to France with my people, we'll drown the bad blood between us, aye, serving King Harry!'

Kerr spluttered with rage, stalking the bank with his fist clenched about the hilt of his dagger.

'Come to France and serve that haggis? I swear you've gone soft to even ask me!'

'I've not softened, nor lost my wits neither!' Howath snarled. 'Come to them maybe. Is that pack of rascals the best you could collect? A dozen damned gallowglasses off the hills? We've bled, we've both lost, but life goes on. Will ye not consider it?'

Kerr swallowed the bile that had swarmed into his throat.

'Life goes on, aye, but as long as I've breath in my body I'll serve neither thee nor your king!'

Howath seemed to swell up inside his cloak, his eyes fixed on the almost speechless Scotsman.

'You're a hard man Sandy, and maybe you've a right to your anger. But Flodden was a fair fight, there might just as well have been ten thousand English slain as Scots. We have to put these damned feuds and fights behind us.

'You have my mind on it warden!'

'You'll not take a day or two to consider what I've said.'

Kerr straightened, took a deep breath. 'Never.'

Beside Glen Craigh,
Teviotdale, Scotland

Alone crow wheeled above the wastes, in the forlorn hope of locating a meal amongst the mosses. The borderlands looked as if they had been razed by a race of blind giants, sworn to topple every hill and tear what little vegetation there was from the bedrock beneath. The crow cawed, tipped its black wing and glided along the dale.

James Eldritch closed one eye and watched the black bird swoop past their shelter, his gloved hand clenched about his horse's wet muzzle. The Ride had dismounted among the rocks further down the slope and backed their mounts into the cave. The chill walls were studded with colourful lichens and scored here and there by ancient dirks. Unintelligible messages scoured by the running waters, filtered by the haphazardly-stacked rocks above.

Their lonely eyrie gave them a superb view of the old reiver road which ran alongside the stream. Mosses and rank weeds had bubbled out of the decaying cart tracks, brambles and ferns creeping over the shrinking pathway. Eldritch peered up at the crowding sky, the drifting storm-clouds swollen with the rain he was banking on to shield their flight south. Twenty miles inside Scotland, and not even the birds of the air had registered his insolent intrusion. Eldritch glanced at his men, wringing their cloaks out in the mildewed cavern. Tired, cold and damn near naked in their light cloaks, the Ride looked more like a band of novice friars than a war party. Sergeant Hobby resembled a wet bear, recently roused from a comfortable hibernation. The lumpily-built Yorkshireman scowled out at the rapidly-deteriorating weather as if he would blame the heavens for their present predicament.

'Stickin' us noses out, twenty-odd mile over t'border wi'out so much as a florin of armour on uz backs,' he complained, just out of earshot of his bedraggled troopers. 'We'll never make old bones harryin' about the moss like a pack o' bloody 'Uns!'

'We're on Kerr's doorstep; he won't know what hit him,' Eldritch growled, peering up at the skies as the punch-drunk rainclouds pummelled themselves black and blue.

It wouldn't be long now.

Auld Sandy's men were well pleased with their expedition over the Border – despite their chief's evident temper. Whatever it was old Howath had told him down by the river had certainly soured his enjoyment of the Truce Day. Kerr rode slightly behind the main pack, mulling over the strange course of events. He hadn't survived twenty years of Border warfare without developing a sixth sense when it came to tricks and trouble.

Where was that damned captain they had heard so much about?

Kerr threw a chickenbone aside and gave a piercing whistle. Young Davey Dunne, riding point on his one-eyed grey, turned his beast and trotted back down the dale, eyes wandering with the strong whisky he had poured in to his water bottle. Kerr frowned.

'Ye make sure and keep your eyes peeled laddie, or I'll peel 'em for 'ee,' he snarled. Davey, sobering up in a moment, sat up straight in his saddle and nodded his head as vigorously as he dared. Kerr rode in silence for a moment.

'These hunters you saw last midnight. We saw no sign of 'em away back at Crow Hole.'

Davey belched.

'No Sandy.'

'Bows.'

'Bows, aye.'

'But no mail, no plate, no bucklers?' The basic require-
ments for a bout of bloody Border mischief. Kerr felt a
shimmering whisper of apprehension. Something was
wrong. He peered up and along the broken ridge line,
squinting at the shattered rock formations which might
shelter Howath's treacherous archers. The sky was boiling
black above the outcrops, the first waves of drenching rain
slanting into the glen from the east. Ten miles into Scotland, he ought to have felt as buoyed as the rest of his men,
cheered by their triumphant but bloodless foray into the
enemy heartland.

'Pass the word, quiet like. I reckon the English are on
our tails.' Davey sat up, startled.

'The English?' The scout turned his scraped head left and
right, wondering if he had heard correctly.

'The English? Yon damsels in all their finery ye mean?
I . . .'

Sandy Kerr rose out of his saddle and leaned over, gripping the drunken youth's eyelid in his steely fingers. Davey
yelped, sprawled halfway out of his saddle as he writhed on
the end of the reiver's arm.

'De'il take ye boy! Take yourself down the line and tell
'em. The Sassenachs are after us, truce or no.'

They rode on, hunched against the coming storm.

The rain had redoubled in fury as if it would lash the
insolent English all the way back to the Border, drive them
home like Autumn leaves beneath a brisk broom. Thunder
rolled over the grey-clad hills, lightning streaked the overloaded skies.

Flashes of the ambush came back to him, pinpoint
images as sharp as a new-honed dirk. Eldritch remembered
the grit and clods thrown up by the reiver's ponies, the odd
coins and trinkets spilling from their flying plaids as they
rode them down the moss, shot them out of their saddles

like straw dolls at a summer fair. A red-haired tyke cata-pulted from his garron, face-first into the rocks. A bearded reiver clutching a brace of arrows in his belly.

And Sandy Kerr lying along his pony's neck, shrieking his name as if it was some magical chant.

'Eldritch!'

He knew he had damned his name, drawing his sword on a Truce Day and shattering his master's long-cherished honour. But what use was a name, exiled up on these damned wastes?

His sister had disgraced it, his father had shamed it.

His crime — if crime it could be called — paled into insignificance compared with theirs. The bitter disgrace which had hung like a rotting albatross about his neck these last three years.

Wine had greased his father's fortune, it was perhaps fitting that it should have so accelerated his downfall. Matthew Eldritch's fleet of deep-bellied carracks had plied the trade routes between Bristol, Lisbon, Cadiz and the Mediterran-ean, exporting rich cargoes of locally-dyed cloth, corn and coal as well as cured hides and salt fish. In return for these staples they hauled home rather more exotic goods: ruby sherries and sweet Spanish sack, Malmsey from far-flung Crete, white Osey and sweet bastard wines from Portugal. Every variety he had imported had returned handsome profits on Bristol's busy quays. But the self-made merchant had resisted the temptation to indulge his eldest son. James had been taught navigation and knots, starting his lessons up to his balls in bilgewater and finishing the day clinging to the topmast rigging. He had learned to use his fists in the taverns along the quays and mastered sword and buckler fighting off Breton pirates who swarmed in the wide Bay of Biscay. His father had insisted he master every aspect of shipcraft and seafaring before he let him loose with a cargo of his own.

But that day never came.

Matthew Eldritch had invested so much of his time in

overseeing his son's future that he had been forced to neglect the rest of his children – including his firstborn, Lillith. She and her younger sister Merron had inherited their dead mother's wild-eyed beauty, but frequent exposure to the seamier sides of life along Bristol's teeming docks had dangerously widened their horizons, replaced their poor mother's piety with a worldly wisdom beyond their years. James had tried to assert some kind of authority over his wayward siblings, but Lillith had indignantly rejected his advice and continued to trade off-colour jokes with the roughest of seadogs as well as flirting with their rather more sophisticated officers.

It had been no surprise to anybody but the poor deluded merchant when his spirited daughter had finally run away with one of Eldritch's merchant captains. The scandal had rocked Bristol's gossiping merchant classes, the stunned master hardly daring to step out of doors in his humiliation. How could Matthew face his rivals – some of them bitter enemies – with his daughter riding like a pirate whore about his own Mediterranean markets?

Instead of fighting back he drowned his sorrows in drink. He swooned while his son fumed, quaffing his own cellar dry and damn near draining his warehouse. James had taken up his sword and stalked the taverns for the flimsiest news of his absent sister, but he had not dared leave his father's side. Within six months of Lillith's elopement, House Eldritch had virtually collapsed.

And then one stormy night the demoralised master had drunk himself blind, found his way along the quay and taken refuge on one of his rival's vessels. They had discovered him in the morning, clinging to the rigging and shrieking threats at the towering heavens. James had been called to the docks and had arrived just in time to see his crazed father's fall.

His broken body had looked ridiculously small to the dumbfounded son. A pitiful sack of blood and brandy.

James had been forced to sell the house for a song, sell off the remaining assets to his grasping rivals. He had scraped enough coin to install his younger brother John at the

Cathedral school in Wells, and had scoured the docklands for suitable work.

For any work.

Edward Kraven had been one of his father's most generous companions – and fiercest destroyers. He had moved with indecent haste, snapping up Eldritch's principal partners in the new markets of Andalusia, Castile and Leon. He had bought his town house at a knockdown price. But above all else, Kraven was a careful, methodical thinker. He knew the wild-hearted James would be left bitter by his predicament, become ten times as dangerous if he and his siblings were simply left to starve on Bristol's streets. His exaggerated sense of duty towards his family – particularly the wayward sister Merron – would drive him into some murderous escapade before the year was out, and there was no telling who might suffer the consequences.

Kraven had thought it best to find a new career for the fiery-eyed hotspur as soon as possible – as far away from Bristol as he could get him. It happened that some years before Kraven had been contracted to transport Sir John Gulliver's antiquated household from its base at Montjoy Castle in North Somerset to its new home on the Scots border. He had kept in occasional contact with the warden of the English Middle March ever since, supplying the lonely lord with a range of hard-to-find goods from firewood to foxhounds. What better place to send an eager young firebrand like Eldritch?

Howath hadn't inquired too closely into the boy's military antecedents. After all, he could shoot a bow with the best of them and his swordplay was unrivalled anywhere on Bristol's murderous waterfront. The younger Eldritch knew full well he was being packed off, but he had little choice but to obey Howath's call. He had packed his and sister Merron's few belongings for the long and lonely voyage to Newcastle, resigned himself to the uninspiring prospect of earning his crust on the border.

'Freezing your arse off with a gang of Jocks in irons

taking pot-shots at you,' the sardonic Kraven had observed as he waved the glaring youth aboard his cog for the long haul north.

James Eldritch, brilliant and bitter, had been sailing against the wind ever since.

Beside Glen Craigh, Teviotdale, Scotland

Eldritch cursed his memories, closed his mind to the guilt and remorse which had come slithering out of his consciousness.

This was no time to piss his piece over the past.

Lillith was long gone and his father was dead.

What was done was done.

The captain shook his head, peered over his shoulder into the drifting rain for the inevitable pursuit. He knew the reivers, once roused, would be riding hard, travelling twice as fast as the Ride. They pressed on over slippery rockslides, through hissing bogs and across swollen streams. Hours of rain had transformed the glen from mossy ditch to waterlogged morass, further slowing their hair-raisingly slow escape.

Eldritch brought up the rear, sodden and sullen as he kept one eye on the prisoners and the other on the valley behind them. Kerr was lolling in his saddle, his legs strapped beneath the pony's belly. His hands were bound behind his back, his torn plaid hanging in saturated folds about his mail. He looked more like a graverobber than a chief; one of those ghouls who appeared as if by magic after a battle to strip and pillage the corpses.

Eldritch hardly cared whether Kerr's capture brought him everlasting fame or eternal infamy. All that mattered was escaping this vast, dreary prison. He wondered for a moment whether he and his disgraced elder sister Lillith weren't two of a kind. Impetuous and selfish, prone to rash actions and bitter recrimination. Perhaps she had felt as trapped by their comfortable existence back in Bristol as he felt cooped up in Crow Hole? Closed in by circumstances, frustrated by complex codes and rules they both despised.

Eldritch grimaced, refusing to contemplate the possiblity that he had been in some way to blame for her wild flight to the Continent. He glanced up at the sky, praying for the night. He had hoped to be riding blind by now, concealed in whirling cloaks of darkness.

Eldritch spurred alongside Jeremiah Hobby. The formidably-built sergeant dwarfed his warhorse, his dripping nose sticking out of the saturated cloak. It was as if he was relying on the gin-blossomed organ to find his way home.

'All this rain. It's a wonder of creation Scotland doesn't just float off somewheres,' Hobby observed, glaring up through the squalls.

'Kerr's cousins'll be on us, if it doesn't get dark soon,' Eldritch said quietly. He didn't want to dishearten the youngsters – still relishing the success of their first foray.

'Aye, and we left all our ironmongery back at Crow Hole,' Hobby complained. Eldritch rolled his eyes.

'I've told you. The only thing which will beat these reivers is speed and surprise. That's why we brought these light bows along, remember? It's no good clattering after moss troopers in a hundredweight of armour plate!' Eldritch exclaimed, attracting doubtful glances from his drenched raiders. William Hacker the beacon guard, a drowned rat in a looted plaid, was helping to herd the prisoners riding along in front of them. He perked up at the captain's edgy evaluation, twisting in his borrowed saddle to study his determined features.

'And who asked your opinion?' the captain snorted, as Hacker stared back over his shoulder, his wet mouth hanging open to reveal a row of splintered black teeth. Hobby twisted around, followed the sentinel's gaze.

Three dozen reivers were coming down the glen after

44

them, armed to the teeth on steaming ponies. Man and beast were soaked to the skin, the relentless rain had turned every filthy coat and patchwork plaid as black as their mood.

'Well I'd swap all these rags for a decent bit of plate now,' Hobby said resentfully, tugging up his cloak to find his carefully-stored bowstrings as if the reivers were some minor inconvenience to be endured like the weather. Eldritch didn't hear him. He swallowed, took a quick look along his own warband. Frightened grey faces peered back at him.

'Get those prisoners spread out in a line,' Eldritch ordered, 'You new men take cover behind them, but stay tight and watch out for tricks!' he yelled. The prisoners, alerted by their frantic captors' urgent shouts, peered back down the glen for their saviours. The Englishmen tugged and kicked their shaggy mounts into a rough skirmish line across the narrow path, keeping the wild-eyed Scots between them and the hard-riding reivers. They were less than a furlong off now, slowing down suspiciously.

Eldritch snatched up Kerr's leading rein and tugged the struggling bandit along behind him. Kerr frothed and chewed at his gag, trembling with indignation. The captain turned his horse around, leading the chief in behind the slowly-moving stockade of horse and men. Hobby and half a dozen of the other archers had already dismounted, Hacker grasping at the herd's dangling reins.

'Use your horse arrows. Drop their mounts in front of them,' Eldritch snapped.

Hobby delved in his leather waist bag, selected a long, heavy arrow with a peculiar fishtail barb, the sharp iron fins bending forwards rather than swept backwards like the more usual bodkins they carried. He had fixed the arrow in a blink, his broad back rippling beneath his soaking cloak as he took the strain.

The reivers had halted now, wondering what to do next. Squabbling and shouting, lashing at one another in their nervous excitement. They knew the first man down the gorge was as good as dead. And the second and third. The miserable prisoners crouched on their ponies, human shields for their despised captors. They retreated another ten yards before the reiver band broke, furious tension getting the better of their common sense. Half a dozen riders spurred their hardy Highland garrons forward, the panting beasts crunching together as they hurtled ahead of the rest.

Hobby dragged back his string and let fly, the barbed missile cutting through the sleeting rain and raking one of the pony's chests. The brute force knocked the beast back on its dead legs, the gutting head buried deep in its vitals.

It was dead before it hit the ground, the screaming rider cartwheeling into the rocks. The prisoners redoubled their efforts, kicking and lunging sideways as the English archers took careful aim, dropped each rider in his tracks. The Scots, realising they would be shooting down the friends they had ridden to rescue, dared not use their own bows. They had to get in close, use their hand weapons. Eldritch heard their hoarse screams of rage; the Gaelic taunts echoed down the glen.

The surviving reivers crawled into cover, leaving a wall of dead horseflesh behind them. The rest of the band held back, torn by bitter arguments as to how to proceed. Moss troopers slumped in their saddles or cowered over their horses' necks, bucklers held up against the terrifying storm.

Kerr was thrashing like a conger on his pony, grunting and roaring behind his gag. Eldritch caught his eye for a moment, pierced with sudden remorse.

'Call them off, or we'll kill them all,' Eldritch snapped, jerking the prisoner's reins. Kerr's eyes blazed back, his shrieks muffled by the dirty twist of cloth about his mouth. Eldritch looked back down the gorge, saw a lone reiver break away from the pack. He narrowed his eyes, squinting into the gathering gloom. The night he had prayed for was upon them, and not a second too soon.

Hobby sighed, raised his bow. Kerr catapulted up and down in his saddle, frantically twisting himself against the ropes which bound him. Eldritch peered at his contorted features, the bitter tears which sprang out of the Scotsman's eyes.

'Don't shoot!' the captain cried. The screeching reiver hurtled toward the improvised stockade, reining up to lash at the archers with a dagger. The bowmen jabbed back at him, the prisoners ducking and weaving in a bid to protect the lone reiver.

Hobby lurched out of the shadows, his dagger between his teeth, heavily-muscled arms hanging by his sides. He ducked under the boy's frantic swing and hurled his arms about the thrashing garron's neck, tipping the beast back on its hind legs.

The boy yelled as Hobby heaved with all his might, tipping the kicking pony on its side and trapping the youth beneath.

The massive sergeant bent over, grabbed the boy by his bunched plaid and yanked him free, twisting his leg from under the furiously-kicking beast. The garron scrambled to its feet and galloped back down the gorge as Hobby hauled the youth into the rocks.

Eldritch stared into Kerr's eyes, saw the reiver's undisguised relief. He leaned out on an impulse, tore the rag from Kerr's scarred mouth.

'Call them off Kerr, or I swear I'll cut the boy's throat,' Eldritch rasped. The boy Hobby had brought down was Kerr's own flesh and blood, or he was a Froglander. The reiver looked into the captain's black eyes, and saw the bitter truth of his words. He went limp, moving his cramped jaw in silent agony.

'Call them off, you bastard, or you son'll be as dead as you!' Eldritch snarled, yanking on his leading rope.

'Aye,' Kerr croaked. 'I'll call them off,' he agreed.

For the first time in his long, hard life, Kerr had met a man more ruthlessly unpredictable than himself. He felt a peculiar, insinuating dread, realised he was afraid.

Beside Mont Gilbert le Galliard in the French Alps

The cell smelled like a bear pit. A ripening brew of body odours and dark urine, spiced with the even stronger scents of garlic and salt fish Scaralatchi thrived on.

Fabrizio almost gagged, walking in there. The great man was wrapped in his ancient patchwork coat, squatting at his paper-strewn bench with his back bent in furious labour. The boy could hear the frantic scrape of his pen, hear him hum the occasional phrase.

'*Crea mundum in me*,' Scaralatchi whispered, pen poised.

'*Cor mundum crea in me*,' Fabrizio corrected, peering over the composer's shoulder. He scanned the dense forest of notes on the troublesome score, an ink-storm of dots and dashes, crossed out and revised a hundred times. Scaralatchi rolled the manuscript back up, turned his eye on his scowling assistant.

'And all these high Cs? There aren't three choirboys in all Europe who could hold those notes, that long,' the youngster pointed out, hands on hips.

Scaralatchi growled, his sagging jowls rippling with irritation. 'There are boys at the Abbey d'Eleron who could hold high Cs for a week.'

'Hah! Foul-mouthed northerners. You would have to cut their balls off first!'

'Maybe we ought to cut your balls off. Fabrizio Ambolini, *primo castrato*, eh?' He dropped his pen and cupped his hand under the boy's crotch.

Fabrizio knocked the grasping fingers away.

'They're attacking the blockhouse on the causeway again. Seigneur Tarsi is worried they might get a lodgement.'

Scaralatchi shrugged.

'We're safe enough,' he concluded. All that mattered now was finishing the score, the masterpiece which had lain dormant in his brain so long, lost in the coiled seams like a good sauce in saturated pasta.

'Oh ho, so you're his general as well as his choirmaster?' Fabrizio inquired.

'This place is as strong as the Crak des Chevaliers! That's why I chose it.' Fabrizio pursed his lips.

'You chose it? I thought Tarsi had chosen you? That night in Novara when he was . . .'

'There are things in this world, Fabrizio, that even you do not fully comprehend.'

He could tell the old goat was pleased with himself. For one thing he always used his full name rather than some feeble diminutive when he was feeling confident of his abilities. The stifling fortress seemed to agree with him, despite the noisy battles which had banged and rattled the walls for close on a month. Cesar was showing flashes of his old genius, the choral expertise which had won him his treasured place in the Vatican. Despite the sleepless nights, the vomit-fits and the bleedings, Scaralatchi was making progress at last.

Fabrizio stared at his lurid coat, the faded patches which had dazzled palaces back in the distant days of his youth. The tired fabric was split and stretched about his broad back. His arms protruded from the voluminous sleeves, spread over the ancient table like hairy hams. He traced his finger along the crudely-cut stubble which ran like a tidemark around Scaralatchi's head, spread his palm over the great bald dome.

'Not now, Favio. Not now,' Scaralatchi murmured, fluttering his fat fingers at his catamite. Fabrizio smiled at the creased skin around his master's neck.

There was a sudden dull boom above their heads.

They looked up, felt the detonation reverberate through the massively-piled foundations. Scaralatchi clicked his tongue, brushed the worst of the disturbed dust from his scrolls and papers.

'Another mine? They would need an army of dwarves to get inside this place!' Scaralatchi said to himself. He pinched his fleshy nose between his fingers, chronically tired.

'Fetch me some more wine, a plate of sweetmeats.'

'Ah, ah! It's bread and water until you finish, on our master's orders.'

Scaralatchi snorted. 'He'll send me wine, or I'll roll this lot up and stick it up my arse! Let him try and play it to his damned delegation then!'

Fabrizio sighed. He knew Scaralatchi would not hesitate to carry out such a threat.

Fifty feet above their heads, the walls were being attacked with pick and mattock, the pitiless granite blocks which supported the soaring fortress chipped and scored by sixty pressed men from the village down the valley. The reluctant pioneers were crouching in a broad ditch beneath the sheer towers which guarded the gatehouse, frantically undermining a small postern door. The black-clad brutes who had driven them to their dangerous assignment had erected a platform of wood and drenched hides to protect them, but every so often a crossbow bolt or arquebus ball would find a gap in the battered framework, knock another of the toiling engineers to his knees. The ditch was already splattered and spotted with their dark, dusty blood.

Constantin Muhlberg, the landsknecht who commanded the attack, roared and raved, lashing about with a bullwhip as the terrified villagers hacked at the scored rock, dug at the iron-bound doorframe. The corporal strode up and down the kneeling ranks, berating their efforts, slashing their exposed ribs like galley slaves.

'Put your backs into it you vermin! You scrofulous donkeys! You idle tarts! You'll dig a way in here or I'll bury you in the spoil, I swear it on the Saints!'

The siege had dragged on a month already, with little to show for their efforts except a slowly-filling gravepit. Black–clad legionnaire and dusty peasant alike had been rolled down the shifting gravel slopes to join the tumbled bodies below. The stronghold was perched on a crag, the only approach along a narrow causeway overlooked by a formidable blockhouse.

The director of the siege – Muhlberg's red-haired commander Francesco Savvi – had turned his guns on the outworks, blasting them into rubble and throwing jars of Greek fire over the remains. But the stubborn defenders had kept up a constant sniping from the ruins, picking off his troops as they made their way across the bridge towards the even more formidable keep.

It was a brutal, remorseless slaughter, a shocking waste of good men. But their master had charged them with re-capturing the tower, and they dared not disobey.

The gangly commander was coated in stonedust, his black tunic and hose turned white by the blowing clouds. Not even the tremendous blasts from his carefully placed culverins could clear the choked air. His gunners had stripped to their waists, their backs ringed with soot and filth. The guns were steaming where the mattrosses had damped them down with wet sheepskins, the vile smoke bitter with the stink of scorched vinegar.

He shielded his eyes and watched his dogsbody Muhlberg lope back along the exposed causeway, attracting a flurry of shots from the top of the tower as well as its forlorn guard-house. The lanky corporal skipped around the flying bullets and chipped stones. The German cursed, wiped the cut on his sleeve.

'Well?'

'We've lost another four this morning. They've some damned hawkeyes up on that tower, poxed Spanish or similar,' Muhlberg reported, breathing hard after his dangerous run from the walls.

Savvi snorted. 'We'll get more. I don't want to waste

men digging holes. Where's the damned dwarf? That's what I want to know. He was supposed to be there!' Muhlberg cursed, spat a dusty mouthful over the blood-splattered wall.

'Tarsi's caught the cross-eyed bastard out. He's no fool, whatever our master thinks,' Savvi grunted.

Where was the damned spy?

The long gallery was filled with smoke, a hateful concoction made up of burnt powder and blazing oil. Two dozen of Alberto Tarsi's best marksmen were busy at the gun-ports, alternately firing and reloading their cumbersome arquebuses. His hired gunners were manhandling a saker around, keeping up a one-sided duel with the culverins the besieging forces had dragged up under cover of the cliffs opposite the gatehouse.

Tarsi hardly noticed the throat-rasping stinks.

He was a big man, his barrel chest accentuated by his richly-embroidered padded doublet and his heavy, black velvet gown. His mantle, trimmed in bands of mink and white fox, had slipped back from his broad shoulders, the luxurious garment smeared with blood and caked with soot. He was directing the fire from the walls, concentrating his arquebusiers above the crude siege engine they had rolled over the causeway and into the ditch. He knew they would kill more of the unfortunate forced labourers than of Savvi's thugs, but war was war.

The poor villagers down the valley should have organised themselves, called out their militia rather than allowed themselves to be driven like cattle to somebody else's slaughter.

Tarsi at once despised and pitied them.

When he was young despite had always gotten the upper hand, now, as he got older and wiser, pity was taking over.

Like any soldier, he had always held the peasants in contempt, a lower form of life barely worth the trouble of extinguishing. A peasant wasn't a man, until he picked up a pike.

He had burnt villages and sacked towns. He had driven screaming populations over cliff edges, slaughtered men, women and children who had been unfortunate enough to remain within range of the ravaging armies. Usually in the name of some emperor or prince, and always in the name of God.

His last campaign, erratically funded by Margaret of Savoy, had taken him to the Low Countries and Spain, from sedge-lined flood plains to sun-baked sierras. Margaret's forces had been stretched in all directions, quashing rebellions and fighting invasions in her homeland and in her fiefdoms in the Netherlands. Tarsi had been one of her ablest warlords.

The weary warrior sighed, wiped a stray speck from his eye as he watched the ant figures scurrying in the ditch beneath the walls. This was the prize for all those bloody labours: Mont Gilbert le Galliard. The fortress was the key to the high pass, a small but highly lucrative trade route from the Vale d'Aosta and the Lombard plains into Southern France. The pass was treacherous enough in summer and frequently blocked in winter, a lonely artery pinched and pulled by the vast white mass of Mont Blanc. The vital stronghold had changed hands many times – but generally through political expediency rather than military conquest. Margaret of Savoy had taken possession of the fortress from one of her rebellious nobles, the notorious Duke de Gueldres. The duke had paid the price for his insolence, forfeiting a whole hotch-potch of territories and possessions all over Europe. Margaret had needed a reliable landlord, and had offered the prize to her able general Tarsi, knowing full well he would jump at the opportunity of advancing himself.

The low-born Italian soldier had transported his gypsy household to the Alpine fastness, well pleased with his splendid new home. But Margaret's decision to elevate him to Seigneur of Mont Galliard had not been based purely on a kindly desire to reward her champion. The castle, just one of a string of fortresses in the valley, was crucially situated to control the high pass and the toll roads which ran through it. Ever since Roman times, travellers had been expected to pay for the convenience of using it. Tarsi had been empowered to collect the tolls, sharing the income with Margaret on a fifty-fifty basis.

Needless to say, the older-established families in the valley had been most put out by their cosy agreement, and several had offered covert support to the old duke's efforts to reclaim his lost treasure. Eusebius della Stroma, Count of Luningiana, owned rich estates just down the valley around the town of Aosta. His finances had been hit particularly hard by the decision. Up until the rebellion it had been Stroma's right to collect the tolls, but as a close kinsman of the treacherous Gueldres clan the count had been implicated in their revolt, and had paid the penalty when the clumsy demonstration had ended in bloody failure.

Now, nine years later, the count had judged it safe enough to challenge that verdict. He had even gone so far as to appeal to the Vatican to arbitrate in the matter, and a papal delegation was due in Novara shortly to rule on his fanciful application.

Tarsi ducked his head as a culverin shot rebounded off the ruined blockhouse and screamed into the surrounding cliffs. He chuckled to himself, listened to the pulverised stone clatter into the chasm below.

It appeared the canny count had decided against leaving the matter solely in the hands of some notoriously fickle delegation from Rome. He would no doubt be portraying himself as the injured party, unjustly punished for his misjudgement nearly ten years before. In the meantime he had encouraged his mad dog ally Gueldres to try and regain the castle by more direct means.

Tarsi leaned over the battlements, squinted down at the hurrying figures in the ditch. Gueldres' creatures, scuttling like black bettles as they tried to dig a way into their master's lost castle.

'Get that oil over here now!' Tarsi called. His daughter Angelica was overseeing the work, wafting the foul stinks from her face as one of his retainers lifted the lid to check the furiously boiling contents. He frowned, remembered the wretched girl was supposed to be entertaining their guests. The Prince of Villefranco had sent a party of ambassadors to begin preliminary negotiations for her hand in marriage. His father Duke Lodovico was notoriously hard-up and Tarsi — surrounded by these vengeful enemies — needed all the friends he could get. But instead of fluttering her eyelashes and demonstrating her embroidery as she was supposed to, Angelica had spent most of her time up on the battlements with him.

She stood back, holding her mantle over her nose as a gang of strapping soldiers in scorched armour heaved the bubbling pot towards the ledge. Tarsi peered over the edge, waved the sweating men at arms into position above the flimsy wooden barricade.

'That's it. Set it down. Are the archers ready?'

The lighter-clad bowmen had waited their turn beside a brazier, holding short, stubby arrows wrapped in tar-soaked rags into the flames. Angelica leaned over the battlement, shielded her eyes at the bright light and drifting smoke. The soldiers hauled the barrel into position, resting the great black tub on the ledge.

'Ready . . . let them have it!' Tarsi bawled. The men at arms tipped the pot on its side. The boiling oil gushed over the white walls, no more than a bird squirt against the mountain but a terrifying nightmare for the unfortunates toiling below. The ugly black smear fell to earth, a gushing spout which splattered over the battered structure the enemy pioneers had erected in the ditch. Tarsi heard their tormented screaming from his lofty eyrie, felt a momentary flicker of remorse as the poor slaves ran for their lives, their clothing scorched, their skin blistered and burnt by flying globules.

'Now!' The archers crowded along the wall fired their blazing arrows at the splashed planking, turning the feeble shed into an inferno. The diggers ran like rabbits as the flames roared up the walls and along the ditch, the fire arrows igniting a bonfire about their bare heads. They were trapped like rats, the soldiers tearing at their flaming black tunics, the villagers they had press-ganged to do their dirty work beating the walls in their ghastly torment.

Tarsi watched for a moment; recognised the sickly incense of roasting flesh. He stood back from the wall, felt familiar gallstones of guilt slide in his belly.

This was his fortress, and this was his business.

But he had had enough. Please God above, no more of this hopeless bloodshed.

'They're running, they've had enough!' Angelica cried, pointing over towards the far end of the causeway. Black-clad figures were hurrying back over the bridge, to be picked off by the mad-dogs he had ordered to occupy the blockhouse. They would be paid treble, quadruple their normal rates for holding on so long. There couldn't be many of them left to pay, after all.

Tarsi raised his chin, his shame souring his sense of relief.

'Savvi must have lost his mind, staging such a pointless assault,' he said, wiping his mouth on his sleeve.

'He's simply doing his masters' bidding, father. The Bastard Gueldres wants his precious castle back; Stroma wants his tolls.' Tarsi was always slightly disconcerted by his daughter's acute grasp of power-politics.

Angelica coughed, spat over the wall as she had seen the soldiers do so many times in the past. Her father frowned, but there was little point in trying to change her ways now. She had been brought up in war, reared on conflict. What did he expect her to do, needlepoint?

The grubby girl had boosted herself up on the ledge to peer down at the destroyed works in the ditch. The flimsy structure had been consumed in moments. The black-backed insect shells she could see strewn about the ditch had up until a few moments ago been human beings. Angelica held her nose.

★

'They were after the postern gate,' she told her father as they strode down the fouled gallery towards the staircases of the inner keep. Tarsi nodded, brushing the worst of the filth from his mantle as he marched. The weary soldiers leaning against the battlements gave him a cheer as he ducked under the stairway, his daughter hoisting her skirts as she tried to keep up with him. Tarsi's liveried body-guards fell in behind, clanking along the echoing chamber in their splendidly-lacquered armour.

'Where do you imagine we're going?' he asked over his shoulder. 'That door is over a foot thick, bound with iron rivets. The tunnel is no bigger than a bath-drain,' he snapped, taking the smoothly-worn steps two at a time.

'A spy,' Angelica theorised.

'As you say, my dear. It's Gueldres' castle, every crack and cellar crawling with their creatures.'

They arrived on a broad stone landing, the only illumination coming from a row of carefully-pared arrow-slits – lancets – in the wall. To their left, the stairs descended into the black pits of the keep. The lower floors housed the garrison, the kitchens, stores, magazine, stables, dungeons and frantically-overworked armourers. The stairwell carried the hot reek of molten lead, sweaty horses and endlessly-boiled cabbage soup. To their right a broad hallway led to their own limited but luxurious living quarters. His major domo, a tall, prematurely-aged Fleming named Julius Furstenbein, strode out of the main hall and fell in beside his master.

'What is it?'

'They've given up, gone home for now,' he growled. 'They seemed to be making for the postern door in the west wall. We'd best take a look, but discreetly,' he warned. The Fleming's features creased with concern.

'Have Strozzi send a squad to the gatehouse tower, tell him to go through the stables and get into the cloister that way. We'll go straight down, but be quick, if there was anybody down there they won't hang about now. *Va Via!*' Tarsi exclaimed.

★

The dim, dank passage ran the length of the tower wall, an arched corridor which connected the warren of dungeons and storerooms in the bowels of the castle. There were whole stretches of plain stone, the bare flanks of the mountain the stronghold had been built up on. Elsewhere, cheap brickwork with powdery mortar mossy and grey with age. Torches had been set in the walls, but only half of them were lit at any one time. The running gutters were convenient highways for the armies of rats which infested the tower. The perfect place to breed treachery.

Tarsi had taken a rushlight and led the way, drawn sword in hand. Furstenbein and his retainers crowded in behind him, Angelica cursing and pushing and peering over their packed shoulders. The long cloister echoed with the sound of their iron-shod boots, sending black shapes scuttling in all directions. They passed long-forgotten rooms, the boarded-up entrances to old tunnels. Tarsi himself had only ever investigated a few hundred yards of the deadly labyrinth.

'We ought to brick these tunnels over. God only knows where they might lead.'

'The postern door is barred, of course,' the major domo replied. Tarsi cursed under his breath.

'Have you changed the locks since we took over?' Furstenbein said nothing. 'So every guttersnipe in the place might have a spare? We should have thought of this before,' he inquired, alarmed now.

'Locks cost . . .' Tarsi held up his sword.

'Don't tell me what locks cost; get them changed, out of your own damned pocket if necessary.' Furstenbein blanched at this unholy prospect.

'Father, look . . .' Angelica had barged the bodyguards aside for a moment, ducked down beside a rusty iron grate in the wall. She tugged at the bars, which held fast.

'Stand back girl. Bring lights here.' Tarsi bent down beside his excited daughter, examined the round gate. The old iron was flaking but sound enough. He bent closer, held his rushlight towards the crude lock housing. Tarsi whistled softly.

'The whole thing's covered in webs and dust, hasn't been touched for years,' he said.

Furstenbein clicked his tongue.

'Well, there you . . .'

'But this lock look; the dust's been smeared off; there's a scratch through the rust here where someone's been trying to get a key in.'

Angelica jumped to her feet, peered down the dark, dank chamber. Tarsi climbed to his feet, waved the quiet guards on.

'Check every doorway now, every hatch and hole.'

They set off down the corridor, quick steps echoing ahead of them.

'There!' Angelica cried. The guards tensed. Her father threw his arm across her chest, pushed her back behind the armoured halberdiers. A thin white shape danced on the periphery of their vision, a spectre lit by the dim torchlights.

'Stand where you are!' Tarsi barked, his voice magnified by the brickwork tomb. He strode forward, sword ready. The white shape seemed to float closer, the invisible limbs moving lightly in the black passage.

'Who's that?' the disembodied voice called back.

'Stand there and don't move!' Tarsi ordered, hurrying forward with sword and torch aloft.

The flickering flames bounced monstrous shadows off the walls, turned the slim youth into a troll of the underworld. The intruder shielded his eyes against the sudden light. Tarsi squinted at the spy, tried to put a name to the finely-boned, olive-skinned features. The pretty boy . . .

'It's Fabrizio, Scaralatchi's . . . boy,' Furstenbein reported.

Angelica had crowded forward once again, touching the startled boy's arm.

'What are you doing down here?' Tarsi demanded. Fabrizio blinked, raised his chin in contempt.

'I'm Scaralatchi's "boy". These are Scaralatchi's quarters!' he said, shrill. Tarsi glanced at the mildewed doorway he had taken for a dungeon.

'Here? My court composer scratching away in the filthiest hovel in the basement?' Fabrizio's eyes smouldered with angry tears.

'Even so, *padrone*.'

'And what were you doing scuttling about, eh?' the major domo sneered. Fabrizio held up a bundle of filthy undershirts. Tarsi recoiled from the ripe stink.

'He's shat and spewed over them. I thought I ought to take them to the washhouse.' Angelica grimaced, gazing intently at the lovely youth. Tarsi noticed the heat in her look. Well it was no use chasing that one, he thought grimly. Not unless she liked . . . he turned his attention on the tearful boy.

The door swung open, admitting a rectangle of lurid yellow light. Scaralatchi, stark naked, stood like a great greased hog on his thick, white and hairless legs. Angelica gasped. Tarsi pushed the wretched girl behind him, snatched the boy's laundry and thrust it towards the fat composer's crotch. His limp penis dangled between his legs like a smoked eel. By God, to think . . .

'Cover yourself in the presence of a lady!' Tarsi barked, furious.

Scaralatchi held the soiled clothing in front of his vast yellow belly, blinking with bewilderment.

'*Padrone* . . . I thought there was trouble . . . the stable boys chase Fabrizio so,' he mumbled, clearly startled by the unexpected visit.

'Who assigned you quarters down here?' Tarsi inquired.

Furstenbein coughed.

'There was very little accommodation available, sir, what with the delegation from Villefranco and all. And Signor Scaralatchi was adamant he needed peace . . .'

'Peace? With a battle going on under the wall?' The Fleming pursed his lips, not daring to contradict his master when he was in such a frightful temper. Angelica was peering over her father's shoulder, still wide-eyed from the dreadful appearance of the composer. Fabrizio stifled a giggle.

60

Footsteps rang down the corridor. Iron-shod boots and the peculiar, staccato tap-tap-tapping of a goat or small pony. Tarsi held the spluttering light up, illuminated a party of soldiers herding a child. Not a child. The dwarf, Obolus.

'We found him trying to crawl under the gap in a door,' the captain reported, steering the lionheaded dwarf with his halberd. The midget cast an immense shadow on the slimy brickwork, and seemed fascinated by the unusual perspective on himself. His head was large, bristling with thick, rusty hair which seemed to stand up from his misshapen skull. His doll-sized body was dressed in an exotic, multi-coloured doublet and bright hose, the sort of outfit favoured by the notorious German mercenaries known as landsknechts. He wore a brightly-jewelled codpiece, the tapering end tied up to a broad leather belt. Tarsi noticed the dwarf's right buttock was bare, his gaudy hose cut out to reveal a hairy backside. The dwarf was wearing little iron-shod shoes, which he seemed to be unable to keep still. Tap-tap-tapping against the cold stone as if he was a clockwork toy.

'What are you doing down here Luciano?' Angelica asked, bending down to bring her bright eyes level with the hatefully-muscled child. The dwarf turned his large head about and grinned.

He held up his chubby paw, a large decapitated rat hanging by its foot-long tail. Angelica paled, swallowed with difficulty as she realised the traces of what she had taken to be tomato sauce about the evil creature's face was actually the rat's blood.

Tarsi glared at the monstrous puppet.

'You were catching rats? Why doesn't the *lusus naturae* talk?'

'Your pardon, *padrone*. But he is not a freak of nature, more a . . . a crude clay pot, poorly thrown, just like myself in fact. He won't talk, he will only sing, but his voice, Gesu!' Scaralatchi murmured, stepping forward to pat the creature's stiff hair. 'He has the finest voice I have ever heard, even in the Vatican choir itself,' he explained, wrapping his filthy robes about his vast waist. Fabrizio snorted. Tarsi scowled.

'Well he'd better sing out what he was about, or we'll stretch his bones for him.'

Obolus made a face.

'*I was earning my keep, seven days a week!*' he shrieked, a frighteningly shrill echo bouncing around the walls. '*Every man, large or small, must make his living in Tar-si's ha-ll!*' The dwarf's voice sank to a rumbling bass, he held the last note and danced a little jig. Tarsi licked his lips, tried to remember when the rhymester had joined their wandering household. He had heard every grand house in Italy had one, a little mascot decked out in the family livery, to sing and clown through the cold winter nights.

'Take him to the torture chamber and shake him out. If you find a key to fit that lock,' he pointed back up the chamber, 'I want to hear about it.'

'*Si, Padrone!*' Captain Strozzi shouted back.

Beside Mont Gilbert le Galliard, in the French Alps

No sooner had the dust from the bombardment begun to settle on the battered gatehouse than Tarsi found himself besieged by whining retainers, buttonholed by outraged house guests and jostled by unpaid builders. The unruly mob seethed through the dustclouds in search of their absent host, professional courtiers in the finest silks rubbing shoulders with white-skinned plasterers from up the valley. They had all heard the electrifying news of Savvi's ignominious retreat into France – and were eager to get on with their interrupted lives as soon as possible.

Their anger was understandable. They had been stranded in the north tower for a month – unable to escape Savvi's legion they had become prisoners of Tarsi's absent-minded hospitality. They had fumed and fretted in the plaster-splattered north hall, apprehensively pacing the wide, airless passages as the Black Band continued its fruitless assault on the gatehouse.

Tarsi's short-tempered guests had been forced to run a gauntlet of flying paint, crumbling plaster and falling masonry as they made their way about their assigned quarters. They had been driven to distraction by the incessant hammering, the constant gunfire and the nerve-racking rasp of wood saws.

They were safe on the far side of the courtyard – only an earthquake could have dislodged the immensely formidable foundations of Mont Gilbert – but it had certainly been a trying ordeal, especially as they had been kept awake all night by Savvi's snipers.

The embassy from the court of the Prince of Villefranco certainly hadn't appreciated the troublesome delay. They had expected to conclude their negotiations inside a week, return to their prince with an immediate offer of Angelica Tarsi's hand in marriage – and a sumptuous dowry into the bargain. House Mounier was chronically short of cash, and might be persuaded to agree the *mésalliance* if the wealthy Tarsi clan could rejuvenate their over-extended finances.

The delegation had not been overly concerned at the battle over the walls – warfare after all was virtually endemic across most of southern Europe – but they had expected to spend rather more time getting to know the young lady in question.

Angelica, however, had spent most of the month up on the walls, gleefully directing her father's hired crossbowmen and arquebusiers as they methodically picked off Savvi's pioneers. Her evident accomplishments with firearms were not likely to impress her prospective husband – a lantern-jawed, in-bred imbecile who was rumoured to have taken an oath of celibacy.

Young Gerhard was, nevertheless, a Prince of the blood. His family had strong connections with the ruling House of Savoy – and therefore the Empire – as well as a long tradition of papal patronage. Such a connection might come in handy, should Tarsi be called to Novara to give evidence in Stroma's forthcoming court case. The Vatican would rule whether he should continue to collect the road tolls on Margaret's behalf, or hand the lucrative rights back to the disgruntled count.

Tarsi longed for a powerful ally. He had fought Gueldres and his wily allies to a standstill, hanging on grimly to his formidable mountain fastness, but he needed friends in high places if he was to carve himself a place at the council tables of Europe.

A clever marriage would help secure Tarsi's connections,

establish his name as a leading statesman as well as a successful soldier. Tarsi had tried to spare some time at least to meet and entertain his prestigious guests, but he had been unable to drag himself away from the walls for more than a few hours at a time.

Arranging a marriage at this level was a delicate process, an art form in itself. If Savvi's attack had achieved anything for his blackguard of a master, it had been the complete disruption of the crucial marriage negotiations.

In addition to the inconvenience, Tarsi had incurred crippling expenses in fighting him off, seriously weakening his own financial position. He had been obliged to hire several companies of Gascon crossbowmen and Spanish arquebusiers to augment his own slender retinue, and they had cost him a small fortune in pay and powder. The four-week siege had eaten through the last of his profits from his outing in the Low Countries – the profits he had intended to use as Angelica's dowry.

Angelica stood on tiptoe to brush the worst of the dust and debris from her father's broad shoulders. He had claimed he hadn't time to change or bathe, insisting they intercepted the visiting delegation before the courtiers rode out of the castle in a fit of pique.

Tarsi's personal apartment was on the top floor of the gatehouse, safely beyond the elevation of Savvi's culverins. The bedchamber, however, still looked as if it had been overrun by a tribe of barbarians, with mouldy food and spilled drinks strewn over his table, soiled clothes and discarded weaponry lying about the floor or leaning against the unmade bed. Its foul-tempered owner was tapping his foot in irritation as his daughter pointed out Prince Gerhard's shortcomings.

'. . . and in any case everybody knows Savoy itself is a house of cards . . .'

'Stop fussing girl,' Tarsi snapped, shoving his argumentative daughter aside. 'I know your mind! Keep me talking up here while Signor Bellatavicci blows hot and cold in the north wing!' Angelica stepped away from her parent, watched him straighten the heavy black mantle. 'We're this close to losing him altogether!'

'*Baie!* What a tragedy that would be!' Angelica retorted, coiling her dishevelled hair about her finger as she glared about the chamber. Hyacinthine, the stylist had called it. He had assured her the intricately-layered kinks and curls would start a fashion which would sweep all Italy. Her father had stumped up in the vain hope of impressing the visiting delegation, but Angelica wished he hadn't bothered. The wretched style required hours of attention if it wasn't to fluff up into an abominable mess. Combing and curling ate up hours of her precious time, and Angelica had never been one for sitting in front of mirrors.

'This Gerhard's no more than an idiot, you know it and you don't care!' she exclaimed, tears springing into her eyes.

'Of course we care!' Tarsi shouted. 'Villefranco might well be a third-rate corner of a second-rate duchy, but it's still a mighty leg-up for a mere mercenary's daughter!'

The insistent major domo took instant advantage of her distress, barging her aside and busying himself straightening the heavy gold chains his master's angry posturings had disturbed.

'Prince Gerhard is a fine, upstanding young man. Rather than being the idiot Mistress Angelica suggests, he is said to have been educated by Italy's leading humanists. He can sing in French . . .'

'Very useful!' Angelica muttered.

'. . . read Greek, play the clavichord and draw in perspective. The Spanish are keen to marry him off to one of the younger Infantas.'

Tarsi scowled at his major domo's good sense.

'Younger Infantas? Good Christ in irons, the oldest is only six!' said a wine-raw voice from the far side of the room. Tarsi turned, smiled at Luca Strozzi's caustic wit. 'They can marry them off all right but they'll never get an heir until the girl bleeds,' he asserted.

Furstenbein looked aghast.

'Even so, my Lord,' the major domo breathed. 'A Spanish bride, of whatever age, would appear to be the Prince's soundest choice. We must endeavour to convince the envoys that Mistress Angelica, already of childbearing years, would make a more advantageous and short-term prospect.'

'Short-term prospect? Uncle Julius, you old flatterer!' Angelica exclaimed, her features flushed with temper.

'Don't start her off again! Bellatavicci's not likely to go home singing her praises as it is, is he? You've barely spoken to him in four weeks, despite the fact that I distinctly told you to wait on them hand and foot!'

'Get Constanzia to wait on them! Here you are trying to talk me up to becoming a princess and yet you send me to do chores you wouldn't give a Turk!'

Tarsi paled, balefully regarding his plain-speaking daughter. Strozzi coughed.

'Well your domestic affairs are one thing, Berti,' he said familiarly, prising himself to his feet. 'But if you ask me we've got more urgent things to consider at home.'

Tarsi waved his broad paw in irritation.

'Spiders and spies. We take over the Bastard Gueldres' favourite fortress; of course there are going to be spies.'

Tarsi had assumed control of the scattered farmsteads and villages up and down the high pass, as well as the proceeds from the busy toll road which ran past the castle. In addition to these crucial sources of revenue, Tarsi had inherited a teeming underworld of serfs, slaves and servants. They seemed to come and go as they pleased, living in the bowels of the castle or in the squalid hovels which had sprung up around the walls like so many mildewed mushrooms.

They had repeatedly screened the surly mob, picking out the more obvious assassins the Bastard Gueldres had left behind, but there would always be more to take their place, more of Gueldres' creatures lurking in the basements.

'Here he goes again,' Angelica accused. 'He said my own maid was a spy! Constanzia, as if!' Strozzi smiled weakly,

67

waved his broad paw in cautious agreement. He had had a fine old time getting to know that mysterious little minx!

'And that poor little midget Luciano. How could he be of any use to Gueldres?'

Strozzi, tall and dark in his lacquered armour and patched surcoat, recovered quickly and held his master's glare.

'Nevertheless, Savvi's dogs were digging by that postern door. It's obvious they were expecting to find it open. If they could have got swordsmen inside the courtyard those hired hands of yours would have run like rabbits.'

'Father caught Scaralatchi's . . . very good friend Fabrizio down there,' Angelica reported mischievously. Tarsi winced. How would he ever make a lady of this wretched spitfire? 'Uncle Julius thinks he must be in league with the dwarf.'

Strozzi shook his head.

'We turned their quarters upside down, searched every inch of the passage. If either of them had a key, they damn well swallowed it.'

Tarsi raised his eyebrows.

'You've locked my court composer up with that snake-hipped sweetmeat and the dwarf?'

'He dotes on the boy, locking them up together for an hour or two is no hardship to either. And anyway, you said yourself. Security first. If one of them was in league with Savvi, they would have had to have had a key. Find the key, you find your spy,' Strozzi declared. Tarsi shook his head resignedly.

'He's supposed to be writing me a masterpiece to present before the Pope himself. By God above, it's not exactly going to fill him full of inspiration is it?'

'Perhaps he ought to write me a wedding march instead? If you insist on marrying me off to that spavin Gerhard, he could call it the "Angelica Requiem"!'

Strozzi brayed with laughter at the girl's bright-eyed sally. Tarsi held his daughter's fiery gaze as long as he could, flapped his arms against his sides in weary resignation.

'Let's go and catch them before they ride out without our

offer,' he said gruffly. 'But if you ask me, there's not enough gold in all Europe to buy us a chance of getting shot of her!'

'Charmed as usual, father dear,' Angelica said, curtsying.

Beside Mont Gilbert le Galliard, in the French Alps

Luca Strozzi ducked under the doorway and grinned at the prisoners squatting against the glistening dungeon wall.

'Signors . . . a dreadful mistake! My master Tarsi has sent me straight down to offer his sincerest apologies for this deeply-regretted misunderstanding!'

The drowsy guards detailed to supervise their ablutions leapt to their feet and presented arms as the locotenent strode into the cell, shaking his head at the evident miscarriage of justice.

The sudden waft of chill air he brought with him from the passage stirred the fetid air in the cell, making the formidable soldier gag.

'You scrofulous harlots! How dare you keep these men in such conditions!' He waved his arms about in an attempt to clear the odious miasma.

The guards recoiled from the stinging rebuke, but dared not contradict the furious captain.

'Gah! What a stink! You keep our honoured guests in a midden!'

Cesar Scaralatchi, squatting on the floor with his fleshy head propped up on his palm, was unimpressed by Strozzi's loud protests. The composer studied the locotenent's antics with contempt.

'Don't blame them! Your men have been waiting for us to move our bowels, on your orders! What did you expect it to smell of, crushed violets and lemon blossom?'

Fabrizio nodded in agreement, his dark mouth puckered up in a furious pout.

'As if I'd swallow some dirty old key,' he piped up. He had been particularly upset by their enforced inactivity, pacing the cell for hours muttering and cursing as the guards waited to inspect their brass chamberpots.

'The very thought!' Strozzi exclaimed, holding his great hairy paw to his short, stiff beard to disguise his amusement.

'Gentlemen, I can only offer my master's sincerest apologies. He deeply regrets ordering such a deeply humiliating examination. The siege, you know. His nerves!'

'His nerves?' Fabrizio yelped. 'He's got a nerve, treating his court composer so!' he accused, snatching up his surcoat from the floor.

Scaralatchi shoved himself to his feet with a grunt, tugged his gown about his vast waistline.

'You can shove your apologies up your hairy arse, signor,' he rasped. 'And you can tell your master his ridiculous suspicions will delay my work for weeks, possibly months!' He clicked his sausage fingers beneath Strozzi's broad nose and barged past the astonished captain. Fabrizio skipped after him, giving the soldier a withering stare.

Strozzi sighed, turned his gaze on the dwarf, rolled in the corner of the cell like a forgotten barrel. He was still swinging the dead rat by its slowly-stiffening tail.

'You're free to go,' Strozzi said flatly.

'If it's all the same to these long-legged shits,
I'll stay here in your dingy pits,'

he sang in a rich, powerful baritone, his fox eyes burning with mischievous fire.

Strozzi grimaced.

'Get back to your sty, you stumpy sneak! And be on your guard, Obolus, I've my eye on you!'

'How kind, how kind of you to say so,
I'll be sure and polish my . . . halo!'

71

the demented dwarf trilled.

Strozzi shook his head in disgust and left him to it.

Angelica Tarsi's Spanish-born servant Constanzia was waiting in the chill passage, a basket of fresh linen balanced precariously on her golden arm. She jangled her bracelets to attract the freed composer's attention.

'Signor Tarsi's orders. New undershirts for our guests. The least he could do, in the trying circumstances,' she said, smiling broadly at the released prisoners. Scaralatchi ignored the gypsy girl's grin.

He grunted something and stalked past the girl, Fabrizio pausing just long enough to give her a lopsided smile before hurrying after his master.

Strozzi ducked out of the vacated cell, picked the fresh linen from the girl's basket and rubbed the quality cotton, between his thumb and forefinger. The veteran campaigner watched the mismatched couple stride off down the corridor, casting strange shadows on the brickwork.

'He hasn't changed his hose since he arrived, the filthy turdskinner,' Strozzi growled, his teeth glinting in his black beard. 'You'd best take these back to the laundry house, *Regina Mia*,' he added huskily, rolling his dark eyes suggestively. She looked away, but Strozzi reached out, raised her pretty chin on his forefinger. 'Maybe now Savvi has taken himself off, we can go for another of our rides down the valley; how would you like that?'

The girl pursed her lips, her cats' eyes flicking over the soldier's familiar features.

'After the last time? We didn't get past the first haystack on the high road!' she exclaimed. 'I couldn't walk for a month!'

Strozzi chuckled, reaching out to lift the girl by her swelling buttocks. He nosed her neck as she struggled to bring the unbalanced basket back between them.

'Captain! Remember where we are,' she scolded, hauling her gown back over her bared shoulder. 'Now what about this dwarf?'

72

Strozzi sighed, jerked his thick thumb towards the opened cell.

'What about him? These shirts are ten sizes too big for his body, but I wager he'd never fit them over his head!' He thrust the basket back towards the maid, leered closer.

'Another time, sweet lips.'

Constanzia curtsied, watched the big man stamp off down the ill-lit passage. She turned her head as she recognised the peculiar staccato steps of the dwarf. Obolus was squinting up at her, his leonine head tipped back on his shoulders, little fists on his hips in grotesque parody of her own stance.

She frowned, nodded on down the echoing chamber. The dwarf tilted his head like some long-extinct species of bird, and clattered off down the passage. Constanzia followed the whistling midget towards a dark recess in the wall, ducked in after her colourfully-costumed companion.

'They found nothing,' she hissed.

> '*They didn't look so closely at my little rat,*
> *They seemed more concerned with what I shat!*'

he warbled, his fiery little eyes twinkling in the half-light thrown off by the torches further along the passage.

Constanzia closed her eyes at his ridiculous couplets, wondering why Savvi trusted the sawn-off freak. It wasn't like Francesco to indulge such idiocies in his creatures.

'They'll be furious you let them down. What happened to you? Where's the damned key?' she snarled, grimacing as the hideous monster began to pick and pry at the decapitated rat's torn throat. He pulled out the thin key – glistening with rank blood – gave it a long and loving lick and handed it up to the scowling servant. Constanzia grimaced, took the key and wiped it carefully on the corner of one of her shirts.

'You'd best lie low. Strozzi suspects.'

'Strozzi, Strozzi Strozzi!' Obolus chimed.

> '*Strozzi is a boiled fish*
> *His ghastly end my fevered wish,*'

the dwarf sang, *sotto voce.*

Constanzia swept her flowing black hair back from her shoulders, shivering with revulsion at the dwarf's bizarre facial contortions.

'I'll get word to Savvi. You'd best think of something quick, little one, or he'll pull your arsehole over your damned head, next time he sees you.'

The dwarf seemed delighted by her dire warning, dancing a jig in the cramped alcove. He bent his head, lowered his voice, and sang:

> '*The fat composer's everywhere,*
> *Running his fingers through the pretty boy's hair.*
> *His fault it was our brave plan failed,*
> *Sniffing round the passage as if he was on our trail!*'

Constanzia tapped her shoe on the cold stone slabs as the wretched creature spread his arms, raising his voice in a shrill falsetto.

> '*I've been locked up with that bore,*
> *The fat composer and his precious score.*
> *I've heard him whistle, hum and sing,*
> *I might have written the wretched thing!*
> *And it's clear it's precious to our Lord,*
> *The money he's invested in his bed and board!*'

'So much noise!' Constanzia shook her head in irritation, narrowing her green eyes as she tried to make sense of the demented dwarf's songs. 'Scaralatchi? That lard ball? What do you know?' she quizzed him, bending down over the chuckling spy. Obolus tapped his nose.

> '*Tarsi's given him a vital task,*
> *To write a special papal mass,*
> *To perform before a doting Pope,*
> *That is our brave master Tarsi's hope.*'

'More riddles! Savvi will skin you alive and feed your entrails to his hounds!'

> '*Savvi will thank his Grecian coin*
> *When he plants his boot in Tarsi's groin!*
> *Stealing a march on his despised rival,*
> *He'd pay a ransom for this trifle.*'

The maid straightened her basket, frowning down at her dangerous intermediary. She knew better than to question the dwarf's demented judgement.

'I'll see Savvi's told all about it,' she whispered.

Obolus leapt like a startled goat, clicked his tiny heels together and clattered off down the passage.

Beside Crow Hole, Redesdale, on the English Middle March

James Eldritch had endured his master's rantings for nearly twenty minutes, staring into the middle distance as the warden strode back and forth. Howath had ordered his subordinate into his private quarters, but his deafening shouts echoed around the keep. Even the dullest scullery hand could make out the gist of his colourful invective. Eldritch hardly blinked, standing in his cloak before his commander as if he was waiting for Howath to draw breath.

'Ye've not much to say for yerself, all of a sudden,' Howath fumed. 'Don't try cocking yer beaver with me boy, I've shat bigger than ye!'

Eldritch absorbed the fusillade of spit-flecked insults, knowing full well the storm would eventually blow itself out. Howath was breathing hard already, face crimson, black beard ruffled.

'What did you imagine you were about?' Howath asked at last, moderating his tone a fraction. Eldritch stared at the mildewed wall hangings with which Miranda had attempted to warm the chamber.

'We have been trying to catch Kerr for more than a decade, my Lord. He's thumbed his nose at all of us, hiding behind his wretched Border code.'

'And it's beneath ye, a damned merchant's boy, to live by that code?'

'Kerr didn't live by it. You bring him before your courts

and he laughs in your face. There's not a man in the whole of the March ready to bear witness against him.'

Howath was nodding his head in mock agreement.

'Ah, so you violate the truce, and bring five score of his friends down on our heads. By nightfall there might be a thousand of them, baying for Kerr's freedom, aye, and our blood.'

'We have his son as hostage my Lord,' Eldritch reminded the warden.

Howath seethed with anger, trying to out-think his troublesome captain. The blackguard was better informed than he was – what had he known about the letter from Northumberland? The new orders to march his retinue to Morpeth ready to join the King's army in the south? Could he have had a clue to its contents, before he had ridden out after Kerr? That would help explain his maddening self-confidence, at least. He might well have broken the damned code – if he guessed he wouldn't be expected to have to live by it ever more.

'You have lost me my honour,' Howath croaked.

'If there is any honour lost, it is mine, my Lord.'

'Your honour? You mean it was your responsibility to say what goes in this march and not mine? This is my march; this is my keep. You don't flout *my* honour, Eldritch!' the older man took a deep, reflective breath. 'You've stuck your damned nose out a tad too far this time, boy. It's not like you to leave yer ballocks hanging free like this.'

'I don't know what you mean, my Lord,' Eldritch said stiffly.

'Hah! You know exactly what I mean.' Howath tore through the sheaf of papers on his desk, held up a heavily-folded parchment still bearing the red shards of the Earl of Northumberland's great seal. Howath waved the offending document in his horsemaster's face.

'D'you ken this, eh? And if you've not seen it, you've heard something about it, if I guess aright. You have your sources Eldritch, don't bother to deny it!'

77

'I have no idea what information you suppose I have acquired my Lord.'

'Ye lying shite! I did you a service Eldritch, giving you a start up here, and this is how ye repay me!' he rasped, his accent becoming more marked as he lost his temper. 'You know full well what this letter says. Scrope's boy is taking over the Middle March and I'm to march to Morpeth ready for immediate transportation to Chatham. His Majesty is raising an army to take to France.'

Eldritch's eyes widened in surprise.

'My Lord, but this is excellent news!'

Howath scowled.

'Don't give me that ballocks! You knew we would be going south, so it mebbe wouldn't matter if you bent a few rules in the meantime! The reivers might be after your gizzards, but you'd be safe, off romping around France!'

Eldritch shook his head.

'My actions were based on . . .'

'Your damned actions? Don't think you're going to boast about your damned conquests! D'ye think I'm about to have it put about that my officers do what they like, while I shiver and drool in my dotage?'

Howath jabbed his finger into Eldritch's chest. 'I'm in charge here, not you. As far as all those bastards out there are concerned,' he pointed at the mildewed banners hanging limply on the walls. 'I ordered you to go after Kerr and bring him in,' he paused, caught his breath. 'The whole ambuscade was my idea, is that clear?'

'Yes, my Lord, always,' Eldritch grated, taking a sideways glance at his master.

'You've brought him in thinking to hang him dead. But whilst you were off setting your damned trap, I was offering our Sandy a commission to command a hundred swords in Henry's army. Aye! Northumberland's expecting me to bring in a full tail. Without 'em that lickspittle Cholmley will take over all the Border horse, and I'll be reduced to squiring behind! There, that's one thing you didn't count on, ye arrogant coxcomb!'

Eldritch's features remained blank, but his ready mind was racing. It was true he had heard from one of his cronies in Newcastle that Howath might be about to be ordered to report to Morpeth. Ambushing Kerr had been a tremendous risk, but it might have been his only chance to make a name for himself before he was swallowed up by the bruising anonymity of Henry's army. The news Howath had actually offered Kerr a place in the very same force had come as a considerable shock. He hadn't anticipated Kerr would survive long enough to revenge his insolent, truce-breaking capture.

'Ah, we've managed to shut your neck for once,' Howath crowed.

Eldritch wiped his dripping moustache as his master regained his temper.

'I mean to offer Kerr a pardon in return for his good service with the Crown. We'll hold his son hostage while the sire comes south with us.' The warden thought for a moment, glanced up at his subordinate.

'And it was my idea, Eldritch, all of it,' he growled.

'Aye, my Lord. All of it,' Eldritch replied, smiling faintly.

PART TWO
The Golden Valley

◆ ◆ ◆ ◆ ◆

'A prudent man should always follow in
the footsteps of great men, and emulate
those who have been outstanding.'

Machiavelli, *The Prince*

Beside the Goodwin Sands, off Dover, June 1520

The wearisome trip had begun in a silt-ribbed creek off the Tyne. Lord Howath, late warden of the English Middle March, had contracted his old friend Edward Kraven to transport his bustling household south in three barnacle-bellied cogs: the *Crimson Tun*, the *Snow Pola* and the *Tower of Strength*. They were slow but spacious, deep enough to take Howath's horses, hounds, stores and accumulated treasures – as well as his warband.

The little fleet had nosed out into the belly-aching chop of the North Sea and begun the long cruise down the bleak shorelands of England. Manacled reivers and English bowmen alike had watched aghast as the sea cut up rough, the evil, white-capped waves crashing and sliding against the formidable bastion of Flamborough Head. They had sailed by the dreary and dispiriting wastes of Holderness, run hard against the sickening pull of the Wash. None of them had relished the tedious voyage, but it was either that or a hellish long walk to London.

'Besides Jack, you're transporting your entire household as well as your men,' Kraven had pointed out. 'You wouldn't want Miranda riding into London with a pack of lousy skelders!' the canny merchant had pointed out, knowing precisely where to prick the old warrior's bristling vanity.

Three-quarters of the noblemen in England had been obliged to attend Henry's overseas adventure. Some of them had been forced to sell off hundreds of acres of precious land – forests, lakes, rivers and all – to bring their household retinues up to the standards Henry craved. The King meant to impress, and good impressions cost money. Knights, lords, earls and dukes would pay dearly for the privilege of plumping their proud liege as he journeyed to meet his counterpart Francis at Guisnes, on the outer reaches of the English Pale.

It wasn't the English king's first overseas venture.

Henry had invaded France seven years before, in league with the Holy Roman Emperor Maximilian. The naive English had agreed to pay the canny German a handsome allowance towards the upkeep of the relatively insignificant Imperial forces, and had been happy to wage war according to Maximilian's experienced direction.

'The Emperor saw him coming all right,' Kraven explained, slipping the cork from a fresh bottle. 'Henry paid through the nose to fight the Emperor's battles for him!'

'Cah, you could hardly call them battles,' Howath said sternly, holding on to the table as the master steered the heavily-laden ship through the waves with stomach-loosening bravado. 'Those piddling fall-outs wouldn't have rated a mention if we'd fought them up on the Border,' he growled.

Henry's French campaign had culminated in the lacklustre sieges of Therouanne and Tournai. The only open engagement of the bitter demonstration of arms had been at the sleepy village of Bomy. The insignificant skirmish had gone down in history as the Battle of the Spurs and had gone some way towards satisfying Henry's thirst for martial glory. But his grand campaign had been thrown into the shade by the stunning news from home: on the very day the King had accepted the surrender of Therouanne, a Scots army had crossed the Border and been brought to battle on Flodden hill. Ten thousand Scots pikemen had been slaughtered by the awesome interaction of English bill and bowmen. Seven years later, Henry had determined on winning similar glory for himself.

That summer of 1520, Europe once again stood on the brink of war, ready and waiting for another bloody bout in the power struggle between France and the Holy Roman Empire. The question was whether England would rejoin the Imperial cause she had taken up with such naive enthusiasm in 1513 or try and establish herself as a continental power through an alliance with the old enemy – France.

The magnificent conference at Guisnes would decide all.

The channel had proved particularly choppy. Howath had been forced to stay in the master's grand cabin in the forecastle and pretend to listen as Kraven argued the rights and wrongs of Henry's European adventure.

'In the long run, it's in everybody's interest if we keep France down. If we once let her merchants get their noses in front of ours, they'll shut us out of every market from Lisbon to Goa.'

Howath raised his chin a notch, wiped his wine-moistened mouth. 'Very well then,' he interrupted, swilling his Malmsey around his goblet. 'We do as you suggest and join Charles against the French. But why in the name of God are we bothering with this charade? All these preparations to go and see Francis, and you say Henry's already made up his mind?'

'My dear Jack, you are forgetting to allow for Henry's basic nature. You know what he's like as well as most, eh?'

Howath nodded ruefully. 'Aye.'

He didn't want that damned tennis court business dragged out again. No doubt Kraven's entire crew were privy to the bitter details of his exile, having heard the gist of his unhappy dispute with Henry over that line call. God's nails, if only he had allowed the King to win the point, he'd be sailing a sight closer to him now!

'He's a bully, a bloat and a damned coxcomb all in one,' Kraven said, lowering his voice to a conspiratorial whisper. 'He means to swagger and pose his way from one ruler to the next, blowing his own trumpet and playing the paladin.'

Howath bristled at the merchant's dangerously treacherous tone. 'Aye, that's as maybe. But you'll lose your head for saying so, if you go broadcasting those opinions to anybody but your friends.' He leaned over the polished oak table, braced himself against the alarming swell.

The vast camp resembled a meadow of white-capped mushrooms, the afternoon sun warming the gaily-painted pavilions and leaning marquees which had grown up almost overnight along the otherwise featureless coastline. The canvas city lapped about the battered walls of ancient Calais – the last remnant of England's once-extensive French possessions.

English soldiers swarmed along the strand below the town, while a flotilla of small boats and lighters sculled between the bigger ships lying offshore. Henry had come intending to overawe the French with the splendour of his army in order to establish his rightful place as Arbiter of Europe. But many of the handsomely-equipped soldiers he had brought with him had no intention of standing around on ceremony. They had come to make red war, not pale treaties.

The crew were busy trimming the sails as the old cog ran in on the tide, the broad-beamed merchant vessel pitching heavily as it was pummelled by the strong offshore currents. The seasick Englishmen had gathered on the forecastle to gaze at the spectacle, clutching the gunwales in awestruck silence. They could see the formidable towers which supported the massive northern wall of the city, the spire of St Mary's Church soaring above the fortifications. A swarming, stinking profusion of intruding humanity, half-hidden by a riot of bright ribbons and streaming colours.

'Merciful Christ, I never thought I'd be as glad to smell horse shite,' Howath growled, taking deep draughts of the breeze as he admired the panorama. He was itching to get ashore, to mingle with the great captains and nobles he had known in the wilder days of his youth. By Gesu, he had been on the Border too long!

Eldritch nodded sourly. They had packed thirty horses in the hold, and he wouldn't care if he never smelt horse shite again. He hung on grimly as the master brought the cog alongside the hastily-improvised jetty. Calais harbour was already chock to the brim with tangled masts and creaking keels – the battleships which were the pride of Henry's rapidly-expanding navy. Edward Kraven climbed up the steep steps to join his guests in the forecastle.

'I'll wager you're happy to see the French coast, gentlemen,' he smirked, glancing at the soldiers' pale faces.

Even Eldritch looked ill at ease. The surly youngster had hardly spoken a word to the merchant in three days, despite their previous extended acquaintanceship. Kraven chuckled, leaning over the side to keep watch as the ship's master completed his manoeuvres.

Packs of damp labourers wearing grey smocks and ill-fitting leather hats were hurrying from ship to ship, lending a hand as their precious cargoes were swung down by block and tackle hoisted from the yardarms. Bales of clothing, stacks of arrows and barrels of salted meats were being hoisted over the sides of the deep-bellied merchant ships and lowered to the jetty to the raucous accompaniment of shouting captains and frantic overseers. Crude wooden ramps were being dragged and rolled into place alongside each ship to speed the disembarkation of the horses, some of them too weakened by the perilous voyage to do more than shake their sweat-caked heads and whinny with relief.

The warden's daughter, dogs, wardrobe and caterwauling pack of serving maids were being carried in the *Crimson Tun*, wallowing heavily a few cables off the stern. Howath had spent hours watching its heavy progress through the swell, hoping to God the master knew his business. He had watched for its bobbing lanterns every night, peering into the North Sea haze to locate its brittle masts every grey dawn.

'I should have had her by me,' Howath muttered, apparently unaware Eldritch had been watching the *Crimson Tun* as intently as he had.

'Packed in with the horses and stores? The *Tun*'s better laden, a sight stabler than this damned tub,' the captain replied, more harshly than he had intended. He had spotted Miranda and his sister a few times, bawled his greetings as they waved back enthusiastically.

Howath bit his lip, somewhat surprised by the taciturn officer's unusual concern. Maybe the candle-wasting spark had set his cap at her? Well, Miranda could do worse, he thought ruefully. But then again, she could do a sight better. And he didn't relish the way Eldritch was making so many of his decisions, either! The old knight looked up from the foam-flecked waves, eyed his subordinate.

'Don't stand there mooning boy! Get yourself below and sort out those horses!' the old man ordered. Eldritch glanced about at the unexpected rebuke, nodded sharply and clambered down the steps towards the busy hold. In another moment they could hear his strident voice barking commands at the toiling crewmen. Kraven fingered the spare hairs on his upper lip, smiled thinly.

'He's as hotheaded as ever, Jack,' the merchant commented. 'Three winters on the Border and ye've not taken much of the wind from his sails.'

Howath grunted in agreement.

The gloomy warden seemed lost in thought for a moment, staring at the straggling carts and wagons making their way from the improvised harbours to the vast camp beyond. Archers, billmen, gunners and knights marched like ants up the bleak ridges. Soldiers, sailors, stevedores, porters, herdsmen, tinkers and whores thronged the harbour.

'I've not seen so many men in one place since Flodden,' Howath said. The merchant leaned over the forecastle to watch the first of the Ride's horses being dragged up the ramp from the noisome hold. Kraven made a face, lowered the neckerchief from his nose as he watched a nervous groom struggling to hold on to a furiously-bucking charger.

'Take a whip to the damned brute or he'll break that ramp!' Kraven shouted.

'Never mind the ramp, use the hoist! You'll feel my steel if you break the bugger's leg!' Howath snarled.

'We'll save his energy for the French,' Eldritch called from the hold, taking a confident grip on the horse's muzzle and leading the sickly animal up the ramp.

'There you are Kraven, Eldritch says there'll be trouble yet!' he challenged. Kraven shrugged.

'Henry's serious. He's come to talk peace, I tell you.'

'Well I'm banking on fighting some bugger,' Howath growled. 'I need a few juicy ransoms to pay for this lot!' The expedition had already eaten through the trifle he had managed to put away during his long exile on the Border. 'Just don't try and bend my ears with all this spy talk about treaties and what have you! I leave all my diplomacy to this,' he slapped the bobbing hilt of his sword. 'I leave everything else to those lisping quill-pushers back at Court!' the ancient warrior boasted, but his words were lost in a sudden squall, his empty threat drowned out by the brazen fanfares of the gulls.

Beside the Golden Valley, Guisnes, June 1520

The sprawling camp at Calais which had so impressed Howath's retinue turned out to be little more than an enormous depot. A teeming mound of shouting men, creaking carts and bellowing animals bound for the main rendezvous twenty miles further inland. Lord Howath had barely been ashore ten minutes before he discovered his Majesty King Henry had already left Calais to meet his French counterpart. The warden decided to press straight on despite the obvious exhaustion of his warband. The horses they had brought over with them were sickly and weak from the trying voyage, lifting their tails to dump piles of steaming green slush over the fouled decks and jetty. The riders were pale and haggard and anticipating a good night's rest. His billmen and archers looked more like lepers than soldiers, propped up on their weapons as if Howath had hired the wastrel knaves from a Thames prison hulk. They might just as well have nailed bells to a stick as tried to march to tuck of drum.

Lord Howath had fumed and fretted as he inspected the dismal troop, Eldritch stalking along in his shadow.

'They put me in mind of nanny house potboys,' the warden growled. 'All that new kit I've bought 'em and all! A fine show they'll make when we get there!'

'A few hours' rest and good earth under their shoes, they'll be mint as new shillings,' the younger man reasoned, rubbing his knuckles into his bloodshot eye sockets. He stifled a yawn as Howath bristled.

'With half the army already marched off to join Henry? I'm not sitting here waiting for this damned crew to get its second wind! They'll be straight enough after I've marched 'em a few mile!'

Eldritch coughed.

'You mean to march them straight to Guisnes?' he protested.

Howath tugged his mantle about his worn armour, flicked his iron-bound wrist in annoyance.

'Calais's full see you, and so will the main camp at Guisnes be if we don't get there soon. Feg's sake man, ye'll not impress their sublime majesties if you're stuck in a field ten miles from their precious pavilions,' he crowed. The older man tugged on his gauntlets with more determination than Eldritch had marked in twelve months.

'I'll take the Ride on, you follow with the foot and our wagons.' Howath paused, looked back down the seething quay towards the clumsily-constructed carriages Kraven had laid on as household transports. More wretched expense!

'And Eldritch, have an eye on my daughter,' he said wearily. 'I don't want these Frenchies breathing their damn love talk in her ears the moment she's off the boat!'

Eldritch was spitting out sparks by the time the groaing company had filed up the strand to join the multicoloured cavalcade snaking away to the south-east. Every road seemed choked with wagons and carriages of every description, every acre crammed with cattle or cannon fodder. Horsehide-covered wains with iron-studded wheels were trundling along behind teams of lowing oxen. Eldritch had detailed the few horsemen Howath had left him to escort the wagons. Sergeant Hobby drove the first carriage – a crudely-built barge which seemed likely to snap its inadequate axles at any moment. Miranda and Eldritch's younger sister Merron were taking it in turns to peer out over the grumpy sergeant's shoulders, pestering the patient giant with ridiculous questions about the countryside.

'But where are all the Frenchmen?' Miranda inquired, leaning so far out of the narrow hatch Eldritch feared she might fall beneth the wheels. Her green velvet neckline was tighter than his codpiece, the wagon-ledge compressing her milky breasts into blushing summer puddings.

Sergeant Hobby followed the captain's moist gaze, glancing over his shoulder and quickly turning back to the road.

'Great giddy goats,' he breathed, 'Put 'em away for the love of Christ or I'll miss the road,' he muttered to himself.

Eldritch nibbled his lip, sullenly contemplating the be-witching prize. Miranda had gambolled in and out of range of his heavily-lidded eyes for the past two years, enticed and then repelled by his stern charms. One moment she seemed delighted by his bristling bad company, the next she chose to ignore his most invigorating conversation. She seemed to be teasing him, but surely such wiles were quite beyond her happily straightforward nature? Why didn't the girl come straight out and say it, if she thought anything of him? Well no matter now, Eldritch thought darkly. This campaign would make his name and seal his fortune. The old warden couldn't live forever, coughing and blushing up like a farmyard rooster at every slight and fancy. He'd miss the old man's bluff grumblings, but as God was his witness he'd served a long enough apprenticeship.

'It's my turn, stand back Manda, I can't see a thing round your great hurdies!'

Eldritch glanced up once more as the object of his wand-ering attention was boosted halfway out of the narrow window by a sudden push from behind.

'Great hurdies? Ouch! Have a care Merry, you'll rip my gown! Don't shove girl!'

Merron avoided Miranda's jabbing elbow and squeezed her slim body between her mistress and the banging shutter.

'There! I said you'd rip it!'

Merron ignored the anguished bleat from inside the cart, frowned up at the darkening sky. She noticed James' fixed scowl was even more pronounced than usual.

'You've not much to say for yourself brother. Sorry you came along?' she called. Eldritch endured his sister's gentle mockery as if it were part of some terrible penance, to be bravely borne along with the rest of his punishing family responsibilities.

'I'm sorry I'm on horseback so soon after the voyage. We've a long ride ahead of us – such a pity you'll miss the most of it.'

Merron chuckled, pulling her mantle up about her shoulders to keep out the evening chill and straightening her lopsided head-dress.

'There's plenty of room up here. I don't mind riding a mile or two,' she offered craftily. Her brother bared his teeth in what passed for a doting smile.

'Do you think I'd let you loose with these scoundrels?' Eldritch asked indignantly.

'You stay where you are missy,' Hobby growled in agreement from the running board. 'We don't know the way, the road, or what bugger's hiding around the next bend,' he added with an authoritative nod of his chin.

Merron ducked back inside the timber-keeled bower, clapping the shutters to and watching her mistress twisting about to examine the back of her gown. Her dark, carefully-pleated hair was hanging down between her cleavage like a well-oiled bellrope.

'Look, I've caught it on a nail,' Miranda complained, pointing out the rent to her careless lady in waiting. 'It's ruined now!'

'You silly whipperginny,' Merron scolded fondly. 'Get it off and I'll put a stitch in it.'

Miranda had never possessed the inclination nor memory required for prolonged sulking. She happily reached behind her back to pluck at her bodice strings. Merron balanced herself against the alarming pitch of the wagon and began to help her mistress climb out of her heavy green gown. The shoulders and sleeves were slashed to reveal a rich red lining, the very height of fashion – several years before. Miranda was lost in thought for a moment.

'I wonder whether father will introduce us to any Frenchmen,' she wondered. 'They say they always make the better husbands.'

Merron smirked. 'Better lovers, maybe. Not that I'll get to look at one, with my wretched brother sitting on my shoulder like the cabin boy's monkey! He goes puce every time I as much as cross my legs!' Miranda chewed the tip of her tongue, lost in reverie.

'I wonder if we'll see a real Prince. A what–was–it, Dolphin?'

'*Dauphin.*'

'*Dauphin.* Precisely,' she said briskly. 'Or that fellow with the funny name . . . the bravest of the brave . . .'

'*Le Chevalier Bayard,*' Merron said dreamily.

'*Chevalier.* Now what's that in French?'

Merron fetched her needle and thread. It was going to be a long journey.

Howath coughed, wiped his gauntlet over his dewy beard. It was almost dawn, and the mist was lying thick on the silent fields either side of the road. Spindly trees appeared out of the morning murk, petrified witches draped in spider–spun silks.

The horizon was a hedgerow.

Howath didn't mind marching into the unknown. He knew English armies had marched that way before. The Black Prince, Good King Hal. But they had marched to battle, to unimpeachable triumph and fortune and the ever-lasting fame of their names.

According to the perceptive Kraven their unworthy descendants were marching to a masked ball, a game of cat-and-mouse where honour and courage and force of arms were to be reduced to empty postures and foolish mummery. He gazed out at the narrow panorama, trying to peer through the drifting mists.

He half wished he was back in Redesdale.

Francis I had indeed assembled a vast army of knights and nobles, a brilliant, gaudy host the likes of which Europe had never seen. The fantastical guard had encamped with the utmost pomp and ostentation, setting up their gaudy pavilions beneath a rainbow of dazzling standards. They had peered over the shallow Golden Vale as the English erected their own marquees, each nation toiling to out-match the other's efforts. Unluckily for the visiting French, a high wind had torn the roof from one of their biggest pavilions, setting their efforts back by precious hours. The English workmen had fallen over themselves with laughter, clinging to their codpieces as they watched the French struggling with their flapping guyropes.

Francis had summoned an impressive army of servants and serfs to set up his tents and hang his bunting, to prepare and serve the extraordinary feasts his specially-recruited cooks had come up with. Francis might not relish facing the boastful monarch's army in a straight fight, but he could always force-feed the arrogant English into the ground.

With Guisnes on the very edge of the English Pale, Henry would technically host the long-anticipated meeting. The King would be staying in a tremendously expensive, beautifully-embroidered pavilion, a vast golden canopy fit to house the English king's monstrous ego. The even grander banqueting house had been painted to resemble brickwork, decorated with gold and silver and hung with the Tudor rose emblem of his house – a fairytale pavilion to surpass the wildest dreams of the most imaginative artist.

Francis had ordered that his own pavilion should be set up across the other side of the shallow arena where the historic meeting would take place. The immense pavilion was surrounded by an extraordinarily-designed, semi-circular marquee in the blue and white colours of France. The tents of his princes, nobles and knights were laid out in meticulously-measured rings about the King's camp, carefully pitched to reflect the owner's social standing and his relationship with his liege lord. As well as the tents and horselines, field kitchens and hospitals, there was an immense tournament field complete with grandstands, archery butts and a frightful display of the latest Spanish- and German-designed firearms. Henry had even ordered that his steel mill at Greenwich be dismantled and rebuilt at Guisnes to provide the forges necessary to repair the swords and lances broken in the tournaments.

There seemed no limit to the mad cascade of money, to the obscene haemorrhage of national wealth.

The colourful complex covered almost a dozen acres, with every precious foot of ground fought over by jealous earls and ambitious knights. The noise and smell from the teeming concentration of men was very bit as intimidating as the awesome view.

It might not have been a battle, but it was the next best thing.

Beside the Golden Valley, Guisnes

Howath had spent six fruitless hours trying to elbow himself some room alongside the tournament field. If he retreated any further away from Henry's pleasure dome he would be pitching his tent in a latrine. The warden had little influence over the courtiers who assigned tent spaces. Neither Eldritch's barely-veiled threats nor Edward Kraven's rather more subtle offer of a bribe had persuaded the Harbingers and Hales keepers to alter their carefully-measured plans.

'Third rank's earls only,' the scrofulous clerk snapped, relishing the opportunity to insult his elders and betters. 'His Majesty's strictest orders,' he had added with a smile.

'Then where am I supposed to pitch my tents?' Howath snorted, rapping his knuckles on his chest to demonstrate his martial capabilities. The clerk shrugged.

'My master Richard Gibson has provided a camp layout for dukes and earls only. Minor nobility and the like, well, they seem to have made their own arrangements, same as the rest of us!' the clerk replied with a sneer. Howath straightened up, his features puce.

Eldritch made as if to turn away, eased his foot beneath the brocaded cloth and gave the table leg a quick kick. The clerk's goblet was knocked sideways, sending a squall of red wine over his papers. The clerk squawked, jumping to his feet and tearing the tent plan from the rapidly-spreading lagoon.

'Ah, you seem to have spilled some of your beverage,' Eldritch snarled, his teeth bared. The clerk cursed under his breath, used his coat sleeve to mop the worst of the wine from the table.

'Master Gibson's instructions were quite clear,' he repeated, stridently. 'If you don't like it you can take it up with the camp provost!'

'That will not be necessary.'

Howath glanced about, squinting against the strong sunlight to identify the immaculately-dressed knight who had stalked up behind them. The suave newcomer inclined his head, gave the discomfited lord an encouraging nod and turned his gaze on the Hales keeper.

'I will report your surliness at the highest level,' he said out of the side of his mouth, as if reluctant to directly address such a worthless churl. 'It is not for the likes of thee to assign this territory where you please,' he accused, fixing the clerk with his viper stare. The clerk swallowed nervously. One glance at the newcomer's evilly glinting eyes convinced him against any contradiction. He glanced over his shoulder at his ink-spotted colleagues, who seemed to be busy giving their quills a minute examination for wear and tear.

'Of course, my Lord, this goes without . . .'

'How dare you address one of our honoured guests as if he was a Spanish donkey seller?'

'My Lord, his Majesty Henry of . . . Master Gibson is . . .'

'Welcome to sample the hospitality of my house, my castle and my bed, if he wishes it! But he did not authorise ink-swilling corpse-molesters to insult his guests!' the noble roared, his wide mouth split into a ferocious snarl. Even Howath seemed taken aback by his display of temper, tugging at his beard to hide his confusion and embarrassment. Why hadn't he dealt with the obstreperous clerk himself? The newcomer was as tall as Eldritch, his fine sky blue tunic inlaid with gold and silver lace as thick as his thumb. His collar, sleeves and cloak were studded with gold buttons and lined with silver fox, the striking outfit topped off with a large, quilted bonnet hung with silver and gold tassels. His features were gaunt, his wide mouth and deep red gums lined with ridges of small, serrated teeth. His dark eyes sparkled with fury as he watched the clerk take a closer look at his plans.

'I meant no offence, my Lord. I have been given precise instructions by . . .'

'Well you have not received any instructions from me, have you? Do you know who I am?' The distraught clerk quailed, the sopping map held to his sunken chest.

'Well then know this, you squirming worm. I am Abelard, Vicomte de Toinueill, elder son of the Duc de Gueldres! You might have heard of him, at least,' the new-comer added with menacing modesty.

'Of course my Lord!'

Charles, Duke of Gueldres, Guelders, Gelders, Gilders. Most of the soldiers present had heard of him, though few had ever mastered the correct pronunciation of his name. The Duke had led a revolt against Margaret of Savoy back in 1511, a revolt which had been partly put down by English troops specially dispatched by the ambitious Henry. Gueldres had also fought with the French during the last outbreak of fighting seven years before.

Eldritch studied the olive-skinned nobleman from the corner of his eye, noting the harsh jawline and close-set eyes. He knew as well as his master that the Bastard Gueldres had aimed the introduction at the three Englishmen – not the bewildered clerk. He quickly turned on his heel, bowed his head.

'My Lord, may I present John Gulliver, Lord of Howath and late Warden of the English Middle March, and our esteemed cousin Edward Kraven, head of the merchant house of the same name, presently serving His Majesty King Henry,' Eldritch said smoothly. Gueldres ignored the young knight, inclining his black ringleted head to Howath and Kraven in turn.

'And this is my captain of horse, James Eldritch,' Howath

warbled, pleased as punch to be rubbing shoulders with a son of old Gelders. The run-ins he'd had with his brute of a father up in the Netherlands!

Gueldres glanced about at the mention of his name – rather too sharply, Eldritch thought.

'Eldritch?'

'Indeed my Lord. Could it be you have already heard of our horsemaster?' Howath asked archly. Gueldres fluttered his fingers.

'An unusual name, even for you English.'

'Betokening magical. Other-worldly,' Howath explained, raising his eyebrows and enjoying Eldritch's evident discomfort. Gueldres nodded, modified his surprised glance into an unnecessarily exaggerated nod.

'Well sirs,' he said. 'Allow me to apologise to you all on behalf of my liege lord King Francis. Sure I am the King would have lent a hand drawing the camp plans himself, if he imagined leeches such as this were to be responsible for their implementation.' The clerk, bent over his table to retrieve his papers, looked up guiltily. Gueldres snatched up the spilled goblet and cracked it down hard on his grasping fingers.

'There! Let that remind you to keep a civil tongue in your head, you serpent!' The clerk paled, holding up his bleeding fingers in horror. He nodded dumbly.

Gueldres turned to his guests, a lazy smile playing about his mouth as if he was unaware of his sudden display of violence.

'Gentlemen, you have been treated in such a disgraceful manner I have little choice but to insist you accompany me to my own crude quarters, where I will soften the hurts this miserable fellow has inflicted with fine wine and some good French fare.'

Eldritch studied the immaculately turned-out nobleman, immediately suspicious of his disarming manner. Howath, however, seemed delighted by the offer, eager no doubt to move a few steps closer to the fabulous quarters of the rival kings.

'Why we would be delighted, quite delighted!' he en-thused.

The abrupt change of plan had thrown Howath's long-awaited arrival into a confused farce. Wagons, carriages and carts belonging to his threadbare household had become hopelessly lost in the snarled traffic, their crude, mud-caked axles entangled with the finest French coaches transporting fabulously-appointed dukes and duchesses to their grand quarters. The drivers had shaken fists and shouted insults at one another until moved on by the hard-pressed sergeants, and gradually, the ill-tempered crowd dispersed about the valley.

Most of Howath's Ride had been obliged to make a long detour around the tournament field to arrive at the meadow Gueldres had reserved as their quarters. The prec-ious acre was situated to the rear of the main grandstand, overlooked by a lone oak. It was soon obvious to the dusty riders why it had been left fallow.

The squalid field was bordered to the north by a reeking zoo, a squawking, screeching, roaring circus of well-travelled tents and rusty iron cages. Lions, leopards and tigers paced behind their grim bars, glaring maliciously at the gawping horse troopers, most of whom had never seen such wonders. A row of latrines had been dug across the southern end of the field to serve the crowds making their way to the tournaments. Grand ablution chambers had been erected for the kings and nobles, small tents put up to preserve the modesty of the minor gentry, and filthy ropes hung up for the soldiers, servants and clamouring hangers-on. The field sloped away sharply to the east, be-coming little more than a sedge-bordered bog beyond the sentinel oak.

Eldritch had taken one look at the stinking morass and knew Gueldres had meant to insult them. He had found the one acre of the Golden Valley nobody wanted, and pres-ented it to the naive Howath on a silver platter. The fuming captain stalked through the quagmire, shaking his head and cursing as the changing breeze blew various foul odours over the soldiers' rough tents and crude shelters. The men looked up as he passed, but kept their comments to themselves.

Hobby had found one of the few dry spots in the sodden field, and had assembled the pick of his archers about him. The bowmen formed an elite guard within the Ride, loudly reckoning themselves the best men in the warband. Eldritch ducked down next to the grim-faced sergeant, holding his nose against the eye-watering stench.

'Aye captain, seems they've put us in a lion's den,' Hobby commented drily.

'Lion's den? Boggard more like! I've not smelt anything like it! He's laughing behind our backs, sending us out here while he entertains the old man.'

Hobby raised his colourless eyebrows.

'Not joining the masters for supper then captain?'

Eldritch frowned. 'Well I might have to later, for appearances' sake.'

Some of the archers chuckled, knowing old Hobby was pulling the youngster's leg. 'Don't you worry about us. After that damned ship and that cussed ride, I'd sleep with the bloody lions if'n I 'ad to!'

Eldritch was pleased to see the wearisome march hadn't eaten through their supplies of good humour.

'Stay sharp lads. I reckon we might have a chance of getting our own back yet. I'll see you at the butts tomorrow morning for some target practice.'

'Practice? Us? We don't practise till we got least twenny tha-zand Frenchies coming dahn on us,' Geoffrey Elver cried.

'You get up at dawn, and you practise,' Eldritch said sharply. The laughter and joking died down, the veteran soldiers glancing at one another. Maybe this Field of Gold wasn't the silly diversion they had imagined.

Good news travelled fast, but bad news travelled faster. Or it did if your master was the Vicomte de Toinueill – the

Bastard Gueldres. Francesco Savvi had worn out half a dozen horses during his long ride up from the south, pausing just long enough to swig a mouthful of wine or wolf some bread while his weary bodyguard organised remounts. He had been in the saddle twenty nights running, hurrying to deliver the news of the abortive attack on Mont Galliard. The veteran commander had not dared to take the most direct route to the north – that would have taken him uncomfortably close to the despised Swiss cantons. Instead, he had crossed the Alps and ridden sharply west, reaching one of his master's string of minor castles – the Chateau Reban near Grenoble. He had picked up new horses and ridden north for the city of Lyons, following the winding valley of the swift-flowing Saône to Dijon. The hard-riding band had then pushed on through the night to Langres before heading south-west to Chalon sur Marne. Sixteen days after setting out Savvi had skirted Paris, taking the bleak road for the northern coast. Several hundred miles of hard riding in virtual silence had given the indomitable locotenent plenty of time to frame his miserable explanations. The fact that the mountain fastness had been a Gueldres possession for decades – largely rebuilt by the old Duke himself – would make Savvi's failure doubly hard for his master to digest. Galliard had been one of the Gueldres clan's most formidable strongholds, and its loss to a sworn enemy like Tarsi had proved especially galling. Both father and son had sworn to get the castle back, even if they had to fight their way through all the forces Tarsi and his precious mistress Margaret of Savoy could throw against them. The old Duke – half-demented by his long wars and suffering from the ghastly effects of the final stages of syphilis, wasn't up to the job any more. If his bastard didn't get it back soon, the old man would die in shame – as well as in acute agony.

Savvi knew it would have been quicker to send professional messengers or make use of his master's specially-trained homing pigeons to send news of the rout, but the veteran soldier preferred to explain his failures in person.

Elaborate excuses wouldn't save his neck – and besides, he had never been a great one for letters.

The Bastard Gueldres would insist on the unvarnished truth. The truth was that six hundred of his master's veteran Black Bandsmen had signally failed to make any impression on Alberto Tarsi's stronghold. The citadel which Gueldres had hoped to reclaim inside a week had held out for almost four, defying every gun they had brought against it. Savvi knew exactly where to suggest the blame lay. An outright accusation would be dishonourable and unseemly, and would only prompt some homicidal tirade from his master. But it had been the dwarf's fault his men had not got in to the fortress. Obolus had been paid to open the postern gate and admit Muhlberg's suicide squad. The spy had apparently been prevented from doing so by some interfering busybody of a chorister. A chorister! He should have strangled the songbird and got on with his job! The Bastard Gueldres would flay his vile hide, the next time their paths crossed.

Savvi had blanched at the thought of explaining his dismal failures, but there was nothing else for it. One hope had kept him going: that the intriguing intelligence his gypsy mistress Constanzia had passed on to him would just save his neck. Intriguing intelligence about Tarsi's intention to impress the papal delegation in Novara with some damned choral composition. The old goat must have lost his mind for even thinking such a thing, but you never knew with these damned Italians. If Tarsi had something up his sleeve, his master would want to know about it. At least, he hoped so.

Francesco Savvi gathered his cloak about him, bent his back and spurred his flagging horse on into the night.

Another few hours and he would be in Guisnes.

Beside the Tournament arena
in the Golden Valley, Guisnes

Half the knights and nobles in Guisnes had ordered their squires to rouse them before dawn, to begin the wearisome business of climbing into their armour. They were childishly eager to get out into the tournament field and stake their claims to fame and glory with lance, war hammer and sword. By the time the breakfast fires were burning at least sixty fully-armoured paladins had crowded into the arena. There was barely enough room for a decent trot − let alone a challenging canter. More knights were waiting their turn at the gate, lifting their visors to try and recognise who they were chatting with as relays of flushed squires hurried up with fresh lances, new straps and half a hundred other pieces of essential gear. The irritable ringmasters, resplendent in jupons carrying the quartered colours of England and France, shouted, bawled and pointed as they tried to draw up lists to organise the chaotic practice bouts. In the meantime the eager knights traded idle blows, lost their tempers and hacked and banged at one another as if they were indeed at war. The latecomers had given up altogether, dismounting to stretch their legs. They had paused at the butts to watch their social inferiors wage their own wars with their opposite numbers; longbow against crossbow, crossbow against arquebus.

Eldritch wouldn't have been able to sleep over the rough and tumble commotion even if he had wanted to. He had been up early in his grey cloak, combing his beard and scrubbing the worst of the mire from his long riding boots. The captain was gratified to see his best archers had been up equally early, eaten a solid breakfast of bacon and biscuits before joining the yawning throng at the butts. A pack of Genoese crossbowmen – all too familiar with the efficacy of their dreaded rivals from over the water, sidled off to find themselves some refreshment. The Englishmen hurried to take their place, peering down the sward towards the four circular straw targets three hundred yards to their front. Eldritch nodded the first four archers forward. Hobby, Elver, Teagues and Ecclestone nocked their arrows and stepped up to their boot-scuffed marks. The captain nodded, and the bowmen raised their forearms, muscles flexing as they took the strain. The best archers had broad, strong backs, well able to cope with the massive strain required to drag back their bowstrings. Foreign princes had tried to copy the English by training up longbowmen of their own, but had inevitably made the mistake of imagining a good archer relied on the muscles of his forearm alone. They had sought out the most formidably-built soldiers in their own armies, and issued them with their deadly six-foot bows.

But good archers didn't grow on trees or fall from the skies. They had to be trained, hour after hour, day after day. Nock, draw, shoot. Nock, draw, shoot. Eldritch's men had been training with their weapons since they were six years old, using special child-sized bows before progressing after many years of practice to full-sized war bows.

Eldritch narrowed his eyes, watched the muscles ripple beneath their jackets, throbbing veins standing out in their necks and forearms. Tiny tremors ran down their arms, beads of sweat broke out on their brows. The bows sighed as the terrific pressures mounted.

'Shoot!'

Hobby loosed first, his fingers opening like a startled crab as he released the string. The arrow flew straight and true towards the first target. The others watched its trajectory with professional intensity, trying to judge the windage. Hobby's arrow hit the outer rim of the circled target. The giant grunted with irritation, bent down and nocked another arrow. Elver and the others let fly, all of their arrows hitting their targets in the blue. Hobby loosed again, his second arrow juddering in the bull. Eldritch sighed with relief.

'Good shot sergeant, in a trying wind!'

The Bastard Gueldres stepped out from the anonymous mob of knights and nobles milling about the butts. His tall frame was encased from head to foot in shimmering black – from his outrageously-curled Turkish slippers to the fluttering feathers in his hat. He went without badge or insignia of any kind, save for a small wolf's head on the pommel of the straight dagger hanging from his belt. Eldritch gave the sardonically grinning nobleman the briefest of bows, returned his attention to the distant targets. Hobby had scored another bull, Elver and Teagues one each.

'Perhaps you English are right to persevere with your, some might say outdated weaponry, Captain. The longbow, in the right hands, is a truly deadly weapon,' the nobleman observed with studied nonchalance.

Eldritch said nothing, clamping his mouth on a dozen blistering ripostes.

'Pray sir, have your men stand aside and let one of my arquebusiers try a shot.'

'At the same target? You'd be lucky to hit it with a saker, at three hundred yards!' Eldritch exclaimed. Gueldres nodded sagely.

'I'll grant you it is not as accurate a weapon over such a distance. Have a target brought forward a little. A hundred yards would make a more realistic shot.' Eldritch smiled faintly. He nodded to Elver, who vaulted over the rail, looked left and right to ensure nobody was still shooting and loped off across the arrow-fringed grass.

'A straw bale's a tough target for an aimed weapon, let alone an arquebus,' Eldritch said archly. Gueldres held his gaze, well aware of the dangerously-veiled challenge. He beckoned to a grubby-looking soldier standing forlorn among his formidably-armed bodyguard. The ruffian doubled forward, bent under the awkward weight of the heavy weapon. Eldritch watched the soldier fiddle with the simple firing mechanism, agitatedly blowing on his match. The acrid, sulphurous stink drifted over the assembled spectators. Gueldres shielded his eyes, watched the attendants at the sharp end of the butts manhandle one of the targets towards them. Even at that reduced range, their features were little more than pale blurs. The soldier lifted his arquebus and squinted down the barrel, his finger crooked about the large, S-shaped trigger. He aimed and fired. Eldritch noticed the brutal recoil almost knocked the soldier off his feet. He coughed and staggered back, squinting after his bullet. The half-ounce ball knocked a handful of straw from the rim of the outermost target, earning an ironic cheer from the curious bowmen gathered about the range.

Eldritch nodded. 'Not bad, given the rather playful wind,' he said.

Gueldres flicked his wrist at the arquebusier, who grinned feebly and began to reload his cumbersome piece. The impatient captain waved his archers back to their marks as he huffed and hawed, uncapped his powder flask to tip a measure of powder down the smoking barrel.

'Nock, draw, shoot!' Eldritch shouted. The forlorn soldier jumped over his complex devotions, spilling powder over the back of his hand. Hobby, Teagues and Ecclestone bent their bows and let fly once more, their arrows bracketing the target.

'Nock, draw, shoot!' In another moment three more arrows had pricked the leaning bale. In another, three more. The arquebusier was reloading his piece as quickly as he was able, but couldn't hope to match their rate of fire. Gueldres kept his eyes on the tall captain. Eldritch wasn't even bothering to check his archers' aim.

'Nock, draw, shoot!'

Fifteen arrows later and the ungainly bale fell over, a

pincushion of feathered flights. The distraught arquebusier had reloaded his piece at last, but Gueldres laid his long hand on the barrel, turned the weapon aside.

'I think Captain Eldritch has proved his point,' he said stiffly.

Eldritch raised his chin in defiant triumph.

'Your man did well enough just hitting the target,' he allowed. Gueldres fingered his moustache.

'Just so, just so.'

'You'll have to train your arquebusiers a little harder, if they're ever to challenge experienced bowmen.'

The nobleman looked puzzled by Eldritch's insolent advice.

'I don't think I ever claimed this man was an experienced arquebusier,' Gueldres said in mock bewilderment. 'This man helps out with my field kitchen. He'd never fired an arquebus at all before last evening.'

The chattering bowmen stopped laughing, stared at the grinning kitchen hand. The Bastard Gueldres took off his glove, waved the velvet fingers down the butts.

'I think you'll find it's the ease with which we can train our soldiers which gives us the real edge over your English longbow. A fine weapon, capable of delivering ten times the missiles at more than twice the range of our arquebuses. But when is it you start training your archers? Three or four weeks after birth, I believe. By the time they are little more than boys they have either mastered the art, or they never will,' he went on, enjoying Eldritch's dismay. He leaned closer, caught the Englishman's darting eye.

'I thank you sir, for such an entertaining morning's sport.'

'Never shot an arky-bust afore? Then 'twere luckiest shot I've ever seen,' Ecclestone complained as the English watched Gueldres' bodyguard take up station about their chief and escort him off towards the tourney field.

Hobby raised his pock-marked chin in contempt. 'He said so 'isself, you can't train archers overnight. Any damned knave can fire an arquebus.'

Eldritch shook his head, cursing his *naïveté*. The Bastard Gueldres had hung him out to dry in front of half the knights of Europe. He seethed with resentment, wishing to God he'd had the good sense to avoid picking a squabble with the cunning nobleman. He had been made to look a fool, a strawhead from over the water. A second-rate captain in the third-rate retinue of a superannuated war-lord.

He strode off in a furious temper, his archers stepping smartly out of his path.

'What's got him so riled?' Geoffrey Elver wanted to know. Hobby frowned after his tormented captain, pondering the youngster's bewildering moodswings.

'I reckon he's just been put in his place,' the heavyset sergeant theorised.

'And he don't reckon an awful lot for it.' Elver, one of the senior troopers in the Ride, shrugged his broad shoulders.

'Hah! So what's new?'

Beside the Vicomte de Toinueill's quarters, Guisnes

Eldritch chewed his beard with frustrated rage, spending the rest of the day brooding in his tent, cursing his miserable destiny. To think he should have been brought to this fabulous gathering, this Field of Gold, merely to be reminded of his own absolute insignificance.

He was nothing and, what was worse, he was going nowhere. Ever since his little escapade back on the border Howath had barely been able to endure his presence, keeping an ever-wary eye on him as if he suspected some vile plot. He seemed set on keeping him at arm's length, treating his captain of horse as if he and Sandy Kerr were blood brothers sworn to conspire against him. Now, the moment he even looked at Miranda, Howath would shout and rant, order him off on some pointless, demeaning errand. How dare he order him about like a horseboy in front of these most prestigious of guests?

He thought so hard his brain throbbed. How on earth would he ever escape this iron-fisted drudgery?

Abelard, Victomte de Toinueill, didn't concern himself with the petty grudges of hot-tempered chaff like James Eldritch. He had proved his point elegantly enough, leaving the bold-eyed foreigner to fume and spit by the butts while he went about his business in his usual dignified and orderly manner.

These English, what impetuous fools they were!

He had kept his own notorious temper in check, over-looking Eldritch's crude challenges as he toured the vast camp on his Majesty King Francis' behalf. He had been charged with spying out his enemy's weaknesses; judging the quality of the troops who had followed Henry across the channel and estimating the braggart's ability to wage a modern war.

He had forgotten all about Eldritch's little outburst, arriving back at his own grandly-appointed quarters in a thoroughly buoyant mood.

But his good cheer had evaporated the moment he lifted the tent flap.

Francesco Savvi had arrived in Guisnes ten minutes earlier and been shown straight to his master's headquarters. The dusty soldier had been easing his buttocks squatting on a padded cushion, but jumped to his feet as his scowling master strode in.

'You? Here! What news of the siege?'

Savvi described their heroic – but tragically unsuccessful efforts to break into Mont Gilbert le Galliard, high in the distant Alps. Tarsi had not only held on to his ill-gotten stronghold – he had slaughtered a couple of hundred of his men into the bargain. Savvi held his breath as the Vicomte paced the luxuriously-appointed tent, his rage absorbed to some extent by the heavy velvet tapestries and ornately-worked screens he had surrounded himself with.

'What happened to the dwarf? This was all arranged, every detail!' he exclaimed, his voice suddenly shrill with fury. Savvi blanched beneath his dust-mask.

'Constanzia sent word he was prevented from getting to the gate. The composer's boy was lurking in the catacomb when . . .'

'Prevented? By a *boy*?'

'Exactly what I said to her my Lord. Obolus couldn't get past the wretch without raising the alarm. He waited for the swine to clear off, but by that time Tarsi had poured a barrel of burning oil onto Muhlberg's pioneers. The blockhouse . . .'

'You should have shot the worthless shits! Call themselves Black Legion? Chicken-breasted sacks, the lot of them!'

'Yes, my Lord,' Savvi growled, head bowed.

'So Tarsi's still wiping his hairy Italian arse on my sheets and we're short a company of good men?'

Savvi nodded.

The legion would need rest and reinforcement before they continued their next assignment, an interesting and lucrative diversion on behalf of their French paymasters against the tiny Alpine princedom of Villefranco. The place was no more than a house of cards, ripe to fall into Francis' hands at last.

The Vicomte had hoped to kill two birds with one stone, ordering the hard-marching legion to stop off during its march south in order to take another stab at Mont Galliard. Now it appeared his ambitious plan to reclaim one of the Gueldres clan's ancestral castles had run badly awry.

Gueldres licked his lips, trying to estimate how much of the money Francis' agents had deposited in his banking house would be left. Not more than half of it. Worse than that, Gueldres knew a contractor who failed to provide the agreed number of men would never work in Europe again. His carefully-built empire would be torn apart by his rivals – Germans, Spanish or those bastard, money-grubbing Swiss.

The Gueldres name would be disgraced, his proud father's dread reputation tarnished and shamed. The Vicomte glowered at the soldier, pawing his buttocks on the cushion beside him.

'Then we need three hundred men, as quick as you like.'

Savvi nodded.

'There are plenty of troops here. We'll hire a few companies from this damned shower,' the locotenant suggested. 'English and French would be better than nothing,' he allowed.

'Hire them? I'm already out of pocket, fool! I paid your rascals to take Mont Galliard, much good that did me. I paid good money for this tent, all these damned trappings!' he kicked a cushion across the room in fury, his fists jabbing the air. 'If I don't get a full legion over the Alps for Francis, I'll be finished, do you understand?' he asked, his voice mangled by anger. 'And if I'm finished you'll be back lugging a pike around Italy!'

'Yes, my Lord.'

Gueldres clamped his hands to his forehead, thinking furiously. 'We'll have to find them from somewhere, and we'll have to keep it quiet. Francis has as many agents here as Charles; they'll soon hear if we're recruiting, if we can't complete the contract,' he fretted.

Savvi waited a moment before continuing his report, glancing sheepishly about his master's quarters.

'Is there anything else you want to get off your chest?'

'Well yes my Lord. You might recall we heard a whisper about the young Prince of Villefranco supposedly marrying Tarsi's daughter.'

Gueldres nodded absent-mindedly, still worrying about his severe shortage of troops.

'He's tried to marry that flat-chested gargoyle off to half the spavins in Europe!'

'Yes my Lord,' Savvi said patiently. 'Well after we lifted the siege the Villefrancan delegation went home without concluding any settlement . . .'

'Hah! I'm not surprised!'

'. . . but Constanzia says Tarsi didn't seem particularly upset by their refusal. It seems he's set his sights a little higher.'

Gueldres snorted. 'He's always had ideas above his station.'

Savvi leaned forward, lowering his voice. 'Constanzia thinks he's trying to tie up some deal with the Vatican, to try and keep Stroma's hands off his road tolls.'

Gueldres froze.

'Tarsi's being squeezed on all sides, my Lord. If the Vatican upholds Stroma's appeal and restores his rights, Tarsi'll be left high and dry in Mont Galliard. Without the tolls, he'll have no money to pay his men. He'll be finished.'

Gueldres acknowledged his locotenent's shrewd assessment.

'But if Tarsi was willing to share the road tolls with the Pope as well as Margaret of Savoy he'd secure powerful political support.'

And Gueldres knew that, with such powerful allies to count on, Tarsi's tenure at Mont Galliard would be extended indefinitely.

'Tarsi's trying anything to ingratiate himself. He's even sending them a score.'

'A score of what? Cannon?'

'A musical score, my Lord.' Gueldres sighed. 'Constanzia says . . .'

'I know all about your contacts, Savvi!' Gueldres yelled, striding threateningly towards the veteran commander. Savvi struggled to keep his voice as calm as his frozen features.

'Constanzia says the dwarf overheard them talking about it. Tarsi and the fat one, Scaralatchi.'

'Cesar Scaralatchi wouldn't get a look-in at the Vatican, you dumb ox! He was thrown out of there God knows how many years ago for buggering the choirboys!'

Savvi sat still, beads of sweat breaking out on his brow.

'But this is his penitential mass, an act of repentance for his entire life! Constanzia says it's a masterpiece and you know what these churchy fellows are like for patronising the arts. They hope the score will convince the papal delegation their old friend Scaralatchi's mended his ways at last. That they'll be in such a state of religious ecstasy to have reclaimed his mortal soul that they'll throw Stroma's application straight out and proclaim Tarsi Chief of the mountains!' Savvi paused. 'So Constanzia reckons, anyway.'

Gueldres looked suitably astounded by his subordinate's elaborations.

'She's an expert all of a sudden? No wonder we pay her so much money!' Gueldres was blowing off steam but thinking fast. There had to be more to Tarsi's scheme than a simple piece of music. Tarsi, the tolls, Margaret of Savoy, the Pope, the pass, the mass!

Savvi was nodding vigorously.

'The papal delegation is due to decide Stroma's application at a special session in Novara. Tarsi's sent that Fleming of his ahead to grease a few palms and keep an eye on the case. He's also got to find a proper choir to sing the damned thing. Constanzia says she's seen the boy training up urchins, kitchen hands and all sorts to rehearse different bits of the score. The boy Fabrizio is supposed to be going to France, some abbey somewhere.'

'Some abbey?' Gueldres breathed. 'Where?'

'They were due to depart shortly after I left to make my report. I don't yet know where or why, Constanzia will go with them and send word as usual.'

'Pigeon post!' the Vicomte cried, shrill with bewilderment at the alarming turn of events. 'For every pigeon we possess Tarsi has a peregrine! Messages can be intercepted!'

'Which is why I came in person to make my report,' Savvi said woodenly.

'What in seven hells is he up to?' Gueldres snorted. 'Making his peace with the Pope through a piece of music?'

Savvi shrugged.

'Maybe the Pope likes choral music,' he suggested.

'Oaf! He likes choirboys, same as Scaralatchi! Tarsi's no fool. But if he ends up earning the blessing of the Supreme Pontiff, he'll be shut up, safe and secure, in my castle, for as long as he likes!' Gueldres exclaimed.

'I'll send word to Constanzia; she'll throttle the fat composer and cut the choirboy's throat! You know how she loves knife-work like that.'

Gueldres had heard all about Savvi's homicidally-minded mistress. She had been working as a spy in Tarsi's household for years.

'An excellent idea, but he's bound to have written it out!'

'Well then she'll burn it!'

'No! Think for a moment. Tarsi's nothing but a boorish peasant, but he must have some idea of the worth of the piece or he wouldn't be wasting his time on it. If it is the masterpiece your brilliant mistress suggests, then maybe it *ought* to be presented to this papal delegation!'

Savvi looked blank,

'And let Tarsi earn this patronage?'

'Not Tarsi, you cretin, me!'

'Steal it, you mean?'

'A score's a score. Any number of composers could have written it. We could have it presented to the delegation in our names, and they wouldn't be any the wiser!' Gueldres rubbed his hands, warming to his theme. 'You're right about Runcini. He'd be tickled pink with a gesture like that. The wise and noble cardinal, first patron of the arts! And if they do uphold Stroma's application we might see Tarsi forced out of Mont Galliard once and for all.'

'Constanzia did right then?'

'I admit she might have earned her money,' Gueldres agreed slyly. 'This once.'

Beside the Vicomte de Toinueill's quarters, Guisnes

'My Lord Howath!' Gueldres cried, 'Welcome to my humble abode!' The nobleman's sumptuous field quarters would have shamed the warden's personal apartments back at Crow Hole, let alone the crude tent he had brought to Guisnes. The hangings, tapestries, carpets and curtains were richer than anything Howath had ever draped on his mildewed walls. The Vicomte's immaculately-liveried household servants hurried in and out of the main chamber with trays and plates, steaming platters and brimming jars as their master greeted his bedazzled guests.

'How could I refuse the kind invitation you extended to me and mine, my dear Vicomte?' Howath asked, bowing his head.

'And my dear friend, Edward. It is an honour, sir, to welcome you once again to my meagre accommodation.'

Kraven bowed. 'You do me the highest honour, my Lord, inviting me into your exquisite home-from-home,' he said smoothly.

'Ah, you mistake me sir. I am no more than a poor outcast, a pariah. What you see around you, is all the home I have left,' Gueldres said pointedly. His overawed guests didn't seem inclined to take his hard-luck story too literally. Eldritch coughed.

'And I see my friend Captain Eldritch has also accepted my invitation to dine, despite his uncommonly early start this morning. I trust you were not overly fatigued by your display at the butts?' he asked casually.

'I was honoured to accept your kind invitation, my Lord,' Eldritch said coolly. Gueldres beamed, ushering the party towards the splendid dining area. He had made the invitation at supper the night Howath had arrived, insisting the warden attend a special banquet to celebrate the historic meeting of their kings. Henry and Francis were due to meet for the first time the following morning, on Corpus Christi Day, the eagerly anticipated grand finale of the whole extravagant performance.

The Vicomte had dressed himself in a flamboyant costume of white satin and gold lace, the ornate tunic parted about a jewel-encrusted gold codpiece. His light Spanish wolf's-head dagger hung from a thin golden belt, the S-shaped hilt encrusted with gems and wound about with gold wire. The nobleman was toying with the scabbard, the blazing candlelight sparkling on his jewel-studded rings.

'You have not yet met my locotenent, Francesco Savvi,' Gueldres said. Savvi nodded, uneasy in the stifling warmth of his master's personal quarters. He hadn't had a chance to change, and was still wearing the dust-encrusted black uniform he had arrived in.

Howath always acknowledged a fellow soldier, and this was clearly a tough customer – the red-headed German's features were criss-crossed with tiny white battle scars.

'Captain Savvi has been busy about my affairs in the south: you must excuse his appearance, the roads are quite dreadful this time of year.' Gueldres smiled at Howath's daughter, blushing with delight on her father's arm. 'And here once again is your dear daughter, Mistress Miranda. You will excuse a soldier's frankness, my Lord, but I am delighted to see your daughter's wonderful complexion has remained untarnished by the trying conditions in which we have found ourselves. Why many noblewomen of my acquaintance would have thrown up their hands in horror and returned to their homes forthwith! Mistress Miranda, why she's quite blossomed amongst all this filth, like the very best rhubarb, if you will forgive me saying so!'

Miranda beamed as the suave Vicomte bowed before her, lifting her white fingers on his jewelled hand. Miranda glanced at Merron, wondering how she should respond to the gallant's flattery. She had complete faith in her, knowing Merron would be sure to point out any breach in etiquette.

Merron's eyes flashed, startled by the sudden movement to her left. Another man had appeared from the interior of the tent. The last guest was a tall, dark-skinned Spaniard, wearing a rather worn but garishly colourful suit of red and yellow quarters. He wore gaily striped hose, one leg yellow and green, the other blue and white, slashed and gathered about his knees.

'And finally, allow me to introduce Capitano Miguel Isolani. Capitano Isolani has an enviable record, training peasants in the art of modern war. And I am sure he would be happy to tell you all about our modern arquebus, isn't that so Isolani?'

Eldritch could barely restrain himself from smashing the grinning Vicomte over the head with one of his handsomely-engraved platters. *Peasants?* He glanced at his master the warden, but Howath appeared to have missed the nobleman's sniping.

'Let us dine,' the Vicomte said, ushering them into the luxuriously-appointed banqueting hall.

Gueldres led the way with Miranda on his arm, his manners as exquisite as his taste in décor. He showed the blushing girl to her seat, nodding to her father as he took his place alongside her. Eldritch was seated next to his master with his back to the draughts coming in from the busy outer chamber. The Vicomte took his place at the head of the table, with Kraven, Savvi, Merron and Isolani packed in – with ever-decreasing elbow room – at the far end. Servants hurried in to fill the crystal flutes Gueldres had ordered up for the feast.

'Before we start, a toast to the historic meeting of our great Princes? To King Henry and King Francis, and the happy conclusion of a lasting treaty between our nations,' Gueldres proposed, raising his glass.

The guests rose, their glasses twinkling in the candlelight. Miranda was flushed with the heat and excitement, looking up and down the table at the fabulously-dressed guests. Her cheeks were as rosy as ripe apples. Merron was pale in comparison, touching her napkin to her lips and taking sidelong glances at the grinning Spaniard sitting alongside her. He seemed bewitched by the girl's cool elegance, delighted by her occasional smiles. Isolani poured her another glass of wine.

Eldritch had noticed his hungry look and tried to catch his sister's wandering eye without success. Howath quaffed his wine, nervous as a novice in the glittering company. The Vicomte seemed to relish his all-too-evident discomfort.

'I had the honour of being introduced to your commander earlier this afternoon,' he remarked.

'Oh yes?' Howath inquired. He hadn't even been called to the headquarters tent yet, much less met any of the army's senior officers.

'You can be sure I told the esteemed Earl of Northumberland how impressed I had been by Captain Eldritch's performance at the butts.' Gueldres raised his glass towards the captain. 'The conversation went on to the general merits of the bow versus the arquebus, an argument with which our friend Captain Eldritch is all too familiar.' .

'Capitano El Dreeg is welcome to try the best arquebuses in my collection,' the Spaniard offered, his voice as fluid as the wine he sipped. He leaned across the table, darkly sincere. 'My armourers can improve the range and accuracy of the mass-produced Italian or German weapons. My fireworker, an Englishman just like yourselves, is a *genius* when it comes to grinding powder! I am sure, once Capitano El Dreeg has tried one, he would never again wish to return to his longbow!'

'My thanks to you, sir, but I will stick with what I know,' Eldritch said icily.

'Quite right!' Gueldres exclaimed. 'Stick with what you know, eh?' He drained his goblet and held it out to the liveried servant waiting patiently at his elbow. He was enjoying himself immensely, antagonising the scowling captain of horse, even though his slow-witted master was proving far too stupid to register his jibes. Eldritch was a sharp one, right enough. Possibly useful, if he could break him away from this dolt of a warden. There was always the possiblity he might be able to persuade a few of Howath's retainers to change their allegiance, to take up arms in his own, critically-understrength legion.

God knew he had to find the men from somewhere, and a mob of mad-dog English would be better than nothing.

The first remove came and went, the guests becoming warmer and more animated with each successive course, every bumper of Gueldres' fine wine. Howath turned his heavy head to follow their crossfire conversations, slowly becoming aware of the tensions between them – and of Gueldres' thinly-veiled criticisms.

'I suggest you go over to the arquebus as soon as possible, equip a few companies at a time,' Isolani went on through a mouthful of chicken, apparently unaware of the vicious interplay down table. 'To guard your camp, your wagons and so on.'

'The Ride does not sit on its arse guarding camps,' Howath replied curtly, noisily draining another goblet. 'Nor does it go into battle with one-shot hagbuts,' he said, his rasping voice becoming slightly slurred. 'Why my division would have been cut to pieces on Flodden hill, carrying lumps of damned wood!' he exclaimed.

'I was at Ravenna back in '13: those lumps of wood as you call them killed ten thousand good men that bloody day!' Savvi retorted, his beard glistening with droplets of mutton fat. Isolani frowned at the German's outburst.

'Firearms have come a long way since Ravenna,' he said

shortly. 'Given the proper tactics, a unit of . . .'

'Gentlemen please! War, war, war! I am sure we are driving these fine ladies to distraction with such diabolical conversation!' Gueldres cried, ordering the wine around once more.

The tent seemed stuffier than ever, the air thick with wine-fuelled tensions. Merron alone seemed immune to the fragrant heat, elegantly poised as she picked at her meal. The Spaniard seemed enchanted with her, offering plate after plate of sweetmeats and trifles.

'Surely, Capitano Isolani, the mettle of the troops is more important than the arms he bears? If one were to give the bravest man a stick, might he not confound the most well-armoured coward?' Eldritch glared across the table at his sister, but Merron was concentrating her attention on the delighted Spaniard.

Gueldres was as surprised as any of them by Merron's confident question, but he said nothing, sitting back in his chair with his fingers steepled over his chest. He studied her cool profile, suddenly struck by the girl's knowing innocence.

No wonder his scatterbrained cousin Claude had fallen for her elder sister, he thought fleetingly. The Vicomte's eyes narrowed as he followed the invigorating argument.

Isolani cracked his goblet down on the table. 'Well said, Señorita! Perfectly correct. The true-hearted knight will always prevail over the perfidious coward!'

'Not on your life, Isolani! Put enough cowards behind an earth rampart and give them an arquebus each, they'll shoot your brave sticksmen down like dogs,' Savvi accused, lolling in his seat as he poked a chewed muttonbone at the Spaniard.

'But one can only do so much with these cowardly dogs of yours. Earth ramparts don't win hearts, don't storm towns, don't conquer nations!' Isolani cried, his dark skin flushed with the heat and the wine. Merron nodded in agreement, a tiny blush staining her smooth cheekbones. Eldritch glowered at her before turning his attention back to the squabbling soldiers.

'I believe that is precisely how the Romans finally beat the Carthaginians,' he said. 'The arquebus is just the weapon for such Fabian tactics.'

'Are you suggesting the Black Legion is made up of cowardly dogs?' Savvi demanded, prising himself to his unsteady feet.

'Absolutely not! The troopers of the *Band Nere* are as fanatical as any in Europe, even the Swiss,' Isolani reassured him.

Howath spluttered, alarmed at the increasingly bad-tempered arguments, bewildered by the bright lights and the heady, heady wine which seemed to be tangling his brain. Miranda was as lost as her father and was looking hopefully at Merron for guidance. But her maid was un-aware, giggling into her hand as the admiring Spaniard whispered in her ear. Eldritch clenched his fists. The wine had gone straight to his overheating head.

'A thousand English bowmen tipped the scales at Flod-den, and would have done exactly the same at Ravenna,' he called. 'I wouldn't give a cup of cold pish for your damned arquebuses!'

Gueldres paled, looking down the table from beneath his hooded eyes. Howath blinked at his captain of horse, out-raged by his dangerous insolence. Kraven leaned over, laid his hand on Eldritch's arm.

'No my Lord, don't bid me quiet!' Eldritch cried, shak-ing himself free of the merchant's placating grip. 'My Lord the Vicomte has played games with us since we arrived: perhaps he'd like to play some more? At cards, perhaps, mumchance, at dice?'

'Dice?'

'Aye, dice! Ours have six sides – yours, my Lord, no doubt have twenty and more!'

'What are you suggesting, captain?' Gueldres asked coldly.

'I beat your man at the butts, my Lord. What about another contest? You said yourself, we should not bring our battles to table. But you made no mention of dice!' he fished in his tunic, tumbled a handful of red cubes onto the cluttered tabletop.

'Eldritch!' Howath warned. Gueldres clapped his hands.

'Excellent! Bring more wine and away with these dishes!' he cried.

Eldritch had gone through the meagre contents of his purse within half an hour, and been forced to borrow a handful of silver pennies from the highly-amused Isolani simply to stay in the game. Howath was winning the lion's share of the pot, scraping his winnings towards him with a grunt of disbelief.

'Damn me, the Gods must be with me tonight,' he laughed, scooping the coins into his fist.

Gueldres smiled thinly. It wasn't the Gods as were smiling on him, it was the wretched dice! He studied each player in turn, their rapt faces raw with wine and excitement. One of them was cheating – the dice were as loaded as a Venetian wine cask.

He had already gone through the loose change he carried in his belt, and dispatched his overwrought major domo to fetch more from the chest he had hidden in his sleeping quarters. He meant to get his stake-money back, and find out which of the knaves was responsible. They were the captain's dice – but Eldritch had already lost a month's wages and looked set to lose more. What sort of fool used loaded dice to *lose* money?

'Seven again! Hah!' Howath cried. Gueldres glanced down at Eldritch, noting the look of irritation which flashed across his furiously-set features.

He was either a very poor loser or a most excellent cheat.

'Fetch me another purse!' Gueldres cried, 'and my own dice while you're about it.' The warden blinked through his alcoholic haze, grinning at his host.

'Your dice? You don't find ours much to your liking, my dear Vicomte?'

Eldritch sat back heavily in his seat. 'They were *my* dice, and they weren't much to my liking,' he said petulantly. 'Go ahead and swap them!'

Merron made a face at her elder brother, scooped up the red dice and dropped them in his empty goblet. Gueldres watched their interplay, fascinated by their barefaced insolence.

His servant hurried to his side, bowed, and tipped a handful of new red dice into his master's palm.

'New dice need a blessing,' Gueldres said, rolling them down the table towards Miranda. He noticed the girl's tongue protruding between her lips as she bent over to retrieve them.

'Mistress Miranda will do me great honour, if she takes my throw for me,' he said silkily. Miranda glanced up at Merron.

'Yes, it's only fair girl,' her father said, trying to disguise a juicy belch behind his fist.

'First throw for the Vicomte,' Miranda cried, blowing over the dice for luck. Gueldres reached out, took her by the wrist.

'But first, my dear, let us make the game a little more interesting. My Lord Howath, would you object to raising the stakes? Giving me a chance to retrieve some of my lost silver?'

Howath shrugged his broad shoulders.

'Lady Luck is with me, why not? A gold piece a throw!'

'A gold piece? I've seen pox-diddled crossbowmen throw for ten!' Savvi cried, forgetting his manners as he too became engrossed in the game.

'Ten it is!' Howath cried, adding more coins to the pile.

'A month's pay to the highest throw!' Isolani suggested, wiping his greasy hands on his backside and sliding his stake across the table.

'Aye, highest takes all,' Savvi agreed, leaning over Merron to flick his own coins into the pot. Miranda looked around the ring of flushed faces, her eyes coming to rest on Gueldres. He released her wrist with a sideways smile and she tumbled the dice over the table.

'Six, five three!'

'Fourteen,' Merron clapped her hands together as Miranda eyed her.

'I can count, Missy!' her mistress scolded. Howath picked up the dice and threw a six and a pair of twos. He grunted, shoved the dice towards Eldritch.

'Three fours!'

Kraven rolled the dice in his beaker as if he was an alchemist preparing some magical formula.

'Two three five! Bad luck, Kraven!'

Savvi rolled six, three and one.

Isolani held the dice up in his dark palm, gazing at the drowsy Merron as if seeking her blessing. 'You'll pray for me, *pistareena*,' he invited, tumbling them down the table and cursing in Spanish as he rolled a one and a double two. Eldritch picked up the stray dice and examined them.

Gueldres grinned. Howath watched the Vicomte throw out his golden arm and draw the heaped coins toward him. The warden was blinking like an old badger lost in a fog.

'That's more like it!' the Vicomte cried. 'What, where's that damned potboy! More wine for my guests!'

He missed the pale glint of triumph in Eldritch's eyes.

Howath was tremendously tired, almost as exhausted as he had been that night on Flodden hill, arms hanging at his bruised sides. He braced himself against the table as if Gueldres' magnificent pavilion had suddenly put out to sea, the canvas pummelled by boisterous currents. His belly heaved and hawed; he could taste sour wine and ripe cheese. The warden could barely focus on the jewelled eye of the dice, relying on Miranda to count his score for him. His pile of coins had dwindled and then accumulated once again.

Gueldres was staring at the dice, wondering if that slow dog Eldritch had somehow managed to substitute them, conjure them away up his sleeves and roll out his loaded originals. He cursed his own lack of attention, racking his brains to try and remember if Eldritch had touched them out of turn.

But the scowling captain was the only man at the table who hadn't enjoyed some kind of winning streak. He had exhausted all his money and a quarter of Isolani's. The warden, still winning, had raised the stakes to a hundred pieces a throw.

'Excellent! You may have won the shirt from my back, my Lord, but by God you know how to play!' Gueldres saluted him, wondering what in seven hells was going on. The new dice seemed to be throwing up the most remarkable set of results. He wasn't losing, but he wasn't exactly winning.

'But my Lord the warden tires, and we all of us have an early start on the morrow,' he said easily. Howath seemed electrified by the prospect of turning in. He leaned over the table, slapped his broad palm into the spilled wine.

'Nonsense! Dawn's an hour off yet!'

'My Lord, I think it best if you retire,' Eldritch suggested, with uncharacteristic benevolence. He half-rose in his seat as if to assist the old warrior to his tent. Howath opened his eye, drew an unsteady bead on his captain of horse.

'Am I in my dotage? Do you mean to milksop me and tuck me up abed?' he snarled, his voice thickened by drink. 'Back where you were sir! You may have frittered all your monies; your master has a few pennies left to him yet!'

Eldritch sat back down, carefully suppressing his irritation.

'I meant no such thing my Lord. I . . .'

'Here, to keep you happy sir, a hundred gold pieces from my winnings,' he counted out the coins and shoved the pile towards the scowling captain. 'Two years' pay in advance, aye, if you'll stow that moaning and join the game!'

'A most excellent gesture!' Gueldres enthused, more bewildered than ever. Eldritch thought for a moment, reached out and scooped the coins into his palm.

'Two years in advance,' he mused. 'Why, how now my Lord, you'll be wagering the services of your entire retinue, if we go on much longer!'

Gueldres blinked like a cobra before a mongoose. Howath missed the significance of the remark, watching his clever captain pulling the rings from his fingers. The

Vicomte's more calculating mind was leaping ahead, still suspicious he was being set up. Wager the lives of his warband? Not even the doltish warden would dare risking all like that, Gueldres thought.

Or would he?

Eldritch weighed the rings in his palm. He had taken them from his father's corpse long years before. Now the tokens of his family's desperate penury would play their part in making his fortune!

'I'll raise the stakes with these rings. Gold and silver, worked with rubies. They are worth at least a hundred each.'

'Aye, throw them in lad! That's more like it,' Howath chuckled.

'Too rich for me,' Savvi complained, gathering up the few coins he had left and draining his glass.

Eldritch, Gueldres and Howath threw again.

And for the first time that long night, Eldritch scooped the pot.

'Ah, my luck's changing,' the captain cried, leaning forward to rake the piled stakes toward him. In one throw he had won back all the monies he had lost, quadrupled the meagre purse he had brought to table. Howath sat back, carelessly quaffing his wine. Gueldres narrowed his eyes, staring at the damned dice.

Duped! The English weasel had swapped the dice when he hadn't been looking, and beaten him at his own game! The nobleman grinned feebly, horrified by his own stupidity. Eldritch was about to launch his long-delayed assault on his fortune, fleece him in his own pavilion!

Edward Kraven, more used than any of them to watching from the sidelines, had followed their bizarre twists of fortune with the quickest eye of all. But not even the canny merchant had spotted Eldritch switch the dice.

The clever captain had lulled both the garrulous warden and the sharper nobleman into a false sense of security, letting them win everything as the stakes piled higher and higher. They had lowered their guard, completely drawn in by his superb brinkmanship, and would surely pay dearly for their lack of attention. Kraven lifted his glass, watched Eldritch take a sideways glance at his master the warden. As if he was wondering what to wager next.

And in a blink Kraven knew what he was about!

The rogue had foxed them all along, pretending to have set his sights on the Vicomte's wealth when all the while he had been aiming to fleece his own master. Kraven lowered his goblet, spilling his wine in disbelieving agitation. The warband, of course! He meant to win Howath's retinue for himself!

'Steady on Ned!' Howath called, misunderstanding his drop-jawed stare. 'It's a drop of good stuff our friend Gueldres is serving up!'

Kraven swallowed hard, shaking his head at the captain's audacity. Eldritch was deliberately chivvying the warden on, tricking him into some foolhardy display of bravado. He had manoeuvred the old drunk on to the summit of a rapidly-collapsing mountain of winnings. And the way things were going, he would be reduced to gambling his only asset – his retinue.

Kraven glanced at Howath, crucified with concern. How in hell would he dissuade the warden from further disastrous wagers?

'Jack, you'll lose the lot if you're not very careful,' he said cheerily. 'We've all an early start this day, let's to bed!' he pleaded, considerately laying a hand on Howath's arm. The warden's moist eyes blazed.

'You and all? If you're pining for your bed away to it!' he exclaimed. 'I've plenty more where that little lot came from!'

Gueldres wondered at this latest change of tack – Kraven warning the old fool off now.

What was going on?

'Come now Edward. Your sensible advice will quite spoil our soldiers' fun,' he cried, maddeningly unsure whose fire he was stoking. 'Bet on, I say!'

'Eldritch has bet his baubles, what about you and I, Gueldres?' Howath inquired, slurring his words badly. 'That brooch of yours for a start,' he went on, turning his wandering attention back on the watchful nobleman. 'Your rings, your own sumptuous quarters!' He thumped his glass down on the table, shattering the finely-wrought stem.

'What about them, my Lord?'

'Why get 'em on the table man, here, against all this! Highest wins!'

It was time. Time to spring the trap he had been preparing all night. One careless word, one angry challenge, and the warband would be his!

Howath was rolling in his chair like a cog in a tempest, cross-eyed and cursing with drink. All he had to do now was raise the stakes, prompt the old fool into wagering the lives of his men!

And he would be there with his loaded dice, to snatch the entire warband up from beneath his nose! It might not be fair, it might not be honourable, but he had been left with little choice. He would not live like some scarecrow, following the old warden into the oblivion of history.

Eldritch looked across the table, the finely-carved chairs the servants had managed to . . . chairs?

Merron and Isolani had gone! Gone? Now???

'Hell's teeth!' he leapt to his feet, his chair toppling over and knocking one of the overworked potboys sideways.

Howath ignored his outburst, his red tongue protruding from his beard as he shoved his entire store of coins – and more besides – into the middle of the gaming table.

'What ails you captain?' Gueldres asked casually. Eldritch, clearly mortified, was peering around the chamber as if he expected to see his wayward sister and her Spanish admirer coiled in the candlesticks.

'Where's he taken her?' He had only taken his eyes from them for a moment – how long had they been gone? He couldn't leave the game now, not when he was on the verge of winning all!

Eldritch stood on the crossroads of his very existence, torn between his duty to his sister and to himself.

Ballocks, ballocks, ballocks!

Eldritch made up his fuming mind in a moment.

'Hold all bets!' he cried. 'I won't be a moment!'

'It's no good dropping out now Eldritch, not now you've finally won something,' Howath jeered.

'I will be back forthwith,' Eldritch said, trying to keep his desperate tension out of his voice. He strode towards the tent flap, barging the flustered major domo aside.

'She's off taking a piss or getting some air,' Howath called, waving his hand carelessly. 'My Lord, you see the stakes before you!'

Gueldres stared at the heap of gold the warden had shoved forward, acutely aware the night's festivities had taken a sinister turn into uncharted territory.

Who was playing who here?

Where was Eldritch going in such a hurry?

Was Howath as drunk as he looked, or merely acting out some elaborate farce they had cooked up between them?

He hardly had time to think, and Gueldres despised acting on impulse alone.

'My Lord Howath is generous to a fault, offering his fortune in such a sportsmanlike fashion,' he said quickly. 'But my rings, my brooch . . . family heirlooms you understand,' he shrugged as if embarrassed by his feeble explanation.

'I've not upped the stakes enough for you, eh?' Howath went on with a fruity belch. Miranda's smile slipped a notch as she began to realise the extent of her father's incapacity.

'*Au contraire*, my Lord.' Gueldres replied, cold as a blade. 'I was merely . . . if you wish to up the stakes, so be it.' He took his rings off one by one, added them to the glistening heap of coins. He unclasped the golden brooch, the wolf's-head device grinning in the flickering candlelight. 'And to ensure things remain interesting to the end, here . . .' He reached for the golden purse dangling along his thigh and fished out a long brass key, flaked and flowering with verdigris. 'The key of my keep at Mont Gilbert le Galliard,' he said, adding it to the bet. He sat in silence for a moment, contemplating the glittering prizes.

Savvi stared, Isolani whistled softly. Miranda's heart was thumping with panic and excitement, but she dared not contradict her father when the drink was on him.

'Will you cover my wager, my Lord Howath?' Gueldres inquired, 'Or am I to take the pot by default?' Howath was blinking fast, peering about the room for that wretch Eldritch. Damn it all, what was he to do?

Gueldres guessed who he was looking for, leaned over to lay his hand over the treasure hoard. Howath lunged forward, grabbed the nobleman by the wrist.

'I've brought nothing to match this, my Lord, as well you know!' he said – without the faintest suspicion of weariness.

'Jack!' Kraven warned. 'Stop now, for God's sake, enough!'

'Then the pot is mine, I think,' Gueldres said icily.

'Wait! You know full well the worth of my men!'

'Indeed. But I am not in the market for secondhand bows and blunt bills,' he retorted.

'They're not bonfire fodder just yet,' Howath growled. 'I'll sign over my entire warband . . .'

'Jack! For the sake of all the . . .' Kraven exclaimed, trying to pull the old warrior away from the table.

'Let him go, merchant man! What's he betting, his retinue? Those ancient veterans of Flodden field?'

'My Lord!'

'AYE!' Howath roared, thumping his fist on the table and almost knocking himself under it. 'Every man, to be taken on their existing pay and conditions as set out in their articles! Every man's service, my Lord, for a year and a day! There, I think that ought to cover your bet!' Howath picked up the dice from the table. He palmed them into Miranda's glass and shoved it towards the scowling nobleman.

By heaven, whose dice were they? Had Howath been canny enough to switch them once again?

'Four dice each, highest total wins!'

Gueldres grinned. There was nothing else for it.

Just then Eldritch sprinted back into the tent, red-faced and panting after his exertions. Gueldres noticed there was a trickle of blood running from the corner of his gasping mouth.

'Roll!' Howath roared, hurling his dice across the table.

'NO!' Eldritch bawled.

Too late.

The loaded dice clattered and rebounded around the piled plates and cold dishes, clinked and sparkled against the finely-cut crystal.

Henry VIII and his esteemed cousin Francis I took up their places at either end of the Golden Valley, each great king surrounded by the pick of his knights and nobles, his most distinguished courtiers. They waited as if undecided whether to go forward into the shallow vale with open arms or drawn swords.

A saker coughed like a slow dog on a frosty morning, shattering the expectant silence. They trotted forward, horses prancing, their richly-embroidered bards billowing, standards and pennants snapping in the breeze.

They picked up speed down the carefully-clipped slopes, their bodyguards hurrying to keep up, pikes and bills and banners shifting and sliding in the drifting smoke from the signal gun. A blaze of trumpets and the kings reined up, gazing at one another as if they had ridden up to some magical mirror, reflecting their fantastic empires in pin-point detail. The tall kings dismounted, stepped across the trampled grass and embraced.

On the Field of the Cloth of Gold.

PART THREE
God's Gift

'Men who are anxious to win the favour of a prince nearly always follow the custom of presenting themselves to him with the possessions they value most, or with things they know especially please him.'

Machiavelli, *The Prince*

Beside Crespin, Provence, Southern France, July 1520

The stark outlines of the abbey cast a shadow over the sun-bleached hills, a gloomy monument in the otherwise glorious Provençal countryside. The terrain was drawn and quartered by steep mountains and sudden, vine-tangled slopes, banded by occasional belts of glistening firs. The rich, dusty earth had been tilled and terraced, silver-leafed olive groves alternately gasping sap in the ferocious summer heat and then whittled by the chill breath of the mistral.

The abbey was as much a fortress as a shelter from the double-edged assaults of the weather, the walls forming acute angles to deflect cannon and shot. The towers were riddled with lancets, the imposing gatehouse dominating the approaches. The monks who garrisoned the grim fastness belonged to the Dominican order, their white tunics and black hoods setting them apart from their brother orders; grey-clad Franciscans and black-caped Augustinians. Their religious zeal and determination to stamp out heresy had earned them a grimly ironic nickname. To the fearful peasants they were known as the Hounds of Christ.

Abbot Herve Odo could claim descent from the great houses of Normandy, and had brought something of their Varangian spirit to the remote hills over which he ruled. But the abbey was much more than a backwater pile. It had enjoyed a long and distinguished history, and had established a reputation as one of the finest training grounds for ambitious churchmen in southern Europe. These church-men had moved on to lucrative sinecures in Paris or Rome, or the great theological centres in Germany.

The Abbey d'Eleron's role at the centre of this highly specialised and extensive network was further reinforced by its reputation for excellence in choral music. The abbey had supplied trainees to choirs all over Europe, fully proficient in all aspects of their wondrous though rather secretive craft. The abbot auditioned a few dozen promising boys every autumn, choosing the very best to join the abbey choir. Abbey d'Eleron's jealously-guarded reputation was as well known in Paris as it was in Vienna. It had even reached Alberto Tarsi, in his stronghold over the Alps.

Cesar Scaralatchi's life's work had been completed at last, the composer dictating the final stanzas to his devoted assistant Fabrizio, who copied out the score in his immaculate Latin script. The composer's drafts were strewn and spotted with wine, sweat and even blood, and were barely decipherable to anyone but the author. As soon as Fabrizio had finished each trying section of the score, Scaralatchi would tear the smudged originals into pieces and toss them in the fire. His work had been plagiarised in the past, and he didn't intend to see his masterpiece go the same way – performed by some vulgar troupe before some ignorant, cloth-eared cardinal who wouldn't know a decent anthem from a fishwife's whistle.

Fabrizio had never heard such stunning arrangements. He had devoted all his spare time to practising different passages of the remarkable work with his own scratch choir – the drummer boy Druzot and little Pilli the kitchen hand. Obolus could remember whole stanzas at the first sight, and sing them back to the amazed youth as if he had written the piece himself. The improvised choir had rehearsed large sections of the complex work, enabling Scaralatchi to make last-minute alterations to the score. But the bemused choristers had not been given the passages in any particular order. They might have been singing the opening stanzas or the last, soaring verses – but only a musical genius would have been able to find any pattern, let alone been able to piece the complex work together again.

The time had come to give the work to a full choir, and Scaralatchi hadn't hesitated to suggest the Abbey d'Eleron.

'My score will demand highly skilled choristers, and the d'Eleron boys are simply the best,' he had told his impatient patron Tarsi.

The soldier of fortune had nodded, idly reckoning what the project might cost him. He had contracted pikemen and artillerymen, engineers and knights, but never a damned choir!

Scaralatchi made a face, wringing out the sleeve of his coat of many colours as if he had inadvertently soaked it in spilt wine.

'I would go and see Odo myself, but I fear my previous *misfortunes* . . .'

Misfortunes? Tarsi thought hotly. That was one way of putting it. Excommunication was a rather more accurate term.

'. . . the ill-advised excesses of my youth,' the composer went on, 'have closed all doors on my rehabilitation. In short, *padrone*, I dare not go to France.'

Tarsi sighed. He had heard all about the composer's previous disgrace. Scaralatchi had devoted all his life to music – all that was left over from his legendary debaucheries, at any rate. Tarsi wasn't about to set him adrift through any misplaced display of moral outrage. So long as the wretch completed his masterwork he was at liberty to indulge whatever peculiar fancy took him. If the score lived up to its reputation and impressed the representatives of the Vatican then Tarsi would procure the old goat half a dozen Turkish boys to sate his damned appetites.

'We have already discussed what must be done,' Scaralatchi said shortly. 'Fabrizio must go in my place. If he can secure the services of Odo's choir we are ten times more likely to win an audience before their excellencies. Believe me, *padrone*, I have had dealings with papal delegations before now. Runcini would cross the Alps on a scabby-arsed mule for a chance to feast his eyes on the d'Eleron choir.'

Tarsi scowled at his heavy-handed innuendo.

'He will be enraptured, watching those boys, listening to my mass. I promise you *padrone*, your investment will reap rich dividends.

'I hope it will be so,' Tarsi said ruefully.

'Fabrizio will convince Odo. He has a silver tongue.'

'Convince them you seek absolution,' the soldier mused.

'Even so. The Scaralatchi *Miserere*, a truly penitential mass,' the composer breathed, an unlikely mixture of bitter cynicism and oily sincerity. Tarsi wouldn't have been taken in for a moment, but then, he was a soldier, not a cardinal.

'How do you know it will be enough to convince the Church you have mended your ways? That you are truly penitent?'

Scaralatchi gave his master a searching look. He knew Tarsi wasn't concerned at the true extent of his repentence. The real question was whether or not the score would win him friends on the papal delegation – due in Novara shortly to rule on the valley road tolls. All he cared was whether the masterpiece he had commissioned would impress the egotistical Runcini, convince him he should reject his deadly rival the Count of Luningiana's bid to secure the tolls. They all knew that without the road revenues, Tarsi would be isolated in his mountain hideaway, forced to return to virtual banditry to maintain his household. Scaralatchi knew his master's mind better than he did himself, but he did not resent his selfishness. Tarsi's triumph would be Scaralatchi's absolution. He did not want to die in the sulphurous shadow of excommunication.

'You had faith in my abilities when we met,' he said flatly. 'Extend your faith a while longer.'

Tarsi frowned. 'But I cannot go any more than you, not with Gueldres and Stroma ready to pounce on Mont Galliard.'

Scaralatchi nodded, losing patience with the uncharacteristically indecisive soldier. Was the great Tarsi having second thoughts? Now he had passed broken glass and sweated blood over the damned score? His Amazon of a daughter would do just as well as her war-weary sire.

'The abbot needs to be convinced of Fabrizio's authority, of his place in your heart and your household. Therefore, *padrone*, he must travel as we have arranged, as trusted companion to your own daughter. And with a suitably powerful escort, of course.'

Not that the little hellcat needed much protection, he thought sourly.

'And the Tarsi signet ring,' the soldier growled.

'Odo must be convinced Fabrizio has your trust, and your blessing. Does he?'

Tarsi flicked his wrist in annoyance.

'He goes with my trust and my blessing. With my only daughter,' Tarsi pointed out with unmistakable emphasis.

Scaralatchi pursed his lips.

'In the circumstances, *padrone*, I imagine she will be safe on that score, don't you?'

Six weeks later the subject of their acrimonious discussion was lounging in Tarsi's finest six-wheeled carriage, reclining in the plush velvet seat as if he was a triumphant caesar come to tour his newly-conquered Gallic provinces. The coach rattled and bumped over the appalling hill tracks, the enormous oaken wheels jarring the occupants' nerves as they were carried towards their remote destination.

'So this is Provence! It's certainly warmer than your father's eyrie,' the youth called, idly holding his hand up so the Tarsi signet ring he wore reflected the strong sunlight pouring in through the carriage window. The beams played over Angelica's features.

'Must you do that?' the girl scolded, averting her eyes from the irritating glare. 'You had better not lose it, flashing it about like a whore's favour.'

Fabrizio held her eyes while he kissed the heavily-embossed ring. He carefully turned the plain band outward to conceal the Tarsi coat of arms. The girl bristled. Her grinning companion hardly seemed to notice the pot-holed road, leaping out of his seat every few moments to study the views. The landscape seemed to have been bathed in warm gold, as if Fabrizio was studying its contours through the bottom of a jar of honey. Every outcrop seemed more sharply defined than the grim granite passes they had left behind, the thorn-backed ridges vividly etched against the sky.

It was as if Provence had its own special sun, casting a diffused glow over a chosen land of olive groves and straggling vineyards. Fabrizio lifted the leather dust flap and waved at some toiling peasants, laughing and hallooing as the sunburnt locals grovelled in the dirt kicked up by the wagon's broad wheels.

He hurled himself back into the seat, putting up clouds of dust and ticks which had accumulated on the upholstery during the carriage's long lay-off in Mont Galliard's stables. Angelica fanned the mote-filled air in annoyance.

'Father will have you flayed alive if you don't bring it back safely. I still think I should take it, at least until we see the abbot.'

The olive-skinned youth flicked his thin wrist dismissively. He was thoroughly enjoying his new-found freedom, relishing the open spaces after his virtual captivity in Scaralatchi's odious chambers.

Angelica sat back in her seat, studied his fine profile. He had sharper cheekbones, and his lips were not as childishly chubby as hers either. His ringleted hair was blacker, finer than her rather coarse tresses. She wondered for a moment if she would ever meet a man who would prefer her earthy charms to Fabrizio's decadent sophistication.

By the Holy Father, she hoped so!

Fabrizio was startled by her sudden glare, clenched his long hands in front of his chest in mock terror.

'I shall guard the ring with my life,' he vowed, misunderstanding the ferocity of her stare. Angelica sighed, patted her hair in irritation.

As she had anticipated, her wondrous new headdress had slipped over her tightly-spun curls, pulled her hair away from her rather severe features. Hyacinthine? She reminded herself not to frown. At least her skin was clear, her quick eyes bold and darting – the colour of a finch's wing.

'Just remember who you are supposed to be,' she scolded. The youth stared back at her, a serene smile playing about the corners of his mouth. Damn his mouth! She felt herself twitch, longing to taste those lips, to bite his impudent tongue.

'Who are you supposed to be, mistress? My guardian, my intended?'

'Intended what?' she snorted.

'Wife of course! Surely even the warlike Tarsi would baulk at allowing his only daughter to travel in the company of a dissolute chorister!' he said archly.

'You're not supposed to be dissolute any longer,' she cried. 'I'm here to vouchsafe for your integrity, your devotion to good Christian morals!'

Fabrizio laughed out loud, his voice as clear and fresh as the mountain streams they had crossed the previous day. 'You are the keeper of my soul, mistress,' he cried, joking again. Angelica seethed, her belly alive with butterfly-winged serpents. She wished it were true. Wished he could want her as she wanted him! Just because he dallied with that disgusting mongrel Scaralatchi did not mean he wasn't a man.

'You don't look much like a pious, Godfearing composer's apprentice! Obolus may pass as House Tarsi's jester, make sure the abbot does not mistake you for his fool!'

Fabrizio frowned, stung by her sudden anger. What was the matter with the girl? Was the heat getting to her? He drummed his fingers on his knee, lost in thought. They rode the rest of the way in silence.

Beside the Abbey d'Eleron, Crespin, Provence

Abbot Herve Odo was in his late fifties but looked older than the hills. Long afternoons in the Provence sunshine allied to the desiccating winds which blew over the ridges had scoured his once-rounded features, hollowed his cheeks and underscored his patient blue eyes. His white hair had retreated behind his ears, the exposed scalp red and wrinkled by frequent strolls in the grounds.

But appearances could be deceptive, especially in the Holy Church. Despite his frail and rather careworn countenance, his breathless rasp and awkward stoop, old Odo was as tough as his sandal leather, as hard-bitten as his valiant Norman forebears and ten times as shrewd as his rather more worldly acquaintances.

The venerable abbot had waited to greet his guests in person, leaning on a cane in the courtyard while the refreshingly moist breath of the fountain played on his upturned face. He looked down as the heavy wagon rumbled over the galleried drawbridge, the hold swathed in belts of white dust. The liveried driver hauled on the reins bringing the carriage to a halt. A small column of riders clattered into the courtyard behind the wain, their iron-shod horses shattering the tranquillity in a moment.

Odo took out his neckerchief and wiped the cold droplets from his face, nodding to the escort commander. The knight sat on a sweat-caked charger, a mace loose in his fist.

He looked about the courtyard as if he suspected an ambush. Apparently satisfied by his brief reconnaissance the captain swung his leg over his saddle and dismounted. He tore off his gauntlets and lifted the sallet from his black locks.

'My Lord Abbot, I am Captain Luca Strozzi, bodyguard to the Lady Angelica Tarsi,' the rider reported, bowing his head. The abbot smiled, raised his arms to welcome the warrior.

'You must be exhausted, the heat, the dust,' Odo sympathised, standing aside as Strozzi waved the liveried postilions forward with the steps. He shielded his eyes as a handsome young man in a striking blue suit swung the carriage door open with a flourish. He peered about the courtyard as if it was the very threshold of heaven. The youth seemed startled by a sudden jolt from the dark interior. He turned and helped his mistress down the steps, fussing over the girl as if she was some broken-backed crone. The young woman pulled her hand back with a flash of irritation, quickly adjusted her features as she spied the bemused abbot.

'My Lady, you brighten an old man's day,' Odo cackled, taking the girl's white fingers in his liver-spotted paw and straightening up, infinitely slowly. His delighted visitor inclined her head in modest acknowledgement of the compliment, patted the back of his warm hand with charming familiarity.

'You must be the Lady Angelica, the esteemed Captain Tarsi's daughter. And the *bello giòvane*, none other than Signor Ambolini, late of the Vatican choir.'

Fabrizio swept his electric blue cloak back and gave the abbot an elaborate bow. Odo smiled indulgently, escorting the young woman from the courtyard and towards the shadowed silence of the main complex.

'You must refresh yourselves after your trying journey. Let's see, it is Tuesday, that means *zuppa di cavolo valpellenese*.'

The old man managed to make cabbage and bread soup sound like some Bacchanalian delight. They watched the rest of the party clamber down from the dusty wain, brush themselves off as best they could. Obolus hopped from one tiny foot to the other and clicked his heels like a playful goat. Constanzia curtsied clumsily as the abbot nodded by.

'Our cook also comes from your Aosta Valley; his soups are something of a speciality of the house!' Odo chuckled.

'We would be honoured to share your repast,' Angelica said brightly.

'However humble,' Fabrizio murmured, falling in behind them as they made their way down the cloister, the old abbot gallantly taking the young woman's arm.

Fabrizio raised his eyebrows, vaguely annoyed at her familiarity. He'd met her type before. So used to a strong father-figure they were unnaturally attracted to bent old men. She hardly seemed aware of *his* presence, and when she was, she slighted him, Fabrizio thought sourly.

He followed behind, making a great show of admiring the peeling frescoes which had been painted along the cloister walls. He skipped up the steps with the dwarf at his heels. Obolus, who had spent the journey sitting in the enormous wagon's oaken hold, had fetched out Fabrizio's hand baggage and was dutifully clutching the tightly-bound chest.

Inside, bound in leather and sealed with red wax, was the master's score. The masterpiece which had brought them a hundred and twenty miles across the sandpaper terrain of southern France.

Strozzi brought up the rear, his boots clattering as he strode down the passageways, peering down the dim cloisters which radiated in all directions about the main courtyard. He studied the abbey's formidable but worry-ingly–deserted defences with professional curiosity.

Odo showed Angelica into his personal quarters, nodded at the suddenly aloof Fabrizio and bent over to ruffle the dwarf's rusty hair. He smiled at the formidable soldier, recognising his momentary concern.

'I trust your charges will be safe enough, within these walls, Captain Strozzi. Your men provided the protection your party required on the road, but there is no evil in this place,' he said not unkindly.

Strozzi nodded, smoothing his stiff black beard. 'Unless it is brought here by unexpected intruders,' he growled. He remembered his manners, smiled quickly. 'Your pardon, my Lord Abbot, but I have been charged with ensuring the safety of my master's only daughter, as well as his servant Signor Ambolini. There may be no resident evils here, but men's hearts can be all too easily poisoned.'

Odo considered this, his hands disappearing into the voluminous sleeves of his gown.

'This is true, this is true. But the Abbey d'Eleron is under the personal patronage of the Chevalier Bayard himself. Any man who commits violence here, will have to answer to him.'

Bayard? A chicken-livered relic in out-of-date armour, Strozzi thought contemptuously. He bowed his head.

'I will rest easier this night, knowing this is so,' he lied.

The abbot's quarters were as spartan as the rest of the abbey, little more than a dungeon if it hadn't been for the large, airy windows. The shutters had been thrown open over the balcony to catch what little breeze there was. The view was magnificent, the surrounding hills bathed in alternately dark then lighter bands of gold. The rich shadows passed over almond orchards and small wheat fields, warmed and then chilled the terracotta tiles haphazardly hammered into place on every rooftop. The slumped beams seemed unable to bear the weight, every cottage and chicken-splattered shack looking as if the roof was in imminent danger of collapse.

The abbey's olive groves shimmered in the midday heat. A donkey brayed beneath a bare-limbed tree in the corner of a field. Monks and peasants were busy in the orchards, spreading calico cloths beneath the hanging branches. An old man was busy beating the trees with a stick, bringing down a storm of black-hearted olives which the crones gathered in their broad baskets.

Strozzi admired the idyllic panorama, looked up as a black-bonneted old woman served the wine. As far as he could tell, the abbey walls were formidable enough. But the guards in the watchtowers appeared to have their feet up on their parapets, clearly enjoying a siesta.

Typical of your idle tart French.

'From our own vineyards, one of the few pleasures we allow ourselves,' Odo declared, lifting his beaker to salute his guests. They had made themselves as comfortable as they could on hard cane chairs, smiling politely as the venerable abbot settled himself and finally dispensed with the small talk.

'I was greatly touched to read your father's kindly letter, my dear, and intrigued by the choral work he describes with such . . . enthusiasm,' he said. 'It is encouraging to all our peoples, when a gentleman of such particularly secular persuasion as Seigneur Tarsi takes an active interest in matters ecclesiastical,' he went on cautiously.

'It is truly an outstanding work – I would even venture to suggest, sublime,' Angelica said, smiling modestly. 'Of course, I am no expert in these matters, and like everybody else, I have only ever heard very small fragments of the work.'

'Which is why you require the services of the Choir d'Eleron,' Odo went on briskly. 'Of course, I am delighted your esteemed father chose to honour us with this commission,' he said, taking a sip of his wine.

'Then you agree?' Fabrizio interrupted, leaning forward eagerly. 'I can assure you, my Lord Abbot, the work is of the highest quality, only the best choir money can buy could possibly do it justice,' he said quickly. Angelica glared at him.

'You composed this masterpiece yourself, Signor Ambolini?' Odo inquired with deceptive innocence.

'I was able to render some technical assistance to my tutor and . . .'

'Signor Cesar Alessandro Scaralatchi,' the abbot observed, spelling out each syllable as if it was some Latin benediction.

Angelica glanced at Fabrizio, then smiled winningly at Odo.

'My Lord Abbot has no doubt heard Signor Scaralatchi's tenure as court composer to His Holiness Leo X proved to be unfortunately short-lived.'

Odo laughed out loud, spilling a little wine over his immaculate habit.

'Young lady, I may be a sworn servant of a closed order, but I know something of life outside the Abbey d'Eleron,' he snapped. 'Let us not bandy words: the gentleman in question was excommunicated!'

Angelica flushed, nodded her head. Her headdress was slipping; she could feel it tugging at the hairs on the back of her neck.

'He was indeed excommunicated, my Lord Abbot. But he was declared *toleratus* rather than *vitandus*, which means that in due course he . . .'

'Please do not presume to lecture me on matters of faith,' he said coldly. 'I am not some backwater *pievano*, taking a handful of coin to hear some shepherd girl's confession!'

Angelica blushed hotly, head bowed.

'He might be tolerated rather than avoided, but the papal bull confirming his excommunication specified it would only be lifted by a senior bishop,' Odo went on, clearly as well aware of the facts of the case as any of them. Fabrizio squirmed, studying his fingernails.

'In fact, I would not be surprised to learn that absolution in this case could only be granted by His Holiness himself.'

Angelica quailed at the prospect of convincing the abbot that Scaralatchi had indeed repented. God might strike her down for overstating the case.

'My sincerest apologies if I have given unintentional offence,' she said carefully. Odo fluttered his fingers in a typically Gallic gesture of dismissal. 'But my father knew of Signor Scaralatchi's history before he took him into his household. He found it in his heart to allow Signor Scaralatchi a chance to redeem himself before the Lord, to return to the paths of righteousness.'

She prayed Fabrizio wouldn't burst out laughing.

'I can confirm, my Lord Abbot, that he has endeavoured

to put his previous mistakes behind him, to find once more the light of Our Lord.' Odo was still frowning, staring into his wine as if it was some Roman oracle. 'He knows he cannot undo what has been done, but he is desperately keen to redeem something of his former reputation. He has one hope, that you will find it in your heart to approve and promote his penitential mass, to offer it up to His Holiness himself in one last plea for forgiveness.'

Odo looked up, his blue eyes sharper than gemstones.

'I am of course gladdened to hear of Signor Scaralatchi's repentance, his desire to seek absolution through this masterwork of his.' He put his beaker down and pressed his fingers together, leaning forward as if he was listening to some whispered confession. 'You are right in pointing out that the principal object of excommunication is to convince the offender to return to the fold, as it were. Punishment has always been a secondary consideration.'

Fabrizio grimaced. Cardinal Amerigo Runcini had known exactly what he was about when he had ordered the bull drawn up and served on the notorious composer. The rehabilitation of the offender had been the last thing on his mind! Fabrizio recoiled at the memory of the cardinal's oily charms. The Fat Salamander, the Vatican choristers had called him. It had been Runcini's agents who had assembled the case against his master, who had crucified the wayward genius for his guileless love. Damn all those hypocrites, they had all been at it, he thought angrily.

'But I must, in all faith, direct a personal question at Signor Ambolini, who I believe was not unconnected with the matters in hand.'

Fabrizio crossed his legs, glancing at his silent mistress. Angelica willed him to speak, to lie without lying, to mislead – indirectly. She knew her father back in Mont Galliard was relying on the boy's answer!

'We have heard so much about Scaralatchi's request for absolution. Does it then follow he has renounced the behaviour, the practices which led to his excommunication in the first place?' Odo asked. Fabrizio paled.

'Signor Scaralatchi has devoted every moment of his life towards completing this work. All other considerations, of love and hate, life and death, have remained secondary,' he said falteringly. 'He has had no time to indulge . . .' Odo cracked his hand down on his writing desk, his kindly features transformed.

'I have already warned you against treating me like some foolish backwater friar!' he cried. 'You are well aware of the question I am asking! I apologise to Mistress Tarsi for the indelicate direction of the conversation, but no doubt she will forgive me!'

Angelica swallowed, limbs trembling at the abbot's unexpected outburst.

'Has Scaralatchi renounced his perverse infatuations, or does he still crave unnatural affections?'

Angelica blushed furiously, hardly daring to look at Fabrizio.

'Well?'

'I am his assistant,' he said, tears burning in his eyes.

'You know what I mean!'

'No, Signor Scaralatchi has not touched anybody in an unnatural manner since we left Italy.'

'Since you left for this abbey?'

'Since we left Novara; since he entered Signor Tarsi's service. Cesar has been too caught up in the emotional intensity of his work to have any time for anything or anyone,' Fabrizio went on, recovering his composure now. He stared straight ahead, his dark eyes locked in contest with the abbot's. He hadn't expected such a humiliating inquisition, but then again, the bastard abbot was a Dominican!

Look what they had done in Spain, in the name of their forgiving God! Thousands of Jews and Moors tortured and burnt until they were ready to renounce their faith in favour of the Holy Roman church.

'Once again, Mistress Tarsi, I must apologise for subjecting your companion to such a gross examination. But you understand Signor Scaralatchi's previous offences preclude any more delicate treatment.' He drained his wine noisily.

'So you say Scaralatchi has given up the vile and unnatural pleasures of the flesh and devoted his life to the worship of God through song?'

'The Scaralatchi *Miserere*, a penitential mass, my Lord Abbot,' Angelica agreed, her colour fading. Perhaps they were through the worst, the abbot would modify his tone and grant her father's wish after all. She so wanted to succeed it was making her feel quite sick.

'May I be permitted to examine the score?' Fabrizio clicked his fingers at the dwarf, who hurried forward with the chest. Fabrizio unlocked the lid and took out the bundled vellum, carefully unwrapped the score.

Odo took the heavy manuscript and gingerly unrolled the cover. He ignored the pious prayer and dedication Fabrizio had copied on the illuminated frontispiece and quickly read the first page.

He looked up sharply.

'You require the services of a choir for this? It does not appear to be finished! What you show me is good – very good indeed – but where is the rest of it?'

'There are other elements, not necessarily included in the score for reasons of security.' Odo clicked his tongue.

'Evidently. But how am I to judge the value of the piece unless I . . .'

'Signor Scaralatchi intends the penitential mass to speak for him, to earn the absolution he prays for. But he has made it clear he intends the full work should only be performed before the representatives of His Holiness himself.'

Odo bristled with anger at Fabrizio's hot-headed interruption.

'The representatives of His Holiness do not possess the time or inclination to listen to every single score presented in His name,' the abbot snapped.

'Nevertheless, my father hopes my Lord Abbot will find it in his heart to speed Signor Scaralatchi's application, undertaken in the knowledge this is his only chance of earning the redemption he craves,' Angelica said, acutely aware the debate had reached crisis point.

She went for broke.

'A papal delegation is due to visit Novara this autumn to ratify details of the late peace treaty between the Count of Luningiana and her Imperial Majesty Margaret, Duchess of Savoy. Their visit would present Signor Scaralatchi with an ideal opportunity to preview the piece, with your blessing, my Lord Abbot.'

Odo seemed startled by her bold intelligence. He turned his brittle blue eyes on the girl, raised his chin a notch.

'They are indeed. But I cannot imagine you will find them a particularly receptive audience. Cardinal Runcini is to chair the discussions.'

'We are aware he will chair the tribunal.'

'And perhaps it is mere coincidence that the Count of Luningiana was the principal ally of the Duc de Gueldres, during his late war with Her Imperial Majesty. I believe your father – Margaret's trusted captain general – is already enjoying the fruits of the famous victories he earned in her name.'

'Fruits he wishes to enjoy in peace, my Lord Abbot,' Angelica said starkly.

'No doubt. But the choir of the Abbey d'Eleron does not perform for a few silver pieces, nor in part-payment for the services of some Italian Condottieri!'

Angelica endured the outburst, holding her breath as the abbot worked out his anger. Then she played her final card.

'My father is well aware of the likely expense, and is fully prepared to meet it. He intends to use the money set aside for my own dowry, in proof of his earnestness.'

Odo was taken aback.

'Your dowry?'

'My father is not, as you have pointed out, a wealthy man. But he is prepared to mortgage his entire household, for the opportunity of earning the patronage of His Holiness. He believes that only with the blessing and understanding of the Vatican will he be able to enjoy the peace he craves.'

The abbot seemed impressed by her ice-cool intellect.

'And he believes he will earn this patronage through his

153

sponsorship of this piece?' Odo held up the immaculately-copied score.

'Yes, my Lord Abbot.'

Odo prised himself to his feet and walked over to the window.

Strozzi made way for him as he stepped out onto the balcony, humming to himself as he leaned on his stick. He thought long and hard before he made up his mind, fifteen excruciating minutes later.

'The work has tremendous promise, that is clear enough to anyone. However, I am not personally convinced Signor Scaralatchi has demonstrated any real repentance, and without some proof of his change of heart, I am reluctant to give it my blessing. Nor am I prepared to forward the work to the papal authorities – not without considerable persuasion,' Odo said briskly.

Angelica closed her eyes, clamping the tears behind the raw lids.

'On the other hand, I am prepared to be so persuaded. I shall seek the opinion of our benefactor, the Chevalier Bayard. Now, my children, I see you are weary. You may rest here the night, and I will furnish you with a letter of introduction to the Chevalier Bayard the first thing tomorrow morning.' The old abbot made the sign of the cross.

'*Benedictat vos omnipotens Deus.*'

'Amen to that,' Fabrizio murmured.

The guests trooped out of Abbot Odo's quarters as if they had been subjected to the most excruciating tortures – their faces drawn and quartered with nervous exhaustion. Strozzi had shaken his head, glanced inquiringly at the pale Angelica.

'Well? Do you think this Bayard will help?' he asked when they were safely out of earshot down the corridor. The exhausted girl shrugged her shoulders resignedly.

'We did our best,' she said faintly. 'Who knows? The letter is better than nothing.'

'I wager I know his answer already,' Fabrizio said quietly. 'Do you imagine the Chevalier Bayard is going to overrule the abbot on the merits of a choral litany?' He scowled and shook his ringleted head, the bitter memory of the hour-long interrogation souring his stomach. Strozzi shrugged in sympathy, not quite in tune with his master's chosen ambassadors. What did it matter whether the fat slug's damned score was performed or not? It was no skin off his nose if it was fed to the abbey's goats!

The three of them followed a shaven-headed acolyte down the quiet cloister towards the north wing of the old abbey, lost in their own thoughts for the moment.

They didn't notice Obolus and the gypsy maid Constanzia falling further behind, conversing in hushed tones as they lurked in a musty alcove.

'Was that a yes or a no? Savvi'll want to know tonight!' the gypsy hissed.

> *'If it were me I'd send us all home,*
> *Drown these dreams of glorious Rome*
> *But then old Odo's a funny fart*
> *That last arrow might pierce his heart,'*

he sang, *sotto voce.*

> *'All that babble about her dowry,*
> *"Oh woe is me" so very flowery*
> *But it might just have done the trick*
> *To save fat Scaralatchi's prick!'*

Constanzia shushed the prancing monster, peering up and down the gloomy corridor for monks or guards or her watchful lover Strozzi.

'Savvi says the whole thing depends on Odo rejecting the offer. If he has done so, then Tarsi would have an excuse for losing his head and ordering a reprisal. That's what the magistrates will think, anyway.'

> *'Tarsi, Tarsi the rhino's horn,*
> *And his precious music scorned!*
> *He'd rather be buggered than let things lie*
> *All these priests will have to die!'*

Obolus cackled, dancing another little jig on the cold stone floor.

'Quiet, you monstrous toad! You'll undo us all!' she cried. 'You know what must be done, but go lightly,' she warned, watching the tiny fool cavort down the corridor towards a couple of startled monks who had just swept around the corner.

'Don't mind him, signors, he's not all there,' she said gaily, rapping her knuckles against the side of her head. The monks gawped, held their fingers to their lips as the dwarf warbled off into the shadows.

She gave the shaven-headed clerics her most winning smile, fiddled with her warm cleavage and sighed like a randy cat. The cold fish never even blinked, hurrying past her as if she had the plague.

'You don't know what you're missing!' she called after them, laughing out loud as they disappeared down the passage.

Beside the Abbey d'Eleron, Provence

Her father would have been frothing at the mouth by now. Tarsi had warned Ambolini to keep a close eye on his daughter, but would not have expected to find him sitting on her cot with his head in his hands, weeping uncontrollably. Angelica was fascinated and appalled by his emasculating distress. She had never seen her father cry, not even when her mother had died all those years before. Despite all the bitter hardships which had shaped their lives, Tarsi had never once shed a tear. Fabrizio was sobbing his heart out over the abbot's rough questioning, and her good heart went out to him.

She felt a delicious thrill of excitement despite his distress, excitement at the thought of having a man in her room. A handsome, dark-eyed and sweet-smelling man at that. She wanted to go to the bed and sit with him, comfort him as Constanzia had comforted her during the nerve-racking siege back at Mont Galliard.

Before she could move, though, Fabrizio had leapt to his feet like a scalded cat and paced the room again, furiously wiping his eyes.

'Questioning me! He had no right,' he said hoarsely, his limbs vibrating with indignation.

'He had every right, when you consider what we were about,' Angelica retorted, more tersely than she had intended. 'As well as everything else he is French, and what we were proposing would naturally strengthen the bonds which exist between my father and three of France's enemies: Margaret, the Emperor-Elect and His Holiness himself!'

'Odo serves the Church before he serves France,' he exclaimed. 'That wasn't the problem. It was me. Me and Scaralatchi!'

He jabbed his chest, glanced up at her as if deciding whether she had understood the thrust of his remark. She had. Angelica smiled, touched his arm reassuringly. The damask silk felt as warm and supple as skin. She felt herself flush as he strode past her.

'And in any case, Odo was right. Even if we were given an audience before the papal delegation, Runcini would never consider absolving Cesar! He'd rather burn as a heretic than give him a second chance!'

'It will all be worthwhile, if we . . .'

'Worthwhile? Who for? Your father maybe! All he's interested in is his precious road tolls!'

'Tolls which have helped keep you and your master from starving, these last months!' Angelica snapped back. Fabrizio waved his hands and covered his face.

'I would prefer starvation to another evening with Odo,' he wailed.

Angelica was torn by his distress. She opened her mouth but closed it again, her wandering mind made up in a moment. Her face was set as she slowly began removing the pins which held her headdress together. She pulled the awkward, pearl-inlaid band away from her forehead and threw it on the bed. She ran her fingers through her itching hair, turning the confoundedly neat tresses into a wild mane. Fabrizio was standing by the door staring at the beeswaxed planking, unaware of her quiet determination.

'Were you seriously expecting Odo to give his blessing to a notorious excommunicant without so much as a by your leave?' she asked, reaching behind her back for the hook and eye which held her gown.

'Notorious excommunicant? Why don't you come right out and say it? Pederast, bed-faggot? What does that make me, eh, his catamite?' The angry youth wheeled around, angry tears coursing down his cheeks. He stopped short — staring in wonder at Angelica's almost supernatural transformation.

She had turned from frosty spinster to fallen angel in a blink, standing in the glow of the massed candles which danced and writhed on the iron stand behind her. The warm radiance suffused the girl in soft yellow light, flattering her previously plain features. She had shaken out her thick hair and unclipped the travel-weary gown, releasing her goose-pimpled arms from the clinging sleeves. He watched in disbelief as she clambered out of the heavy dress, trampling the green folds about her ankles. She straightened and glanced up at the youth, nervously picking at the seam of her suddenly-transparent shift. He could see her nipples, brown and hard as date stones as they brushed against the soft calico. He looked lower, staring at the dark delta between her smoothly-defined thighs.

She swallowed nervously, terrified he would fling open the cell door and run for his life.

'I was proud of you; proud of the way you stood your ground back there,' she said, blushing fiercely as he continued his astonished inspection. Hadn't he ever *seen* a girl before? She took a step closer to him. Fabrizio held out his hand, brushed his finger down her cheeks. She was crying too.

'I wanted to show you,' she said hoarsely. Fabrizio swallowed.

'Show me,' he croaked, closing in on her like a nightmare shadow come to life, engulfing her in candlelight and sandalwood.

They could hear the subdued chanting of the monks at evensong, a soothing ambience which seemed to pulse and fade through the very foundations of the abbey. Even the hard-hearted Strozzi had been entranced, half-hypnotised by the soaring rhythms, the glorious cadences which were the lifeblood of the colony.

The heavenly choir hadn't taken the edge from Strozzi's rather more worldly hungers, however. If anything, Constanzia would have said he seemed unusually invigorated by the barren surroundings.

Perhaps it was the closeness to God. Like when they hanged a man. She'd heard men came in their codpieces, as if they would fertilise all the women who invariably flocked to an execution.

She squirmed beneath the big captain, her white teeth clamped on his leather scabbard in a fruitless attempt to keep the noise down. He thrust hard, banging her head on the bedstead, gasping for breath as he hammered away inside her. Constanzia raked her nails down his shoulders the way he liked. Strozzi groaned like a trapped bear, sweat standing out on his creased forehead like salt pearls. The naked girl spat out her gag, the urgent rattle in her throat smothering Strozzi's senses, finishing him off with a howl which must have woken every damn monk in the place. He gave one more battering-ram heave and collapsed over her, sweat dripping on to her mauled breasts.

Constanzia hauled him sideways, felt the sticky throbbing thing between her legs fall away like a drowning man's arm.

They were lying in the last guest room, the smallest of the three the abbot had set aside for his guests from the valley. The mistress was no doubt saying her prayers in her shift by now, trusting that idiot Fabrizio with the precious score.

The score Savvi had sent word to steal.

All she had to do now was get rid of Strozzi and slip into the boy's room, relieve him of the manuscript and signet ring. Constanzia didn't anticipate the sulky catamite would give her any trouble. The dwarf would find his way to Odo's quarters and signal Muhlberg's assassins. Odo's balcony would be the last place from which the watchmen would expect to see any sign of treachery. Having attracted Muhlberg's notoriously elusive attention Obolus would make his way to the scullery, where they had located a small and poorly-secured door. He would then admit Muhlberg's legionnaires into the heart of the complex, and direct them wherever they were needed. If all went well, she would meet them there with the ring and the score. The *Band Nere* soldiers would then escort them to safety over the wall, keeping any over-enthusiastic guards at bay. And then another sticky reunion with her other soldier, the red-haired Savvi. The man she had loved and served since he had picked her out of a travelling show at the age of fifteen.

Well, that was the plan, at any rate. These things had a nasty habit of breaking down at the last minute – like Savvi's abortive attack on Mont Galliard. With luck, though, they would be off into the night before the abbey was aware what had happened.

'Where are you off to now?' she asked languidly, watching the other captain struggle into his damp shirt and fasten his unravelling hose. They were alike enough to make their secret liaisons interesting, though Strozzi lacked Savvi's finesse, preferring the battering ram to the other loco-tenent's rather more subtle approaches. Savvi's speciality was undermining. He'd brought her towers tumbling down often enough!

'To make sure we haven't set their alarm bells off, hollering to wake the dead,' he chuckled.

'Me? You were snorting like that donkey in the yard! I thought he'd join in at any moment.'

'What, snorting or fucking you?' Strozzi asked with a leer.

Constanzia sat up quickly and slapped his dangling codpiece. He jumped back with an oath.

'For shame captain – such language in this house of God!'

Strozzi finished dressing, replaced his sword and belted it round his waist.

'Ah, you'd be surprised the games they get up to in places like this,' he said darkly.

'Oh no I wouldn't,' she assured him, tugging her shift over her tousled hair. She wiped her forearm over her face, rubbed the soft calico between her sticky thighs.

'You might treat this as a holiday, spend the night for

once,' she said petulantly, shuffling over to the plain dresser and pouring water into the pewter washbowl.

'I'm needed on the wall. If they're still awake, maybe I'll come back and mess you up again!'

Constanzia muttered something, lifting her shift to splash water over her chafed crotch.

'That gate overlooking the olive groves, they might as well put out a welcome sign,' Strozzi said with a sigh, watching his mistress complete her hasty toilette.

'So you're going over to keep them company. Do me a favour, lover, and find me some bread and wine, a little cheese. That muck they served for dinner – I wouldn't give it to a pest–house rat.'

Strozzi laughed, opened the cell door a notch and looked out.

'Ah, someone has to look over the place, I don't see the Chevalier Bayard taking a turn around the wall, do you?'

'I'll keep a lamp burning in the window for him,' she called, watching him wave saucily and slip out into the passage.

She waited for a moment and then threw on her clothes, rifled in her bag for her knife. The seven-inch blade was notched and worn but as sharp as a surgeon's razor, glinting in the candlelight.

She crouched over him, fascinated by his sleekly-muscled body. His skin was several shades darker than hers, a deeply satisfying amber compared with her bone-white flesh. There wasn't a blemish on him, just the occasional tuft of soft black hair, sleek as a cat's pelt. She ran her finger down his sternum, over his flat belly and into his belly button. A trail of slick black hair led her hand lower, to the peculiarly throbbing muscle which stood half cocked over his belly. He looked as if he had the plague, all bright and shiny and purple like that. Surely it wasn't normal? He grabbed her wrist and tugged her towards him, manoeuvring her hand towards the wretched implement. It was as hot as a poker and about the same colour.

Fabrizio grimaced in peeved pleasure.

'You look as if you're going to be sick!' he hissed, raising his dark head from the rumpled bedding. She giggled, pulling the stiff stalk one way and another.

'Does that hurt?' she asked as he slumped back down, a low moan escaping between his dry lips. It jumped in her hands. Angelica squealed, lifting her fist and then lowering it. Fabrizio writhed in response as if the simple movement had somehow been . . .

'What was that?'

'Don't stop now! I feel like a cadaver in some Florentine medical school! Don't you know what to do?' he asked, propping himself up on his elbows. Angelica had leaned away, her hair hanging in a great sweep over his belly as she tilted her head, listening.

'I heard something at the window,' she whispered.

'The window? We're two floors up and we don't have a balcony. Not that you'd get out onto it, this place is built like the *Stinche*!'

'I'm sure I heard something.'

'You heard a rat in the wall, a starling on the roof. Here,' he pulled her down over him, brought her startled face close. 'My throat's raw, my lips are sealing over. Kiss me before I die,' he said, comically melodramatic.

Angelica felt a frisson of terrorised excitement speed through her nervous system, every inch of her skin tingling in sensual suspense.

She leaned forward, and pressed her lips to his mouth.

Eel-breeches wasn't in bye-bye, he had slipped in with the Squinter to jaw-jaw into the night, making up their own verses as the lonely bald men sang sad, sad songs.

Obolus paused on the threshold, held his fingers to his lips.

Constanzia cocked her head, listened to their interrupted loveplay with mischievous delight. So she wasn't the only woman bending backwards that night! Who would have thought – Mistress Angelica and Fat Scaralatchi's snake-hipped bedmate?

Obolus made an obscene gesture, impatiently pulling at the Gypsy girl's skirts.

'Hold your water you scrawny little shit!' she rasped, tugging her clothing back as she tried to think. Fabrizio would have taken the precious chest into Mistress Angelica's quarters. And he'd stuck his finger in a pretty ring and all, she thought lewdly. It might make things difficult, if Ambolini was up to the hilt in her virgin mistress. On the other hand, she might be able to take them from behind, garotte the pair of them before they were aware she was there.

The dwarf seethed with manic glee, picked his nose with the point of his dagger as Constanzia pondered the unexpected development.

'As you were. I'll get the score; you let Muhlberg in. Go carefully!'

The conspirators retraced their steps down the corridor and slipped into Fabrizio's empty chamber. She quietly closed the door, watched as he hurried to the window, positioning a chair beneath the leaded panes and hauling himself up. The window was too small for a man, so it hadn't been barred. He opened it, wincing as the rusty hinges creaked. She boosted him up. The dwarf kicked his little legs, squirmed over the sill and pulled himself through the tiny gap. She pulled the window to and crept over to the door to wait.

He could see the pale shapes of the trees in the moonlight, the glimmering lanterns of the watch out in the tower. Somewhere out beyond the wall, Constantin Muhlberg, old mule-face himself, was waiting for his signal. The slow-witted German would spirit them away, score, signet ring and all.

But first, a little mischief to blacken Tarsi's name forever.

Obolus giggled at the prospect, looked right and left and then stepped out onto the thin brickwork ledge which ran the length of the north wing. He could see the dark balcony beneath Odo's window, faintly illuminated by the lamplight leaking through the shutters. The abbot's quarters were in a corner tower overlooking the dark grounds. The dwarf flattened himself against the cold stone and tiptoed along the ledge, his little boots grating on the crumbling brickwork. The blowing wind carried the faint trace of garlic sausage. The ledge gave out two yards short of the protruding tower wall, slightly below the iron railings which ran around the balcony. Obolus held his breath, adjusted his footing and leapt into the darkness.

Abbot Odo finished the letter and sat back, pinching the bridge of his nose between his thumb and inky forefinger. The guttering candles had almost given out, plunging the venerable abbot into virtual darkness. He set the pen down, blew over the crisp paper and re-read the short note. *To my brother Bayard, greetings . . .*

He looked up sharply, wondered at the sudden scrape he had heard from the balcony. It sounded as if one of his geranium pots had toppled over in the wind. Odo frowned, continued reading the letter. Bayard might just find it in his heart to support Tarsi's insolent proposal, especially if it were made by his charmingly naive daughter. He had been impressed by the offer of the dowry. That had taken grit and . . .

Odo looked up once more, a rectangle of silver light sliding into the cell. The shutters creaked open, filling the room with moonlight. Odo squinted, his tired eyes almost useless after his exertions at the writing desk.

'Who's there?' he called. A dark shadow, a child, stepped into the room. Odo tilted his head, watched the strange figure . . . it was the dwarf! He recognised the stiff red hair, the over-large head on the narrow shoulders.

'Luciano, how . . .'

Obolus was singing softly, walking along the bookshelf, running his finger down the leathery spines. The abbot stared, unsure whether to cry out or laugh out loud. The dwarf picked up the abbot's walking stick from beside the shelf, twirled it about his head like an ornamental halberd.

Odo could just see his jagged white teeth in the feeble light.

'What are you doing here? How did you get into my room?' he snorted, angry at the foolish interruption. He had backed behind his writing desk, groping for the pen-knife which lay among the quills.

Obolus darted forward, thrusting the gnarled stick to-wards the base of the desk and levering himself forward. Odo gaped as he vaulted up onto the desk, scattering the quills and spilling the ink over Bayard's letter.

'Da da!' he gave himself a round of applause, leapt up and clicked his heels. Odo watched, hideously bewildered, as the dwarf whistled and hummed to himself, danced a mad jig on the table.

Odo grasped at the inkpot, lifted it from the ruined vellum.

Obolus stopped dancing and took a deep breath, clicked his tongue and wagged his finger under Odo's wrinkled nose. Before the abbot could blink he had whipped a stiletto from his tunic and lunged with all his might. The thin blade pierced the old man's eye with a sickly pop, grated against his skull as it slid up to the hilt. Odo screeched, hurled backwards by the dwarf's momentum. The old man crashed to the ground, his chair sliding away into the wall. The jarring crash brought a guard running from his station along the passage. The cell door flew open, filling the room with fragrant yellow candlelight.

'My Lord!' a clumsy spearman peered into the abbot's plainly-furnished quarters, squinting at the dancing shadows in terror. Perhaps the old boy had been dreaming? He sometimes shouted out in his . . .

The dwarf came in low, from his left. The spearman looked down just in time to see the cackling midget duck under his quivering spearpoint and thrust the abbot's pen-knife through his knee joint. The blade sliced through his hose and bit into the soft cartilage, sliding against the dis-located kneecap. The spearman fell to one side, screaming in agony as he lashed out at his slavering opponent. The awkward blow sent the dwarf tumbling across the room towards the abbot. The guard fell back in the doorway, blood running down his leg in noisy streams. The dwarf was up again, bowling forward on his horrid little legs, his boots ringing on the stone floor. The spearman prised himself away on his backside as his attacker grabbed the discarded spear, lifting the heavy shaft over his tiny shoulders. The wounded guard shouted a warning as Obolus hurled the spear with all his vindictive might. The six-foot pole juddered into his chest, the blade biting through the muscle and shattering two ribs before burying itself up to its neck in the soft tissue of his right lung. The guard fell back, the spear quivering between his grasping fingers.

Obolus darted past his kicking legs and hurled the door closed, dropped the bolt with a rusty clang. He could hear angry shouts down the corridor, barked orders and slammed doors. The guard gurgled and cursed, felt his arming jacket swelling up and turning cold with his lost blood. The abbot had rolled on his belly, hands pressed to his wounded eye. Obolus put his shoulder against the desk and shoved it over the floor towards the door. He could hear them thumping the studded oak, bawling at him to open up.

He pushed the desk into position, grabbed a handful of papers from the abbot's desk and held them up to the flaming lamp. In a moment he had a blazing torch. Obolus paused, snickering to himself. He picked up the lamp and tipped the oil over the softly moaning abbot, then turned and poured the dregs over the priceless contents of the bookcase.

Odo was moaning now, pulling at his dappled habit; the greasy spots blossomed as he tried to elbow himself away. Obolus bent over and held the flame to the abbot's clothing, jumped back as it ignited in a flash of fire. The abbot screeched, rolled onto his back to try and extinguish the flames. His right eye was a bubbling mass of blood and tissue, his flailing hands smeared with gore.

Obolus slipped sideways on it, steadied himself and hurried back onto the balcony. He lifted the torch into the night air, waved it to the right and then to the left.

Light poured out of windows further down the north wing; dim figures were running about the abbey grounds.

Obolus tossed the flaming torch back into the room, clambered back over the iron railings and disappeared into the night.

Beside the Abbey d'Eleron

Luca Strozzi had inspected three of the guard towers along the northern perimeter, satisfied himself that at least the guards were awake, when he heard the sudden commotion behind him. He paused, peered back at the massive pile of the abbey, its monolithic fortifications eerily lit by flaming torches and hidden lamps. He could see the fiery signal from the tower, a restless pendulum of orange flame. He stood in astonishment for a moment, watching as the signal was swallowed up by a sudden bright glow from within. He could hear shouts now, the angry clang of a bell away to the left. Dim figures were running across the open sward to his right, guards from the north tower hurrying to answer the alarm. Strozzi tugged out his sword and doubled over the closely-clipped grass. He glanced at the soldiers loping alongside, wondering where Odo had found such strapping fellows. They certainly didn't look much like . . . he leapt back in surprise as the first soldier jabbed at him, a glinting boar spear coming within an ace of his chest. The soldier grunted with the effort, overbalanced by the desperate thrust. Strozzi yelled, parried the stroke and yanked his blade back across the soldier's face. The intruder toppled sideways clutching his throat, his jaw hanging away from his teeth like a broken mouse-trap. Another soldier darted in from behind, throwing his arms around the captain's neck and hauling him to the ground. Strozzi writhed beneath him, trying to free his sword. He could see black–clad figures scurrying past with drawn swords, arquebusiers following behind, their matches bobbing like will o' the wisps.

Band Nere, here?

The brute on his back was biting his ear, his garlic-riddled breath assaulting Strozzi's senses. The captain feinted to the left and then rolled right, tipping the bandit from his shoulders. He thrust backwards with his sword, a reverse blow which caught the wretch in the groin. Strozzi leapt to his feet and looked around him. An arquebusier took careful aim and fired, the hot lead singeing his beard and tearing his collar away. Strozzi hurled his sword at the black–clad rogue, bent down and recovered the wounded man's boar spear. The bell clanged above the sudden tumult, drowning out his panic. The arquebusier hadn't finished, the dog! He came on with the clumsy weapon held high, ready to club the captain into the grass. Strozzi ducked the blow and ran him through on the boar spear, desperately aware he shouldn't be fighting out here in the grounds. Whatever the hounds were after, it was inside the abbey! He planted his boot in the dying landsknecht's chest and dragged the heavy spear free, standing sideways as a great gout of blood erupted from the killing wound. Strozzi ducked down, grabbed the man's catgutter and loped towards the flaming mass of the abbey.

'Mistress, mistress!' Constanzia shrieked, banging her fists on the door. Angelica was electrified with terror, her shift thrown over her shoulder as she struggled to unbolt the door. Fabrizio was hopping into his hose, groping for the dagger he had left under the bed.

Angelica threw the door back, terrified Constanzia would be trapped by the screaming intruders who had so ruined her loveplay. Thank God, Constanzia was alone. She had brought her pewter washbowl . . .

Fabrizio drew his dagger with a curse as Angelica fell back into the room, an ugly cut above her eye. Constanzia followed her, staggering after her poleaxed mistress. The washbowl clattered away into a corner as she recovered her balance, held up the gleaming knife. The choirboy gaped back at her as if she had sprouted wings.

'It's us, you fool! Me, Fabrizio!' he cried, misunderstanding her savagery. The gypsy leapt around the bed like a Florentine acrobat, the curved blade cutting the air in front of Fabrizio's face. He staggered back, shocked by her terrible, malignant intensity. He pushed and shoved, hacked at her arm with his own blade as she spat and kicked, trying to work her knife into the panic-stricken youth's belly. Blood spouted but he couldn't feel any pain, just a mad terror which ballooned in his throat like overbaked dough.

Constanzia rolled sideways, dragging her victim over towards the jagged dagger. Her wrist was scored, blood flowing freely over her fist.

Her face had been transformed, less than human in the weirdly-shifting candlelight. Fabrizio tore himself away from the deadly point, the effort allowing Constanzia to change her grip. She brought the knife up towards his throat, caught him a glancing blow on his jaw.

He elbowed her aside, raising his knees to ward the mad bitch off. Constanzia scuttled away, one arm hanging loosely by her side, the other menacing him with the knife.

'You're Savvi's spy! You're the one who tried to let them into Mont Galliard!' he gasped, his various cuts and hurts shrieking agonies at his troubled skull.

'You're damned quick on the uptake,' the girl rasped, her voice barely recognisble. Her eyes glowed red with fanatical fury, a shrieking need to kill him off. Angelica groaned, rolled over on her belly grasping her bleeding head.

'I've no time for this. Drop your dagger and I'll make it quick, otherwise I'll cut her slow in front of you!' she threatened, working her damaged shoulder. Fabrizio still had his knife. His blood was dripping onto the floor. His head was banging, eyes brimming with tears.

Why should the girl hate him so? What had he ever done to her?

Constanzia circled around him, backing off towards the open door. She bent down over Angelica.

'This low-born bitch has queened it over me for years! She's no more right to order me about than I have the Pope!' she snarled.

Ambolini screeched a warning, launched himself across the chamber at the beautiful assassin. Constanzia leapt to her feet, bringing up her blade to parry his desperate thrust. She caught his wrist and hauled him on, doubling his own momentum. Fabrizio felt a sudden cold wetness in his belly. His legs went rubbery as he staggered on, grasping at the doorframe for support.

Constanzia let him go, jumped over Angelica's flailing hand and darted towards the bed. She picked up the chest which they had left beside the rumpled cot, cramming the box under her wounded arm and retrieving Ambolini's knife.

She threw back her head and yelped with triumph, leapt over her swooning mistress and landed beside Fabrizio, writhing in the doorway with her dagger protruding between his bloody fingers. She smiled evilly, quickly knelt down on his forearm, pinning him down in his own blood.

She gripped his wrist, leaned over and cut away his forefinger, snatching up the bloody token complete with its fouled signet ring. Fabrizio was weak with loss of blood, his senses reeling at the terrible savagery of her assault. He stared at his mutilated hand as if he couldn't comprehend his own wounds, the bloody stump dripping on his up-raised face. Constanzia howled like a banshee and jumped to her feet with skirts flying, her long brown legs stretching away into the dim distance of his blurred vision. She jumped over his sprawled body and raced off down the passage. Fabrizio stared at the grey stone ceiling, icy threads of pain stitching complex patterns across his belly, up into his chest and around his cold heart. The knife was sticking out of his belly, a hand's breadth above his pubic hair. The black hair which had so fascinated Angelica was sopping with his warm blood. He tilted his head, made out the naked body of his mistress slumped beside the cot. He couldn't focus on her face, much less tell whether she was still breathing. He could hear heavy footfalls echoing down the passage, furious shouting. He tried to call a warning, but every time he opened his mouth he felt the knife bite deeper into his belly. Howling pain assaulted his skull, black fogs of agony boiling up behind his eyes. He knew no more.

The dwarf had hurried through the chaotic galleries towards the kitchens, monks in various stages of undress hurrying this way and that as they fled the terrifying tumult echoing down the passage. He skidded into the deserted scullery. Great copper pots hung from the roof beams next to bunches of aromatic herbs and strings of eye-watering onions. Pheasants had been garotted on wire hooks, rabbits hung upside down, their lifeless eyes glazed. The vaulted kitchen rang with shouts, flames danced at the narrow windows. Obolus hurried to the scullery door, lifted the heavy brass bolts and swung the door open.

A stone path led towards the abbey vegetable plots and herb gardens, scene of a viciously comic struggle between half a dozen French spearmen and a squad of Muhlberg's assassins. The spearmen had formed a small schillitron among the cabbages and beans, fighting back to back amongst the trampled, tangled roots. They were thrusting and parrying like madmen at the screaming intruders, holding the advance up for precious seconds.

But the *Band Nere* came on like iron men, black-clad demons swinging great two-handed swords. The saw-toothed blades lopped the tops from their spears as if they were made of matchwood. Their leader – a gangly brute in black-lacquered armour – screamed their blood-curdling warcry.

'*Hut, dich, baur ich komm!*'

He ignored their desperate lunges and waded through trailing beanstalks to get in amongst them. His massive, six-foot scythe sang through the night, cutting through bean tendrils and canes, slicing through muscle and shattering bone. The steel whirlwind harvested the guards one by one, left half a dozen bloody bundles in the ruined garden.

Muhlberg kicked the last defender aside, waved his troopers up on the path towards the capering dwarf.

'There he is! Follow Obolus!' he bawled as his legionnaires packed in around the small doorway like giant beetles invading a termite mound. They bent down and ducked inside the scullery, carrying the attack into the heart of the abbey.

'Where's Hutter? Where's Horst?' Muhlberg shouted.

'Over on the north wall. One of the Frenchies must have been quaffin' horse glue, he's gone as mad as a march hare!'

'Cut them down and secure the wall!' Muhlberg ordered, watching the bloodied soldier lope off into the darkness.

Obolus was looking up the wall watching the north tower burn. The fire he had set in the abbot's quarters was raging out of control, the iron railings assaulted by belching flames and searing smoke. The dwarf cackled and danced as he watched the flaming demons sweep through the grim tower. Muhlberg had seen his signal, come hot-footing across the lawns to answer his call. A bell was clanging in the tower to his right and he could hardly hear the dopplesoldner's gravel-throated bark over the desperate tumult from the ransacked abbey.

> '*Get the score, get the score, get the score,*
> *Grab it from the funeral pyre!*
> *Get the score, get the score, get the score*
> *Rescue it from the fire!*'

Obolus brayed.

The landsknecht captain tilted his head, the damned bell ringing in his ears. He cursed the mad dwarf in five languages, grabbing the runt by the collar and hauling him up in front of his scarred features.

'Get the what? The pyre?'

One of his panting arquebusiers was watching his back, squinting at the dimly-discerned shadows silhouetted by the burning tower. The guards had put up a stiff fight and there were more of them hurrying up from the main gatehouse.

'Hurry up Muhlie! This place is crawlin' with bleedin' Frenchies!'

Muhlberg swatted the shouting soldier aside, tried to concentrate on the chirping dwarf. The disgusted soldier couldn't make out what he was babbling about, the blazing inferno must have stolen his wits.

'Get the fire? It's already on fire!' Muhlberg shouted.

The noise was tremendous. Shots were ringing out now, waking the entire neighbourhood, no doubt. Obolus dangled from his fist like a freshly-caught perch, grinning and twittering as he admired the flames.

'They've got men moving in from the other side Muhlie; it's time we got out!'

'The choir, the choir!' Muhlberg bawled. 'He must have said choir, not fire! Get in and find the little wankers!'

'What, kill 'em?'

'No, grab 'em, one each! Savvi must want them!'

'I didn't know he was that way inclined,' the arquebusier said, shaking his blond head. Obolus swung around and sank his teeth into Muhlberg's wrist. The dopplesoldner cursed and flung the vampire dwarf into the flower beds. Obolus prised himself to his feet and darted off into the inferno, dashing between the black-clad legs like some hound of hell.

'Not that way! Ah, good riddance,' Muhlberg growled, sucking his wounded wrist. Obolus had left a ring of bright white marks in his dark skin.

He'd mark the little bastard, when he caught up with him.

The choristers had sat up in their narrow cots, listening to the growing tumult with a mixture of excitement and disbelief. Nothing of note had occurred there in living memory, and now all hell was apparently breaking loose. They remained in their beds, wondering what to do and conversing in desperate undertones. Giacomo Sabatini, their bullying chief, had gone as far as flinging off his bedclothes before he had remembered the dire punishments meted out to wandering choirboys. Brother Johan would paddle their behinds, if he caught them up and about after lights out – no matter the distractions. The youth shook his head in bewilderment as shots and screams ruptured their midnight tranquillity. They leapt out of bed now, their crystal voices shrill with terror.

'Who's shooting?'

'They're slaughtering the brothers!'

Aldus had flung off his bedclothes and hauled himself up onto the table to peer out of the dormitory's single leaded window.

'The grounds are full of soldiers!' he shrieked, sparking a stampede towards the doors. Giacomo planted his feet on the cold floor, electrified by uncertainty. Soldiers? Here? He pushed and shoved his way through the screaming mob, the anxious boys stepping out of his way as if relying on the strapping youth to defend them.

'What is it? What do they want?' Fillio the Greek inquired, his brown eyes bulging in alarm. Giacomo opened the door a notch, squinted into the passage. He glimpsed flaring torches and hurrying men – and slammed the door shut again.

'Bar the door! They're coming this way!' he cried, beside himself with terror. Little Fillio had pissed himself with fright, the rest milled like blind children caught in a flood. Giacomo raced to his cot, bent down and began shoving the heavy wooden frame towards the door. The rest packed in about him, wide-eyed lemmings in white shifts, anxiously apeing the head chorister.

They hadn't moved the cot more than a few feet before the door was kicked open. The boys screamed in terror and stampeded towards the other end of the dormitory, a pack of black-clad soldiers swarming after them.

Giacomo stared at the heavily-armed legionnaires, big bearded men in lacquered armour, swords bloody in their fists.

'Against the wall! The lot of you!' one of the bandits roared, stalking through the cringing press of boys cuffing and kicking the terrified choristers out of his path. Giacomo ducked under his grasping arm and made a dash for the door, straight at a grinning arquebusier. He tried to dodge around him but the soldier was a second quicker. He reversed his cumbersome weapon and cracked the youth on the jaw as he dashed past, laying the boy out cold. The rest of the choir stood still as if transfixed by his fall.

'That's it my pigeons, nice and quiet and nobody gets hurt. Get the little buggers out front and pile them in Tarsi's wagon, and look lively!'

The Abbey d'Eleron's world-renowed choir had been silenced at last.

Strozzi had been forced to take a wide detour around the defences to avoid the black bandsmen swarming over the northern wall. As far as he could judge they had been attacked by at least a company of seasoned troops, well used to receiving orders and not in the least bothered by the prospect of a good scrap. They had been kept under tight rein until now but they were becoming distracted, eager to loot the abbey of anything worth carrying before their leaders called them off. Strozzi had killed three of them as they made their way back towards the wall, loaded down with altarpieces and candlesticks from the chapel. The last had died defending himself with an ornate, gold-leafed cross. The tower on the north wall was burning merrily, the careless garrison among the first to be slaughtered. As far as he could tell at least half the abbey had been set ablaze, the greedy crackling punctuated by collapsing timbers and crumbling masonry.

The old abbey had proved less formidable than it had seemed.

Strozzi paused to catch his breath in the middle of the garishly-illuminated lawns, watched the abbot's balcony collapse in a cloud of showering sparks. By Christ, the dogs had caused as much damage as a brace of culverins.

Bare-legged monks, servants in tattered, soot-smeared nightclothes and semi-naked soldiers were fleeing the sudden inferno, stampeding towards the southern end of the complex. Strozzi cut across the terrified mob, kicking and barging his way towards the kitchen block, which seemed to have miraculously survived the deadly flames. The last of the fugitives raced past him, shouting incomprehensible warnings. Strozzi ducked down as a shot rang out, threw himself into a tangled flower bed behind a rampart of bleeding Frenchmen. A couple of them were still moving, groaning and hissing in the darkness. The ground was sopping with their steaming blood. A laughing legionnaire staggered out of the drifting smoke, bent beneath his looted load. The soldier had wrapped himself in bolts of cloth, tapestries and curtains taken from the ransacked ruin. The grossly-swollen arquebusier didn't see Strozzi hiding behind the slaughtered Frenchmen. He seemed intent on getting back to the wall with his loot, dropping his arquebus and cursing in Italian. He bent down, came face to face with the alert captain. His eyes flared as Strozzi plunged his dagger into his stretched throat. Strozzi grabbed the raider by his bunched clothing and wrenched him down into the trampled vegetables, snatching up his weapon.

His friends didn't miss him, equally intent on escaping with as much as they could carry. Strozzi pressed himself down over the feebly-kicking arquebusier as another squad of legionnaires doubled through the smoke, carpets and looted bedding rolled under their arms or slung over their shoulders. They were accompanied by another squad of arquebusiers, looking sharp as they marched backwards, menacing the blazing ruins with their weapons as their burdened comrades made their escape.

Strozzi tilted his head, sure he had heard shouts, muffled cries for help.

He had!

The bundles he had taken to be carpets were bound boys; the filthy legionnaires had gagged them with lengths of calico or clamped hands about their mouths. They were kicking and writhing, tugging at their pitiless captors. Strozzi's blood boiled, but he could do nothing. He could not oppose a score of arquebusiers alone. The captain lowered his head, his mind racing. Stealing the choir? Is that what the *Band Nere* was about?

He had heard tales to chill the blood, but kidnapping children had never featured on their terrifying roll of dishonour. The captain felt his clothing go cold with the blood of the Frenchmen. He could hear their voices now, guttural with smoke and their own ferocity.

'Keep 'em moving! Where's the fucking wagon? Horst! Leg it round the . . .'

'There it is!'

'About time! Its Savvi's bitch driving, look – might have guessed she'd be late!'

'Busy screwing the abbot, I'll wager!'

'Anything with a pizzle, that one!'

Their filthy laughter was drowned out by the spine-jarring rattle of wagon wheels. By God Strozzi knew that sound well enough! They were using Tarsi's carriage to carry away their captives.

He lifted his head from the dismembered corpses, spied the familiar hulk looming through the bitter incense of the burning abbey. Strozzi stared, unable to comprehend what he saw.

Constanzia, his own precious gypsy sweetheart, was standing up on the running board, the reeking reins belted about her narrow waist. She held on grimly, raising her arm in a clenched-fist salute to the admiring legionnaires. Strozzi prised himself to his knees as the leader stepped up in front of the carriage, waving his leering charges forward.

'Get the boys loaded. If they squeak, slit their throats!'

One of the Black Legionnaires spotted Strozzi emerge from the piled corpses, furiously intent on confronting his treacherous mistress. The landsknecht raised his arquebus and fired, but the lead ball missed the charging captain.

'*Pestilenza!*' Strozzi roared. 'Whore! Cheat! Traitor!' He

raised his clumsy weapon as the alerted guards wheeled about to face the unexpected onslaught.

Strozzi doubled forward, smashing a path through the twisted canes.

Constanzia saw the bloody apparition and screamed in terror.

Muhlberg peered about, his two–handed sword useless at that range.

'Shoot him down!'

Strozzi closed his eyes against the squalling storm, felt a cold thump in his shoulder as the enemy soldiers opened fire. The fearsome impact knocked him sideways. He pulled the trigger as he lost his footing. Strozzi rolled into the wall, the wind knocked out of him. The garden was filled with sparks and acrid fumes. Constanzia sat down heavily, slumping on the running board with the reins about her waist. The panicked horses bolted, the heavy cart bouncing and sliding as they stampeded for the open grounds. Muhlberg leapt aside as Constanzia gave a small groan and toppled off the wagon. Her skirt billowed, the flying hem catching in the wheels. The horses plunged on, terrified by the noise and assaulting smells, the reeking smoke which belched from the burning ruin of the abbey.

The gypsy girl was tugged beneath the wain, her arms extended in mute appeal as she was grasped by the iron–shod wheel–rims. She screamed then – a thin, piercing shriek which cut through the night, jarred Strozzi's shocked senses.

'Enough! Leave them!'

Strozzi covered his head as the arquebusiers emptied their weapons at the wall above his head, showering him with razor–sharp chips.

'Grab those horses! Get out of it, I said!'

Strozzi gasped, assaulted by thrusting spears of agony. He could feel hot blood coursing down his arm. He raised himself weakly on his elbow.

The legionnaires were hurrying away over the littered grounds, dragging their loot and their wounded with them.

They had brought the terrified carriage horses back under control, and a grinning legionnaire had taken Constanzia's place on the running board, whipping up the team with a series of bloodcurdling oaths.

The leader bent down over the girl's broken body, clenched his fist in her blood-drenched gown and dragged her along for a few paces.

Strozzi watched in paralysed fascination as the legionnaire gave up in disgust, peering down at the smashed corpse.

The gypsy girl's beautiful brown legs had remained where they were, her golden skin splashed and splattered in blood.

Strozzi had been able to encircle her slim waist with his two hands. The wagon wheels had made short work of that wondrously smooth belly, the tantalisingly taut muscles he had kissed so often in the past.

The legionnaire looked back, made out Strozzi's huddled body in the lee of the burning wall.

'She's no use to any of us now, captain!' the brute called, waving his bloody hand in ironic salute. He bent down, lifted something from the girl's torn clothing. The soldier held it up like some magic talisman and then slipped it inside his black tunic.

Strozzi closed his eyes, listened helplessly as the foundations of the burning abbey creaked and groaned beneath him. Masonry was falling all about his cowed head, burning timbers toppling from the upper storeys of the black ruin.

A tower struck down.

PART FOUR

Into the Valley

◆ ◆ ◆ ◆ ◆

'Mercenary armies bring only slow, belated and feeble conquests, but startling,
sudden defeats'

Machiavelli, *The Prince*

Beside La Grouchelle,
Auvergne, France, August 1520

The horse were to come in across the meadows to the north of the chosen village, crossing a lily-choked river either side of a hump-backed bridge. Their only real obstacle would be the dripping fir plantation, planted as a windbreak decades before. The marauders had taken a long look at the drowsy hamlet before setting their trap, the shrewd chief ordering half his men off on a gruelling flank march to bottle the peasants up in their valley.

'Take them from the rear Eldritch, I don't imagine your people will have much difficulty with that, eh?'

Gueldres – the Bastard Geldray to the tongue-tied Englishmen – managed to turn the most straightforward battle order into outright mockery. Kerr, Isolani and the rest sniggered into their fists at the Vicomte's witticism. Eldritch drummed his fingers about the wire-wound hilt of his sword and said nothing.

How he longed to plunge the blade into that rapscallion's throat! It had been Kerr who had found out the hidden route in the first place. He had come trotting back like the dutiful hound he was, reported his discovery to Geldray. Auld Sandy – the Vicomte's newly-appointed chief of scouts, by God, had taken great delight in emphasising the difficult nature of the ground, the virtual impossibility of dragging their warcarts through the foot-deep mud.

Warcarts! The unwieldy vehicles had been the final humiliation. Geldray had taken a great delight in reassigning the Ride – possibly the finest light cavalry raiders in Western Europe – to the ponderous battle wagons. He knew full well the massively-fortified vehicles were practically obsolete, but it had tickled him to think of the fleet-footed English cavalry reduced to going into battle locked inside their own, fully-armoured coffins.

The Ride had become the laughing stock of Geldray's highly cosmopolitan camp. The last nation to successfully employ the slow-moving carts had been the Hussites – Czech extremists battling the knights of the old empire two centuries before.

Geldray's ingenious jest had not been lost on Sandy Kerr. He and his reivers had been allowed to keep their horses, further enraging their English colleague.

'Ye might just as well plough with dogs, as take yon tubs down there,' Kerr had ventured, chewing a piece of twig and jerking his thumb at the ridiculous contraptions they had hauled down from the north.

It had taken a week and more to convert the wagons to military use, reinforcing the heavy oak ribs so that they would deflect all but a direct hit from a cannon. The oxen teams which would pull the ton-weight carts had been trained to walk on between specially-designed panels which would protect them from enemy fire. The heavy boards could be removed from their brass fittings and hung from the side of the cart while on the march.

Eldritch dreaded taking the bloody things into battle.

The Vicomte relished his anxiety, never missing an opportunity to test the scowling captain's resolve.

'Too boggy? Nonsense,' he exclaimed, seizing on Kerr's thinly-veiled challenge. 'The flank march will give us the element of surprise! These peasants aren't stupid, they don't lie abed snoring all day like you English yeomen. We've passed this way before, my friends!'

Eldritch shielded his eyes, peered down the heavily-terraced slopes. The woodlands wound away down the valley, following the course of a meandering brook. It was not unlike Redesdale – back home.

Eldritch suppressed a sigh of agitation.

'Block the end of the valley look, pinch out their escape route, and we shall bag ourselves a fine set of likely lads!'

The Vicomte had left Guisnes with four hundred troops – a hundred hired thugs, two hundred and more of Howath's bewildered warband, and his own, black-clad bodyguard. But they had recruited hard as they marched south, pressing every waif and stray they could lay their hands on into his black-clad legion. They had snatched fishermen from their nets, shepherds from their flocks, potmen from their inns.

The English had looked on in confusion, jeered and ridiculed by the grinning legionnaires. They had marched the length of France as if it was an enemy state, despoiling the villages as they went. Geldray was in the pay of the French king, and yet here they were brutalising his subjects, taking whatever they wanted from the villages which had the misfortune of lying in their path.

The Ride wouldn't have behaved with such reckless abandon on a jaunt over the Border, let alone in their own peaceful shires.

The callous robbery had quite sickened them – and the sicker they got of it the more Geldray gave them – as if he was daring his newly-won recruits to refuse him.

'Ah, it's a bad business, captain,' Hobby complained, leaning his vast unwashed bulk against the wagon's heavy planking. It had taken them an hour and a half to haul the war carts along the muddy floor of the valley, following the wide detour Kerr had pointed out. The rabbit track had been easy enough going for the Scotsman's ragged ponies, but it had been sheer bloody murder for the English wagon teams. Pushing, hauling, cursing their clumsy vehicles through a virtual morass, whipped by brambles and stung by clouding horseflies.

Eldritch gave the old soldier a sidelong stare.

'You don't say,' he rasped. Hobby hadn't stopped moaning since they had left Guisnes nearly nine weeks before. The sergeant overlooked the captain's irony, gazing down on the narrow gullet they had blocked with their unwieldy wagons. Hannibal would have sobbed with laughter, to see the crudity of their tactics, Eldritch thought blackly.

'We've done some shit-rag things lately my Lord, but rounding up honest peasants . . .'

'We'll do as we are told,' Eldritch growled, sickeningly aware who had gotten the Ride into their current predicament.

If only his wretched sister had been able to keep a lid on her damned farmyard passions, they might have been humming a different tune now. 'You know the score, Hobby. The Bastard Geldray won our contract of indenture fair and square,' he lied. 'If we renege on them now, refuse to serve him as our rightful lord, then it'll be the warden who'll suffer. He signed the transfers, he'll lose what honour he's left. Is that what you want?' Hobby frowned, bewildered by the unexpected turnaround back in Guisnes. He had served Howath for a dozen years, and had yet to fully comprehend the Ride's abrupt change of allegiance.

''Course it's not what I want, what any of uz wants,' he complained. 'It's just this bugger Geldray . . . ay up! Here we are!' Hobby raised his chin, spotting a blur of movement in the distance. Eldritch narrowed his eyes against the bright afternoon sun, made out the first of the fugitives from the village hurrying down the slopes on either side of the road. The steep, rocky ground and uneven drystone walls which interlocked the surrounding hillsides would make flight difficult. They were bound to risk the quicker route out of the valley, head for the road before it was too late. They could hear the village hounds yapping now, and muffled gunshots. Screaming too.

Eldritch imagined the terrified wives and screeching infants, the madly-barking dogs and lowing cattle.

A hundred and more leagues from the nearest open ocean, but these Frenchies were about to learn some harsh lessons in piracy. And God help the Ride, because they would be teachers this day.

Eldritch watched the latest of their unfortunate victims

bound down the slopes towards them, tripping, rolling down the creeping hillside in sheer panic, completely oblivious to the clumsy barricade.

'No shooting. We'll let Kerr push them on to us, club any bugger who wants to mix it,' he told the waiting troops. They glared back, as gloomily defiant as they dared.

By God, he'd not made many friends, that black night in Geldray's tent.

Everything had been going exactly as he had planned. He had used his own loaded dice to lose a pouchful of coin, drawing the foolish warden into his cleverly-laid trap. Geldray had suspected him, of course, but hadn't worked out why he should cheat so hard and lose so heavily. Howath had gone on betting beyond his means, picked and prodded by his captain's caustic wit. He had strung him along like a fat carp, played him out of the snaggy reeds only to lose him in open water. He had been within a dice-roll of triumph, betting his winnings against the warden's only asset – his warband. The poor warden had been driven to distraction by Geldray's barbs and boasting, his powers of judgement undermined by Eldritch's deliberate and dangerous advice. He would have gone belly-up in another moment – if it hadn't been for his own spitfire of a sister, fleecing her beaver at the first man to give her a second glance. He had been forced to lay down his bets, leave the warden at table with the razor-sharp Geldray.

And Geldray hadn't wasted a moment, taking his place to rake in the fattest prize of all. The Ride should have gone to Eldritch – God knows he'd worked hard enough for it. But the Vicomte had taken it by default, plucking their destinies out of Howath's dithering grasp.

Eldritch had cursed and cried, wept bitter tears of frustration and shame. He had wept for the warden and for his own sorry part in the Ride's betrayal. By Jesu, his trickery would have been hard enough to bear if he had triumphed. But the knowledge he had been to blame for its unintended transfer to the Bastard Geldray had tortured his soul, stolen what little peace of mind he had ever enjoyed. Now he would have to live with that shame for evermore . . .

The men suspected him, Miranda and Merron despised him, and the warden . . . Eldritch cringed to think of the poor, bewildered old man, the hopelessly confused fool who had sobered up that dawn to the news that he had lost his entire retinue through an ill-advised wager. That he had bet the lives of more than two hundred of his men against a sackful of Geldray's coins.

The Vicomte had been magnanimous in his victory, assuring the horrified warden he would indeed look after the men as he had promised, employ them on the terms and conditions they had agreed.

'A year and a day and you shall have them back, my Lord!' he had cried, slapping the table as the first feeble glimmers of Corpus Christi Day had illuminated the dew-soaked pavilion.

But anybody who had seen Howath's face would have known the truth: that the warden would be rotting in his grave long before he ever got his precious warband back.

The news had been all over the camp before sunup, the whispered details hungrily devoured by the gossiping troops.

That the Lord Howath, fatigued by long decades of loyal service to his liege lord Henry of England, would be handing over the command of the justly-famed Ride to a younger, fitter, chief – rather more suited to the new tactics King Henry was keen on introducing.

Who better to instruct Henry's Border Horse in the arts of *modern* warfare than the noted continental commander Abelard, Vicomte de Toinueill, Bastard son of the legendary Duc de Gueldres?

It was put about the camps that the Bastard Geldray would oversee the adoption of the arquebus, and phase out the outmoded longbow.

Henry himself had been only too keen on the idea, tickled by the prospect of getting some of his men trained in the new firearms – while they were safely out of range of his own deerparks. And Henry wouldn't exactly regret Lord

Howath's passing either. He had never forgiven the warden for beating him hollow on the tennis court all those years before.

Eldritch was acutely aware that the only person who had offered the bewildered warden any real comfort had been his old mentor, Edward Kraven. And Kraven, more than any man, knew exactly who to blame for Howath's misfortunes. He had known what Eldritch had been about from the beginning, and had tried to warn Howath from the foolish wager which had cost him his retinue and his self-respect. Kraven had offered to put the sickly warden up in his own town house back in Calais, at least until he recovered his damaged health. Miranda would of course be welcome to remain behind and nurse his sickly father.

Eldritch hadn't anticipated that the girl he had paid considerable attention to for the past three years would be snatched away from him, confined to the merchant's house like some overdressed drudge.

Kraven's bitter accusations still rang in his ears.

'You must have known your reckless gamble would result in the warden's humiliation, no matter which one of you usurped control of his retinue!'

'Nobody forced him to make that bet, you heard me warn him off!'

'He gave you a start, boy, when you were set to starve on Bristol's wharves. He treated you as a son and this is how you repay him!'

Eldritch had been stung by the merchant's all-too-accurate barb, horribly aware of the consequences for himself if the truth ever leaked out to the men.

But Kraven had no right talking to him about betrayal. It had been mightily convenient for the merchant, packing Eldritch off to the north. He'd snapped up his father's business, his house and by Christ he would have had him and all, running around doing his errands!

And besides all that, he would now have Miranda to entertain him these dark, wintry nights!

★

And if Kraven's accusations hadn't hurt enough, Eldritch had been forced to endure an even more vicious tongue-lashing from Merron. Deprived of her only friend, his young sister had found herself alone in an alien world. She would be forced to accompany the muttering warband into the unknown – following Geldray's merest whim about a foreign land. Eldritch, in a towering rage after his un-satisfactory interview with Kraven, had absolutely forbidden Merron to remain behind in Calais. Leave a headstrong sixteen-year-old at the mercy of every petty-captain and ragged-arsed underling in the garrison? Did she think him mad?

'Not mad no,' Merron had bitten back, her eyes flashing dangerously. 'Isn't madness generally caused by feverish humours? How could a cold fish like you be suffering from hot blood?' Eldritch, already goaded by Kraven's insidious taunts, had somehow managed to control his whiplash temper. Merron had ignored his glare, pressed on while he fought the urge to batter her on the nose.

'Shooting your mouth off and hitting people for no reason! No wonder Lillith couldn't stand it any longer! You would have seen her in a nunnery, and now she's gone you've got your pious claws in me!' she shrieked. Eldritch felt his heart thump in agitation. He held his breath for a moment.

'I've a moral duty to our dead parents, don't you see that?'

'You ought to be more responsible for yourself, and let me worry about my morals! If it had been left to you Lillith and I would have been locked in the attic at home, sewing stockings while you went away on your self-right-eous crusades! By God, you were born out of time, brother!'

'You go too far,' he rasped. 'If keeping you and your sister from playing the whore on the waterfront's a crusade, then I'll gladly wear the cross!'

'Well I'd rather play the whore than live like some monastic Templar! It's not natural, the way you shun everyone! Poor Miranda thinks you've done it all to get away from her.'

'Done what?' he asked dangerously, wondering how much his clever sister had managed to work out for herself. Her sideways scowl had told him she had guessed – or been told – everything.

'She might not have your wits, brother, but even she worked out you were to blame! She's convinced you mean to escape from her, fly to the far ends of the earth to avoid marrying her.'

Eldritch sighed with exasperation.

'I did no such thing. I would have married her,' he hissed, gripping his sister by her elbows.

'You thought you'd win her and the warband, with your damned cheating!' she exclaimed, driven beyond endurance by her brother's icy reserve. Eldritch saw red, backhanded the furious girl across her mouth. Merron staggered back against the tent post. She would have fallen if he hadn't held on to her gown, which tore up the seam exposing the pale flesh of her forearm.

'I'm surprised you've such a clear recollection of the game, seeing as how you spent most of it playing poopnoddy with that Spanish prick Isolani!'

'Well at least he's got a prick!' Eldritch hurled her to the floor, as much to save her from any further blows as to shut her up.

'For God's sake, watch your mouth! Do you want the whole camp to know our business?' He panted with anger, holding on to the leaning tent pole as if he was at the rudder of a drifting ship. He held his hand to his brow, hot as a glede despite Merron's accusations to the contrary.

'You say so because I don't go haughmaganding every maiden I meet? It doesn't mean I'm not a man, damn you!'

Merron held her fingers to her lip, examined the smeared blood on the back of her hand.

'I've never given Miranda any expectation of an offer,' he said, trying to hold his brittle temper in check.

'But you just said you'd have married her!'

'If she'd ever shown any damned interest in me, aye!'

Merron's spiteful accusations had wounded him deeper than any of Geldray's caustic taunts, than Kraven's bitter indictment. He willed himself to stay calm, terrified he would take out all his anger on his scowling sister. And punish her for Lillith's elopement, the subsequent ruin of all their fortunes.

'I am sorry, I should not have struck you,' he said hoarsely.

'No, you should not!'

Merron picked at her ripped sleeve.

'Miranda told me she loved you, but I warned her from such foolishness. He's in love with himself; he lusts for nothing other than power and position. You say you despise Gueldres, brother, but you're more alike than you imagine. Than you'd ever dare admit.'

Beside La Grouchelle

'Captain Eldritch sir!' Hobby was tugging at his arm. He glanced at him, half perplexed by the sergeant's concern.

'They're coming sir!' Hobby cried. Eldritch peered over the wagon rim, saw that the fugitives had spotted the trap. They turned and tried to run back up the steep slopes to avoid the ambush which had been set for them. Eldritch swallowed, made up his wandering mind in a moment.

'Up and after them! Geldray's too far back, they'll get around us otherwise!'

'That's what we thought sir,' Hobby muttered, rising from the fortified cart like an unshaven colossus.

Eldritch led his men out of the wagonburg, waved them into a skirmish line across the slopes. Half of them were arquebusiers, dressed up in their fantastical harlequin costumes, some of them sporting slashed hose with bared buttocks. His own men looked more like beaters hired by some English squire, loping forward with their bows held out like hurleysticks. They wore olive green or mustard-coloured tunics, leather jacks and mail shirts. The peasants they had been sent to capture would hardly recognise them as soldiers. Until they knocked them to the ground, Eldritch thought.

'Go steady, we don't want to break their heads!' he shouted, as the first desperate Frenchmen gave up any idea of escape and turned to fight. They were halfway up the steep hillside now, smoke from their burning homes drifting down the terraces.

They grabbed whatever came to hand – earth, lumps of sod, flinty rocks – and opened a fierce bombardment against the pursuing soldiers. Eldritch ducked as a jagged stone whistled past his head. A damned woman had thrown that! He doubled forward, scrambling on his hands and knees to get at the bawling peasants. Hobby staggered as a stone ricocheted off his helmet. One of Isolani's handgunners was toppling back down the way they had come, his garish garb caked with clay.

Eldritch could see why the peasants had given up hope of escape. A line of horsemen had appeared on the ridge, cutting them off from the woods where they might have hidden themselves.

Kerr!

The canny Vicomte had heard all the sorry circumstances of the Scot's capture, and shaken his head at the unsporting trap Eldritch had set for him. Eldritch hadn't done anything he wouldn't have done himself, of course, but it had been another handy stick to beat the Englishman with – promoting his bitterest enemies from the ranks! Geldray had restored the reiver's privileges, made him chief scout of all the Horse as were left – Scots and English alike. He had even made his red-headed dolt of a son Angus a corporal!

It had been a particularly bitter pill for Eldritch, watching dangerous rivals raised up against him, but he had no choice but to obey his new master's commands. To do otherwise would have been to rob Howath of what little respect he retained, exposing him to allegations that he had welched on his bet. Eldritch had sworn he would serve his sentence, serve his new master Geldray for a year and a day as Howath had promised.

He owed the old bugger that, at least.

The Scotsman had taken an equally extensive diversion away from the main body, arriving on the heights just as the villagers had become aware of the trap in the valley. They were riding down across the slope now, the treacherous descent hardly bothering their hardy bog trotters. They had reversed their lances and some carried heavy nets ready to catch a kicking codfish of a Frenchman.

The villagers bunched together in desperate panic, grappling with the noisy hunters as the horsemen cantered down behind them. They kicked and threw rocks, grabbed at saddles and wielded their pitchforks where they could.

It was over in moments.

The Bastard Geldray's black-hearted legion had absorbed another seventy more or less able-bodied recruits. The Vicomte had ridden down the valley with his grinning bodyguard, inspecting the bloody and bruised volunteers as if he was Charlemagne himself, come to save the west. Eldritch fingered a bruise above his eye where a toothless old devil had clocked him one with his hoe.

'They're not Gascons, it's true, but beggars can't be choosers. Well done Captain Eldritch, have them bound to the back of your carts. I imagine you might need a helping hand, getting your wagons back on the road, eh?'

Eldritch stared at the grinning Vicomte as he pranced past on his charger. Hobby shook his head.

'Like I said, captain. It's a . . .'

'Bad business. I noticed,' he growled. 'Now do as he says and get these muck-raking rabbits lashed to the wagons. I don't want them running off home the moment it gets dark!' Hobby saluted, hurried off to do as he had been ordered.

Isolani threw his arquebus in the back of a wagon, gave the Englishman a curious look.

'A successful afternoon's hunting, Capitano El-Dreeg,' he observed. His raw eye was still discoloured from the right hook the captain had given him back at Guisnes. The Spaniard didn't appear to bear any grudges, but then again, the warning blow hadn't stopped him from making doe eyes at Merron either. Despite their arguments his younger sister was still infatuated with him – taking him his supper and pouring his wine like some Carthaginian slave girl. Their hair-raising rows had kept half the camp entertained, whether they understood the ripe English expressions or not.

'We didn't come here to hunt,' Eldritch grunted, and stalked off towards his waiting horse.

The slack-jawed recruits hardly seemed aware what had befallen them, and their anxious appeals hadn't cut much ice with their English guardians either. Hobby scratched his head as he listened to their guttural imprecations. He only knew half a dozen words in French and the prisoners' thick southern dialects quite defeated his inadequate vocabulary. The sergeant tried to explain that they had only been obeying orders of their precious Vicomte.

'He's on your side, you daft buggers,' he'd shouted, in the vain hope of convincing the peasants they weren't about to be loaded aboard some Turkish galley. 'He's a Frenchy like you! Frenchy, eh!'

Eldritch left the sergeant to explain the situation as best he could, and spurred on ahead to catch up with the Vicomte's senior officers. He had determined not to be isolated within the rapidly-expanding legion's cosmopolitan command structure – forever on the receiving end of whatever mischief Geldray could devise. He might get kicked in the teeth, insulted and landed with the filthiest assignments the thrice-damned rogue could dream up, but he refused to simply hide in the wagontrain like some miserable churl, gloomily awaiting the inevitable humiliations.

He would face out the dangerous dandy, and try his best to keep abreast of his bewilderingly fluid affairs.

The captain caught up with his new chief at a crossroads a few miles down the valley at a place called Montbrison. The main road followed the ever-deepening gorges turning to the south-east, cutting through a range of mountains whose fir-clad peaks were still capped with snow.

They had come further than Eldritch thought. Another hundred leagues or so would see them at the Chateau Reban near Grenoble, the Gueldres stronghold they had heard so much about in the last few weeks. It was the only decent-sized castle the clan had left. From what little Eldritch had been able to discover, it appeared the old duke had been stripped of his best estates following his ill-advised rebellion against Margaret of Savoy. But he had not been able to find out what the Vicomte had in mind for his assorted recruits this far south.

Eldritch cantered up to the Vicomte's extended party, brought his panting rouncy to a halt with an unnecessarily elaborate flourish.

Sandy Kerr was the only officer to even acknowledge his arrival, raising his scarred chin to give the captain the most contemptuous of greetings. He was in his element now, squatting on his hairy horse like some latterday Ghengis Khan, his lank moustaches hanging about his misshapen mouth.

'Ye found us then, captain. Ye've niver got yerself too bogged down with yon wains?' he asked, his amber eyes glittering with malice.

'No Sandy. Not with you here scouting a path for us,' he snapped back, irritated by the Scot's smug self-assurance.

Geldray had turned the tables on them all, but he'd never dilute the bad blood between them, not if he marched them right around the earth.

The Vicomte's black-surcoated bodyguards had dismounted a short way off, the tired riders lounging on a grass verge about a roadside shrine. They seemed unaware of the irony, sitting about belching and laughing as their sweat-caked horses tore at the surrounding vegetation. The peeling Madonna gazed serenely down on them as they munched looted wheat bread and swigged the wine they had captured back at La Grouchelle. The Vicomte himself had remained in the saddle, his expensive black suit gilded with a fine layer of golden dust. He was nodding his head soberly, listening to his locotenent's somewhat breathless report. Eldritch hadn't seen the taciturn Savvi since that terrible night back in Guisnes. He knew Geldray had sent the captain on ahead to make preparations for the legion's arrival at the chateau. Judging from Savvi's fixed stare, he'd not found things organised entirely to his liking.

'HE DID WHAT?' Geldray exclaimed, sitting up so suddenly his horse took a nervous sidestep. Eldritch urged his own mount alongside the scowling nobleman's stallion, as close as he dared without obviously eavesdropping. Eldritch tilted his head, tried to follow the Vicomte's exotic *lingua franca* – the cosmopolitan mother-tongue of the camp.

'The little bastard! Since when does some damned freak make up my mind! What was that shit-eater Muhlberg doing?'

Savvi, ever alert despite his cow-eyed expression, nodded his head towards the Englishman. Geldray jerked round and stared at him.

'And here's another bugger itching to give the orders! I thought I told you to see to the wagons?' Geldray snarled, his features contorted with rage. Eldritch looked up, wide-eyed.

'I came to make my report, my Lord,' he said dutifully. Geldray waved him away with a curse, waited until the clever Englishman had turned his horse towards the weather-ravaged shrine. He was already deeply suspicious of the captain's motivations, unsure how far he could trust the newcomer to carry out the assignments he had in mind for him. The Vicomte narrowed his eyes, watched Eldritch take off his bonnet before the shrine and cross himself, mumbling a brittle prayer. The simple piety of the gesture looking strikingly out of character.

Savvi leaned closer, his red hair stuck with bits of dust and debris he had collected during his thankless ride south.

'He's taken them all back to the chateau. He thought it was for the best.'

'For the best?' Geldray cried, his dark eyes flashing dangerously. 'I'll tell you Savvi, I'll see you fattening the crows for this! What in the name of God do I want with a dozen bastard choirboys?'

The Locotenent looked somewhat abashed by his master's dire threat.

'Well I've been thinking . . .'

'There's a first!' Geldray snarled, drumming his velvet-clad fingers on the raised pommel of his saddle as he pondered Savvi's distressing intelligence.

Couldn't he trust these moronic trolls with anything? The moment his back was turned the fiends ruined all.

'I've thought of a way we might turn the situation around, as it were.'

'Turn it around? We get Muhlberg to take them all back, eh? Apologise to the damned abbot?' he asked with leaden sarcasm. Savvi shook his head in apology.

'I'm afraid the abbot's dead, my Lord.'

Geldray clapped his hand to his forehead. 'Dead? He's a personal friend of that pious swine Bayard! Do you imagine he'll let this lie?'

Savvi shrugged.

'What I thought was, we could turn the tables on the boys, so to speak. We could tell the choir we rescued them,' he explained, smiling wanly at the Vicomte's terrible expression.

'Rescued them from what? What could be worse than being kidnapped from a blazing abbey by a gang of garlic-chewing apes in black harness?' Geldray demanded, the angry colour leaching from his pinched features as he began to ponder the appalling consequences of his servant's actions.

'Castration, my Lord. That'd be a sight worse, in my book.'

Beside the Abbey d'Eleron, Provence

The toiling peasants who had been put to work clearing the rubble from the devastated abbey had crossed themselves in mortal fear when they saw the grim caravan arrive – post-haste from the great city of Avignon. They had heard tales about those smartly-painted black and red wagons to turn their hair white.

Tales of torture and terror, of religious genocide on a biblical scale.

The Holy Inquisition had been set up to persuade the teeming infidels of southern Spain to turn to the paths of righteousness. But the all too willing agents of Torquemada had not been content burning screeching Moors at the stake, or stretching Jews on the rack.

They had broadened their bloodstained horizons, extending their inquiries south into mainland Italy, north into the lush valleys of France and then east into the superstitious villages of southern Germany. The all-powerful agents of the Inquisition had burnt out the black hearts of witch covens and wizard chapters, rooted out the vile ivy of heresy and stamped it underfoot.

Without mercy. Without pity. And without question.

The peasants knew those colours only too well, and were not taken in by the gaily-painted wheel spokes, the gaudy maypoles which bore the bloody banners of the Inquisition.

They had dropped down into the dust, taken care to

avert their eyes as Briconet of Avignon had cast his shadow over their crude hovels. They had all seen the sinister black wagon at the rear of the dreaded caravan, and heard the horrifying jingle of equipment as the heavy wheels rattled over the uneven road.

They could only guess at its deadly cargo: forges and boiling cages, back-breaking chains and thumbscrews. Wrenches, knives, branding irons and hammers. Bone-cutters and ankle-biters, straps, manacles, whips and wires. And a great, blood-drenched table, a rack bristling with hoops of iron and complex levers, an altar to unspeakable pain and torments. They had watched the laden wain clutter up the hill towards the black skull of the abbey, and prayed to God they would not be called before its overseers.

Angelica almost envied Fabrizio's delirium – at least his surely terminal sufferings had prevented the authorities from subjecting him to hours of interminable questioning. Unable to extract the information they sought from the badly-wounded boy, they had instead turned all their attentions on his heavily-bandaged but otherwise able companion. The black-robed fiends had seemed friendly enough at first, shaking their tonsured heads in dismay as Angelica had outlined the bare bones of her fantastical tale. But their grave compassion had been a smokescreen, a haphazardly-cast net to catch odd sprats they might use against her later. They had soon returned to her bedside, pulling up cane-backed chairs to begin their interrogation in earnest. Brother Avila, the desperately-overworked orderly, had tried to keep the in-quisitors at bay, insisting the girl needed complete rest. But the agents had shooed him out, told him to take his bowl and poultice elsewhere.

There was no shortage of patients requiring his attention. Over a dozen of the brothers had been wounded during the massacre, along with any number of guards and servants. Many had already succumbed to their injuries and others would surely follow, despite the best efforts of the gentle Avila.

Angelica leaned forward as the taller agent plumped her pillow, bringing her pale face within range of his piercing gaze. He sat down beside her and glanced at his stouter colleague. The second agent, Master Souris, had balanced a small portmanteau on his broad lap, and was busy scratching notes, his crow quill shorn of feathers. She could see the tip of his red tongue protruding as he dipped the business-like pen in the small silver ink pot. Angelica tried to focus on his extensive jottings, but all she could make out were spidery trails compressed within wavy margins.

'Mistress Tarsi. We very much regret having to interrupt your deserved rest, but you will understand the magnitude of what has occurred here precludes such inconsequential considerations.'

Angelica frowned, trying to concentrate on the agent's brusque Italian.

'Your pardon, gentlemen, but I am unable to recall your names,' she said, raising her fingers to her well-wrapped forehead.

'I am Abandando Briconet of Avignon, the Papal Legate. I have been appointed to investigate this incident as a matter of the utmost urgency on behalf of his Majesty Francis I and His Holiness Leo X,' the agent retorted, staring intently at his blinking prisoner as if he would unravel her mind along with the bandages wound about her head.

'You have already admitted you came to the Abbey d'Eleron in company with the chorister Ambolini and Captain Strozzi,' Briconet told her. She noticed his front teeth were badly streaked, like the dirty marble steps in some old alley. Briconet's gaze was fixed on hers, noting every expression, weighing every flicker of her eyes.

'Of course I admitted it, Monsieur Briconet. I have never made any secret of the fact. My father . . .'

'Your father sent you here to hire the abbey choir: that's your story, in a nutshell,' he snapped. His companion paused, dipped his pen in the ink as he puzzled her reply.

'Gentlemen,' she said uncertainly, 'surely there is no question you believe our party had anything to do with the attack on the abbey?' she asked, her features turning chill at the prospect.

Briconet allowed himself a pained smile.

'All we seek is the truth, my dear,' he said. 'Now is it or is it not the case that you were sent here by your father, Alberto Tarsi, to hire the services of the abbey's choir? A choir which has only performed on a handful of special occasions during the last decade?' Angelica nodded her head.

'And naturally you were disappointed when Abbot Odo declined to allow the choir to perform for your father?'

'I was disappointed . . . he didn't immediately decline our offer.' Angelica corrected herself, horribly confused. She could recall isolated incidents as if they were still-life portraits from a Florentine art school. Picture faces, grotesquely distorted by flaming candlelight. Fabrizio, naked and erect. Constanzia in the doorway, the pitcher held above her head, droplets of water falling over her braced shoulder like slow pearls. Fabrizio again, lying by the door with his hands in his stomach, head bent at an awkward angle as he looked out for her . . .

'Of course you were disappointed. Your father had made up his mind he would hire the choir. It had not occurred to either of you Abbot Odo might refuse your patronage.'

'He hadn't!' Angelica cried. 'Not entirely! He had promised to write on father's behalf, to . . .'

'So he had agreed to your family hiring the choir?' Briconet interrupted.

'No! Not just like that! He said he would write to the Chevalier Bayard, seeking his opinion on whether or not Signor Scaralatchi should be given the chance . . .'

'Scaralatchi? *The* Scaralatchi?' Souris asked, raising his quill from his grubby notes.

'The very same,' Briconet sighed, reaching over to push the clerk's quill back down again.

'Abbot Odo was unconvinced of Signor Scaralatchi's repentance, but he had agreed to write to . . .'

'And you have this letter in your possession?'

'He was to deliver it to us the following morning.'

'And of course, it was destroyed in this *terrible* fire.'

'Are you suggesting my father and I had a hand in the attack on the abbey? That we slaughtered defenceless children, attacked the Brothers as if . . .'

'Signor Tarsi, your esteemed father, served the House of Savoy in the Low Countries and Spain. He is no stranger to violence of this nature. He is a mercenary who fights for the highest bidder. Is this not so?'

Angelica fought to control her feeble-minded outrage, barely comprehending the seriousness of the charges they were laying against her.

'My father would never have set his hand to an unprovoked attack on a defenceless abbey,' she replied as calmly as she could.

Briconet's blue eyes seemed to be gazing straight through her.

'Defenceless abbey?' the inquisitor repeated. 'A rather arrogant assessment of the abbey's defences, if I may say so. A company of Gascon spearmen as well as any number of local volunteers? Only a serious professional soldier would even contemplate such a confrontation. These mysterious attackers you *claim* to know nothing about. They appear to have been remarkably well informed of the layout of the abbey, the distribution of the soldiers whose duty it was to defend it. They also knew the internal layout of the main complex. It seems to us something of a conundrum, that your completely innocent arrival should coincide with their particularly vicious assault.'

Briconet paused, took a shallow breath. He reminded the quailing girl of a weasel, poised to destroy some hopelessly-entranced rabbit.

'Mistress Tarsi, perhaps you do not fully comprehend just who we represent. I am Briconet of Avignon. The filthy Jews and Moors of Spain, the blood-spewing heretics of Germany have every reason to dread my name. I am Papal Legate and senior Inquisitor of the Holy Church.'

He paused, licked his dry lips. 'So do not oblige me to

prostitute my considerable talents on a worthless farmyard bitch like you!' he snarled, the terrifying hatred in his voice forcing her back into the cold pillow. Angelica swallowed, tears of fright blurring her vision and rolling down her chin to stain the thin sheet Avila had brought for her.

'Now, let us begin once more. You arrived at the abbey with Strozzi and Ambolini, the servant Constanzia, sadly deceased, and a *lusus naturae*, who has not been seen since the night of the attack.'

Angelica clutched her frail cot, her assaulted mind racing in different directions. Obolus. He hadn't been seen since the attack, she thought foggily. She knew Fabrizio had been wounded – possibly to the death. Strozzi had been dragged out from beneath a cairn of smoking stones, a roast ox in seared leather. Constanzia had been killed in the grounds, her graceful body wrecked by the wheels of Tarsi's grand carriage.

'The dwarf!'

'Has not been . . .'

'The dwarf's the spy! Captain Strozzi suspected him all the while!' Angelica exclaimed. Briconet blinked once. The simple gesture seemed ten times as sinister as his rigid but unseeing stare.

'Are you suggesting he devised this sickening barbarity? Your servant Obolus may well be buried in the rubble. It might take months to clear the northern walls.'

That was no exaggeration, at least. The apocalyptic blaze had blown out Abbot Odo's personal quarters, toppled the northern tower and brought down the curtain walls between the kitchens and the empty dormitories. All that remained were stark black slabs, rising like tottering soldiers from the heaped rubble and blackened beams. The flames had turned the most formidable spars into skeletal ash, the pock-marked wood branded by rills of soot which cracked and crumbled under the soldier's boots. They had hauled bodies away in barrows, the well-cooked flesh parting like the most succulent roasts . . .

The gagging peasants had been hurried up the hill to

help, pressed into service to clear the wreckage and locate the pitifully-burnt survivors. One old crone had come across the grievously-wounded Ambolini and the Tarsi girl, huddled together beneath a sooty cot in one of the miraculously-untouched guest rooms.

Miraculously untouched, while a quarter of the main complex had been completely gutted? Barely singed, while almost a hundred others had been turned into lamp-black effigies by the terrible flames? Briconet could practically taste the girl's guilt, as acutely aware of her poorly-concealed lies as he was of the girl's cloying, bedridden fragrance.

Angelica closed her eyes, ran knuckles into the raw sockets.

'I swear on God's books, on the eyes of my unborn children, that neither I nor my family had any knowledge of their cowardly attack,' she said as steadily as she could. Briconet was unimpressed. He stood up, gathered his hands inside his great sleeves.

'You can swear on what you like, my dear. But I shall have the truth out of you, one way or another.'

They drifted out of her blurred vision like fish swimming beneath a sunlit bridge, lost in the crowding shadows of her consciousness. By the time Brother Avila had arrived to mop her fevered brow, she had relapsed into a deep, but not a dreamless, sleep.

The gaudily-painted carts belonging to the papal legate were not the only traffic on the hill that day. The dust had barely settled on the heavily-rutted road before more riders hurried up from the river. The frightened villagers peered between their shutters as the bright host rode by. At their head were three score Gendarmes in white surcoats, their closed helmets sporting colourful ostrich plumes. They rode beneath silken gonfalons, streaming swallowtail pennants which snapped and jangled as the riders urged their mounts up the slope towards the abbey.

The silver and gold banners were embroidered with biblical scenes and bore Latin inscriptions of almost fanatical piety. They rode like the crusaders of old, caught up in the whirlwind of history.

Briconet watched them from the ruined tower, narrowing his eyes as the strong afternoon sunlight glanced from their burnished armour. The papal legate didn't need to read their pious devices to know who they belonged to. He turned to his clerk, blinking myopically as the reflected sunlight startled his sore eyes.

'Bayard,' Briconet breathed.

'He must have flown down from the north, to get here this quickly,' Souris observed admiringly, standing on tiptoe to peer over the sill.

The shining horsemen materialised before their eyes, gathering shape and form as they rode into the jagged-edged shadows cast by the ruined abbey.

'Behold the Angel of the Lord,' Briconet sneered. 'But those brave knights of his might yet prove useful,' he allowed.

Ten minutes later the agent had welcomed the legendary chevalier into the hastily-cleared dining hall – the only room in the abbey in a fit state to receive such a distinguished visitor. Pierre du Terrail, the foremost knight in France, was a tall but rather lightly-built man of middle years, his sinewy body completely encased in a superb, closely-fitting suit of armour.

Briconet wondered if the chevalier ever took it off, or whether he slept in his mail like the effigies back at Avignon cathedral. Bayard had placed his closed-faced helmet on the table and greeted the papal legate with reserved courtesy. Briconet noticed the ravishing Provençal climate hadn't even brought a blush to his cheeks. His skin was supernaturally pale, almost feminine. His features, however, were rather broad, his nose prominent and well fleshed. Bayard's sorrowful brown eyes were widely spaced, exaggerating his lugubrious expression just as his brutally-tonsured hair made his ears stick out like a backwater priest.

But bucolic clergymen did not usually present themselves at the Abbey d'Eleron wearing a finely-crafted suit of 'Maximilian' armour. The modern, fluted suit was covered in deep grooves and every joint was heavily embossed to deflect lance and arrows. It must have cost the pious knight a king's ransom. Briconet imagined the chevalier's servant must have given his master a brisk rubdown at the bottom of the hill, because his immaculate equipment was as spotless as his reputation.

Briconet despised him; despised his undoubted faith and despised the chivalrous code he had chosen so loudly to live by. A code for the meek and mild which had little relevance to the world they lived in.

The Holy Church could not afford such selfish indulgence, times being what they were. Heresy was rampant in Germany, the heretic Luther undermining long centuries of patient church-building in an afternoon. The Turks were swarming in the Eastern Mediterranean, and the great kings who should have been uniting against them were busy squabbling among themselves. Bayard was a relic of a never-ever age, the epitome of a true-hearted crusading knight. The Church could not afford to place such spotless fools at the helm of its storm-racked ship of state.

The Church required men of the world to determine its course in the modern world — men who understood the treacherous shoals of international politics, who had the correct respect and appreciation of the vitality of trade and finance, and above all, men who understood what it was to be a man. Here was the perfect Christian hero, entirely unaware of the all-too-human reek of his own shit.

Bayard had accepted a goblet of wine to wash the road dust from his mouth. The bottle was one of the handful which hadn't been smashed or looted during the recent attack. The knight smacked his lips, nodded appreciatively.

'A good vintage. I was always partial to the d'Eleron grape. Unique to the region, I am told,' Bayard sighed. 'I doubt it will ever taste the same, now the vineyards have been bathed in the blood of your brother monks.'

Briconet compressed his lips, nodded piously.

'I am both gratified and astonished by your prompt arrival, my Lord Chevalier,' Briconet said smoothly. 'I had heard you were still with His Majesty in the north. Little did we imagine you would answer our prayers so speedily.'

'I was in Dijon. We took horse the moment we heard of this unspeakable outrage. Is it true you have apprehended the perpetrators? The female who led the expedition?' Bayard inquired. Briconet folded his hands in front of his chest, nodded ingratiatingly.

'We believe we have gone a great way towards establishing the guilty party,' Briconet agreed. 'My investigations have uncovered the beginnings of a vile plot. An ambitious Italian soldier of fortune with grandiose ideas far above his station. It appears this rogue attempted to force our cherished Abbot Odo to allow the abbey choir to perform some scurrilous musical composition, written by a disgraced composer who has already been excommunicated from the Holy Church. When the dear departed Odo refused their impudent overture, this man's agents slaughtered him and kidnapped the choir for themselves. We have found dozens of witnesses who speak of a large black carriage bearing the House Tarsi insignia.'

'House Tarsi?' Bayard wondered aloud.

'Even so, my Lord Chevalier. The tyrant has set up his own bandit kingdom in a remote pass near Mont Blanc. He changes his allegiance on a whim, first serving the Empire, and then her enemies. He holds his usurped territory open to the highest bidder, inflicting swingeing taxes on all who would travel the pass. It is a busy route, my Lord Chevalier, and crucial to our military and commercial well-being.'

Bayard nodded his head, his monastically short hair veined with silver threads.

'I am sure His Majesty King Francis would join me in offering his most sincere thanks for your efforts on our behalf,' he said, sipping at his wine. Briconet tensed. 'However, the abbey was under my personal protection, and I could not possibly burden you with the impious duty of hunting down those responsible for this crime.'

'The duty of tracking down these barbarian murderers is, as you say, an impious one. But I feel it is *my* duty to offer all my experience as Holy Inquisitor to hasten the inquiries already in hand. The dreadful crime was, after all, perpetrated on land administered from the papal headquarters in Avignon.' Bayard nodded graciously, but his wide brown eyes were set.

'This man Tarsi must be brought before the proper authorities forthwith. You are of course most welcome to accompany me to the Alpine frontier.'

Briconet acknowledged the chevalier's stiff invitation.

'Perhaps you could arrange an interview for me with the Tarsi girl, at your earliest convenience?'

'Of course, my Lord. Once she has recovered from her . . . injuries.'

'Injuries sustained in the attack? Does it not strike you as odd that Tarsi's soldiery should harm their own master's flesh and blood?'

'It is all too often the case with savages such as these, my Lord Chevalier. There is no honour among theives.'

Briconet should not have had to tell the foolish chevalier that!

'I believe the youth Ambolini was injured during a struggle. Mistress Tarsi's injuries might have been self-inflicted in order to confuse our investigations.'

Bayard nodded soberly. 'Then she is not excessively hurt?'

'Not excessively. It is possible she received some further hurts when the fires her own troops started raged out of control, trapping her in a burning room. She must also have been troubled with falling masonry – several of the brothers received similar injuries about the head and shoulders. That would explain the burns on her arms and feet, and weals on her chest and abdomen.'

Bayard looked up, his widely-set eyes mournful but fiercely acute.

'You have already interrogated her yourself, I imagine.'
Briconet smiled coldly.
'She helped us with our inquiries,' he agreed.

Beside Le Col Galliard,
in the French Alps

belard, Vicomte de Toinueill was riding along happily, a mischievous smile pulling at the corners of his mouth. Every now and again he would chuckle to himself and then burst out laughing, his uncharacteristically unrestrained braying magnified by the rocky gullies they were negotiating.

His closely-packed bodyguard wondered if he had finally lost his mind. He had been in an unusually jolly mood ever since they had left the chateau at Grenoble.

In actual fact their chief was thinking about castration.

He wasn't planning to castrate anybody in particular – although there was no shortage of suitable candidates in his household, he remembered with a sign of irritation. No. Old Savvi had hit the nail on the head for once, coming up with the perfect answer to the conundrum he had been left by his over-zealous servants.

'Castrate them! As if!' he cried, wiping tears of mirth from his chilled cheeks. 'Ah, good old Savvi!'

The red-haired locotenent glanced nervously at his highly-amused commander, wondering what crazy notion had tickled the Vicomte's foolish fancy now.

'That was a good one. You should have seen their faces, Francesco! A picture, a real picture,' Gueldres enthused.

'They took the bait, my lord,' Savvi observed uneasily.

'Took the bait! A ha ha ha! I couldn't keep a straight face! The big one – what's his name? – Giacomo. Standing before me with his hands on his hips and his legs wide! He snapped 'em shut quick enough when I told him what Odo had in mind for him. "My poor boys, my darling sons," I said. "Thank our sweet, merciful Lord we were in time." "In time for what?" he said. "In time to save you from Odo's inhuman scheming!"'

Savvi smiled awkwardly as Gueldres rocked about on his nervously-prancing horse. They had drawn some way away from the bodyguard and the rest of the legion's inquisitive officers, and the chief was clearly relishing the opportunity to gloat over his latest piece of trickery without being overheard – particularly by the snooping Englishman Eldritch.

'I had to bite my moustaches to stop myself laughing out loud. They were standing there like three-legged sheep outside a butcher's shop, hopping from one foot to another. I've never seen such terror, not even in the middle of the bloodiest battle!' Gueldres hooted.

'I thought it might shake 'em up a bit, the prospect of losing their tackle,' Savvi admitted, beginning to see the funny side himself.

'Picture it Savvi,' Gueldres invited, wiping his nose. 'A company of black-coated rogues has just abducted them from their cosy little buggery nooks, slaughtered their mucky-minded guardians before their very eyes. They've been bundled into the back of a wagon at knifepoint, kept on bread and water for three days before being unceremoniously thrown into the deepest dungeon in the castle. All I had to do was convince them to overlook it! "Boys, boys," I said. "Another few days and you would have been under the knife." "The knife?" What knife was I talking about? Where was Abbot Odo and their dear Brother Avila? "Burning in hell where they belong," says I. "Don't you realise why they had kept you all together? Why you weren't allowed to wander outside the walls of the abbey? Because you were to be castrated like young bullocks and sold into slavery, sold to the grasping Turks for a hundred gold pieces a head, or rather, a prick! Ah, ha ha ha!"'

'And they swallowed it, did they?'

'Hook line and sinker! They were clutching their balls as if they'd turned to golden goose eggs! And then Giacomo, he says he'd suspected as much all the long!'

The Vicomte's bodyguard shook their heads as the two commanders fell over their saddles, holding onto their horses' manes as they howled with debilitating laughter.

'I said Tarsi had sent his ambassadors up to the abbey to fix the price and arrange their transportation. I realised this Giacomo was the ringleader, and told him he'd been specially picked for the Sultan himself! Ah ha ha ha ha ha!'

'Tarsi pimping for the Grand Vizier!' Savvi exclaimed.

'Well he'd have more luck selling choirboys than that piglet's arse of a daughter of his!' Gueldres snorted. 'And then to cap it all this Giacomo fellow scratches his head and asks if I'm sure I've got it all right. "Because that fellow with the long face said he'd cut our throats if we as much as farted!" Well, I said, he often employs some rather colourful invective. I expect he meant it as a figure of speech! Cut your throat – a figure of speech!'

Savvi guffawed, almost toppling out of his saddle as Gueldres mimicked the bewildered choirboy. The two of them held one another up, shook their heads as their skittish horses carried them around a rocky bend and out onto a broad, furze-studded ridge.

The sudden magnificence of the view stilled their laughter, the fresh wind sobering them in a moment. The shallow valley ran away to the east, the featureless plain dwarfed and dominated by the towering peaks beyond,

'The Alps, my Lord,' Savvi observed rather unnecessarily.

'Ah, it's been too long.' The Vicomte breathed deeply. 'Way too long.'

The breathtaking pinnacle of Mont Blanc soared into the cobalt blue sky, its white-tipped spires tangling the clouds which drifted west on the stiffening breeze. Eldritch shielded his eyes, gazing at the awesome mountain, the mighty

216

crown thrust towards heaven on the shoulders of its lesser brothers. The brisk mountain air caught in his throat and made his eyes water.

'By God, it's beautiful,' he thought aloud. Gueldres glanced at the English captain, amused by his drop-jawed reaction. He and Savvi had halted their tired horses on the stony plateau, allowing the toiling legion time to catch up with them.

Gueldres had marched out of the Chateau Reban at the head of five companies of his veteran landsknechts, the arquebusiers and pikemen alike kitted out in their distinctive black harness. The *Band Nere* could be seen coming a mile off in the rolling foothills, and the few inhabitants had made good and sure to leave them a wide berth. They had passed narrow stone enclosures and snowbound sheep folds, but saw no sign of the flocks which roamed the rugged slopes – nor the canny shepherds who looked after them. Behind the veteran fighters came three companies of fearful militia – slow-witted peasants, alehouse drunkards and pressed men the legion had absorbed through fair means and foul during the long march down the Rhone valley. They were cannon fodder – impure and simple minded – still wearing the filthy smocks they had been captured in. Gueldres had equipped them from his lavishly-appointed armoury at Reban, issuing the green recruits with a handful of javelins and small round bucklers. The bigger men – sturdy farmhands well used to heavier tools – had been given a simple steel helmet, a sixteen-foot pole and turned into pikemen.

The nervous militiamen were easy meat for the sergeants. The scowling demons in their black-lacquered armour watched their every move, and punished every whimper with pitiless brutality. The few fools who had tried to desert the column on the march had been dragged back to camp, and forced to run a gauntlet of bawling legionnaires. Not many of the bewildered fugitives had survived the vicious drubbing.

Eldritch had taken up station just behind the grumbling

mob, riding at the head of the accursedly slow-moving war carts. Sergeant Hobby was in the leading wagon, shaking his head as usual in gloomy contemplation of their mission. The Spaniard Isolani had stretched himself out on the oaken deck behind him, conversing with the archer in stilted camp-English.

Eldritch didn't hold with Isolani's lackadaisical approach to soldiering, but at least he could keep an eye on him. If he hadn't been so busy sunning himself on top of the cart he might have been hanging about the baggage train trying to cadge a few moments with his sister Merron.

The lovelorn captain's arquebusiers had been distributed along the creaking column, several to each wagon. They were forced to share the cramped holds with an equal number of scowling Engishmen clutching bills and bows. The troopers spent most of the day cheerfully insulting one another in their own tongues, nodding and laughing at one another's incomprehensible banter.

It was a miracle the murderous crews hadn't fallen out among themselves, but as none of them had the faintest idea what their comrades were chattering about, the long march from the north had gone off without undue incident.

The Vicomte's personal baggage brought up the rear of the column with the provisions wagons and artillery. There were a dozen and more carriages of all shapes and sizes, including one vast black wain drawn by eight powerful Flanders mares. The heavily-shuttered caravan was guarded by an entire company of legionnaires under the personal command of Corporal Muhlberg, who glowered and shouted if anybody approached within twenty feet of his lumbering vehicle.

Eldritch had been given strict instructions to keep his men away from the wagon, and had no idea what fantastic treasures it might contain. They had loaded the wain under cover of night, out of sight of the cold halls where they had spent their all too brief rest days at the Chateau Reban. Loaded with gold and silver to pay the rapidly-expanded legion, Eldritch supposed. That would add up to a pretty penny and all, considering the huge number of men the Vicomte had felt necessary to employ on his mysterious jaunt to the south. As well as his captains, sergeants and double-paid dopplesoldners, Gueldres would be obliged to maintain hundreds of pikemen and arquebusiers, a dozen and more gunners and a platoon of pioneers.

The Englishman still hadn't managed to work out where they were going, let alone what they were intended to do once they got there. But you didn't bring a thousand troops along on a sightseeing tour of the local hills. They were going into action, it was as plain as the . . .

'Rather more impressive than the hills you were used to, I imagine?' Gueldres asked, interrupting the English captain's reverie.

'I've not seen anything like it,' he admitted, feeling the cold wind biting at his limbs. Gueldres raised his hand, pointed out the great mountains marching off towards the east.

'Mont Blanc, the mother of all the mountains,' the Vicomte went on, transported by the breathtaking spectacle.

'Our road will take us beneath the peaks?' Eldritch inquired.

Gueldres was on his guard in a blink.

'We'll see captain, we'll see,' he said slowly.

The officers turned in the saddles and watched the mile-long column work its way across the rubble-strewn plain below. Eldritch narrowed his eyes, imagined they were being followed by a great black-backed python, its glistening scales undulating, colourfully uncoiling in the strong sunlight. Clumps of pikemen sang as they marched, their steel-tipped poles glittering and flashing. Long files of arquebusiers followed behind, clumsy weapons chafing their shoulders and worrying their straps. The militiamen marched in compact squares, a watchful sergeant positioned on each flank with his ornamental halberd. They loped along with effortless determination, bullying and badgering their charges.

Behind them came the wagons and carts and rumbling culverins, creaking and rolling and leaving a cloud of gritty dust in their wake. A cloud any observer would see fifty leagues off, Eldritch thought sourly. Clearly, the Vicomte wasn't banking on achieving any degree of surprise, wherever in hell they were headed.

The road wound up into the white mountains, a simple silver thread against the slate-grey and bright green slopes. The same roads which had carried Caesar's legions into Gaul and Hannibal's elephants into Italy. Eldritch was delighted to be following in their tracks, to see the very same peaks the long-dead general had ridden by in all their glory.

'We've mountains of our own, aye, back in Scotland,' Sandy Kerr piped up, his rusty plaid wound about his wiry body. The Vicomte indulged him with a sideways smile, nodded his chin at the sheer face of Mont Blanc.

'But not like this, my friend. This is one of the highest peaks in the whole world, and surely the most dangerous and beautiful.'

Eldritch was surprised to find Gueldres in such an expansive mood. He had been in a foul temper when they had arrived at his castle near Grenoble the week before. His hectic – and largely nocturnal – activities must have cheered him up, though he hadn't offered the flimsiest explanation what he had been up to, nor what he had in mind for his recently-reinforced legion.

'She's more dangerous than beautiful,' Savvi growled, his red beard bristling above his bearskin cloak. 'And more so by the day. If we don't press on into Italy, the weather will come down and we'll be trapped like wolves,' he said morbidly. Gueldres glanced at Eldritch and Kerr.

'Don't let Savvi worry you unduly,' he advised. 'You'll have plenty to keep you warm.'

Eldritch frowned. What did he mean to do then, leave them in the pass through the winter? He'd heard the snows came early, in these high valleys.

'You may yet be following me on to Italy, but not before you have carried out a small assignment on my behalf.'

Eldritch raised his eyebrows.

'And what would that be, my Lord Vicomte?' he asked, uncharacteristically courteous.

'I would have thought that would have been obvious. I have already told you this pass is my home, and that it is held by my enemy.'

'Tarsi,' Eldritch observed. Gueldres seemed to flinch at the name.

He must be quite a character, to have such a hold on him, Eldritch thought fleetingly.

'Tarsi indeed. He makes sport in my valley, and lays with his damned whores on my father's bed in Mont Galliard. But he'll be laying under six foot of cold sod, when I've got my castle back.'

Eldritch nodded soberly.

'You want us to storm this Mont Galliard for you?'

The Vicomte swivelled around in his saddle; smiled winningly.

'You know captain, the mountain air seems to have done wonders for your powers of deduction.' His wolfish smile evaporated in an instant. 'Why in God's name do you think I brought you along? I don't keep dogs and bark myself!'

The straggling legion had barely reached the next ridge when Kerr's light horsemen returned from their reconnaissance, setting up dirty knots of dust as they whipped their ponies across the plain.

Sandy Kerr noticed them first, shielding his eyes as the scouts hurtled towards them. Gueldres frowned, turned his horse about as the outriders reined to a halt in a shower of stones. Davey Dunne, their keen-eyed corporal, pointed back over the grim wasteland towards the foothills.

'Captain Sandy, riders sir, hundreds of 'em!'

Gueldres overlooked the hairy Scot's breach of military etiquette. The horsemen hadn't seemed to grasp the fact that their scar-faced chief was no longer in command.

'Riders? Where?' Davey Dunne gaped at the Vicomte as if amazed he could understand his rough brogue.

'Hundreds, coming up hard against yon burn! Goin east waes us!'

Gueldres pulled at his black moustaches as he digested the reiver's report. The youngster had been ordered to watch the flanks, follow the bluffs along the north bank of the River Isere a dozen miles to the south. The turbulent stream was fed by the mountains, and would be practically impossible to cross without risking life-threatening chills. If the riders were following the river as the young Scot maintained, they could only be headed one way. To Le Col Galliard, one of the few routes over the Graian Alps into Italy.

Eldritch urged his horse closer to the brooding Vicomte, puzzled by his bewildering strategies. Gueldres didn't seem unduly perturbed by the scout's intelligence. Mysterious riders over the horizon, herding the slow-moving legion toward the rat-trap pass? What was the cunning hound up to?

'Did you see banners, colours?'

'Aye, and grand knights in white, like greet silver swans!'

Gueldres raised his eyebrows at the excited youngster's poetic report. Grand knights in white, with the freedom to roam where they willed about southern France? It could only be Bayard. His agile mind considered and discarded various plausible explanations.

But there could be but one sensible conclusion: the grand chevalier was hot on the trail of the foul bandits who had ravaged his abbey at d'Eleron down in Provence.

The only question was whether his unfortunate quarry bore House Tarsi devices or his own – the snarling wolf's head of House Gueldres. Well, that little conundrum would be settled soon enough, he thought drily.

'Captain Savvi, lead the legion on into the valley. You had better fortify the camp, form a wagonburg hard against the north slope – it's steeper on that side, easier to hold.' Savvi frowned.

'And where are you off to?' the bewildered locotenent asked abruptly.

'I'll take a ride over the plain, and see what's become of our dear brother in Christ, Bayard.'

Eldritch, Isolani and Kerr rode just behind the agitated Vicomte, Gueldres' black-coated bodyguard packed in behind them. They could clearly see the trail Kerr's scouts had left in the rocky ground, and followed it straight back towards the pale grey bluffs.

The Vicomte checked his pace as they approached the slope, anxious their pursuers hadn't already beaten them to it. He turned his panting horse into a cairn of tumbled rocks and dismounted.

Eldritch followed the athletic nobleman towards the summit.

They threw themselves down behind a windswept furze bush, shielded their eyes and peered towards the river. The sun was almost overhead, throwing young Dunne's mysterious, white-cloaked riders into stark relief. Just as his own legion stood out like flightless crows in their lamp-black livery, the splendid horsemen bringing up their rear could be seen from miles off. Their slim lances glittered and winked, the devices they bore snapping and cracking in the wind. Gueldres peered to left and right along the ridge, but he couldn't see any scouts. They were clearly trusting in their own arrogant grandeur and the churning white waters of the River Isere to safeguard their progress.

Typical.

It was Bayard all right. He could clearly make out his shining emblems, his close-faced helmet crowned with lancing light.

He'd certainly lost no time in picking up the trail, Gueldres thought sourly. The last he had heard from his far-flung agents, Bayard had been riding hard for the ravaged abbey, galloping through the night at the head of his sworn companions.

The chevalier had been Abbey d'Eleron's principal patron and protector for many years, and the recent massacre would cast a terrible blemish on his spotless reputation.

Gueldres had anticipated Bayard would find himself duty bound to avenge the cowardly attack – he would surely forfeit his precious honour otherwise – but he certainly hadn't expected the chevalier to act with such uncharacteristic haste.

They would never have time to break into Mont Galliard now, not before Bayard had arrived in a blare of trumpets to sort matters out for himself.

Gueldres cursed, realised he would have to revise his constantly-fluctuating plans all over again. Damn Bayard to hell! He took another look at the imperious horsemen as they trotted along the riverside track.

The shining column reminded him of newly-opened clams, their silver harness and snow white surcoats as dazzling as any mother of pearl in the cold afternoon glare.

The Vicomte frowned, pondered the unexpectedly rapid development for a moment. At the present rate Bayard's men would arrive outside Mont Galliard a few hours after his own vanguard. He would hardly have time to set up the damning clues, the bloody evidence which would incriminate his rival Tarsi, set the swine up to take the blame for the piggeries back at the abbey.

Gueldres had laid the most infernal trap imaginable, dug a tiger pit fit for the arrogant Tarsi himself. But the trap wasn't ready yet, the bait not quite ripe enough.

Bayard, Eldritch, Tarsi . . . they all had a leading role in his deadly play. He could set all the lines he wanted, but who would be caught on his cruelly-barbed hooks?

Beside Mont Gilbert le Galliard, in the French Alps

Alberto Tarsi hadn't heard from his daughter Angelica in well over a week, and was becoming increasingly concerned at the outcome of her mission to the Abbey d'Eleron. Surely he would have heard something by now, even if Odo had refused their hopeful application? He had immediately regretted his precipitate decision to send her on such a fool's errand. He and Scaralatchi had hatched the ridiculous idea – they should have followed it through rather than entrusted it to their youthful loved ones. Angelica had brains but little experience of the complexities of court, and her generous, open nature would make her vulnerable to clever men. Tarsi and Scaralatchi had banked on the fact that she would only be dealing with half-men – the abbots and his celibate brothers – and that her apparent worldliness would help balance the scales when it came to striking a deal. Young Ambolini might have had the experience – he had been in the Vatican long enough to acquire all the courtly skills he would ever need – but he surely lacked the patience required for successful negotiation with his elders, especially with officers of a church which had excommunicated his own master. Fabrizio was vain, waspishly temperamental and given to sulking. By God, the boy had been Scaralatchi's catamite for going on four years, how had he expected the youth to turn out?

Tarsi cursed himself for imagining the ill-matched pair would achieve anything at the abbey. They should have

225

ridden directly to Novara, and presented Scaralatchi's reputed masterwork to the visiting papal delegation themselves. They might well have been able to secure some kind of preview of the piece, through a combination of his own forceful negotiating skills, Furstenbein's bland calculation and Strozzi's strongarm methods. If all else failed they could have resorted to a little oil of angels, bribed the crocodile-faced agents and secretaries who flocked about the cardinals like maggots on a ripe cheese.

Ah, it was no use fretting now.

But they fretted anyway, forced into one another's company by their acute sense of guilt and the heartfelt absence of their companions. Angelica and Ambolini had been sent out to recover their reputations while they remained in the subdued safety of Mont Galliard, their unease growing with every passing day. Scaralatchi was morose, spending the evenings drowning his sorrows in sack, alternately snarling with rage or sobbing into his goblet. He reminded Tarsi of the old hands he had so admired in his youth, squatting around campfires entertaining the young soldiers with tales of wine, war and women. But this was his court composer, not some arthritic old landsknecht. It was difficult to reconcile his divided personality, to believe the wheezing fat man was the genius he claimed to be. Tarsi grew more doubtful, slumped in his chambers listening to the slobbering oaf vent his spleen on the devilish methods of the Holy Church.

Why hadn't they heard from Angelica? Surely she could have spared one of the guards to ride back to the pass. Perhaps the messenger had been intercepted? Angelica's carrier pigeons might have fallen prey to a falcon. Peregrines were common enough in the high valleys.

He had spent most of the day pacing up and down outside the fragrant pigeon loft – built into a gallery on the northern tower – peering up at the wintry skies to spot her winged messenger. He had held his breath when he had finally spotted it, a tiny black and white speck winging in along the razor-backed cliffs. The pigeon veered and dived over the outcrops as if guided by some invisible string, beating its short wings rapidly despite its long and trying flight. Tarsi stepped aside as the exhausted bird glided up towards the machiolations and made a perfect landing on the bird-speckled ledge beside the loft.

'Don't scare her off now m'Lord,' the handler advised, waving his impatient chief away from the quietly cooing bird. He had waited another age while the pigeon made up its mind, hopping into the wire entrance and resuming its place in the crowded roost. The handler opened the door a notch and slipped inside, emerging a moment later with the bird cradled in one hand and the tiny silver message tube it had carried in the other. Tarsi had snatched it up and unravelled the brief note.

'Abbey d'Eleron has been attacked. Odo dead, the choir taken. House Tarsi widely reported responsible. Angelica alive, with Briconet and Bayard riding to Mont Galliard from north. Papal delegation now at Aosta with Stroma, forces closing in from south. Suggest evacuating Mont Galliard immediately. More soonest, Furstenbein.'

Tarsi read the note three times, wondering whether he was the victim of some appalling prank. D'Eleron attacked? What on earth for? His fingers trembled as he held the tiny fragment, the brittle rice paper which heralded his disgrace and doom. House Tarsi reported responsible? By whom? Why would the papal delegation assume he had played any part in Odo's death? Terrifying possibilities sprouted in his mind. Gueldres?

He cursed himself blind, tore down the stair to the half-built courtyard bawling orders as he went. He called out the guard, two dozen retainers in House Tarsi livery. He dared not strip any more men from the castle walls, not with the Bastard Gueldres up to his filthy tricks again. He would put out that grasping serpent's eyes, when they met again.

Tarsi had been fuming with rage, his heart beating erratically as he jumped up into the saddle and led the way out of the fortified gatehouse. The narrow causeway dividing the tower from the flanks of the mountain was covered in white scars where Savvi's culverins had blasted out whole chunks of masonry. The blockhouse which overlooked the exposed bridge – and played such a key role in delaying Savvi's assaults – had been partially rebuilt, with new gunports dug for the mad-dog garrison of Spanish arquebusiers. They had lost three-quarters of their number during the vicious siege, but the survivors had shared their fallen comrades' pay, and had seemed please enough with their bargain. Tarsi had decided to keep them on – they were surely more use than half the mercenary troops in the main keep. Tarsi could hear them laughing and singing, holding an impromptu party in the battered redoubt as he led his bodyguard over the narrow causeway and out into the valley.

Angelica alive, he thought furiously. Thank the Lord for small mercies.

The old soldier frowned, wondered how the notorious inquisitor Briconet had become involved with the evil affair. But of course the abbey was under the nominal control of the cathedral at Avignon. Abandando Briconet, papal legate and agent of the Inquisition, would be an obvious candidate to lead any investigation into the attack. The abbey had also been under the personal protection of the Chevalier Bayard, which would explain his interest in the matter. But why should those unlikely allies head for Mont Galliard? Unless they had been given false information as to Tarsi's involvement, set off on his trail by Gueldres' devilish whispers.

Tarsi spurred his horse on down the narrowing pass, great columns of tortured rock towering above the valley floor. He knew he would be trapped like a mouse in a bottle if his unsuspecting enemies could seal either end of the pass. He peered over the rearing cliffs, watched the clouds swallow the last of the afternoon sunlight. It would be fully dark in a few hours: please God he would be able to hide himself in the night, and be granted a precious hour or two to think what on earth he should do next.

The thought of Angelica at the mercy of the deranged Briconet . . .

Tarsi hauled back hard on his reins, cursing his own stupidity as his sweating horse came to an untidy halt in a cloud of dust.

The note might have been an elaborate forgery, dispatched to tempt him out of his mountain hideaway! How did he know Bayard was on his way to him, that his old enemy Stroma was hurrying north from Aosta? The warlord cursed, tugging at his beard as he tried to think clearly. No. He had recognised Furstenbein's handwriting, the tiny characters carefully spaced and as neat as his immaculately-maintained ledgers. The major domo might have been caught up in a blind panic, but he would never compromise his own exacting standards. Furstenbein would not have reckoned the most desperate crisis as a suitable excuse for shoddy handwriting. Tarsi smiled grimly, wishing the worrying Fleming was by his side. Aye, and Strozzi with him. What was his captain at arms doing about this wretched business? Tarsi waved the bewildered escort on into the twilight.

Fifteen minutes later the column was approaching the rock-bound throat of Le Col Galliard. The mouth of the pass was no more than a hundred yards broad, the steep slopes piled with loose scree and long-fallen boulders. The cliffs reared right and left, sheer and black as trash glass, scored and fluted by the ancient glacier which had scoured its own path down the mountains. The clatter of their hooves echoed off the walls, a sinister counterpoint to the hellish fanfares in his brain. Tarsi paused, cocked his head.

That was no echo! He yanked the unfortunate charger to a halt, the horse throwing up a shower of loose stones as its astounded master stared on down the winding trail.

A black-clad army was pouring into the pass, like winter floodwater hurrying along a dust-choked drain. Tarsi gaped, hardly daring to reckon their numbers. The officers were prancing out on dark horses, black and red gonfalons snapping overhead. He saw stands of pikes and long files of arquebusiers, half-screened by the dust they kicked up as they came.

The Chevalier Bayard didn't ride beneath the *blutfahne*. Gueldres! What damned trickery was this?

'Back to Mont Galliard, we're too late!' he cried, tugging the charger about and savagely spurring the beast back the way they had come. His bodyguard, more confused than ever, packed in about their chief, increasing their pace as Tarsi rode hard for the temporary sanctuary of the keep. A trap! Furstenbein's warning note had come within an ace of ruining him, sending him rushing towards the gaping jaws of his resourceful and vindictive enemy. The warlord reined in on the causeway, waving the riders towards the looming mass of the castle. Tarsi whistled at the drunken Spaniards manning the blockhouse, trying to attract their wine-fogged attention.

'Have a care, the enemy is upon us!' he roared. Quizzical faces appeared at the gunports, peering out at him as if he had grown an extra head.

'Light your match, set your cannon! Gueldres is back!' Tarsi snarled, turning his horse and following his rearguard into the fortress.

The reivers had spotted the cavalry heading out of the pass, and had taken off in immediate pursuit when the mysterious horsemen had turned tail and fled. Davey Dunne and young Angus Kerr had whipped their mounts on as best they could, but the nervous fugitives had easily outpaced them, galloping back down the vast crack in the earth as if every fiend in hell was at their heels. Geldray had followed on with his mounted officers, squinting into the drifting dust clouds as their quarry beat a hasty retreat.

The Vicomte sucked his teeth, realised with a surge of savage excitement that his old enemy Tarsi had been moments away from riding straight into his unwary vanguard. The close escape of his deadly rival seemed to invigorate him all over again, banish the worries which had weighed him down that afternoon. The Vicomte waved Kerr's light horsemen on ahead, ordering them to pursue the fugitives up to the fortress gates making as much noise as possible.

Kerr's reivers had obliged with Highland enthusiasm, yipping and hallooing to wake the dead. Their dreadful warcries rebounded from the walls of the gorge, set up a howl which seemed to strike forgotten chords deep within the surrounding mountains.

Geldray peered around at Eldritch, urged him to take his carts after the excitable Scots. The English captain sensed Geldray's almost animal hunger, his feverish determination to regain his stronghold – at whatever cost.

Eldritch knew the grinning Vicomte wouldn't hesitate to climb a mountain of corpses to reach his foe, to cut out the heart of this usurper Tarsi. Daylight was running down fast – and it seemed to Eldritch it was carrying their own future, their very destinies, with it.

Accelerating into the unknown on some fool's errand, risking their lives on the Vicomte's whim? Eldritch was paralysed with doubts, undermined by the desperate uncertainty of their Alpine adventure. And what was this Bayard up to, riding up fast to close the gorge behind them? To drive the heathen English onto Mont Galliard's guns, he presumed. He was acutely aware of his lack of experience. How many times he had been outmanoeuvred by the subtle noble. But this wasn't a game of dice or a contest at the butts.

'What are you waiting for?' The Vicomte snarled, turning his horse in front of the thoughtful captain. 'We've caught them with their hose round their ankles, don't you see?'

'What about Bayard?'

'Ballocks to Bayard! He's no concern of yours. This is between Tarsi and me.'

Eldritch sat back in his saddle, conscious of his comrades riding in the wagons behind him. They would be buying back Geldray's stronghold with their blood.

'Captain Eldritch, I gave you an order! Light your torches, ride hard! You can overturn their defences before they're aware we're here!' he exclaimed.

Isolani loped up, peering down the pass like a hound on the scent.

'Have your man Stitchwort ready with those grenades! Every tenth man to carry a firepike,' Geldray bawled. 'If you get in close enough you can blast the bastards away from the gunports.'

Isolani turned on his heels and ran off to his waiting troopers, apparently satisfied their commander had carefully considered every aspect of his abruptly-altered plans. Geldray glared at the captain, annoyed to find him rooted to the spot. He leaned over his saddle, beside himself with the prospect of delivering the *coup de grâce*.

'Take your wagons after Kerr and use them to screen the fire from the blockhouse on the end of the causeway. Isolani's men will rush the gunports. I'd draw you a damned map but we haven't time!'

Eldritch stared down the gorge, gnawed hollow by uncertainty. He sensed his choices were being snatched away from him, thrusting him into the careless embrace of chance. Doubt was no use to a soldier.

'Get those wagons moving!' Geldray bawled. 'I don't want Bayard claiming the credit for taking my castle!'

'Why should Bayard help you?' he could hardly help the questions popping into his head.

'By Christ, is this how you English serve? Pondering the whys and wherefores before you do what you're bidden?'

The Englishman concentrated hard, trying to look beyond the Vicomte's angry posturing. Why the haste? Why should Bayard be interested in Geldray's precious fortress? The Vicomte's features paled menacingly. This was no act.

'Captain Eldritch, either you will lead your men into the attack or I'll call your friend Kerr back to take over your men. You have your orders, sir.'

Eldritch made up his mind. They couldn't back out now.

'Prepare for action! Fix your boards and batten down your hatches!' he cried, turning his horse along the stalled convoy.

His relieved troopers jumped down from their carts and began unloading the heavy screens which would protect the patiently waiting ox teams. The awkward labour would prevent them from dwelling on their captain's all-too-obvious misgivings.

Geldray turned to Savvi, who had ridden up to see what the commotion was about.

'You take four companies on down the pass and wait for me there. I'll get Muhlberg to form a wagonburg this end, blocking the road.'

Eldritch noticed the red-haired locotenent obeyed his orders without question. Why should they need a wagon-burg? It was Tarsi's men who needed to defend themselves. Geldray gave the Englishman one last stare, and spurred his horse back down the column.

Eldritch braced himself in the open hatch as the clumsy wagon picked up speed, their spine-jarring descent boosted by the rocky slope.

The valley ahead had blossomed with muzzle-flashes and gunsmoke, the sinister tranquillity shattered by the vicious crossfire. Half a dozen sakers and culverins belched and rocked, sent churning roundshot ricocheting around the deadly arena. Eldritch could hardly see their objective – the squat blockhouse was wreathed in smoke, bone-white fur-rows scored in the defiant walls. The garrison was keeping up a spirited bombardment, raking the exposed ground with snarling volleys of shot. Lead bullets and flying chips swarmed like wasps before their nest, furiously stitching through the choking smoke.

A wagon blazed to their right, its slaughtered ox team crumpled up like bloody bone-sacks, impaled on the broken shafts as if they had been snatched up by a great, black-billed shrike. The matchwood cabin had folded up on itself, trapping what was left of the pulped crew in a funeral pyre. Eldritch couldn't tell whether the waxwork dolls were Isolani's arquebusiers or his own Borderers. Their ferociously-roasted flesh had melded them together, uniting them in death.

He held on grimly as the driver tugged their team about the obstacle, the wheels clattering over the ruts hurling the nauseous crew into the panelling. Another squall of shots lashed the rolling smokes, the lead balls beating a hellish tattoo on the vulnerable planks. Eldritch gripped the sides, determined to wait until the last possible moment before ducking back inside the wagon. The light was fading fast now, but he could see the causeway clearly enough. The grey stone seemed to glow in the twilight, illuminated by the flashes of the cannon which had been wheeled up to support their attack.

Geldray was right. They had lost precious moments preparing the wagons for their baptism of fire, whipping the uncomprehending oxen into position for their clumsy charge. The blockhouse reminded him of a penny loaf set on its side, the sooty gunports bored by giant rats. The redoubt was garishly lit by flashes of fire, rocked by hurtling cannonballs which sent up fountains of angry sparks. The fiery smoke was shredded with every shot, blown this way and that by the withering gunfire.

One half of Isolani's harlequin arquebusiers were being carried into battle in the wagons, the rest were following behind, using the clumsy crabs as cover. Eldritch glanced down at the unconcerned oxen, tramping along inside their oaken coffin oblivious to the furious barrage. A bullet scored the oak planking and whined off into the night.

'Driver, left, left! Bring it up under the gunports!' Eldritch yelled. He took one last look at the monstrously-spouting blockhouse and ducked down inside the wagon. Hobby made room for his chief, tugged the hatch over their heads. It settled into place with a satisfying thunk, sealing the crew inside the airless hold. The driver was squatting in front of them, bent down beside the small port cut in the front panel. He had wrapped the reins about his waist, and was guiding the team by tugging the leather one way or the other. It was every inch as crude as Eldritch had feared, but a driver on the running board would have been a sitting duck for the keen-eyed defenders. A rain of bullets drummed against the hull as the wagon began to pick up speed. They must be near the bottom of the slope! Eldritch hung on grimly, eye glued to one of the small spyholes they had cut into the panelling. All he could see was fire and flame. He hoped the wretched driver knew where they were going.

Suddenly, there was an almighty crash which stuffed the hold with sparks and splinters. The arquebusier squatting behind was hurled aside, his mouth smashed by a chance shot. The tennis ball-sized round had crashed through the panelling as if it were rice paper, struck the anxious soldier in the right cheek. The Spaniard slumped down between the legs of his companion, his jaw tangled up in a scorched noose of bubbling muscle. His teeth shone horribly white, pearls in a torn necklace. Blood jetted against the oak planking from half a dozen smashed arteries and veins as the dumb victim thrashed and writhed, hands clawing at his ruined face.

'Get a grip on him!' Eldritch bawled as the driver cursed, yanking the reins to his left. The heavy wagon rolled on its side, Eldritch could sense the right-hand wheels spinning in space. They grasped at one another in terror, deafened by the bellows of the unscathed arquebusier and kicked in the back by his struggling comrade. The heavy wain careered over the dead ground and collided with the blockhouse wall. Steel fittings and swinging chains meshed against the crudely-dressed stone, squealing until the wagon came to a sudden halt.

'Out and at 'em!' Eldritch bawled, flinging the hatch open and forcing himself out of the reeking hold. He blinked against the smoke, the hot stink of burning match. The wagon had hit the side of the blockhouse, the two wheels on the right trapped against a rock ledge which had lifted the mad contraption off its axis and stopped the lowing oxen in their tracks.

The barrel of an arquebus swung out of the smoke like insect antennae. Eldritch grabbed the hot wood and hauled it around. The surprised gunner let out a terrified shout and stumbled away from the gunport, his half-drunken companions hurled sideways by the tremendous impact of a culverin round. Stone chips razored through the smoke, thudding and splintering the panelling. Eldritch hauled himself clear, realising he was crouching beneath the main gunport. Hobby rose out of the stalled cart, his face splashed and spotted by the wounded arquebusier's blood.

'Where's the grenades?' Eldritch shrieked, electrified by the bombardment. He ducked down as an invisible defender jabbed at him with a boar spear, thrusting the glimmering blade through the smoking mouth of the gunport. Hobby handed up a heavy, canvas-wrapped pot. Eldritch grasped it in two hands, held it steady as Hobby lowered a length of glowing match to the carefully-tied fuse.

The stinking pots were Stitchwort's handiwork. The eccentric Englishman looked more like some back-street alchemist than a soldier, with his peculiar leather headgear and soot-scorched eyebrows. But Captain Isolani swore he mixed powder ten times finer – and ten times more power-ful – than the sulphurous muck they had shipped down from Germany. Eldritch noticed his hands were trembling, crouched on the unsteady cart while Hobby squinted at the fuse.

'Be careful where you're putting that match, you beef-witted turd! You'll blow us all to hell if you're not careful!'

'Keep the fucker still then!' Hobby bellowed, lowering the glowing taper to the deadly fuse. Eldritch ducked down as the boar spear scythed the smoke above his head, the spearman thrusting blindly at the foreign voices he could hear over the tumult.

The defending soldier saw something fall from the gun-port ledge, stared down in amazement at the spluttering keg. His comrades threw themselves down. The enorm-ous force of the explosion was trapped within the formidably-built blockhouse, doubling the deadly effect of the pellets, nails and stones Stitchwort had packed into his dangerously unstable bomb. The bewildered defenders, deafened by blasts, half-drunk on cheap wine, were obliterated in a tearing inferno of razor edged destruction.

Alberto Tarsi had a grandstand view of the battle, peering out over a parapet as the harebrained convoy crashed down the slopes towards his impregnable blockhouse. He had been on the point of laughing out loud, tickled at the prospect of being assaulted by deranged peasants in Hussite war carts. The old soldier had watched in disbelief as the enemy commander had marched the larger portion of his black-clad army on down the gorge, leaving the mad fools in their ridiculous carts to waste their lives in a futile demonstration against the walls.

Perhaps the Bastard Gueldres had hired himself some Swiss. Either that or the wain-riding fanatics had been at the rye bread.

'Where's he off to? He'd better support those carts damned quick!' Tarsi called to the grinning master gunner. 'There! We hit one of 'em!' he cried, pointing his drawn sword as the unfortunate vehicle came to a convulsive halt in a welter of flying blood and ox guts.

But his disbelieving grin vanished when he saw the rest of the unlikely contraptions pick up speed about their burning comrade and rumble down the slope. The black-backed beetle trucks careered to a halt beneath the flaming gunports, one wagon snarled against the next in a logjam of broken-axled wrecks.

Tarsi squinted through the smoke, made out a mob of arquebusiers and pikemen hurrying to second the outrageous manoeuvre. The pikemen had fixed long leather buckets to their spears, the devilish contents sparking and spewing flame. Firepikes! The wagons had wrecked themselves under the gunports, giving the attacking troops the cover they needed to cross the bullet-swept no man's land which had defied Savvi's best efforts.

Tarsi felt sick with dread, unmanned by the diabolically sudden attack.

'Get the sakers around! Fire at the blockhouse!' he bawled.

237

The sweat-drenched gunner peered over the parapet at the merrily blazing target.

'That's our men in there!' he cried indignantly.

'Fire at the wagons, fool! Or your . . .'

Tarsi's instructions were drowned out by a cataclysmic explosion. He peered about in time to see the structure lifted from its foundations, the black mouths of the gunports jetting flames twenty feet into the air. The massive detonation sent half of the carts skittering away over the rocky ground, sideswiped like children's toys by the appalling force of the blast.

He reeled back, his face scorched by the intense heat which belched from the ruin. Tarsi choked on the smoke, realised the enemy firestarters must have set off the blockhouse magazine.

The gunners threw themselves down behind the parapet, stunned by the speed and scale of the audacious attack. Their commander fought for breath, his coat singed by flying fragments. His mouth seemed full of powdered acid, the bitter bile of imminent defeat. He knew the foul aftertaste well enough. Tarsi hauled himself to his feet, watched the blockhouse boil, engulfed by its own powder.

The treble-time garrison must have been wiped out to a man.

Beside Mont Gilbert le Galliard, in the French Alps

All their arguments had been forgotten in a muzzle-flash, the campfire mutterings and drunken boasting which had divided the cosmopolitan warband set aside while the men got down to the task in hand.

And what was she supposed to do in the meantime, knit? Sew? Tear up old shirts for bandages?

Merron Eldritch watched the cannonballs describe fiery crosses in the night sky, fascinated and appalled by the shriek of the roundshot. The culverins were blasting the castle's foundations, biting away jagged mouthfuls of the leaning cliffs onto which it had been built. The rockfalls were slowly but surely undermining the gatehouse, leaving great heaps of sooty slag piled about the foundations.

The broad ditch about the foot of the main tower had been partially filled in with rubble, the hot stones sliding into the moat with a diabolical hiss of steam. Merron watched the assault from the relative safety of the wagonburg, sitting up on the running board while old Ruthie the herbswoman muttered and rummaged in the interior. There would be wounds to bind and poultices to apply before the night was out, and the goodwife was busy preparing her favoured remedies, reciting the unlikely ingredients as she worked.

Merron flinched as a massive detonation erupted in the gorge, the very bones of the mountains jarred by the tremendous blast. Even old Ruthie was stunned into silence, opening and closing her mouth as the night air was sucked up in the enormous fireball. Merron covered her face, knocked over the running board by the sudden surge of air.

'By Goar, that were a big 'un,' Ruthie commented, holding on to the chest as the wagon stabilised once more. Merron picked herself up and peered towards the boiling heart of the fire and destruction. A pillar of black smoke was streaking towards the heavens, belching flame and engulfing the billowing warclouds. She opened and closed her mouth to clear the furious ringing in her ears, wondered for a moment where her daft brother had got to. In the thick of things as usual, she imagined.

And Miguel would be out there somewhere in his colourful costume, his bared buttocks no doubt singed black by the flames.

Well it would serve him right and all, chasing about the pass like a mad thing. Nobody had bothered to take the time to tell her what the siege was about; who it was locked up inside the towering fortress and why the Bastard Geldray had ordained they should be trading body blows with them. It was no good asking James – he hardly gave her the time of day. Miguel wasn't much better, babbling on in Spanish when she eagerly pressed him for details of their adventures,

Where was the point in all this fighting? Hobby hadn't a clue, Ruth Malahide didn't give a tinker's cuss one way or the other, and there were precious few others prepared to discuss developments with a silly girl like her.

Merron frowned, acutely bored of the firework show.

She stared at the tower, defiant as ever in its girdle of filthy smoke. The sheer stone walls soared into the sky – she could see tiny orange flashes erupting along the towers as the defenders kept up a one-sided duel with the determined gunners below. The smoke and fireworks would have been devilishly exciting – if Miranda had been here to share the frightening fun. But the warden's daughter had been left back at Calais, reduced from prospective princess to nursemaid by her father's sudden disabilities. Without her friend to share in the excitement, Merron's eagerly-anticipated tour of France had turned to a tedious trudge, a miserable excursion to the ends of the earth. The trek south had been bad enough, but this siege would be even worse. She had been ordered to the rear with the women and the children, waiting about the campfires while the men – her men – played the poltroons under the walls.

Merron picked herself up and glared out of the garishly-illuminated wagon. The weather-worn canvas stretched over the untidy interior glowed saffron, illuminated by the fierce fires raging beneath the castle. The taut screen was busy with swift, sharp shapes – the hurrying shadows of Geldray's legionnaires. The black-clad apes were loping on down the pass – away from the actual fighting, Merron noticed with a flicker of irritation. The Vicomte hadn't committed any of his thugs to the attack on the castle. The girl paused, leaned out to watch the column pick its way down the path. They moved surprisingly quietly when they wanted to, despite their lamp-black armour and clumsy weapons. The sergeants – grim-faced trolls wielding enormous double-handed swords – were hurrying them on through the camp, keeping their men well away from the carnage beside the blockhouse. Some sort of ruse, Merron supposed. She was about to duck her head back inside when she saw a sudden movement over by the big black wagon. Her brother had pointed the great wain out to her during the march from Grenoble, told her its deep hold had been filled with coin to pay Geldray's marauders. She hadn't believed him at first, but it certainly seemed important enough to warrant a constant guard of up to fifty of Geldray's most intimidating troops. The soldiers were on their feet the moment anybody wandered within a dozen paces, ordering the curious camp followers away in their peculiar camp-dialect.

But the wary guards had wandered off – or been ordered along the pass with the rest of the black-coated crew. The treasure wagon stood alone, silhouetted by the flames, every shaft and spar as sharply defined as a raven's wing. Merron narrowed her eyes against the fires boiling up about the wagonburg perimeter, and caught sight of a small child making his way between the black wagon's massive wheels. She could have sworn he'd dropped down from the running board, bent double as if he was searching beneath the wain's oaken belly. It seemed odd Geldray would have gone to such trouble guarding the great wain, if a child could come and go as he pleased the moment the guards' backs were turned. She slipped over the side of Ruth's provisions wagon, her inquisitive nature dangerously engaged by the sneaking youngster. She ducked down behind the water butt, took a cautious peek over the rim. The busy child hadn't seen her. He had ducked beneath the black wagon's hold and was tugging at something hidden up behind the axles. Merron frowned, puzzled at the young thief's brazen forced entry. The abandoned wagon seemed to swell up in her vision. A few stragglers hurried past, oblivious to the mysterious intruder scurrying beneath the wagon. She picked up her skirts and tiptoed towards the wain, tilting her head to listen to the intruder's sinister whispers. His voice seemed hoarse – maybe he had got too near the drifting smoke. No, the little fiend was singing to himself! Merron reached the wheel, fascinated by his warbling commentary. She ducked down and peered beneath the black-lacquered panelling.

And screamed at the hideous, pug-faced monster she found crouching there, his tiny arms clamped about a leather portmanteau.

The little demon stopped singing, sucking his breath with a series of scalding hisses as he glared at the astounded girl.

Before Merron could flinch the dwarf had swung the heavy case at her face, catching her a glancing blow on the jaw which knocked the terrified girl on her behind. The demon scuttled out after her, a knife glinting in his little fist. Merron prised herself away, kicking out at the murderous midget. The dwarf capered away, dancing between her scissoring legs.

'Get away from me! Help! James!' Merron screeched to wake the dead; screamed louder than the bursting shells. Camp followers, cooks and half-deafened servants material-ised out of the drifting fumes, popped out of their merrily-lit wagons like startled bugs. The dwarf growled with rage, his voice as harsh and guttural as a wildcat she had once found trapped by its foreleg in one of the war-den's gins. She kicked out as he swung the blade, tearing at her travel-weary skirt. People were shouting and hallooing all around and the dwarf was panicking. He glanced around, ducked his head and scuttled off beneath the wheels, disappearing into the shadows. Merron sat back and, staring at the packed carts, twisted her head fearfully as her rescuers hurried out of the murk.

'Whatever is it?'

'Captain Eldritch's daft sister! Must have seen a rat or something.'

Merron was dimly aware of dark figures lifting her from the ground, dusting the worst of the grit from her gown. They were either beaming at her with a twinkle in their eyes or muttering to their colleagues, nudging one another in the ribs. She ignored their brusque inquiries, concentra-ing hard and clenching her fists as she tried to control her laboured breathing. Her knights in shining armour began to melt away into the night, convinced she had taken mad from the shelling.

'I saw a dwarf, hiding under the wagon,' she panted. The stragglers had learned to give the wagon a wide berth, and seemed reluctant to investigate any further, despite the girl's furious prompting.

'He took something from underneath. I heard him sing-ing,' she explained testily.

''Tis only a few bangs girl, no need to go wettin' theesen!' one of Howath's ancient retainers observed sourly.

Merron caught her breath and strode back towards the deserted wagon. The camp folk who could be bothered packed in behind her as she climbed up the steps, tilted her head to listen at the closed door. Merron could hear them, whispering and hissing to one another, a whole nest of the little devils! She waved the curious servants closer, lifted the heavy bolt which had been left to secure Geldray's invaded treasure house.

'Watch it, there's more of them in here,' she hissed. Merron held her breath, yanked the bolt back with a rusty squeal and tugged the hatch open. The wagon immediately erupted with frightful screaming. Merron leapt back in alarm as the terrified occupants bolted for the garishly iluminated doorway. The grizzly old retainer – a veteran of half a dozen bloody Border battles – elbowed the girl to one side and thrust his brawny arm across the hatch to trap the shrieking boys inside.

'Hold hard there me beauts!' he yelled, knocking back their gasping hands with his stick. 'Get back there I say!'

Merron peered over the old man's shoulder, relieved to see the hold was teeming with ordinary boys rather than the demons she had suspected. The frightened youngsters were wearing grubby shifts, scraps of blanket and discarded coats, their grubby faces pinched with fear and smudged with dirt and dust. The boys at the front had pressed back into their companions, clutching at their bellies as if they had been taken short with sheer fright.

'Quieten down ye little buggers!' the ancient ordered, cracking his stick against the side of the wagon. The terrified prisoners seemed paralysed with fear, retreating against the far wall of the wagon thrusting their smaller companions to the fore.

'What they sayin'?' the ancient asked, turning towards the intrigued girl for a moment. Merron shook her head, completely bewildered by their barely-comprehensible babble.

'Sounds like French, but I might be wrong.'

'Well? Get back ye little bleeders! We'll not harm yer!'

'They're pleading with us,' Merron announced, cocking her head as the tallest boy took a fearful step forward before falling to his knees, convulsed in terror. He reached up, tugged at her torn skirt.

Merron bent down, took his grubby hand in hers, reassuring him they meant no harm.

'What ye telling him? Get yer paws off her!' the ancient barked.

'Get back you blubbering oaf,' Merron snarled, elbowing the old retainer away from the steps.

'Can't you see they're terrified? He's begging you not to cut his balls off, you ignorant turd!' The ancient stood back, glowering down at the boys as if he was tickled by the bloody prospect. Merron turned back to their terrified spokesman, her fingers pinched in his petrified grip.

'*Nous sommes amis*,' she insisted, trying to pull her hand away. The wild-eyed boy clung to her sleeve, imploring her with his brown eyes. His tears had cut clean channels through the grime on his cheeks.

Merron hardly dared imagine what hells they had been promised, when and if the wagon door was ever opened.

James Eldritch, crouching in a ditch three hundred yards away from his bewildered sister, had made startling discoveries of his own. The arquebusiers in the tower had found their range now and were peppering the shallow trench with bullets, kicking up little whirlwinds of stinging grit. Hobby, Elver and half a dozen others had taken cover beside him, blinking against the sulphurous winds which belched out of the ruined blockhouse. They had brought their bows along, but there was little prospect of a decent target in the midnight murk. Isolani's arquebusiers had given up the one-sided fight and were crouching down with their weapons between their knees, waiting for the fogs to clear before resuming their hopeful sniping against the lower galleries.

Half a dozen of the carts which had carried them into the battle had been smashed to matchwood or set ablaze by the tremendous explosion of the redoubt, the dazed crews huddling behind the ruins, anxiously awaiting the supporting troops.

But the reserves hadn't arrived to exploit their breakthrough, to carry the attack across the exposed causeway and up to the walls. Without the protection of the carts, they could do little but retire the way they had come. And face the Bastard Geldray's vindictive rage.

'Zee 'spectin' us to git on over that bloody bridge by us'selves?' Hobby asked, nervously fingering a specially-honed arrowhead. Eldritch raised his head an inch over the crumbling parapet, took another anxious look at the bullet-riddled causeway. The stone bridge linked the formidable foundations of the keep with the surrounding cliffs. Geldray had assured them it was the only way into the fortress. A bullet whistled off the scarred parapet, screamed off into the night. Eldritch ducked back down, realising they would be shot to pieces before they had gone another hundred yards. He cursed the absent Vicomte to the pits of hell. Geldray had set them up for this, hurled them into his own private war with this Tarsi character. But he would be damned if he would waste the Ride in pursuit of somebody else's feud, no matter what Geldray reckoned to their courage.

He scrambled down into the ditch and peered back towards the brightly-lit camp. He could just make out the defensive ring of wagons and carts, drawn up on a slight slope across the far side of the narrow pass. He frowned. Where had the damned Vicomte hidden himself? Inside his precious commissariat wagon? Eldritch peered to the left and right, but could seen no sign of Geldray's Black Legion. Four companies of crack troops might have made all the difference, thrown against the walls while the garrison was still reeling from the loss of their blockhouse. What was the strutting turkeycock thinking of? Elver the archer noticed his anxious expression.

'I reckon 'ee knows an easier pass or summat. Took off down th' gorge wi' the rest of 'em,' he reported. Eldritch turned on the undernourished archer.

'What d'you mean? Took off? Where?'

'When we got chucked on uz' arses, I saw 'un riding back that aways with the red 'aired feller. Mayhap they knows another way in?'

'There is no other way in,' Eldritch snapped, realising he

only had the Vicomte's word for that. They certainly hadn't had time for a proper reconnaissance of the approaches. The captain cringed at the prospect of being hornswoggled all over again. The black-hearted bastard had sold them all down the river! Hobby had rolled on his back to follow the bad-tempered debate. He shook his head and jerked his thumb towards the causeway.

'No bugger would dig out a bridge like that, if there was an easier way up behind,' he argued with his usual gloomy logic. 'And why stick a blockhouse this end, if old Gelders can get five 'undred men in the back door?'

Eldritch frowned, slightly reassured by the experienced sergeant's gruff assessment. But his prickly sense of relief was spoiled a moment later when Elver gave an anguished shout and pointed back over the burning wilderness.

Eldritch twisted about, squinted through the smoke towards the abandoned laager.

'What is it now?' he hissed.

'Riders, coming down behind us.'

'In another moment Eldritch made them out too. They weren't exactly inconspicuous in their immaculate white mantles. The leaders came on in a tight arrowhead, helmets lowered and lances at the ready.

The Chevalier Bayard had caught up with them at last.

Their trumpets blew a brazen fanfare which rebounded in hellish echoes down the pass. Eldritch had doubled back towards the merrily-blazing blockhouse and found Captain Isolani crouching beneath an upturned wagon. He was sitting splay-legged, his dark eyes watching intently as one of his arquebusiers tied a crude dressing about his gashed forearm. The Spaniard gave him a lopsided grin.

'You've seen our reinforcements then, Capitano El-Dreeg?' Eldritch nodded grimly.

'Bayard. Geldray said he was on our heels. What in the name of hell does he want?'

Isolani cocked his head, listened to the rasping blasts of Bayard's heralds.

'I would venture to suggest the brave chevalier would like a word with the author of this charming diversion,' he said in his sardonic, heavily-accented English. Eldritch grimaced.

'Geldray's buggered off along the pass. He's left us to it,' he reported.

Isolani shrugged, apparently unconcerned by their bewildering predicament. Did the cock-happy Spaniard know something he didn't?

An arquebusier shouted a warning in Spanish, raised his weapon as a vanguard of white-clad crusaders spurred their horses into the arena. They trotted along the track, placing themselves between the alarmed camp and the assaulting soldiers. They didn't appear to be overly concerned at the risk they were taking, riding into the middle of a bloody battle as if they were back on parade at Guisnes. Eldritch hadn't actually met the legendary chevalier himself, but like everybody else in France he had heard a great deal about him. Judging by the self-assured smirk with which they rode forward, the chevalier had rather too much regard for his own reputation.

Eldritch watched the herald steer his horse between the carts, disdainfully examining the huddled corpses strewn in the no man's land between the cliffs. Eldritch helped Isolani to his feet and the pair of them stalked out to greet the arrogant messenger. Bayard's man wore a spotless white surcoat, white hose and long, pointed boots of supple white leather. The tapering toes were secured by a fine silver chain to his gleaming shins. The blank-faced Frenchman wore his hair in a cruelly-cut tonsure, clipped up high about his prominent ears. He regarded the scarecrows down his beaked nose. Isolani's arquebusiers menaced the herald on all sides, but the flamboyant messenger didn't seem in the least put out.

'I am the Mouth of Bayard,' he said in a rather shrill falsetto. 'I am instructed to bid you cease fire forthwith, and attend upon my master.' Isolani glanced at the Englishman, who was scratching his chin with all the careless dignity he could muster.

'Your master finds us engaged in a trying siege,' Eldritch

replied in halting French. 'Perhaps he would like to wait until we have carried out our orders and received the surrender of this castle.'

The herald looked pained by the Englishman's pronunciations. He shook his head.

'My master travels in company with Briconet of Avignon, in the name of Francis I, King of France and His Holiness Leo X. I believe his instructions supercede your own, captain,' he said witheringly.

Eldritch took a threatening step forward. The herald blinked, but his overweening arrogance prevented him from imagining that Eldritch would dare lay a finger on him. The captain grabbed the herald's bridle, gave the snorting horse an abrupt tug.

'Go tell your master *our* master has proceeded on down the pass. Perhaps he would like to take the matter up with him,' he growled. The herald bristled.

'And who, pray, is your master?'

'The Vicomte de Toinueill.'

The herald smiled.

'Come sir, you must know we have intercepted your messengers, or at least, the packages they bore. We know you to be in the service of Alberto Tarsi, Condottieri.'

Eldritch grinned, showing his teeth.

'Well if that be so, perhaps you could explain why you find us presently engaged in laying siege to Signor Tarsi's castle?' Eldritch asked triumphantly. But the herald hardly blinked at the captain's sullen inquiry.

'Sir, we have intercepted all the correspondence which has passed between you these last weeks. Tarsi employed you to carry out a certain mission on his behalf. You fulfilled your end of the bargain; Signor Tarsi did not. Which is precisely why, sir, we find you presently engaged in besieging his castle.'

Eldritch's smile slipped a notch, disconcerted by the herald's bland self-assurance. Eldritch stepped from one foot to the other, scratched his nose.

'What correspondence?' he asked at last.

Beside Mont Gilbert le Galliard

Eldritch thought furiously, racking his brains at the bewildering conjunction of fortunes while smiling beatifically at the scowling herald. He longed to punch the insolent dog on the snout, but he knew the brigand's way out would see them all dead by nightfall.

'Captain Isolani, please take yourself around our siege-lines, and inform the men they will immediately pull back to the wagonburg to await further instructions,' he ordered curtly — with far more assurance than he actually felt. The Spaniard held his level gaze for a moment, nodded and trotted off towards the quietly fuming trenches. Eldritch glanced up at the herald, who was making a minute examination of their arms and equipment.

'War carts?' he asked, suppressing a snort of laughter. The Englishman grinned good-naturedly. Let the French prickster think what he liked. He needed time, time to think! Why would Bayard believe they were serving Tarsi? Did they imagine the blood spilled on the scorched stones was fake? Some concoction boiled up in one of Ruth Malahide's cooking pots? They had blown up the block-house on the causeway, opened the way for what ought to have been a straightforward assault on the gatehouse. Hardly the work of soldiers in Tarsi's pay, Eldritch would have thought.

But the herald had second-guessed them. He seemed marvellously well informed of their situation — a damned sight better informed than he was, that was clear enough. Eldritch's bowels turned over. His growing sense of foreboding had completely extinguished the fire of battle which had burned in his belly.

'I don't know what you are talking about,' he said blankly. 'We are bound to serve the Vicomte. He ordered us to attack the castle, and I am sure he will be only too pleased to clear up any misunderstanding.'

The messenger smirked to himself.

'Misunderstandings? You . . . but I have said all I was bidden to say,' he decided, glancing over his shoulder at his patiently-waiting bodyguard as if he would say a sight more if called upon.

'You will call your men off, confine them to the camp and attend my master forthwith.' Eldritch made a face, carefully calculated to convince the arrogant messenger he was as subservient as the herald himself. He didn't have to try too hard.

'I must have time to alert my master the Vicomte. I have no doubt he will be anxious to explain the situation in person.'

The herald raised his chin in acknowledgement and turned his horse. He followed the attendant knights back towards his master's camp, swinging in his saddle like some cocksure squire entertaining the ladies. Eldritch gave him an ironic salute and turned back to the battleground, wondering what on earth to do next.

Bayard's herald finished his report, bowed low and backed out of the chevalier's hastily-erected pavilion. The company had set up camp half a mile from Mont Galliard, and waited for their infantry and wagontrain to complete the rapid march up from Provence.

The superb host Gueldres had spotted from the ridge that afternoon was but the vanguard of the formidable force Bayard had collected to punish the perpetrators of the massacre at the Abbey d'Eleron. As well as his own immaculate escort, Bayard had enlisted the services of half a hundred lords and knights, complete with their retinues. Mailed spearmen, peasant pikemen and veteran Gascon crossbowmen had toiled after the fabulous crusaders, choking on the dust thrown up by their chargers.

Their masters had sworn an oath never to rest until the mad dogs responsible for the outrage at the abbey were brought to swift and immediate justice.

The chevalier's careworn features were furrowed with fatigue, his eyes swollen in their shadowed sockets. His long lashes were clogged with grit which he wearily wiped away on the back of his gauntlet, staring at the minute fragments as if he was reading his own destiny in the dust. The urgent chase from Dijon had crucified him and almost killed his silent companions. They had barely rested, laying prostrate beside the road while the hollow-eyed squires and grooms brought up fresh horses. He had snatched what sleep he could, propped in his high-backed saddle like a sack of flour, mile after mile of sun-baked hillside and broken-backed plain. He barely managed to lift his aching head as Briconet coughed politely, anxious to elaborate on the herald's laconic report.

'My Lord Bayard,' Briconet observed, an unstable compound of grovelling humility and savage temper. 'Here we have all the evidence we need: clear proof of the Englishmen's guilt,' he said, bowing his head as if astounded by their continued existence. Bayard noticed his gleaming tonsure was coated in a fine layer of dust. 'Surely the time has come to strike at the serpents, to grind the filthy robbers of d'Eleron beneath the boot of the mighty Chevalier?'

Briconet folded his hands into his voluminous sleeves. He tried to preserve an air of sublime indifference, but Bayard could still make out the agitated palpitations of his fingers – drumming against his arm beneath the rough sacking.

'Is it not as the letters suggest, they have fallen out over the spoils like the bloody vagabonds they are?'

Bayard sucked his cheeks, his weary brain barely able to follow Briconet's twisted logic, let alone ponder the motives of the renegade English. The scouts had spotted the undersized messenger trying to slip out of the pass to the north, carrying the offending documents in his satchel. The leather portmanteau had been almost as big as the messenger himself, according to Briconet's colleague Monsieur Souris, who had happened to be riding nearby when the outriders had raised the alarm.

Bayard blinked to clear his vision, rubbed his palms into his eye sockets.

'Tarsi sent English mercenaries to capture the choir and return them to Mont Galliard,' he said slowly. 'The English carried out their end of this hellfire bargain, but Tarsi refused to settle their account, and so the English turned on him.'

Briconet shook his head at their disgraceful record.

'I pray to God His Majesty Francis I will one day rid our shores of these upstart English, these unholy *Transmarini*,' he said piously. 'Not even a Turk would make such a hellish bargain.'

Bayard nodded.

'But why on earth should Tarsi send his own flesh and blood to d'Eleron if he was prepared to employ such methods in his extremity?'

'Precisely because he was *in extremis*, my Lord Bayard,' Briconet said smoothly. 'His daughter was relying on being able to persuade our dear brother Odo to release the choir into her father's service. Failing that, she had banked on being away from the abbey before the attack took place.' Briconet shook his head in dismay.

'The fact we arrive to find the *Transmarini* banging on Tarsi's door demanding their pay confirms the whole disgraceful tale, though I confess, I would never have expected to hear such a demonic catalogue of criminality.'

Bayard shook his head in reluctant acknowledgement. Certainly these English had displayed remarkable ferocity during their bloody march down the Rhone valley. Half a dozen villages had been put to the sword, the fields strewn with their slaughtered inhabitants. If he had been ten years younger, Bayard would have snatched up his lance and ridden directly into their encampment. But Bayard was older and wiser now, as well as stiffer in the joints. He well remembered the fiasco at Bomy, when the French nobility had once again been humbled by the filthy English, sent spurring from the field in abject defeat. He himself had been captured and ransomed, subjected to a dishonourable parole by his grinning captors. He would never make the same mistake again. The English might be dirty, verminous mongrels, but only a fool rode into battle against them without adequate attention to the ground. He knew in his bones there was more to this conumdrum than met the eye. Souris, for instance, Briconet's myopic clerk.

How had he come to be riding at the head of the column, accompanying the scouts as they reconnoitred the narrow entrance of Le Col Galliard? How on earth had he managed to spot the fugitive dwarf hiding among the loose rocks and tumbled boulders about the mouth of the pass? He had been unusually fortunate to spot the midget creeping in and out of the shadows – and to alert the dozing troopers to his presence.

Sadly, the miserable trickster had managed to hide himself away in a fissure, but not before he had dropped his dispatches. The signed, sealed and delivered evidence of Alberto Tarsi's guilt. The letters were clear proof of Tarsi's involvement, the wax seal had been stamped with his own signet ring. But the rogue's daughter had insisted the robbers had stolen the ring during their attack at the abbey. The letters might be an elaborate forgery, aimed at incriminating the innocent Italian.

Bayard sighed with fatigue.

'You heard the herald, Monsieur Briconet. The English captain claims the Vicomte de Toinueill is his master.'

Briconet smiled evilly.

'Exactly as he was primed to say,' he said triumphantly. 'Remember the Tarsi woman under our interrogation. Presented with overwhelming evidence of her guilt she too blamed this unfortunate Vicomte. If only he was here to lay these scurrulous lies to rest, I am sure my Lord Bayard would find it all the easier to search his heart for the truth.' Bayard's tired eyes flashed with their familiar fire. Briconet hesitated, aware he had gone too far.

'Meaning no offence to you, my Lord. The Chevalier Bayard's reputation for dispensing justice is rightly legendary. But allow a humble servant of the Inquisition to observe how the purest heart can sometimes – in complete innocence – overlook evidence of the vilest nature. In short, my Lord, you might not imagine what some men are capable of, whereas I, Briconet of Avignon, have been obliged to swim the foulest waters, to lift the filthiest rocks in order to locate the dark secrets which coil so close within inferior hearts. I am all too aware what men like Tarsi are capable of.'

Bayard grunted in annoyance. 'The Englishman said he would be coming along shortly. They can't get away from us now, that's certain.' Briconet looked pained.

'Assuredly not, my Lord. But I believe an instant assault, an immediate charge by your brave Gendarmes, will scatter the fiends as they deserve.'

Bayard sat back in his stiff-backed chair.

'You might have the edge on me when it comes to interrogating prisoners,' he said, making a veiled reference to the inquisitor's frightful methods, 'but allow me to decide what tactics to employ on the battlefield. These are Englishmen. I have charged into narrow valleys after their kind before now, and lived to regret it. Many of my comrades were not as fortunate as I.'

Briconet nodded, smiled serenly.

'I would not presume for a moment to suggest tactics to the great Bayard,' he said. 'But is it not possible they might be scuttling away into the rocks, hiding their wretched selves from your bright lances?'

'Like the dwarf you mean? As far as we can tell, there was just the one midget, the rest seem fully grown men.'

Briconet showed his teeth at Bayard's sardonic sally. 'Even so my Lord . . .'

'There is no point in riding in there, in the dark, to be

shot to pieces in some confounded trap. We know well enough where they are,' he said finally.

It was some time after three o'clock in the morning, by his reckoning. The blockhouse was still burning, casting a lurid light over the pass. The soaring rock faces resembled twists of bitter toffee, the sheer cliffs the grey faces of diseased old men. Scaly skin stretched over crumbling bones and yawning fractures.

But Eldritch knew there was no way through, out or over the formidable mountainside. The only escape would be down the pass, abandoning their entrenched encampment and attempting to outrun a mounted enemy while burdened down with weapons, women and wounded. He had dismissed that possibility out of hand as he hurried about the confused camp, trying to get the bewildered company into some kind of order.

Isolani had obeyed his instructions, had the assaulting troops pull back to the main wagonburg. They had heard ragged cheering from Mont Galliard as the relieved garrison realised they were retiring for the night.

'Never mind Mont Galliard,' Eldritch had snapped. 'That's the least of our troubles. We're stuck between a rock and a hard place now,' he reminded the Spaniard. Isolani had shrugged, as if every battle he had ever joined had been interrupted by the arrival of a third set of bloodthirsty combatants. 'Geldray's buggered off with his rogues, left us to face Bayard. If we don't hurry along and see him soon, he'll be riding in here with two hundred Gendarmes.'

'Not if he has any sense, Capitano El-Dreeg. We still have half a dozen serviceable carts and any number of ordinary wagons to form a perimeter, just like those Hussites of old, eh? Bayard would be cutting his own throat, riding down the pass.'

Eldritch rubbed his chin, gloomily contemplating Isolani's assessment. As far as he could gauge, the pair of them had about three hundred men left on their feet.

Between thirty and fifty had been wounded in the initial attack on Galliard, and there were an equal number of non-combatants with the baggage train. As well as his stubborn sister, Eldritch reminded himself. He looked up sharply as Merron came skipping along the perimeter of the wagonburg, her skirts hoicked up about her legs. Eldritch closed his eyes. He couldn't trust her to remain in the wagon, not even in the middle of a damned battle!

'James! Thank God, I've been looking everywhere!' she cried, resting her palms on her knees, breath sawing between her spittle-flecked lips. Isolani slipped his paw beneath her elbow and helped her stand. Eldritch frowned at his familiarity.

'I thought I told you to . . .'

'The wagon!' she panted. 'The black wagon you told me was full of gold! It's not. Geldray brought a choir with him,' she explained breathlessly.

Eldritch waved his hands.

'I've no time for your fun and play now Merron,' he began. His sister ignored his indignant objection.

'Geldray captured the choir at an abbey in Provence. They killed the monks and burnt it to the ground! They told the boys they were rescuing them from a butcher named Tarsi, who wanted to cut off their ballocks and . . .'

'Whoa girl!' Eldritch cried, stepping between her and the Spaniard. 'This isn't the place for telling tales!'

'It's not a damned tale! Go and see for yourself, a dozen choirboys beshitting their shirts because they think we're working for this Tarsi!'

Eldritch tried to concentrate on his sister's insistent sobs. Tarsi? The herald had understood they were working for Tarsi, and Merron's mysteriously misplaced choir had thought the same. He bristled with unease, realising the elaborate hoax could only be the work of one man – Geldray!

He shivered with frustration, fists clenched at his sides as he tried to think his way through the baffling puzzle, the trap Geldray had led them into. Merron was babbling on, energetically pointing to the wagon.

'Geldray had it watched all the way from Grenoble: nobody was supposed to go anywhere near it. Then Geldray marches all his *Band Nere* off down the pass, leaving it high and dry with us. I went over to have a peek and saw this dwarf,' she shuddered with revulsion, unaware of the closeness of her own escape, 'I went to ask him what he thought he was doing, fiddling around beneath the wagon – and he went for me, with a knife!' Eldritch wasn't really listening.

'The boy, Giacomo. He was the head chorister at the abbey. They were taken almost two weeks ago; they saw the abbey burn! The men who took them wore black, black all over. Geldray did it all right, but he told them he'd rescued them from Tarsi. He said he'd saved them from being castrated! He showed them letters, sealed letters, to prove it!'

Isolani scowled, muttered something in Spanish.

'But why not take the choirboys with him? What do we want with them?'

'They've been left behind,' Eldritch waved his hand distractedly, 'to prove our guilt. To implicate us in the attack on the abbey.'

'It's going to look pretty bad for us if they find us in charge of them,' Merron piped up. Eldritch realised his sister was right. They had been left with a wagonload of living evidence, left to face whatever accusations had pursued them into the pass.

'We must go directly to this Bayard, this chevalier,' Isolani snapped. 'Let him get to the bottom of it!' Eldritch held his arm.

'He's been drawn in like the rest of us, don't you see? Geldray's off into Italy, leaving us to face the chevalier alone. God alone knows what Bayard thinks we've done, but it's bound to have something to do with the abbey, these boys.' The Spaniard's usually cheerful expression crumpled with doubt.

'But what? What are we to do? Take cover behind the wagonburg and pray for the winter?'

'Wait. For God's sake let's think a moment,' Eldritch ordered himself. 'Geldray's been one step in front of us ever since we left Guisnes. He's been planning something like this all along, and now he has us where he wants us, up against the wall here.' He peered over the deserted trenches, over the blockhouse towards the lantern-lit mass of the castle. 'There are two men that might have a clue what's going on. Geldray for one, and Tarsi there, for another.' He pointed towards the silent keep, its galleries eerily lit by tiny pinpoints of light. Isolani growled into his beard.

'And what is he going to do for us? We have just slaughtered half his men!' Eldritch forced himself to think clearly, calmly. He knew they would be dead for sure, if they didn't start taking lessons in statecraft from their gifted master the Vicomte.

What would Geldray do now? That was the question.

He'd look around; he'd discover a way out, dig himself one if necessary.

'We have to get in to see him, to warn him he's in as deep as we are.'

'Bayard won't wait all day! It'll be sunup in a few hours!' Isolani exclaimed, his Latin bravado completely undermined by the conspiracy.

'Well then we'll have to hold him up a while,' Eldritch announced. 'Get everybody back behind the wagons, my archers to shoot at long range, your arquebusiers to fire only if they ride too close. With a little luck Hobby'll be able to hold them out of range before we kill too many of Bayard's men.' Isolani looked doubtful.

'For the sake of Christ, Isolani, they'll hang us as soon as look at us if we're not damned careful! Don't hurt *any* of them until you've absolutely no choice.'

He pointed at the four culverins Geldray had transported to the pass, only to abandon them when he had made his hasty withdrawal down the gorge.

'Get your man Stitchwort to double load those cannon. Bread, wood, turf, anything to make a good loud bang. I haven't met a Frenchman yet who'd ride down the throat of a loaded culverin.'

'Bread?'

'If we open fire with roundshot they'll be all over us; it'll be over in a few hours. They'll never forgive us for slaughtering their men, whatever the rights or wrongs of our case.' Isolani nodded, apparently resigned to their fate.

'We must keep them at arm's length. Don't kill any of them until you've got to,' he repeated. The Spaniard narrowed his eyes.

'Trust me. Keep them away however you can for as long as you can. If it comes to blows, give up before you spill any more blood.'

'Hah! We Spanish . . .'

'I'm in command here Captain Isolani!' Eldritch barked. 'Damn my eyes sir, you'll do as you are told!'

Merron jumped back at her brother's outburst. Eldritch calmed himself.

'Do as I say; buckle yourselves in behind the wagons and keep your heads down. I'm going to try and get in to see our dear friend Tarsi.'

The soldier in question had remained at his post in the gallery which ran the length of the gatehouse tower. The tiled floor was pooled with blood, the sticky splashes scuffed and smeared where his anxious soldiers had slipped on their comrades' gore. Half a dozen of his hired gunners had been hit by flying splinters, cut down by rock chips hurled into the air by the pummelling bombardment. Cracks had already appeared in the stable wall – through five feet of well-bedded stone. Mortar dust had coated everything and everyone with a sinister white shroud, reminding all but the most resolute of their own mortality. The shocking speed – and initial success – of the last assault had surprised Tarsi and demoralised many of his remaining men. The terrible explosion in the blockhouse, and the immediate extinction of a fifth of his available manpower, had sapped the will of all but the most devoted Tarsi retainer.

The rest, hired hands and canny mercenaries, would only stand so much slaughter. He might offer them all the coin in Europe, but money was no good to you if you were lying in a shallow grave in a remote Alpine pass. But the looming crisis had been averted, the lightning assault which had spread such havoc abruptly called off.

Instead of being trundled up over the causeway to fire point-blank at the heavily reinforced gate, the culverins which had caused such damage had been left idle, the gunners taking cover in the bewildering chaos of the enemy camp. Tarsi, keen-eyed in his mountain hideaway, had watched the bulk of Gueldres' legion march away down the pass, sending them on their way with as many roundshot as his sweating gunners could manage. He had hardly considered the rearguard he had left behind worth worrying about – a few hundred fools shut up inside their oak coffins, hurling themselves down the slope in a comic charge worthy of old Ziska's Hussites. But their hare-brained courage had wiped the smile from his face in a moment. By the time he had registered the danger to his outer works, the fiends had thrust charges into the block-house and wiped the garrison from the face of the earth. The cautious soldier squinted through the smoke, trying to follow their baffling manoeuvres.

After an interminable stand-off, the rogues had drifted back towards their wagonburg, apparently content with their night's work. What was Gueldres thinking of, allowing him such a respite? Tarsi had brought up extra troops from the inner keep, moved his lighter guns to the threatened sector and had his pioneers begin to shore up the crumbling walls in the basement. His retainers had worked like ants to prepare the castle for the deadly struggle to come.

And then more puzzling developments.

A company of knights, resplendent in their shining white surcoats, had followed the rag-tag warband into the pass, and set up their own camp half a mile from Gueldres' rearguard.

Bayard, just as Furstenbein had forecasted.

But the two forces hadn't united to launch a new attack. They had faced off as if they were about to come to blows over the mountain prize – unless it was another of Gueldres' endless tricks. Tarsi hardly knew what to think.

Now though, with the first feeble glimmer of dawn illuminating the rocky summit of the cliffs opposite, he knew the long-delayed attack would be released in earnest. Perhaps it was time to seek out one of little Luciano's tunnels, and save his skin while he could. Tarsi was a realist, and had never been one for foolish gestures. If fate had decreed he would lose his home this day, so be it. But he would not contemplate a pointless death, hacking about in the ruins of his ever-hopeful empire.

'*Padrone!* Enemy skirmishers in the ditch!'

Tarsi had been half-expecting the warning shout. He crossed over to the battered parapet and took a peek between the machiolations.

He could see the enemy archers working their way forward, taking cover behind one of the burnt-out wagons they had left on the causeway.

Tarsi rubbed his eye, peered closer. One of the rogues had torn off his shirt, and was waving it above his head on a broken pike.

By God's bowels, Gueldres was toying with him even at the moment of his victory!

'Have a care! There'll be more of them any moment!' he warned. The weary troopers stationed in the gallery prised themselves to their feet and dusted off their weapons. They went to their posts like dead men.

Tarsi cursed under his breath.

'They're waving!'

What?

Tarsi peered down at the corpse-cluttered causeway. A tall captain in a filthy white surcoat was striding over the bridge as if he already owned the pass, the Tudor rose emblem on his chest shining brightly in the weak sunlight. He went bareheaded, long black hair pulled back from his severe features.

He was a long way from home, this Englishman.

His servant picked his way along behind him, holding the dirty flag aloft. He seemed to be trying to keep the arrogant officer between him and the sharpshooters in the castle.

'Hold your fire!' Tarsi called. The newcomer walked out briskly, a longbow stretched over his broad back, one arrow free in his fist. The scowling captain paused, held the arrow up in some bizarre demonstration. Tarsi noticed the quiver he wore around his waist was empty. Some kind of peace gesture then. Perhaps the bastard had come to demand his surrender.

But surely Gueldres would have reserved that pleasure for himself?

Well, perhaps not. The Vicomte was far too clever to make such a target of himself. The Englishman had come within fifty paces of the battered wall. Maybe he was spying out the damage? He was shouting something. In French.

'What? He comes in peace?' one of the Gascon crossbowmen sneered, raising his weapon. 'I'll give the bastard peace all right.'

'Hold your fire, I said!' Tarsi shouted. The intruder was making a great play of wrapping his remaining arrow in paper. The captain peeled the longbow from his back, nocked the message arrow and raised his arm.

'He's going to shoot!'

'He's firing a message, you turd! Leave him be.'

Tarsi watched the unlikely errand boy loose his arrow. It rose into the dawn sky, turned over gracefully and flew over the battlements, skittering away over the stones.

'Let's have it here!' Tarsi called. A lightly-wounded arquebusier lifted the heavy arrow and tore the parchment from the point. He seemed appalled by the six inch bodkin, running his thumb over the razor barb.

Tarsi snatched the note and tore it open. The Englishman's spoken French was bad enough, his written French almost indecipherable. 'Incoming peace you are on. I friendly yours am (underscored). My enemy is on top of your enemy.' Tarsi shook his head, agitated by the Englishman's terrible grammar. He strode back to the battlements and peered down at the anxious soldier.

'What do you want?' he bawled in heavily-accented but quite clear English. The intruder waved.

'We need to talk!'

'Hah! Go tell your master Gueldres he'll have to try harder than that to get in here!' Tarsi bellowed.

'He's no more my master than you are!' the spirited captain roared back. 'He's tricked the both of us!' Tarsi shook his head in contempt at this feeble sally. Is that the best the rogue could come up with?

'He's walked out, left us with this damned choir!'

He'd done what? Tarsi struggled to decipher the captain's furious bellows. Left them with the choir?

Tarsi opened his mouth and then paused for a moment, the flimsiest outline of an explanation beginning to materialise in his weary imagination. Slowly, the glistening filaments stitched themselves together – names and events crystalising in the chaotic floodwaters which ran about him. The choir?

'We stand accused of kidnapping the choir – in your name!' the captain shouted. 'He's tricked the both of us!'

'Drop your weapons and come forward!' Tarsi roared.

He needed to speak to this arrogant Englishman.

The Chevalier Bayard watched the sun peek over the clifftops, the dawn light throwing twisted scarves of silver and gold over the soaring rock faces. He crossed himself, giving thanks to God he had lived to see another blessed day. The knight finished his earnest devotions and picked himself up from his knees. Briconet made a play of crossing himself.

'The rogue. He will not come. What can one expect from a back-stabbing Englishman? They have no honour,' Briconet observed. Bayard raised his chin, ran his fingers over the stubble he found there. They had waited up half the night for the English officer to show himself, to obey the herald's invitation. The foot soldiers had arrived, dusty company by dusty company. The wagons had creaked and clattered into their camp, bringing food and water for the weary troops. His knights, crossbowmen, gunners and skirmishers had snatched what sleep they could while their masters paced their pavilion.

Briconet had urged an immediate assault, a bloody charge through the enemy's matchwood defences. But Bayard had ruled out such foolish heroics. For one thing, he was far from satisfied the bloodthirsty Briconet had correctly assessed the facts of the case.

It was no good interrogating corpses, after all.

'I didn't think he would,' Bayard said simply.

Briconet tried to hide his frustration, nodding his head in wise agreement while he seethed with restless energy. Bayard saw straight through him. Here was a true disciple of Torquemada, an unquestioning devotee of the fanatic Bernardo Guy – bloody high priests of the Inquisition.

Briconet had inherited all their hysterical ferocity. He remembered the terrified girl, curled up in the corner of her noxious cell back at the abbey, her shift wrenched over her bleeding knees. She had tucked her arms inside the grubby gown as if to protect her skin, huddled herself up with her feet protruding from the ragged hem. The prisoner had shrunk away from him, flinching from his gentle touch as if he bore burning brands. Bayard had been shocked by the terror in her eyes, the gleaming whites criss-crossed by burst blood vessels. He hadn't dared examine her any further. The slowly spreading pool of urine on the stone floor was eloquent testimony to her torment.

Bayard had technically exceeded his authority by forbidding the wretched inquisitor from making any further 'inquiries', but Briconet had not dared to challenge the chevalier. He had ordered his ancient to escort the terrified girl back to his own carriage where she had remained ever since, wrapped in a blanket and hiding beneath the simple planking on which Bayard made his bed.

'He mocks us, my Lord,' Briconet insinuated. 'We

should send in the skirmishers . . .' Bayard held up his hand.

'Do not presume to lecture me on battlefield tactics, my dear brother in Christ,' the chevalier repeated, making the title sound like the filthiest curse. Briconet and others like him had turned huge tracts of countryside into pits of suspicious hatred, neighbour turning against neighbour in their haste to divert the inquisitors. Bayard wondered how many naive peasants had borne false witness. How many had been betrayed, tortured and finally burnt at the stake after being reported to the roving agents by some jealous friend or relative. Just occasionally the terrified peasants would hit back – ambush the agents of the Inquisition or vent their fury on some wandering Hound of Christ. The order he had tried to influence by example had long borne the brunt of the people's anger, whipped into a frenzy by Briconet's infamous methods.

Nevertheless, he had ordered the Englishman to report to his pavilion and he had signally failed to do so. It was time to teach the rogue a lesson.

'Bring up my horse!' he called. 'Crossbowmen to the van, followed by the pikemen of the militia reinforced by one hundred gendarmes on foot. The rest, mounted, about the standard with me.'

Bayard's captains clattered off to their men. Horns blew and horses whinnied. Briconet smiled indulgently.

The Genoese and Gascon crossbowmen came on in three ranks, their arbalests already loaded with heavy, foot-long quarrels. The fearsome missiles would fly through an inch and more of solid oak, and impale a soldier to the man behind. But the clumsy, spring-loaded crossbows were slow to make ready, and the nervous mercenaries in the front rank weren't used to marching into battle first. The French nobles generally placed themselves in the van, leaving the ill-assorted peasants to queue behind them. Maybe old Bayard had lost his nerve? The muttering skirmishers certainly weren't impressed by the sight of the chevalier's famous standard being carried by a hundred and more gendarmes well to their rear.

The host shuffled on, eyeing the rearing cliffs, the loose heaps of scree which seemed to possess a sinister existence of their own, rolling and rattling as they marched past. The ranks parted, the nervous mercenaries looking over their shoulders to see the great Bayard pressing forward.

'What's this? Steady the front rank!' Bayard called. The men gave him an ironic cheer, which rebounded back around the tight gorge and encouraged them on.

'Advance!' Bayard roared, his silver sword raised towards the barricade the enemy warband had hidden behind. The crossbowmen stepped out, increasing their pace as they closed ranks bearing down on the haphazard stockade.

Suddenly, the silent wagonburg seethed with furious life. The enemy troops popped out like rats in a burning barn, raised their arms in dreadful challenge. The astonished crossbowmen checked their pace, tilted their heads at the peculiar *whoosh*.

The arrowstorm landed ten feet in front of them, the yard–long missiles bouncing and skittering over the bare rock or thudding into the patchy vegetation. An old log bristled with bodkin points, its back broken by the fearsome impact. The front rank stopped dead.

'Shit!'

'Who said that? On, on, they cannot even judge the range!' one of their red–faced captains bawled. Bayard glanced at him, unimpressed by his inexperienced ardour. The archers had judged their range only too well. They had deliberately fired short. Why on earth would desperate fugitives waste so many arrows?

The sluggish host rolled forward, compressed by the slowly-closing cliffs, impelled by the pressure from the mounted troops bringing up the rear. There were shouts and curses on all sides. Bayard, good soldier that he was, knew their hearts weren't in it.

'These are the killers of Abbot Odo, the butchers of priests and children,' he shouted. 'Who dares turn their

267

backs on such vermin?' The crossbowmen stepped out again, weapons raised. Another few yards and they would . . .

The wagonburg erupted with orange flame, the narrow pass immediately blocked solid with the screaming discharge. Four guns belched smoke, the terrifying blasts bringing down rockfalls all around them. The front ranks went down under the withering barrage.

And then picked themselves up again, astonished to find their legs and bellies hadn't been blown out by shattering roundshot.

Instead, the enemy gunners had double-loaded their pieces with wedges of loose turf, torn books, even hard-baked bread. The ill-assorted ammunition had battered and bruised the front rankers, but hadn't killed any of them. Bayard held up his sword, mystified by the enemy soldiers' reluctance to come to blows. Outnumbered by a far superior force, the ragged band ought to have been running for their lives by now.

His horse shied as the closely-packed crossbowmnen seethed and writhed away from the rolling smoke. For many of them it was their first taste of powder, and they didn't seem to be relishing the sulphurous stink. Bayard's little army was stuck fast, the terrified wounded trying to elbow their way back through the following ranks, throwing the entire force into confusion. Another volley of stones and rubbish turned the squirming legion into a panic-stricken mob. Bayard held on as his horse was carried up in the flight, lifted from the ground by the sudden press of men.

The last thing he saw before he fell off his charger was a crowd of women, children and servants fleeing the wagonburg. Archers and billmen herding their camp followers out of their temporary sanctuary. He hardly had time to wonder at this puzzling conundrum before he was tossed and tumbled on the shoulders of his troops, kicking and punching and gouging their own way out of the pass.

Bayard could have cried in shame.

'Halt! Stand your ground!' he bawled, carried along like a sack of meal on the backs of the routing mercenaries.

The renegade English must surely have been driven mad by their ordeal, because he could have sworn he had spotted the victorious wagon-riders hurrying towards Mont Galliard.

Beside Mont Galliard

He thought for one dreadful moment the order to evacuate the wagonburg would ruin everything. The weary soldiers looked at one another, unable to believe their own ears. Abandon their defences and take cover in the very fortress they had marched so far to assault? The English bowmen were convinced the idiot Spanish had got it wrong, misunderstood Isolani's bawled instructions. The Spanish were adamant the Engish were about to send them to a slaughter beneath the walls of Galliard, fill the breach with their allies before closing in for the kill.

'Don't stand there gawping Hobby, get them moving! Women and children first, straight over the causeway!' Eldritch bawled, his face contorted with rage.

'Where over the causeway?'

'Where d'you think, you great ape? The Bastard Geldray's tricked us all the long, don't you see? Get them into the castle before those fancy turds yonder realise we're firing rubbish rather than roundshot!'

Hobby jumped to it, dragging his men from the fortified wagonburg and kicking them along the inner perimeter. The broken ground beyond the ring of wagons was littered with discarded equipment and scoured by smoke. The battlefield sloped away towards the ruins of the blockhouse, narrowed towards the slim causeway.

'What's he on abaht? They'll shoot us dahn like dogs afore we've gawn 'alf 'n ell!'

'Get moving Teague, damn your eyes! The castle's our only hope!' Eldritch roared back, propelling the archer along with a swift boot to his backside.

Wilfrid Stitchwort the fireworker was clever enough to work out their peril for himself, calmly loading his well-travelled dogcart while the suspicious soldiers bickered and pointed. He jammed the last few barrels of his specially-ground black powder into the basketwork hold and lifted the shafts with a fierce grunt of effort.

'For Christ's sake give me a hand,' he called, back bent as he tried to manoeuvre the cart through the sullen mob. William Hacker threw down his halberd and snatched up the second shaft, helping to tug the well-laden cart over the strewn ground. He had spent a good deal of time with the eccentric fireworker, and had become his unofficial apprentice during the march through France. Hacker wasn't keen on getting involved with the sharp end of the fighting, but his quick wits made him a handy helper, and he was fascinated by Stitchwort's fanciful stories of rumbling demolitions and crumbling towers.

'It's the last of the good stuff,' the leather-hooded alchemist explained.

'D'you mean to blow the causeway up in their faces then?' Hacker asked doubtfully.

'It's an idea,' Stitchwort admitted. 'But without the causeway we'd be stuck up there like flightless crows, unless our new friend's got a secret passage under the mountain.'

'Well maybe he has at that,' the cheerful scout replied, face flushing with effort as he manoeuvred the cart towards the gap Eldritch was tearing in the wagonburg wall.

'There's no time; make for the causeway!' the captain yelled, helping a couple of bemused arquebusiers tear down the heavy boards which had been positioned between two of his stalled carts.

'Shove this one back, let them through!' he shouted. The Spanish troopers didn't understand his English but they quickly grasped his intentions. Wilfrid Stitchwort drew his head into his wrinkled leather shell and began to drag the cart through the gap.

'What in seven hells are you doing with that?' Eldritch demanded.

'It's the last store of my special blend. It might come in handy yet.'

'Well for the sake of St Peter hurry, they'll be after us in a moment!'

The terrified defenders needed no further urging. They ran for their lives, women and camp followers hurrying to keep up as they struggled along with babes in arms or clumsy bundles of essential goods.

'Come on, we haven't got all day! Save yourselves!' Eldritch cried, hauling soldiers by the scruff of their necks and hurling them on down the slope towards the causeway – their last, precarious lifeline.

Edlritch cursed, trying to master the frenzied chaos which threatened to swallow him and the entire band in one bloody gulp. They were trapped, hemmed in by treacherous enemies, closed down by the rocky-shouldered pass. The wagonburg which had helped them stave off the first onslaught had been set up at the centre of a three-pronged crossroads. To the north, the narrowing gorge climbed towards the soaring, snowbound heights. Bayard's army had disintegrated but his milling soldiers still blocked the passage.

To the south, the toll road wound through sheer chicanes before descending gently towards the main valley. But the warband would never have reached the peaceful slopes on foot – not with a well-mounted enemy snapping at their heels.

Their only escape route lay directly behind them: the slim stone bridge which spanned the gorge, linking Mont Galliard to the outside world.

It was along this fragile corridor which the warband would have to flee. Eldritch watched, heart in his throat, as the first of his troops ran the gauntlet. He realised their frantic commands had succeeded in getting the uncertain herd moving. But the desperate measure quickly turned disciplined defenders into a panic-stricken mob, every man intent on saving his miserable hide. The bowmen and arquebusiers who had stood their ground before Bayard's ill-fated assault were caught up in the rout, clambering over their own defences in their haste to get away. The few officers who were left could do nothing but try and direct the mad stampede, laying about with the flats of their swords as they tried to drive their berserking troops towards the bridge, channelling them towards the unlikely sanctuary of Mont Galliard.

Isolani was knocked aside in a moment, clattered about the forehead by the wildly swinging barrel of an arquebus as he tried to impose some order on the chaotic retreat. He staggered back, pinned against one of the massive wagon-wheels, and would have been trampled underfoot if Merron hadn't been there to haul him down. The wild-haired girl had been carried along in the flood, pulling herself hand over hand down the inner perimeter of the wagonburg. She had just ducked under the dirty belly of one of the wagons in time to tug the dazed captain back by his belt. Isolani lost his balance, landed heavily on his buttocks.

'Get in!' Merron cried, frantically tugging at the Spaniard's dishevelled tunic. Isolani prised himself up into an awkward crouch and scrambled under the wagon as the mob careered towards the narrow gate Eldritch had created. The wagons began to slip and slide, pushed aside by three hundred and more furious troops seconded by their own frantic wives and sweethearts.

The gate gave way at last, a stream of terrified humanity spewing over the slope and running for their lives towards the castle. They weren't sure whether they were being driven to a slaughter, but the promised protection seemed preferable to remaining in the hatefully-exposed pass.

Isolani coughed on the choking dust, dabbed at the bloody gash on his forehead. Merron held on to him, arms crossed about his chest as he panted like a broken-winded nag between her legs.

'We can't stay here,' he croaked. Merron glanced about, spotted the narrow gap beneath the wagon's shot-proof screen.

'This way!' Merron ducked her head to the gap, saw the mass of fugitives streaming away down the slope towards the blockhouse. The smoky ruin was half buried in a litter of smashed carts, as if the English had come to make a bonfire of their precarious bolthole. She wriggled beneath the heavy oak planking, using her forearms to push the board up on its creaking hinges. Isolani lay on his back, propelled himself free with his heels. The two of them rolled out in a shower of choking grit, leapt to their feet and chased off after the fleeing warband.

It had taken the Chevalier Bayard precious moments to recover his footing, but it would require long years of shameful penance to recover his dignity. He had been dragged along like a sack of straw, tumbled head over heels by the crush of soldiers in the pass. Only his bruised and battered armour had saved him from cracking his ribs or splintering bones on the boulders which protruded from the rattling scree. His horse caught him a passing blow as it careered away through the press, sending him sprawling into a tangled thorn bush. Bodies tumbled down on top of him, shrieking and cursing. Somebody trod on his head. His sword had snapped beneath him and his mouth was full of filthy grey dust. He rolled onto his knees, back and pelvis prickled by the thorns which had worked their barbs beneath his expensive plate. The great warrior spat the worst of the grit onto the floor and hauled himself to his feet, jostled and barged by his foolishly-humiliated troops. He found himself surrounded by a gang of nervously-staring crossbowmen, some of them nursing minor injuries, others seeking the weapons they had accidentally discarded during their ignominious flight down the gorge.

Bayard glared at them as if he would melt their hearts

within their breasts. He fumed and cursed, but the dust he had swallowed strangled the sounds, transforming the legendary knight into an eerily-moaning man of the mountains. The crossbowmen shied away, unable to hold his critical gaze. Bayard shook himself off and stalked off through the disordered mob, locating his youthful officers in the confusion and slowly restoring some kind of order to the feeble legion.

Ten minutes later he was back in his pavilion, boiling with anger while his frightened squire pulled and tugged at his jammed fastenings. The chevalier tore his arm free and waved the white-faced herald away.

'Damn your eyes, Mountjoy, leave me be!' he croaked. 'The thorns will remind me of the disgrace I have borne this day,' he said, voice shaking with dangerously-repressed emotion.

Abandando Briconet had wisely evacuated the chevalier's pavilion, leaving him to cool off before he risked poking his head around the tent flap. He found Bayard slumped in his rigid armchair, his armoured legs stretched out before him, his comically pointed toes sticking up like caltrops. His cruelly-hacked hair was white with dust, his hitherto immaculate Maximilian armour scored and grazed by the rocks. His scabbard was empty, his helmet and headdress missing. The papal legate had to press his lips together to stifle a giggle. The great chevalier brought down by a rabble of cutthroats skulking in some Hussite war wagons! It was too fantastical to be true.

Bayard looked up, scowled fiercely as the inquisitor hesitated on the threshold.

'My Lord Bayard. A terrible disaster. May almighty God seek out and punish the craven few who disgraced your arms this day.'

'Craven few? Did you not see their cowardice for yourself? The wretched crew turned tail and fled at the first whiff of powder!' he bunched his fists, banged the arm of his chair. 'You know what they were firing? Bread and books! Bread and books, my dear Briconet!' Bayard snarled, running a trembling fist across his nose. The chevalier tensed, turned his dazed gaze on the gloating devil.

'And what does the Inquisition make of that, eh?'

Briconet frowned.

'The swine had run out of ammunition.'

'Wrong!' Bayard prised himself to his feet, stared into the inquisitor's darting eyes. Briconet grimaced, unused to being so interrogated.

'The craven dogs sought to appease your anger by sparing your men,' he suggested. 'They will throw themselves on your mercy, knowing you to be the gentlest knight in Christendom!'

'No, that won't do at all! They had powder and ball enough to kill the front three ranks with a single volley. You know Briconet, one should always endeavour to learn from one's mistakes. The lessons of Crecy, Agincourt, aye, and Bomy of ill-repute which I have taken to heart.' Bayard tapped his chest and coughed a wad of grey-flecked spittle onto the floor. 'I refused my gendarmes the honour of leading the attack, knowing they would be shot down by the score before they had come to grips. But the scum I sent to do the work of true-hearted men turned tail and fled the moment the enemy turned their cabbage-cannons on them!'

'Scum in truth, my Lord Bayard!'

'Put to flight by slabberdegullions hiding in war crates,' Bayard snarled, shaking his head in disbelief. 'Slabberdegullions who possessed the training and discipline required to hold their fire even in the face of our attack.'

'Fanatics to a man,' Briconet agreed.

Bayard turned on his heel, pressed his dusty face up close to Briconet's ashen features.

'Would fanatics hold their fire when charged by an overwhelming enemy, sworn to bring them to justice for their vile crimes? Would desperadoes capable of cutting down innocent monks and kidnapping children possess the self-control to use bread and books for cannon shot?'

'They must have been drunk, in their delirium they . . .'

'Their archers were ordered to fire short! Ten paces short when they could have cut down my men like new corn! Does that sound like the work of fanatical killers and child murderers, well sir?'

'My Lord Bayard is dismayed by the perplexing defeat, he is understandably . . .'

'Is it true I am perplexed, my dear Briconet.'

'The scum have taken cover within the walls,' the agent reported. 'Even while your men carried you away against your will, the fiends abandoned their wagonburg and fled into Mont Galliard, their master took pity on his misguided creatures.'

'Wrong again!' Bayard cried, his eyes aflame with indignation. 'You have led me to believe that rabble of English bandits was responsible for the outrage at my abbey. You have extracted a pitifully unlikely confession from the Tarsi girl. You have a bagful of letters which might have been counterfeited the day before yestereve, and yet you present it as damning evidence of Tarsi's guilt.' The chevalier paused to catch his breath, holding Briconet's angry stare.

'I wasn't convinced of their guilt, and now I'm almost convinced of their innocence! Guilty men would have opened fire with every round and arrow they had, determined to kill as many of their enemy as possible before they were rounded up and butchered like dogs! They have taken refuge with Tarsi, united in unjust accusation!' he accused, his features flushing purple beneath his dusty mask.

'My Lord Chevalier is mistaken. The evidence clearly shows Tarsi to be responsible! He refused to pay as he had contracted so the English fiends turned on him. Tarsi saw the might of our forces from his battlements, and thought better of his own duplicity. Better to pay out his fortune and drag out our siege rather than have us storm his precious fortress!' Briconet paused, moderating his tone. 'You have suffered a cruel reverse, and your judgement has been understandably clouded by the misfortunes of your men.'

Bayard shook his head.

'*Au contraire* my Lord. My clouded judgement has miraculously cleared. I see, everything,' he said heavily. Briconet smiled weakly at the bizarre transformation. Bayard appeared to have put himself into some kind of trance.

'See all, my Lord?' he inquired. The nervous inquisitor would normally have added, 'you blaspheme sir,' but the shrewd agent thought better of it. 'Perhaps I have been, overzealous, in my desire to see the wrongs of d'Eleron avenged,' he admitted, turning himself from white knight to black bishop in a blink.

Bayard snapped out of his daze, turned his brittle stare on the papal legate.

'I believe we have been hunting the wrong fox. I am deceived.'

'Surely not deceived, my Lord Bayard,' Briconet said hopefully.

'Aye, deceived. Mountjoy, get back on your horse. I want you to carry my personal greetings to this fellow Tarsi, to speak with him at his earliest convenience. If he's as innocent as I think he is, he'll have no objection to answering the charges in person! We will order him to attend a full inquiry into this hideous conspiracy.'

Briconet winced at this unforeseen tactic.

'He'll jump at the chance to lie his nose off and save his neck!'

'He'll be tried sir, by his peers! And now, my dear sir, you will bring your prisoners into my presence, right away.'

'I am afraid the girl is weak, my Lord Bayard. The journey . . .'

'Journey? Your damned attentions more likely! I will not ask you a second time Briconet. Bring the girl to my quarters, now!'

Bayard began to tear at his bruised armour as the seething inquisitor backed out of his tent with a sickly grin. Briconet was cursing under his breath, bursting with righteous indignation.

That Bayard would dare question the word of an inquisitor of the Holy Church! The sneering herald strode off, straightening his surcoat as a groom prepared his dusty charger for his new mission. Briconet watched the youth tapping his ridiculous slipper as he waited impatiently for the boy to adjust his saddle girth.

Damn him and his high-handed master, there was still time to finish this wretched business – clarify their enemy's appalling guilt before too many more unnecessary questions were asked. He turned back towards the mass of soldiers milling like agitated ants about the camp, intent on finding himself some rather more pliable servants. Terror would do where reason had failed!

The nervously-shuffling infantry had pressed most of Bayard's gendarmes back down the pass, separating the heavy cavalry from their supports – a squadron of lightly-armed stradiots. The outlandish raiders were armed with an assortment of weapons – light crossbows, spears and javelins – ideally equipped to ride down a fleeing foe.

There was still time!

Briconet strode towards their chief, a grinning imp with drooping black moustaches and a painstakingly-embroidered, full-length riding coat.

'What in Christ's name are you waiting for?' Briconet cried, snatching at the rogue's jingling bridle. 'Did you not hear the order? Pursue, pursue the cowards! Ride them down before they reach the gates!'

The Croat captain glanced down at the dreaded inquisitor, unable to understand a word he was saying but all too aware of his exalted position in the Holy Church. He crossed himself, nodding eagerly.

'How dare you sit gawping?' Briconet lifted the ornate cross from his chest and pointed it towards the bridge, still jammed with refugees from the abandoned wagonburg.

'Ride them down, destroy them! Kill them all!'

There was one word the Croat understood all too well.

'*Kill?*

'Kill, kill, kill!' Briconet shrieked. The captain smiled,

twisting about in his fantastical saddle to bawl something at the misbegotten crew slouched behind him. The inquisitor jumped back out of the way as the horsemen brandished whips, waved their weapons and catapulted out of the camp after the helplessly-stuck fugitives.

Eldritch watched the warband run, panting with relief as he saw his sister and the lanky Spaniard catch up with the press of soldiers crowding about the neck of the causeway. He had been carried along in the rout, kicking and punching the fugitives as they babbled and pushed, desperate to escape the exposed slopes. The lean captain held on to the balustrade, digging his nails into the chipped stone to hold his place as the mob packed onto the bridge and forced their way past him. He hauled himself up onto the narrow ledge, waved his arms about his head to catch his sister's attention.

'Merron! Over here! Run!' he called. He peered about him, taking in the bewildering details of the battlefield in a moment.

His jaw dropped as he saw the dustcloud hurtling down the pass after them. A band of horsemen had forced their way out of the bottleneck gorge, beating a passage through Bayard's milling infantry. Lightly-clad stradiots on swift horses, not unlike his own precious Ride. So Bayard hadn't given up just yet, he thought fleetingly.

'Isolani, hurry for the love of Christ!' Eldritch bawled. The leading riders galloped through the abandoned wagon-burg and turned down the slope to be swallowed up by the streaming smoke belching from the blockhouse. They emerged a split second later, light crossbows held across their chests, long spears trailing bright pennants and fox-tails. They wore steel sallets wound about with colourful ribbons, looking more like mummers than soldiers. But Eldritch knew the latches they carried could skewer a man at a hundred paces.

The last of the fugitives reached the causeway, pushed their way into the press of stragglers. Eldritch tore his bow from his back and ran along the narrow ledge towards them, nocking an arrow as he ran. He glanced down at the soldiers hurrying in the other direction, picked out some faces he recognised.

'Give them covering fire or we'll all be cut down!' he yelled, jumping down into a gap between the struggling men. He peered back down the perilous bridge, saw the first of the fugitives hurry beneath Tarsi's massively-fort-ified gatehouse. The iron-jawed portcullis reminded El-dritch of a monstrous pike, lurching out of the shadows to snap up a shoal of sticklebacks.

The stradiots were whooping with delight, their bawling captain anxious to please the devilish shaman who had ordered them into the pass. They rode through the twisting smoke, levelling their latches as they came. Eldritch fended off a gang of shouting Spaniards and raised his longbow. He watched the first rider loose his bolt, the heavy quarrel seeming to hover in mid-air as if it possessed a deadly will of its own. There was a blur of startling colours as the harle-quin on the bridge threw himself behind his sister. Merron's mouth was red and wide, her silent scream resounding in her brother's head. Eldritch automatically switched his aim to the second rider, bringing the barbed tip of the arrow to rest on the rider's padded hauberk. He let fly, his arrow skimming above the heads of the terrified mob between them, burying itself with a whistling thud in the man's ribs. The jarring impact lifted the rider from his saddle. He threw out his arms, dropping his latch before he was lost to sight in the swirling crush.

Eldritch tugged a second arrow from his belt-bag, fran-tically searching for another target. The fugitives pushed past in blind panic, spurred to one final effort by the prox-imity of the whooping horsemen. Isolani had wrapped his red and gold arms about Merron, propelling her forward while he shielded her back. Eldritch grabbed her arm and dragged her on, hurling her towards the yawning gate. Out of the corner of his eye he noticed the dusty back of her gown was spotted with blood.

'Merron!'

Isolani staggered after her, the cruelly-barbed quarrel protruding from his shoulder blade. The jagged wound was spouting blood, bright red jets squirting between the Spaniard's dark fingertips.

Eldritch shoved his free hand under his armpit and boosted the pale-faced captain on down the causeway, a knot of archers forming a bewildered rearguard about them. Hobby was walking backwards, nocking his bow as he went. The stradiots had reached the bridge but hesitated to charge, knowing they would be forced to ride one or two abreast, sitting targets for the keen-eyed foreign devils. Their hesitation gave Eldritch's men the bare moments they needed to reach the sanctuary of the gatehouse. Soldiers in wide-brimmed, riveted helmets and strange scarlet and black livery were clattering out from the huge doors – even as the last of the fugitives threw themselves into the slowly-closing jaws. A bareheaded knight in a bulky black gown was waving his sword at him. Eldritch wondered for one desperate moment if they had run straight into a trap, shot down like dogs on the very threshold of their sanctuary. The inner courtyard might have been a killing ground, overlooked by crossbowmen and swept by cannons. The big soldier swept his arms about his screaming sister, ushering her towards the doors. His beard looked red in the light from his troopers' burning torches, his wild eyes bright with tension.

Eldritch blinked, stunned by the fearsome apparition.

'Under the walls! Get under the walls, fool!' the gaudily-dressed chieftain screamed. The English captain hesitated, bow hanging loose in his fist, Isolani coughing and spluttering as he hung like a dead weight on his arm. Crossbow bolts were whining and clattering about the shot-blasted bridge, embedding themselves in the formidable oak doors as the riders at the far end of the causeway dismounted and found their range.

The heavyset knight cursed in Italian. He dashed forward and bent down, threw the swooning Spaniard over his shoulders in one fluid movement. He glanced round at the captain, mouth agape in the chaos on the bridge.

'For the love of Christ, get into the castle!' Alberto Tarsi roared, spittle flying from his broad red mouth.

Eldritch nodded dumbly, helping the furious commander in through the narrowing gap.

The iron hinges shrieked in protest as the massive doors were swung shut. There was a last angry splatter of crossbow bolts – bee-stings on a mammoth. Eldritch staggered on, looking up at the square of light above the fortified courtyard. His warband had thrown themselves down where they could, tripping the hurrying garrison soldiers as they sprinted back to their posts on the walls. The noise was terrible, soldiers shouting in three languages, orders and counter-orders bellowed over the chaos.

Merron was crying freely, hair hanging over her face like tarred ropes as she reached out to hold on to the unconscious Spaniard. Tarsi had lain the captain out on one of the litters beside the door, waved the bloody-aproned orderlies away with their wounded harlequin. The warlord was panting hard, staring at Eldritch as he propped himself on his bow, caught his breath beside the rusticated stonework around the guardhouse.

'You are welcome to Mont Galliard,' he said in his mangled English, sheathing his sword and striding off to organise the defence. The Englishman gazed around the formidably-built courtyard, bitterly relieved by their close escape.

'And you're bloody welcome to it and all,' Eldritch breathed.

Beside Mont Galliard

The grim Englishman followed Tarsi about the castle like a long-legged wolfhound, shadowing him as he toured his restless but relatively quiet fortress. Without Strozzi to rely on the commander had to order the defences himself, hurrying from the courtyard to the walls. His legs ached and his head was thumping, his mind turning cartwheels as he attempted to digest the conflicting reports he was receiving, weighing what he read against what he could see with his own eyes.

A large force of fighting men had encamped on his threshold, their numbers growing every hour. Another – far more desperate – crew had taken refuge in his courtyard, galley slaves washed up on the barren slopes of Mont Galliard.

The enigmatic Englishman who commanded them was telling him all he wanted to hear – but hardly dared believe. He had taken an immense gamble, opening the his doors to this rabble. Was it possible this Eldritch was right, they had both become victims of the Bastard Gueldres' dastardly scheming? By Christ, he hoped so, or he would be dead or worse, a prisoner, by the morning.

Tarsi rubbed his beard, his limbs leaden with the tension. But he dared not relax, not with his precious stronghold girdled about with troubles and strife.

'Tell me again, how you came to be there,' he invited his troublesome guest.

★

Eldritch watched the chieftain stare down into the pass, the rocky strait which might so easily have proved their own Thermopylae. Trapped like mice in a wine bottle, surrounded on all sides by grand knights on prancing chargers – he dreaded to think what would have become of the Ride, if they hadn't been able to fortify themselves within the wagonburg. The Bastard Geldray had inadvertently saved their lives, ordering them to march the length of France in the ridiculously clumsy but surprisingly effective contraptions. Eldritch looked down at the wrecked wagons, so much firewood littering the valley floor now.

'He thought to make fools of us, riding those carts into battle. If he had not been so keen to humiliate us, we might be lying down there among the ashes.'

Tarsi looked askance at him, not sure whether or not he liked the sardonically-smiling Englishman, or whether he could trust a tenth of what he told him.

He was apparently unaware of the damage he had caused with his mad-headed charge down the slope. With the blockhouse ruined the stronghold wasn't the impregnable eyrie it had been.

Eldritch and his blasted warcarts had caught the Spanish defenders napping and left the causeway open to direct assault.

Worse than that, the enemy commander would now be able to set up his guns alongside the ruined redoubt, bringing his culverins to bear on the walls of the main fortress.

Tarsi contemplated the likely course of the assault which would surely follow. If he was in Bayard's shoes he would have his pioneers construct snug emplacements for their guns and pound the vulnerable gatehouse to dust before ordering an all-out charge through the ruins.

He had watched as Bayard's infantry had been reformed into large squares, waiting patiently under snapping colours. New contingents were arriving every few minutes, filing into place between and behind the chevalier's original forces. The lightly-clad militia – papal troops according to their streaming gonfalons – kicked up clouds of dust as they marched up from the south. Tarsi knew Runcini wouldn't be far behind – just as his Major Domo Furstenbein had predicted in his note.

The army assembling in the pass was ten times the size of Savvi's Black Legion. He had held Mont Galliard through one trying siege, but he doubted the battered fortress would stand up to another without repair and reinforcement. Hundreds of men might perish, when Bayard chose to sack the stronghold.

But sack it he surely would.

The two soldiers had little choice but to think of themselves as brothers in arms – thrown together by Gueldres' elaborate plotting. The unlikely allies spent the short interlude they had been allowed trying to solve the desperate puzzle, discover a way out of his infernal trap.

To Tarsi's obvious frustration, Eldritch hadn't been able to shed much light about the events at the abbey – nor the bizarre kidnap of the choir. As far as they could make out the Ride had been making its way down the Rhone valley when the attack had taken place – many leagues to the south.

The grubby-faced altar boys at the centre of Gueldres' sinister web were being fed and watered in the rear courtyard, safe and secure for the moment. The Vicomte had clearly intended to connect the fate of the choir with Tarsi and Eldritch, implicate them in whatever devilry Gueldres had devised. Would he have stopped short of murdering the boys beneath the walls of Mont Galliard? Or forcing one of the terrified youngsters to bear false witness against him?

He could no more read his wasps'-nest mind than he could understand the hoarse calls of the crows wheeling about the death-house castle. Tarsi stared at the enemy encampment, the newly-arrived troops being ordered into position, the artillery being wheeled up into hastily-fortified batteries, pack animals being unloaded by sweating labourers.

And maybe somewhere down there amongst that noise

and bustle was his precious Angelica. Surely the wily inquisitor Briconet wouldn't have passed up the opportunity of parading the poor girl before her father's walls. Tarsi closed his eyes, tried to banish the emasculating idea from his restless imaginaion.

Eldritch let the older man think in peace. He reckoned they were safe enough for now, holed up in Tarsi's rock-girdled fortress, but he hated the hopeless and unfamiliar sense of isolation. They had found a sanctuary of sorts, but it was a sanctuary none of the armies massing in the pass below were likely to respect very much longer.

'Back home, when we found ourselves outmanned like this, we'd simply turn tail and ride, every man for himself.'

Tarsi sighed.

'In the old days, up in Flanders, Italy, Spain, we would always give way to the larger force. I've fought entire campaigns before now, without drawing my sword.'

Eldritch glanced at the old adventurer, his broad-shouldered presence reminding him sharply of his own father in his heyday – before Lillith had eloped and ruined all. Back when House Eldritch's streaming colours would have been carried in the vanguard, or hoisted above a fleet of oceangoing carracks.

Now those same, sad colours were wound about his own pirate lance, serving strangers in a stranger's war.

'Why should mercenary armies lay down their lives in a lost cause? You might buy a soldier's duty, his devotion even, but a sensible man can't afford to throw away his livelihood. What good's a pouchful of coin, if you have to cut your way through that little lot to spend it?' Tarsi inquired with careless reason.

Eldritch frowned, watched another column of heavily-armoured knights make their way up towards the causeway. How many more did this Bayard need before he launched his assault?'

'You mean you can't trust your own men?' Eldritch inquired. It had not occurred to him the Ride might find itself defending the fortress alone. Tarsi chuckled.

'They'll wait around to see how it falls out. There will be a parley soon, a formal invitation to surrender. If I let them blast off some of that powder and then beat the drum, they'll be happy enough. But if I hang out the *Blutfahne*, bid Bayard do his worst, they'll be over the walls like shithouse rats.'

Eldritch digested this intelligence in silence. He didn't like the sound of the *Blutfahne* one little bit. Typical German buffoonery, telling the world it would be death or glory . . .

Tarsi smiled at the young captain's *naïveté*, the blunt honesty which had helped convince him he had been correct to take the dangerous step of admitting his band into Mont Galliard. Tarsi had spent a lifetime dealing with two-faced courtiers and grasping clerks, lying locotenents and lisping lieutenants. They had always made it their business to treat truth as a weakness, to shun straightforward explanation as some kind of womanly vice.

But the Englishman, whisked from the deadly perils of the causeway, had told Tarsi everything that had occurred over the past three months, going into details Tarsi wouldn't have dreamt of admitting himself.

At first he had suspected the shrewd captain was making it all up, insulting him with his unlikely tale of bragging commanders and drunken, campfire challenges. Perhaps this was yet another of Gueldres' tricks, the ultimate assassin sent into the very heart of Tarsi's stronghold.

The chieftain had found himself drawn in to Eldritch's outrageous story, concluding Eldritch was either a Prince among liars or a complete imbecile. Surely he hadn't expected to out-cheat the legendary Gueldres, fool a shark like him with the old loaded dice routine?

'And your sister was off with this Isolani fellow? The one who stopped that crossbow bolt?'

The last time he had inquired, Eldritch had been told Isolani was very weak from loss of blood. The surgeon hadn't been able to say whether he would last the night.

Eldritch didn't have to be told his sister would be mortified if her Spanish lover succumed to his wounds. Maybe he had misjudged the captain. He had certainly saved Merron's life, flinging himself between her and the pursuing crossbowmen. Merron hadn't left his side since, bathing his wounds with potions and unguents supplied by Tarsi's busy surgeons. They had removed the barb, but taken a great hunk of his shoulder muscle with it.

He frowned, answered Tarsi's query with a gruff nod.

'She ruined all,' he admitted.

'What I can't understand is why this 'Ow . . . Owith . . . why this warden of yours risked his entire retinue, the lives of all his men, on such a harebrained wager?'

Eldritch's jaw tensed. He hadn't quite told Tarsi everything. His disastrous attempt to rob Howath of his warband would remain a matter for his own conscience.

Tarsi noted his momentary hesitation. Why would the old warhorse have been betting so heavily? Risked his only asset?

Eldritch realised Tarsi was staring intently at him, wondering whether to accept his story or throw him over the battlements to Bayard's white-coated wolves.

'Gueldres wagered the keys of his castle. He said Howath would have Mont Galliard for his own, if he won.'

'So. You were using your ill-earned stake money, 'Owith had staked the lives of his men, and our friend the Vicomte had wagered my fortress,' he breathed. It was so preposterous it must be true, even if this lean Englishman was keeping something back for himself.

There was a clatter of hooves on the causeway. Tarsi peered out between the machiolations and watched a small company of knights dismount beside the blockhouse. They began to pick their way over the rubble-strewn bridge towards the fortress. Tarsi sucked in his breath, noting the streaming gonfalons they bore above their heads.

The Chevalier Bayard's herald had arrived at last.

★

289

Bayard's gendarmes had polished their armour so bright it stung their eyes. Ensigns held on to their fabulous standards as the proud colours were worried by the strengthening wind. Chill currents turned their breath to dragon vapour, lifted the herald's unmistakable surcoat. He held the flapping hem down, glanced nervously at the piled fortifications which seemed to rear out of the rock.

Mountjoy's mission had been delayed for half an hour by the unauthorised attack on the bridge. The stradiots – a rabble of gypsy cutthroats recruited from the far corners of Europe – had been unable to resist the temptation of such an easy kill and had charged out of the camp to harry the English fugitives.

But the English archers had turned hunters into hunted. The stradiots' moustachioed commander had perished in the sudden arrow-storm, pierced through the eye by an English bodkin.

His agonised demise had at least saved him the trouble of explaining his sortie to the furious Bayard.

Mountjoy leaned back in his saddle, peering up at the dimly-discerned faces on the wall.

'Alberto Tarsi, Seigneur of Mont Galliard, knight of Savoy!' he cried. He was fidgeting with the hem of his coat as if he expected to get an arrow through his heart.

'You are summoned to a parley with my master, the Chevalier Bayard. Will you come down from your walls, under a drum of truce?'

Tarsi stepped back from the wall, his weather-worn features creased with doubt.

'Well? What do you think?' he asked. Eldritch tugged his nose, cursing his own uncertainty. He didn't want to appear utterly at a loss before the formidable soldier of fortune. He decided on bravado – God knew it had got him out of scrapes in the past.

'I wouldn't trust the bastards as far as I could piss. If Bayard wants to talk, let him come in to us.'

Tarsi chuckled.

'We'll be safe enough, so long as Bayard's on the

causeway. If they shoot first, your archers can put an arrow through his damned halo.'

Eldritch turned to his morose sergeant.

'Hobby! Get your best shots up here on the wall. If there's any trouble, you shoot every one of them down like dogs.'

'Aye, right you are. But where are you going?' the bewildered sergeant asked, hanging on to the captain's arm.

'Out to see what they want.'

Hobby tugged the younger man closer, whispered warningly in his ear. 'There's no way out of here, if it comes to a fight.'

Eldritch glanced in the old soldier's wrinkled face, his pale blue eyes moist with cold.

'I know. That's why we're going down to talk,' he said.

The nervous ambassadors met in the middle of the bridge. One of the crossbowmen they had shot down earlier in the day lay in the gutter, a thin stream of black blood running away towards the castle. The causeway was littered with broken bows and spent missiles. The stone balustrade along which Eldritch had performed his dangerous stunt had been chipped and scarred by flying fragments. The black chasm to either side echoed with its own emptiness.

Eldritch stood just behind Tarsi, partly concealed by the Italian's cloak. William Hacker had taken up Eldritch's weather-ravaged colour. His personal device looked mean and ragged in comparison to the handsome gonfalons Bayard's heralds had brought with them.

Tarsi narrowed his eyes, recognising the great chevalier and his sinister familiar, Briconet, his gaunt features concealed under a heavy cowl. What an odd conjunction of heaven and hell they were, he thought sourly.

'Alberto Tarsi, I am come in the name of our Sublime Majesty Francis I, King of France, and in the name of His Holiness Leo X, to lay charges against you. I bid you set aside your arms, and prepare to answer these charges forthwith,' Bayard intoned.

The chevalier's armour had been polished and cleaned,

every trace of his eventful charge into the valley removed. Briconet had wrapped his spare frame in a plain brown cloak, his eyes glittering with malice.

Tarsi pursed his lips.

'May I be permitted details of these charges?'

Briconet stepped forward, briskly unrolled a small scroll.

'By all means, Seigneur. Firstly, this indictment alleges that you, Alberto Tarsi, conspired with others to kidnap the choir of the Abbey d'Eleron in Southern France. It further alleges that you conspired with others to murder Abbot Herve Odo, and twenty-five of his brother monks listed separately, along with forty-six members of the abbey garrison. It is also alleged that you, Alberto Tarsi, conspired with others to trade the above-mentioned choirboys as slaves, with a party or parties presently unknown, for purposes of perverse sexual gratification.'

Tarsi trembled with rage, his furious passion barely contained by his fur cloak. He could barely speak, opening and closing his mouth like a freshly-landed fish.

'What say you, Alberto Tarsi? Will you lay down your arms and attend trial upon these matters, or must we fetch you out ourselves?' Briconet jeered.

'You could try, you snivelling shit!' Tarsi snarled. Bayard held up his gloved hand, stepped between the furiously-staring combatants.

'Seigneur Tarsi, you must understand your position is quite hopeless. More troops are hurrying here as we speak. There is no escape. As a soldier and a man of honour, I urge you to lay down your arms forthwith, and answer these charges as best you may.' The knight paused for a moment, his bright eyes burning. 'I urge you sir, to prove these charges false.'

Tarsi missed Bayard's heartfelt appeal to see reason, failing to recognise the chevalier's doubts.

'I'll answer them right now! They are false, all false. You have been led here by the Vicomte deToinueill, who has borne false witness not only against me, but also against Captain Eldritch and his company.'

Bayard stepped back, his urgent appeal dismissed. The anxious soldiers tensed, hands straying to their sword hilts.

'You may produce whatever evidence you care to refute these allegations,' he insisted, imploring the fiery Italian to accept the inevitable.

'Can I? And who will hear them? Who will try these trumped-up charges?

'I do not need to remind you of the gravity of this allegation. Your case will be heard by a tribunal of your peers.'

'Abandando Briconet for one; the Cardinal Runcini for another?'

'As you say, Seigneur,' Bayard agreed, stiffly formal in his glowing armour.

Tarsi bristled.

'You expect me to walk out here to answer such a ridiculous set of lies?'

'I would,' Bayard said simply.

'Before you make your mind up, my dear Lord Tarsi, perhaps I could read a list of prisoners currently held on matters relating to the present indictment,' Briconet said smoothly, clicking his fingers at the nervously-staring clerk. Souris hurried forward with another scroll, handed it to his gloating master. Tarsi noticed Bayard's fierce scowl, as if he had not agreed to the employment of such a devious strategem.

'Currently accused of conspiracy to murder and kidnap,' Briconet read quickly. 'Angelica Tarsi, maid. Fabrizio Ambolini, courtier.'

'Damn you Briconet, you know full well she had nothing to do with any of this!'

'Then surrender yourself and she will be released without charge! Admit your part in this disgraceful affair and I will set the maid free this very night, you have my oath on it!'

'Your oath? I'd rather trust a . . .'

'Seigneur!' Bayard called. 'We have not come to this parley to trade insults.'

Briconet smirked, continued reading.

'Further, captured in the Valley d'Aosta by forces of His Holiness Leo X and charged with aiding and abetting the above accused and also of diverse banditry, Alexander Kerr and divers Scotch-men in the employ of Alberto Tarsi.'

'I've never even heard of the bastards!' Tarsi shouted. Eldritch grasped his arm.

'I have. They were further down the pass when we were attacked. I saw them ride south,' he said urgently. Bayard straightened up, a silver statue come to life before them.

'You have one hour to decide. If you do not give yourself up I will order my guns to begin the destruction of the fortress. This is the final parley we will attend upon.'

Tarsi drew in his breath. So it would be no quarter asked or given, once the guns had made their breach?

'And I will insist on the immediate trial of Angelica Tarsi, for her part in this dreadful conspiracy.'

'You wouldn't dare,' Tarsi said hoarsely. He turned to Bayard, instinctively aware the chevalier had no stomach for Briconet's medicine.

'I beseech you, my Lord, to prevent any harm being done to my daughter. I swear on all the books she had no part in this.'

'Hah! Then you admit it! Have the girl freed!' Briconet snapped.

'I admit nothing. My Lord Chevalier, in the name of God I beg you to ensure my daughter is kept from any harm.'

'You have my word she will not be harmed,' Bayard mumbled. 'Any further,' he added, *sotto voce*.

'Assuming she is not found guilty of the crimes she is charged with,' Briconet piped up.

'You filthy leech, if you've laid hands on her I'll . . .'

'My Lord Seigneur,' Bayard said hoarsely. 'I urge you to think of your position. You will be given a fair trial on these matters, and may call any witnesses you see fit.'

'The parley is over,' Briconet decided. The chevalier ignored his anxious objection.

'I think it ought to be made clear that should your daughter be released this night, she will not be permitted to give evidence in your defence.'

Tarsi thought quickly. 'So even if you give her back and

I ride out to answer my parole in the morning, she will not be able to help me disprove these lies?'

Bayard nodded.

'This is your choice, Seigneur.'

'I have not granted Tarsi parole!'

'I have,' Bayard snapped, ignoring the interfering inquisitor.

'If you give me your word you will ride out of Mont Galliard at sunup, and accompany us to Aosta to answer these charges, your daughter will be released forthwith.'

'What about Ambolini, the chorister?'

'He will also be freed upon your word of honour.'

'But he will not be permitted to testify either?' Bayard shook his head.

Tarsi made up his mind in a moment.

'Then keep him until the trial. He will be the only witness I can call to disprove these foul allegations.' The blustering soldier tugged his cloak about him, as if suddenly aware of the chill crosswinds playing about the exposed bridge. 'I give my word,' he said wearily. 'Return her to me, this night, and I shall accompany you in the morning.'

'What? We'll give her back and he'll see us in hell before he shows his face!' Briconet shrieked.

'I gave my word!' Tarsi bawled.

'And I accept your word as a man of honour, Seigneur,' Bayard intoned. 'But be aware, the youth Ambolini was wounded in the attack. It is conceivable he might not survive the journey to Aosta.'

Tarsi looked up, held the chevalier's stare.

'My only witness is on his deathbed, is that what you are saying?'

'I am merely keeping you informed of the situation,' Bayard said coldly. 'I would not want to be accused of any deception.'

'Perish the thought,' Tarsi muttered.

'I would not trap a Turk in such a manner,' Bayard insisted, his eyes blazing. Tarsi waved his hand in annoyance.

'I'll trust to God Ambolini will testify. In the meantime, I'll take my daughter.'

It was another of Briconet's tricks, damn his eyes! Tarsi watched the frail, spiderweb creature being carried along by a pair of Bayard's retainers. They had taken hold of the girl under the armpits, the hatefully-stained shift hanging about her wasted frame. Tarsi didn't dare imagine whether it was blood or traces of half-digested food. Her hair was a mass of greasy knots and tangles, hanging like rats' tails over her drawn features.

It was some serving girl they had sent out from the camp to bait the trap! Tarsi gripped his sword, a feral growl building up in his throat. Bayard followed his gaze, held his gloved hand to the Italian's shoulder. Hot tears had sprung into the mercenary's raw eyes, slicked the shadows beneath the sunken sockets.

'Angelica?' he croaked.

'There is no lasting harm. She has received treatment from my own surgeon,' Bayard said, shamefaced.

The grandly-armoured gendarmes held the frail creature upright under the fearful examination of her horrified father.

Angelica's hands had been wrapped in grey linen bandages, but her thin arms were still covered in sores from the ghastly bands with which she had been restrained. Her hollow cheeks were grey with pain, eyes blank with the unspeakable suffering she had endured.

Eldritch gaped at the poor thing, wondered what hellhole she had escaped from. What manner of man could commit such abominations on a defenceless woman? Tarsi was beside himself with rage, lifting his sword and then sliding it home with a dangerous clang. He took a step forward. Briconet retreated behind the scowling chevalier.

'The girl insisted on sticking by her story. We gave her ample opportunity to tell us the truth,' he shrilled.

'There was nothing more I could do,' Bayard said. 'Apart from prevent her from any further harm.'

'Further interrogation! The girl was questioned according to the statutes laid down by the Holy Inquisition,' Briconet insisted, eyes flickering about the blank-faced soldiers – ready for action around him. 'I am a papal legate and agent of the Inquisition. I act with the absolute approval and authority of the Holy Church,' he cried.

Tarsi stepped forward, lifted the stick figure into his arms. She weighed less than his shield.

'You starved her into submission!'

'She refused to eat!'

'What have you done to her hands?' Tarsi wailed, grasping at the bulky bags which had been fastened about her pale arms.

'We were forced to employ several methods of persuasion.'

'Persuasion?' Tarsi breathed, grasping for his sword as he held his daughter up with his left hand. Angelica whimpered like a beaten cur, barely able to stand on her bare feet. Eldritch leapt forward to support her, bending down to lift the frail body in his arms. He was appalled by the vacant terror in the girl's unrecognising face as she stared up at him, flecks of spittle at the corners of her mouth.

Bayard stepped in front of Tarsi, arms opened wide to prevent the raging soldier from exacting an immediate revenge on the cowering inquisitor.

'He speaks right Seigneur. Briconet has the authority of the Holy Father himself.'

'Does the Holy Father approve the piggeries you insist on committing on innocent maidens?' Tarsi snarled.

'You forget yourself sir. Do not presume to lecture me on my duties,' Briconet cried. Bayard held up his hand.

'I expect you to honour your promise, and meet me at the end of the bridge at first light tomorrow. Be ready to ride to Aosta, and you may answer *all* the charges made against you.' He stepped back, ushering his bodyguards and standard bearers away. Briconet made sure he went with them.

Tarsi glowered on the causeway, Eldritch at his side.

'I'll kill him now, have done with it!' Tarsi breathed, beginning to draw his sword. 'They mean to hang me anyway!' Eldritch shook his head.

'There is yet hope. I convinced you to let us into your fortress didn't I? A child could have seen Bayard's heart isn't in it. He looks as if he's come along to keep that venomous snake in order. And besides, you have given your word.'

'A pox on my word! That's my daughter you're carrying, my own flesh and blood. Look what they've done to her,' he choked, ramming the sword back in his scabbard and gently lifting Angelica's bandaged arm.

'She needs warmth and care. She's safe enough for now,' Eldritch advised, oddly moved by the girl's mute predicament. He gazed into her ravaged face, the tortured hurt lurking in the bloodshot corners of her eyes. Tarsi relented.

'Take her back to the castle,' he agreed, exhausted and crushed by the terrible tensions of the last hours.

'You're right, she'll be safe, and that's as much as I can hope.'

'I told you. There's always hope. Bayard won't stand by and see us hung for crimes we did not commit.'

Tarsi glanced at the gaunt Englishman who had dropped into his existence so abruptly. Despite all, the old soldier was strangely reassured by his calm determination. Eldritch hoicked the moaning girl higher in his arms, and strode towards the castle.

Tarsi wept in bitter frustration when he saw what Briconet had done to her hands. Turning those delicate, tapered fingers into sausages of split meat. The manicured nails to broken crusts in blistered beds of oozing pus. Eldritch hung on to the raving chief's arm, hauling him back as he strode towards his chambers to fetch his axe. A sword was too good for Briconet, he shouted, hardly comprehensible amidst a stream of foul-mouthed threats and blood oaths. The furious father had gazed at the Englishman, barely recognising him through his hate-haze.

'You have given your word! You have given your word to Bayard!' the captain insisted, refusing to be shaken free. 'Killing Briconet will drag you down to his level, to the gutter where he belongs!' Eldritch had reverted to English, unable to master the necessary French. Tarsi hadn't a clue what he was saying, but he understood his meaning well enough. The powerfully-built soldier had been at the gate before Eldritch's imprecations had finally penetrated his consciousness.

'Get your hands off me!' Tarsi snarled. 'What would you do, if it was your sister, if it was Merron up there, crippled by that rat-puke bastard of an inquisitor?' he demanded, pressing his bearded face against Eldritch's.

'The same as you. I would sneak into their camp and cut his throat over his soup.'

Tarsi nodded savagely, his teeth glinting in the gloom.

'Aye! And here you are telling me to remain indoors, answer my parole like a naughty schoolboy caught raiding orchards?'

'Even so. You've more to lose than I, Seigneur,' Eldritch said calmly, watching the dangerous flush drain from the soldier's mortified features.

'I would have gladly taken her place. They could have tortured me!' he croaked. Eldritch nodded.

'They tortured you, my Lord. They tortured you here,' he tapped his temple, 'hurt you far more deeply than they could have done with all their thumbscrews and burning tapers.'

Tarsi recoiled at the images which pierced his tumbled mind.

'Aye,' he grunted.

'If you open the gate, ride out after him, Bayard will have you shot down like a dog, and he will despise your name forever.'

'I don't give a sewer rat's spleen for Bayard!'

'You gave your word. If you kill Briconet, you kill yourself, your daughter, your name.'

'You seem to have mastered the art of intrigue very rapidly, for a *Transmarini*,' Tarsi sneered. Eldritch realised he was succeeding, deflecting the furious knight from his bloody revenge.

For now at least.

Tarsi remembered his daughter's hands – bloody strips in swaddling, and gripped the hilt of his sword in seething resentment. 'They'll roast us at the stake before we can prove anything. And you'll not slip the noose by pretending you were only obeying my orders!' Tarsi accused, scarlet with fury. Eldritch swallowed his anger at the jibe.

'I will be on trial for my life as well as you. The suggestion I was only obeying your orders, Seigneur, would be no defence against such charges,' he said coldly. 'You heard Bayard. We are charged together. Co-conspirators to God-knows what. You trusted me on the bridge, when I realised we had all been duped, when I called you down to talk. Would you yet believe I would steer such a craven course?'

Tarsi blinked. He wouldn't have hesitated to do so, if he thought for a second it might work. What was this gaunt scarecrow to him – a foreigner, a mercenary blade who had turned up on his doorstep with fire and sword? He was just another soldier and no more.

His anger subsided.

'We will be climbing a mountain of lies. Gueldres has made sure of that,' he said miserably, sliding his half-drawn sword back into the scabbard with a ring of steel.

'These letters, the business at the abbey. Gueldres won't have left any stone unturned. He would have been utterly thorough. You don't know half he's capable of.'

Eldritch nodded wearily.

'I can well imagine. But Bayard seems to me to be as honest as they say he is. He went out of his way to assure you we would receive a fair trial. He'll sit on the tribunal, with this cardinal fellow.'

Tarsi snorted.

'Runcini. Aye. The Fat Salamander. And our dear friend and ally, Abandando Briconet, Prince of Shits, to prosecute! D'you think he'll be keen to let me go, now, after tearing my Angelica's fingers from their sockets?' Tarsi fumed.

'I am assured this Bayard carries immense influence with the French king. He will ensure any evidence is considered fairly.' The words seemed like fragments of paper in his mouth, half-lies dressed up in spit. 'You returned the choir as you promised you would, unharmed. Bayard won't forget that, we won't let him!'

'Briconet will argue we had no choice but to let them go! We could hardly cut their throats and expect Bayard to overlook it!' Tarsi retorted angrily.

Eldritch nodded, determined to remain as calm as possible. If the vicious experiences of the last weeks had taught him anything, it was the need of a cool head at all times. Throwing fists or swinging a sword was no answer to devilish webs such as those cast by Geldray and his ilk.

'The choir was unharmed, and we spared as many of Bayard's men as we were able. The chevalier knows full well we could have drowned the pass with blood, if we'd wanted to. He's our only friend, our only hope.'

Tarsi chuckled resignedly as he contemplated the legal ordeal to come. The ritualised murder they dared term justice.

'To think my future depends on the evidence of a half-dead choirboy. Scaralatchi's catamite,' he shook his head. 'He might not even live as far as Aosta. He might already be dead!'

'Bayard would have warned you if he was. Briconet wasn't going to say anything about the admission of witnesses!' Eldritch clung at every windblown straw in his bid to reassure the brooding knight. He knew he was wasting his breath. When it came right down to it he and Tarsi were out of the same mould: soldiers, not thinkers.

Perhaps it would have been better after all to take a picked squad and raid the camp, drown their shadow crimes in a logjam of bodies? Bayard's and all, if he got in their vengeful way.

Tarsi sighed, tugged his great mantle about his broad shoulders.

'I wish Luca was here. I wish that fart Furstenbein was here, he'd have an idea what we were up against, at least.'

'I think we all have an idea what we are up against. We've got the rest of the night to figure it out.'

PART FIVE
Mea Culpa

◆ ◆ ◆ ◆ ◆

'It cannot be called prowess to kill fellow citizens, to betray friends, to be treacherous, pitiless, irreligious. These ways can win a prince power but not glory.'

Machiavelli, *The Prince*

Beside the Palazzo Salassi, Aosta, Italy, September 1520

The weather had suddenly turned colder, the first rasps of winter gusting down the valley and lifting the last russet harvests from the trees. The Aosta valley was one of the most beautiful, fruitful regions in all Italy, but the steep passes brought chill winds as well as wanderers down from the mountains. The busy trade route had also brought horrifying news of the massacre at the Abbey d'Eleron.

The papal delegation en route to Novara had been stunned by the shocking details and had immediately diverted north to the old Roman town of Aosta. According to their flourishing network of spies and agents the culprits would try and cross the Alps – hide themselves away in the lush wheatfields and vine-clad hillsides of the Lombard Plain. If their predictions proved correct then Aosta – centre of the entire valley – would make a logical base to direct the vengeful pursuit.

Cardinal Amerigo Runcini never left Rome without a large body of troops. He had plenty of light cavalry to spare to assist the search for the killers. But he was a busy man, and he did not relish being trapped in the north by the fast-approaching winter. While his captains were busy scouring the high valleys for the despoilers of d'Eleron, he would occupy his time with a little local litigation.

The troublesome Count of Luningiana had been waiting for eighteen months for his appeal to be heard. He had called upon the church to reconsider the terms of the peace treaty concluded between himself and Margaret of Savoy almost ten years before. The treaty, which had been brokered and subsequently ratified by His Holiness himself, had robbed Stroma of his road tolls, left him virtually destitute in his once-magnificent palace. Now he claimed he had suffered enough, that the Vatican, in its infinite wisdom and mercy, should return the precious tolls to him.

Runcini didn't consider himself a greedy man – he could think of half a hundred cardinals who wouldn't get out of bed without a generous bribe. But he had expenses the same as everyone else. One could not make this sort of decision lightly. He had no doubt the grateful appellant would ensure his earnest deliberations did not go unrewarded.

The cardinal's newly-arrived caravan had sought refuge where it could. A sprawling, squalling shanty-town of red and gold tents and horsehide hovels had sprouted up almost overnight amongst the fluted columns and triumphant archways of the old town.

Modern Aosta had retained the grand monuments which had been built in honour of its namesake Augustus, preserving the rigid Roman street plan. The main gate – the massively-fortified Porta Pretoria – led travellers on to the main avenue, the Via Sant'Anselmo, which passed under the Arch of Augustus and over the River Buthier before arriving at the central piazza. The other main street, the Via Sant'Orso, ran from the gate towards the grimly gothic Collegiata dei Santi Pietro ed Orso. The cardinal's personal suite had been given rather choicer quarters in the Palazzo Salassi – taking over an entire wing of the count's down-at-heel home.

Stroma didn't mind the temporary inconvenience – nor the astronomical cost of their visit. He knew the delegation's ruling on the road tolls would make or break his fortunes – not to mention those of half a dozen other families further down the valley.

But there were bigger issues at stake than family pride.

The delegation's long-awaited decision might alter the whole balance of power in the region. If the looming war between France and the Empire were to break out again, possession of those same Alpine passes would assume critical international importance.

The cardinal had as usual brought a legion of servants from Rome. Swiss guards and secretaries, clerks, food tasters, alchemists and astrologers had swollen his gaudy host. They had thrown themselves down where they could, taking over every nook and cranny in the rambling palace. The overcrowded quarters rang with their snores, sluggishly circulating air pungent with their combined body odours. Stroma had ordered his own household servants to clamber through the blocked passages with incense burners, to try and clear some of the stink.

'Gah, they smell worse than a holdful of Turks!' the count complained, helping himself to another goblet of wine. He was a small, tightly-bound soldier, with tapering legs and pointed beard. His small eyes were mischievously bright. He moved like a night beast, small, quick steps taking him back to his roost beside the range.

His friend and ally, Abelard, Vicomte d'Toinueill, was reclining in the well-upholstered chair opposite, his long, leather-clad legs stretched out on a footstool. The Vicomte had arrived that forenoon at the head of a small troop of mounted bodyguards, the rest of the expanded legion — minus Isolani and Eldritch's contingents of course — had taken the *alta via*, the high road to the south-west. He had ordered the loyal Savvi to march them to Champorcher on the first leg of their deliberately roundabout route to the coast — and the blissfully unaware Gerhard Mounier, Prince of Villefranco. The feeble-minded fool wouldn't know what had hit him, when Savvi's landsknechts came swarming out of the mist!

The sneak-attack would earn a handsome profit, and go some way toward restoring his grievously-emptied coffers — or so he hoped.

'Runcini brings a thousand men to a tax tribunal! No wonder the Vatican's so short of money,' the adventurer mused.

Stroma resumed his seat, stroking his carefully-barbered beard.

'He's worried about being attacked by brigands,' he smirked.

'And so he should be: they're our brigands after all, hah!'

Stroma had given covert encouragment to several bandit leaders, hoping to convince the Vatican that the rival House of Savoy was unable to exercise proper control over the passes. As far as his spies had been able to make out, the policy had been extremely successful, stoking the age-old animosity between the two camps.

Gueldres smiled at the count's intrigues.

'We can link all their attacks with Tarsi's English renegades. My agents are already spreading the word about the attack on the abbey, mentioning their names in every back-street bar and knocking shop. If Runcini's spies are half as good as they are supposed to be, the cardinal will know exactly who to blame for the massacre. *Il Zazzera*, the long-haired Englishman!'

He laid his palm over his fluted goblet. 'Runcini plugs the valley this end and Briconet hurries down from the north. Tarsi is holed up like a genie in a bottle. Believe me, Stroma, this time, he's finished.'

Stroma didn't share the Vicomte's confidence. He sipped his wine, glancing at the younger man staring into the fire opposite. Neither the Duke de Gueldres nor his bastard son had ever blamed the count for his decision to abandon the rebellion they had begun almost a decade before. It had turned out to be a bad war, devilish bad for business. Stroma had advised the Gueldres clan against the revolt, warning them that in taking on Margaret of Savoy they were lining up against the Empire itself. The duke's small army had been chased about the Spanish Netherlands by Margaret's far more numerous forces. An army which had included Italians, Germans and even a few thousand longbowmen sent over by Henry of England. The shrewd count had quickly realised the revolt was doomed to failure and had withdrawn his own forces from the field. Other ringleaders – his old friend and ally the Duc de Gueldres for one – had not been blessed with his foresight.

They had been outcast ever since.

The Vicomte could sense Stroma's doubts, the catastrophic hesitations which had cost them all so dearly in the past. He watched the count adjust his cushion, knew their small talk was over.

'So. You think you have done enough to see our friend Tarsi and his new friends burned at the stake for his crimes?'

Gueldres steepled his long, olive-skinned fingers, his features lit by the flickering flames. The blazing logs popped and hissed beside him.

'If he gets out of this one,' he shrugged his thin shoulders. 'He's a better man than either of us. He'll swing, alongside that arrogant bastard Eldritch.'

Gueldres had explained all that had happened since his party had arrived in Guisnes, describing the dice game with the bragging English, the long march south, and the shocking news of Muhlberg's assault on the abbey. Even Stroma had been taken aback to hear of the murder of old Odo.

'You're sure you can't be connected to the business at the abbey? Muhlberg's a good soldier, but he's a big-mouthed cretin same as the rest, when he's got a few barrels in his belly.'

Gueldres nodded. He had torn himself in two worrying about the unauthorised assault, the bizarre kidnap of the choirboys. But those same choirboys would be sitting on Tarsi's doorstep by now, and the finger of guilt would naturally be pointed at the Italian. The discovery of the choir, together with all the incriminating evidence the Vicomte had left behind, would surely be enough to convict his enemies. He had prepared another set of variously-suggestive documents, ready to send away or produce as evidence – just as soon as it became necessary.

All of them had been stamped with the stolen signet ring: surely this would be taken as damning proof of Tarsi's guilt.

Gueldres had left no stone unturned, determined to destroy the pair of them once and for all.

'You don't make a fortune betting on favourites. Our dear friend Alberto's sitting in a sling. We've hung him up like a Parma ham!' Gueldres lifted his glass, took a sip of his mulled wine. 'Maybe if Bayard had his way, there would be a show trial, accusations, evidence. He might even dig some dirt on our involvement. But Briconet is shadowing him every step, with all the evidence he could possibly need,' Gueldres went on. 'He won't look any further into the business than our dear friend Runcini.'

Stroma took a deep draught of his wine to calm his nerves. Gueldres was playing a dangerous game. Too dangerous for his liking.

'Don't worry. I have people in Briconet's headquarters as well as the cardinal's. They know what to do.'

Geuldres lifted his legs back to the floor and leaned forward, his gaunt features turning from red to black as he was silhouetted by the shadows.

'We'll finish the business, once and for all. Take back what is rightfully ours.'

'Aye,' Stroma said with a sigh. 'It's just . . . this damned choir business I don't like. You're pushing your luck, trying to steal his thunder. Don't you think Runcini will suspect something? The Bastard Gueldres sponsoring a choral requiem?' Stroma shook his head.

'Runcini is a vain, self-centred egotist. You fill his purse, I'll inflate his ego.'

'But if he thinks for a minute this masterpiece of yours could be connected to the business at the abbey, we'll be done for, ego or no.'

'How will he ever find out? Odo's dead, Tarsi's messengers as good as. By the time Briconet's finished with them they won't know their arse from their elbow, let alone be able to give evidence as to the authorship of some bloody score!'

'But you're proposing to have the very same score performed in Aosta,' Stroma snarled.

'Yes, yes. But there's nothing to stop us claiming Scaralatchi, miserable, excommunicated schemer that he is, sold us a copy as well as Tarsi. But no matter. Briconet will shut them all up before the cardinal gets so much as a whisper of it.'

Stroma was still not convinced.

'No, my friend. This Tarsi, he's clever. He was aiming to impress the cardinal with this choral masterpiece. But it won't be Tarsi who gets into Runcini's good books, it'll be you and I!'

Beside the Church of St Orso,
Aosta, Sunday Mass

Julius Furstenbein leaned forward to peer down the street. The tall Fleming had disguised his outlandish features beneath a large, fur-trimmed hood. The bulky disguise ought to be enough to fool the spies and lookouts abroad in this damned crowd, he thought drily. The excitable Aostans flocking and barging about the ancient cloisters seemed more interested in catching a glimpse of the renowned cardinal than worrying about some stranger.

Hawkers were selling pies and sweetmeats, shouting their wares and making a few pennies while they could. Busy tinkers dipped in and out of the crowd like waterfowl dabbling in a ditch, stretching on tiptoe to pass their produce up to the resourceful townsfolk perched high on the whitewashed walls.

The elegant cypress trees which lined the Via Sant'Orso had been hung with bunting, decorated with twists of paper left there by the superstitious populace. Pleas and petitions, promises and prayers written in barely-legible French or Latin. The local peasants believed the visiting clergy would ride along and pick the papers from the trees, grant their every wish with a flick of their ring-encrusted fingers.

The average citizen stood as much chance of being admitted to the superb Gothic Church of St Orso as they did of flying to the moon, but it hadn't stopped the worthy townsfolk from turning out in droves to see the gorgeously-appointed papal delegation arrive for Sunday mass.

Swiss guards led the way, scowling in their scarlet and black livery, tasselled halberds over their shoulders. A vanguard of white-robed bishops followed, stalking through the bitter fumes left by the swinging censers like gaunt herons wreathed in a morning mist. Trumpets blared, brazen fanfares which shook the old houses to their foundations. Cardinal Amerigo Runcini himself was being carried in a sedan chair clad in shimmering scarlet silk and hung with knotted tassels. Now and then he leaned forward, tugged the heavy curtain aside to jerk his wrist at the gawping peasants who had lined the streets all the way from the Palazzo Salassi.

A hundred and more knights and nobles formed a colourful rearguard, their prancing horses bedecked in flowing bards bearing the colours of their houses. Pennants fluttered in the wind, vast silken gonfalons billowed like sails above their toiling bearers.

The canny Count Stroma had distributed several chests of small coin to the crowd in order to improve their fickle mood – and help ensure his distinguished guest got a warm reception. It wouldn't do to have the fat leech booed and whistled by a bunch of half-starved harpies. Instead, the stinking mob seethed like a delicate anemone imprisoned in a rock pool, waving their arms and punching the air as the grand procession came to a halt.

Furstenbein elbowed himself some room beside a fluted column, glad his unusual height enabled him to see over the bobbing heads in front of him. He watched the principal guests climb down from their coaches and make their way up the rich carpeting towards the church. He watched the bishops make their way under the immense gothic archway, censers swinging to disperse pungent clouds of aromatic incense. Runcini followed behind, his magnificent robes stunningly scarlet against the drab crowd. He wore a large, almost flat hat, hung with tiny red leather tassels which moved like some Turkish veil about his plump, oily features. Furstenbein watched the leading noblemen pack in behind him — Stroma, short and severe in black-lacquered armour. And then his master's serpent of an enemy, the Bastard Gueldres himself, resplendent in a kingfisher suit of turquoise and gold.

What could those unscrupulous dogs possibly want here? he thought sourly.

Glory, patronage, power.

The crowd lurched forward taking Furstenbein with it. Liveried attendants dug in their heels to hold them back as the rainbow congregation swept past his cloister and on into the church.

The massive doors swung shut.

Furstenbein wondered about forcing his way down the cloisters and finding a side door, but there were guards at every window charged with keeping the nosey Aostans out. He turned away, clicking his tongue in irritation that his covert mission continued to be dogged by such bad luck.

His master had sent him south to try and arrange for Scaralatchi's mass to be previewed before the papal delegation due to visit Novara. But the shocking news of the assault on the Abbey d'Eleron had persuaded the cardinal to march his vast cavalcade to Aosta instead. The old Roman town was in the very heart of the Count of Luningiana's jealously-guarded territory, obliging Furstenbein to take lodgings under the noses of his master's sworn enemies.

The dispirited Fleming had toured the back streets incognito, overhearing snatches of conversation, whispered innuendo. He had been deeply alarmed to hear that the outrageous attack on the abbey was widely believed to have been Tarsi's work.

His master, responsible for the piggeries the excited Aostans were describing in such lurid detail? He had understood at once that the attack could only have been the work of the Bastard Gueldres — perhaps working in hellish compact with Stroma to discredit their rival. His suspicions had been confirmed when his highly-paid informants had told him that he wasn't the only agent interested in arranging a musical appointment with the visiting cardinal.

Furstenbein had been appalled to hear Stroma himself had invited the cardinal to a special preview of a new choral work at the church of St Orso that very Sunday!

Furstenbein had bribed and cajoled his informants, but none of them possessed the wherewithal to have his name added to the prestigous guest list. He had come along on the off-chance of slipping past the guards, but one look at the Swiss had convinced him his thankless mission was doomed.

He cursed his own helplessness, turned to make his way back to his lodgings. There was nothing more to be done here. He must get back to Mont Galliard as soon as possible and warn his master – in person this time – of the sinister conspiracy surrounding him.

Furstenbein was so engrossed he failed to notice the sinister figure slip out from behind the grand column he had been leaning against. The little man moved in a series of peculiar spurts, dodging and diving through the crowd as he hurried to match the Fleming's purposeful stride. The distinctive, staccato rattle of his iron-shod shoes was quite lost in the fearsome tumult.

The interior of the church was as awesome as its soaring exterior promised. Massive, ornately-worked arches spanned the central dome, framing superbly-rendered frescoes within each outflung arm. The elegantly-proportioned buttresses had been painted with complex, symmetrical diamonds in bright blues and lush golds, endless helixes stretching this way and that over the superb dome. A shaft of wintry sunlight speared the oculus, bathing the glittering company in a soft golden glow.

Gueldres strode up the nave, raising his dark head to marvel at the spectacular artistry. He narrowed his eyes against the bright light, following the bewilderingly beautiful visions until his eyes smarted at the effort. The coffered ceiling panels had been painted eggshell blue, each biblical image framed in gold leaf.

'A grand sight, eh? My family coughed up for most of it you know,' Stroma remarked, taking his place in the deeply-stained oak stalls.

'Our friend the cardinal seems impressed,' Gueldres commented, nodding down the packed nave toward the superb altar. The massive structure dominated the building, dripping with gold and silver, bristling with candelabra and heavily-gilded crucifixes. The altar panels had been meticulously painted with scenes of quite staggering horror. Some half-demented artist's idea of hell, no doubt. A German, most probably. They seemed surprisingly well-informed of what the fiery pit should look like. Bird-headed demons and dagger-spewing fish roamed a bleak landscape of drooping towers and flying windmills, peopled by fabulously endowed – but clearly hopelessly lost – souls. Human beings with heads growing from their arses, many-legged children fleeing a fire-breathing porker.

He shook his head, watched the immaculately-appointed choir file past and take up their positions.

He wondered for a moment what had become of the choir Muhlberg had kidnapped from the abbey. Had Bayard caught up with them yet? Had the resourceful Briconet made up his narrow mind as to who was to blame for the massacre?

Gueldres smiled to himself as he imagined his old enemy Tarsi trying to explain away the mountain of evidence they had collected against him. He wondered where the old soldier would begin, faced with such a bewildering catalogue of incriminating documents and sworn affidavits. Clear proof, if proof was required, that the greedy Italian warmonger had snatched those innocent boys for his own perverse amusement.

Gueldres held his gloved hand to his mouth, stifled a roar of laughter. Poor old Tarsi!

'Something amusing you Gueldres?' Stroma leaned closer, whispering confidentially.

'I can't wait to see Tarsi's face when they bring him to trial,' he explained.

'This is what we've waited for right enough.' Stroma nodded toward the shuffling choirboys, their angelic faces the living image of the frescoes around the walls.

'Let's hope he likes it. I've gone to a good deal of trouble arranging this.'

'You'll get your reward my friend, when Tarsi's balls hang from my gatehouse.'

Stroma smirked, briskly wiped his clipped beard.

'Aye, well. Hello, you're wanted.' The count nodded down the ornate pews towards the aisle. Corporal Muhlberg was hopping from one foot to the other. Gueldres sighed, propelled himself along the bench toward the drowsy-eyed landsknecht. Muhlberg was clutching his black hat to his chest, nodding apologetically.

'What is it?'

'It's Obolus. He's gone after a spy in the crowd. Tarsi's Fleming.'

Gueldres frowned. Furstenbein was it? What was that gangly stormbird doing down here, apart from poking his nose in where it didn't belong? The Vicomte thought for a moment, wondered whether the Fleming might be able to spoil any of their complex arrangements at this late stage. He couldn't think how, but it didn't pay to take any chances.

'Obolus is going to follow him, see where he's hidden himself.'

Gueldres nodded grimly.

He'd had another idea.

They had already prepared another bundle of documents – the incriminating details lavishly waxed and stamped with the stolen Tarsi signet ring. He had been thinking of sending some half-daft messenger to the north, allowing the bundle to fall into Briconet's grasping hands. But the documents would seem far more authentic if they were captured on a Tarsi insider, on his lanky agent Furstenbein! If they could discover where the Fleming was lodging, they might be able to plant further proof of Tarsi's nefarious dealings on his inscrutable servant . . .

Gueldres grinned, delighted at the prospect of reinforcing the body of evidence against his old rival.

'Send after him and don't let him out of your sight. Send Obolus back to me as soon as possible, with the black leather portmanteau from my locked chest. Is that clear?'

'Black leather portmanteau. Right.'

'Make sure it is, I don't want any more cock-ups! I'll see Obolus outside in about an hour.'

Muhlberg's sloping brow furrowed in concentration. He nodded and loped off down the aisle. Gueldres turned to resume his place beside Stroma. His smile slipped a notch when he saw the count was deep in conversation with the mealy-mouthed master of the St Orso choir, Father Bembo. The newcomer was leaning across the heavy pews, his immaculately-tailored white habit thrown back from his pock-marked features. Stroma looked up sharply as Gueldres sat back down beside him.

'He says he needs more time!' Stroma growled. 'You certainly pick your moments, Bembo. I thought I made it quite clear extensive rehearsals were out of the question?'

Gueldres held his breath as the nervous choirmaster bent lower, hand held across his mouth to ensure confidentiality.

'With respect my Lord, I did ask if I could at least preview the work in question.'

Gueldres pricked up his ears, wondering what was wrong now. Couldn't the fool read music?

'We're previewing it before the cardinal. All your boys have to do is sing it!'

'We tried . . . I mean, we went over the piece as far as we were able, given the fact you only saw fit to hand it over this morning!'

'I didn't want one of your precious little angels selling it off to the highest bidder! We've been plagiarised before now. We've moved heaven and earth for a chance to perform it!'

'What's the matter with it?' Gueldres hissed.

'He says it doesn't sound right.'

'Right? I'm assured this is one of the most stunning compositions ever to be sung anywhere in the world! And you can't understand the score?'

Gueldres was acutely aware every head in the entire church had been turned their way, anxiously wondering what the commotion was about. He peered down the aisle, saw the cardinal and his flock of attendant bishops moving towards the altar to begin the long-awaited service. Runcini's falsetto voice rose and fell as he intoned the familiar phrases which would begin that morning's elaborate liturgy.

Gueldres felt black hairs prickle the back of his neck, sensed his carefully-laid plan was going unexpectedly awry.

'Never mind your fussing, Bembo. It's a piece of music. Sing it!' he snapped. The red-faced cleric swallowed hard.

'I am not sure we have been allowed adequate time to prepare the piece. I think it best we skip the . . .'

'No!' Gueldres cried, gripping the monk's fat hand. 'We have asked special permission to perform the mass to welcome Cardinal Runcini! He won't wait around while you practise the damned thing!' Father Bembo pulled his hand back and tucked it under his voluminous sleeves.

'I warned you Gueldres, I warned you they'd need more time!' Stroma fretted.

The count had no damned backbone, never had, Gueldres thought blackly.

'Very well,' Bembo said. 'On your head be it.'

The Vicomte wasn't sure at what point the choir had finished coughing and started singing. Surely they were simply warming up, stretching their throats for the treat to come?

An expectant silence had fallen over the congregation, the serenity of their surrounding settling every conversation in a moment. Gueldres listened to the choir practise. Shrill bursts of Latin phrasing, stuttering fanfares of notes which chimed like sweet bells for a moment before abruptly giving out. He stared at the pale-faced choristers, wondered when on earth they would finish their tomfoolery and begin to sing the piece properly. How much more warming up did the little bastards need? He would warm their hearts for them, aye, over an open brazier! He'd sell the little shits to the Turks!

Gueldres gripped the pew before him, his gloved fingers flexing about the carved oak as the horrible noise droned on. His body was vibrating with anger from the tapered tips of his fashionable shoes to his constricting collar.

The angelic imps were doing it deliberately now, singing half a bar and then closing their mouths, forming tiny red Os in their cockeyed insolence. He'd give them Os. They would Oh! right enough, when he squeezed their balls in a set of nutcrackers!

Stroma turned around slowly, his jaw sagging. His tongue protruded like a bolt of red velvet.

'What on earth are they singing?' he hissed, inadvertently grasping Gueldres' forearm. The Vicomte couldn't speak. He could only listen in helpless mortification.

The choir faltered now, realising just how dreadful they sounded. Bembo swung his arm this way and that, stared at his newly-copied score in horror. The choirboys began to look around, disconcerted by the drop-jawed stares of the disbelieving congregation.

Gueldres couldn't see the cardinal's face. Runcini had clearly been looking forward to the long-awaited premiere, licking his moist red lips as the choir had fidgeted and coughed. But his admiring glances had turned to shock and then to bewildered anger. He held his hand up to his head, resting his creased forehead against his thick, sausage fingers.

'By God Gueldres, stop it,' Stroma hissed, elbowing his ally in the ribs. 'Stop them, do something,' he implored. Gueldres remained transfixed, his mind sliding off on bloody tangents of his own as the choir stumbled and hacked around the jumbled work.

Tarsi had tricked him! The rat-buggering lout had set him up for this appalling fall from grace. Fall? He was tumbling, tumbling out of control! Tarsi would be holding his fat belly now, coughing his bastard lungs out with great gales of demonic laughter.

And then Runcini looked round.

His fleshy features were creased and slick with a combination of warmth, wine and unflattering sunlight, his eyes dark – piggy pools half-buried in folds of fat. A slimy salamander who had crawled forth from his own pit of fiery corruption, attracted to the butterfly choirboys like a death's head moth to a candle flame. But the dismal cacophony had turned him away from the beautiful youths, forced his beastly eyes heavenward. Agonisingly slowly, the cardinal lowered his hand and turned his face back towards the hellishly-painted altar panels.

Gueldres and Stroma had been dismissed with a grimace, ruined with a look. All their hopes, all their scheming dashed to nought in seven minutes. Gueldres cringed, ground his teeth in mortification.

Father Bembo was shuffling the pages now, his thin face flushed with embarrassment. Some of the choristers were crying openly.

But most of the congregation were laughing.

It had started over on the far side of the nave, some giggling idiot ducking his head behind one of the concealing columns. His fruity laugh sent a frisson of amusement rippling along the pews. The grand dames decked out in their flamboyant Sunday best raised handkerchiefs to their mouths and bent their heads as if in prayer.

The head choirboy lifted his chin, throat muscles rippling as he yodelled a tremendous, soaring solo. A perfectly flowing stream of notes followed by a ridiculously extended silence.

Then he did it all over again.

It was unbearable. Terrible. Laughable. Insufferable.

Gueldres hung on to the oaken pew as if he was in danger of being sucked down through the solid marble floor.

A black-clad knight of Novara guffawed, excused himself with a series of embarrassed nods at his distracted neighbours.

He was followed by a set of Aostan squirelings, dandy man-boys clad in the latest Florence fashions, wrists cocked like dying fish before their sunken chests. They were rocking down the aisle now, staggering into one another and steadying themselves on the pews.

The murmurs, the whispers built up like an onrushing tide, filling the pews, flooding the nave, rising and falling about the serene ceiling like a neap tide of mirth.

The Vicomte glared left and right, murdered the laughing congregation with his stare. His angry glances sparked choked chuckles and stifled giggles. Sudden uncontrollable bursts of laughter set off tiny explosions of merriment wherever he looked. Somebody at the back started clapping. One wag in a red velvet suit joined in, whistling at least an octave out of key.

Gueldres shrivelled and died, grasped his knees in his anguish.

Stroma cracked his elbow into his aching ribs.

'Out! Get out, I'll not sit here and endure the laughter of the court! You've made me a jackass sir!' he snarled, prising himself to his feet and clambering past the petrified Vicomte.

Father Bembo turned the page of his bloody score, waved his arm for silence. The choristers sobbed with relief, bitterly humiliated by their ordeal. The boys seemed to shrink, their stiffly-inflated chests sagging beneath their viginal cassocks.

'We'll do the *Gloria Sanctus Agnus Dei*,' Bembo intoned, capturing their wandering attentions in a moment. The boys swallowed, collected their breath and began to sing once more, complex Latin chants with superbly-phrased responses.

The last flicker of unsuppressed laughter was driven out of the church like a puff of foul smoke, blown out on a ringing chorus of praise. Bembo looked up, encouraged his young charges with an urgent nod of his chin. The boys sang out with gusto, the soaring cadences filling the church with celestial light.

Gueldres got up, bowed his head, and stalked out, the heavenly chorus ringing in his burning ears.

Runcini didn't even see him go.

But the gleeful Aostans relished every moment of his shameful retreat, turned the aisle into a never-ending avenue of flaming torment. Men and women sniggered and pointed, cupped hands about their neighbours' ears to whisper and hiss. Small children, delighted by the unusually light-hearted mood of their parents, squealed like butchered piglets as he stalked past.

The doors loomed at last out of the blurred corners of his vision. The crisp air bit into his mortified features, nibbling his face like a randy whore.

He stepped down from the vaulted threshold and quickly elbowed a passage through the sagging crowd. He kicked and punched the staring peasants aside, tugged his black hat down about his ears as he avoided their spiteful glances. The moment he was through the pressing throng he took to his heels, hurrying towards the nearest alley to hide himself away from their howling laughter.

Somebody would pay for this humiliation.

Somebody would wish to God they had never been born.

Beside the Via Sant'Orso, Aosta

Deprived of the chance to hear the new choral work, the cheerful townsfolk had decided to entertain themselves. Wandering players worked the bustling crowd, setting up improvised stages on walls and verandahs, and launching into spirited performances which soon had the local *pievani* shaking their heads in disgust at their antics. Their crude pastiches were little more than pagan folk tales brought up to date, with greedy friars and wicked landowners preying on honest woodsmen. Randy wives ran away with soldiers or servants while their boorish husbands counted their money. The teeming crowds loved every minute of it, hooting and laughing at every tasteless revelation. The actors – disguised with a variety of outrageously-enlarged organs – hammed it up for all they were worth, bringing a smile to the face of the pious burghers who scowled about the fringes of the crowd, secretly revelling in the wickedness of their lowly neighbours and wishing they could join in the fun. The ripe banter and raucous laughter echoed back and forth between the stern façades of the town's churches, attracting more and more people out onto the heaving streets.

The general good humour acted like a sour sauce on the raging Vicomte. He strode through the press, pushing the grinning peasants aside with bloodcurdling oaths which brought the revellers up short. Life was hard and celebrations few and far between, and the townsfolk didn't take kindly to being cursed by some upstart northerner.

'You've had your fun master, piss off and let us 'ave ours!' one anonymous wag shouted behind his back. Gueldres leapt about to catch the brute, but the crowding mob had grown a thousand filthy faces.

'Back off you swine, or I'll cut your tongues out,' he snarled, hand on his sword hilt. The surly crew gave him some room, muttering and jeering as he stalked off towards the palazzo.

'Bloody French. Think they own the place.'

'I thought they did.'

Obolus had spotted Alberto Tarsi's spy straight away. A stooping night-black heron amongst the drably-plumaged flock which thronged outside the church. He had kept out of sight, following the intruder all the way back up the Via Sant'Orso to his lair in a seedy, three-storey tenement on the corner of the Via Sant'Anselmo. The tall, swiftly-moving spy had been in a fearful hurry all right, and Obolus had almost lost him in one of the labyrinthine alleys which branched off the main thoroughfares of the old town. But he had finally caught up with him, spotting the tall Fleming darting down a back lane and into his hovel.

Planting the evidence should be easy enough.

As far as Furstenbein knew, Obolus was Tarsi's fool. He might have been sent down to Aosta on a special mission, or to give the Fleming vital new information.

As well as being a superb tenor, a convincing mimic, an energetic tumbler and a first rate jester, Obolus was a gifted counterfeiter. He had helped Gueldres prepare the letters and documents which would help establish Tarsi's guilt, prove his dastardly involvement in the plot to kidnap the choir. He had already left one highly incriminating selection in the pass outside Mont Galliard – where it had been conveniently retrieved by the alert agents of the Inquisition.

The new bundle had also been stamped with the stolen Tarsi signet ring – clear proof of their authenticity. All

Obolus had to do was fetch the bag from his master's quarters and plant it and the precious ring on the unsuspecting Fleming. He could then whistle up some of Count Stroma's guards, and leave the worm to wriggle on his hook!

Furstenbein could curse and plead and whistle all he wished. The forged documentation would speak for itself.

The dwarf's fractured mind was crackling with animal excitement, a kaleidoscope of sights and sounds which would have bewildered most mortals. He was acutely aware of a whole range of subliminal signals, vague images and ghostly impressions which danced on the cracked glass of his consciousness like skaters around a frozen pond. He reacted to each stimulus like a hound on the scent, or a shark closing in on a shoal of panic-stricken mackerel – blocking out every other sense to concentrate on his fleeing prey.

Obolus could sense the slight changes in air temperature as the crowd ahead seethed and divided about some unknown obstacle. He could feel the shifting passions of the closely-packed mob as a series of tiny shocks which vibrated through his clumsy body as if it was a twisted tuning-fork.

The posturing threats of the rival street gangs, shouting and gesturing at one another as they paraded beneath their ragged gonfalons. The sudden, pungent frisson of lust as a goodwife brushed past a knowing stable boy, or a leering barman grabbed the buttocks of his overworked serving girls. The air was ripe with their raucous body odours, pulsing with their unspoken conversations.

Obolus saw and heard all, felt every shout of anger, every anxious mother's cry as a chill knife along the knots of his spine. He had felt the geese walking over his grave, watched a topsy-turvy world go by through their roving amber eyes. If he tilted his head he could block out the clamouring humanity, and concentrate instead on the delightful song of the cypress trees as they bathed the winds with their fragrant, sap-glad branches. He could bend down and listen to the grunts and grumbles in the walls, itching and aching on their powdery foundations, hear the panic-stricken splash of a rat as it swam head-up through the flooded catacombs beneath his feet.

He was only just aware of the choir, singing their hearts out in the church, well out of earshot of the cheerful Sunday crowds.

The place was pulsing with signals the majority of the bumbling peasants were only ever aware of in the utter black of the darkest night, or out alone in the wild woods.

They would have burned him at the stake for his trouble, if the blockheads could have guessed a fraction of the things which went on in his outsized head. Obolus might have earned his crust as a cap-and-bells jester, but he knew he should never boast of his supernatural skills, or demonstrate his wonderful talents to the superstitious townsfolk.

The tingling choral music – echoing faintly through the crumbling bones of the old town – stopped abruptly. The sudden hush brought him to a surprised halt. There were pages and pages of the stolen score left yet – hadn't the cardinal relished his grand mass? Perhaps the congregation had heard enough? Driven to distraction by the dismal, finger-in-the-ear screeching and tired silences?

Obolus giggled. He could have warned Gueldres the score was flawed, but that would have spoiled his fun. It was the dwarf's delight to wreck and ruin their grand designs, to shove a stick in the wheels of their mighty carriages of state. It didn't matter to him who he betrayed or who he served. Masters were as interchangeable as old hose – one could mix and match according to their stinks. One day he might advance Tarsi, the next he might assist Gueldres to pull off some cunning coup. It suited Obolus to see them fight like cats in a sack, to show up their well-laid plans for what they were: pitiful trickery. Childish amusements to while away the winter nights.

Today, he had decided to play Gueldres, shifting his pieces about the board while the master wasn't looking.

Tomorrow – who knows? – he might counter his own manoeuvrings by sweeping the bastard's pawns from the board, lifting them from their precious squares one by one, as if he were pulling the wings from a fly . . .

The wary townsfolk stared at the cackling dwarf, made the sign of the evil eye as they watched him capering about on the pavement. Obolus whistled one of the raucous peasant tunes, tilting his head to listen to the faint echoes in his head.

In another moment the tiny tremors broke out again, fresher, more confident. A surging, celestial spring gushing from every crack in the pavement as if the foundering choir had been granted a reprieve, cast a lifeline of glorious notes. Obolus listened approvingly, recognising the familiar plainsong. He could just make out an even dimmer noise, a faint chiming on the outermost limits of his remarkable hearing.

Bells!

His broad brow creased in bewilderment. He sensed a sudden change in the supercharged air, a distant murmur carried by a thousand anxious voices. And then he was aware of the sudden quiet, an expectant silence advancing over the ochre rooftops like an eclipse of the sun.

He heard the distant peals long seconds before anybody else. The crowd paused about their games and brawls and backgammon, cocking an ear to the unexpected alert.

The dwarf threaded his way between them, crossing the main road and following his nose back to his master's temporary lair at the Palazzo Salassi. The crowd had become more animated than ever, loudly discussing the import of the bells. Obolus slowed down, spreading his hairy hand on the cool, whitewashed wall which ran along the outer perimeter of the palace.

Now he felt the unmistakable thunder of hundreds of hooves, a tiny flutter through the stones. Horsemen, coming this way fast.

Obolus digested the bewildering signals. He wondered

about waiting for old horse-face Muhlberg, finding out what was up from the slow-witted landsknecht. Or maybe he should seek out his mad-tempered master? But there would be no time to get back to the church in this crush, he decided. And Gueldres might not be entirely pleased to see him, after the humiliations he must have endured at St Orso.

Obolus cackled with glee and set off again, his stocky, heavily-muscled legs beating a fierce tattoo on the worn pavement. He'd been dawdling, misled by his own acute awareness. He knew what he had to do now.

Obolus trotted under the main gate of the palazzo, ducked beneath the sleepy sentry's halberd and cut across the artfully-laid lawn before the wretch was aware of him.

The mob seethed about him, all black teeth and bad breath. Gueldres lowered his shoulder and jammed his way through the reeking mass, heading for the grey towers of the palazzo. He was tripped and shoved, elbowed and spat on, but he finally pulled himself out on the tree-lined street which led to Stroma's palace. His triumphal outfit was scored and smeared, his slashed sleeve hanging from his shoulder.

Gueldres clenched his fists, breathing hard to control the blazing rage threatening to blow his swollen eyeballs out. The pressure seemed to be swelling with every nervous step he took, a hateful pustule ready to burst through his cracking skull. He could have sworn he could hear the rolling thunder of hooves, echoing down the twisted canyons of his brain. He grasped at the wall and steadied himelf, shook his head to clear the maddening rattle.

A band of latecomers hurried up the street. The careless peasants laughed and hooted, careering past the shabby show-off bent double by the wall. They ignored the reeling drunk, imagining he was some squire trying to find his lodgings after a long night on the tiles.

The Vicomte sank to his knees, panting with fury as he remembered his humiliation, the laughter and jeers of the court bouncing about his throbbing skull. He clenched his hands about his head and wretched, great sour sobs rung from the very pit of his belly. He crouched in the running gutter, teeth clenched, drooling his fury onto the polished flagstones.

Ruined! Wrecked like the proudest ship adrift on a whiptide of jeering, jostling humanity. All his petulant conniving had been in vain, the childish scheming of a schoolyard bully. The score he had anticipated would herald the rebirth of his own fortune had been turned into a great, ringing raspberry.

Gueldres cursed and cried on his hands and knees, cracked his head against the crumbling plasterwork in his frantic frustration.

And that was when he saw Obolus.

If he had remained standing he would have missed him altogether. The dwarf was hurrying along, a hairy satyr in bright silks. He was heading towards him, working his own way through the milling crowds with the large black portmanteau under his arm. Darting between the trampling legs, ducking under the vendor's carts as he made his getaway from the palazzo.

But instead of continuing towards the Via Sant'Orso, the little fiend ducked down into a side alley. Where was the little beast going now? He was suppose to be bringing it straight to the church! Damn that moron Muhlberg, he'd given him the wrong message! And damn Obolus, for snatching the wrong score in the first place!

Gueldres blinked with rage. He prised himself to his feet and ducked around the blind side of the corner tenement, wondering if the dwarf had discovered a rat-run back to the church. He hurried past the mouldy ruin on the corner, thinking to intercept the verminous gnome as he emerged from the lane.

Gueldres pressed himself against the mossy wall and held his breath, listened for the dwarf's staccato footsteps. He heard his strange song, a mad tumble of words sung to the tune of one of the wandering musicians' country ballads.

'Obolus is over here, Obolus will never fear
run and fetch the leather sack
stab the bastard in the back
And hurry, hurry hurry hurry!

'Obolus!' Gueldres shrieked, launching himself out of the noisome alley and diving full-length for the capering fool. The damned bells in his head must have played tricks with his hearing, because the dwarf wasn't where he should have been. Obolus stopped dead ten paces away from the sprawling nobleman, cocked his rusty red head in malicious bewilderment.

Gueldres peered up at the freak, tried to smile.

'Obolus, I thought it was you. So you've found that scab Furstenbein, eh?'

The dwarf knew something was amiss, his complex, swirling, demented brain analysing explanations as he capered towards the doorway of Furstenbein's lodgings. Bells were ringing all over the town now, the tumultuous street fair drowned by the brass-tongued peals welcoming the mysterious riders from the north. The leading squadrons had passed beneath the Porta Pretoria and were forcing a passage down the Via Sant'Anselmo, through crowds of curious Aostans.

Gueldres could hear their clattering approach over the mad roaring in his head.

'Cavalry, hundreds of them,' he panted. 'It must be Bayard.' The dwarf was humming urgently, poised by the rickety entrance to the Fleming's corner hideout.

'You've brought the documents, eh? We'd better hurry then.' He took a step forward. Obolus took a step back.

'Hang on Obolus, I didn't realise it was you,' Gueldres called, prising himself to his feet.

'GUELDRES, YOU BASTARD!' The frantic bellow shook the grimy window panes, shattered his concentration in a blink. He peered round towards the main road, saw a closely-packed company of riders trotting along the Via Sant'Anselmo towards the town square. A flock of fine knights in startling surcoats, pennants snapping above their heads. Their chargers were roped with sweat, their ornate harness coated with white dust.

The Vicomte narrowed his eyes against the slanting winter sun, recognised the mighty chevalier by the blinding silver halo reflected from his fine armour. But the diabolic shout hadn't come from Bayard's tightly-compressed mouth. Alberto Tarsi was standing in his stirrups amongst the lesser mortals riding a few lengths behind the knight, a squat black bear in his travel-weary cloak. His arm was raised, his gloved finger quivering with fury and pointed in his direction.

'There's the bloody traitor!' Tarsi roared, his bearded face puce with anger. In a split second Gueldres recognised the gaunt features of the English captain, riding alongside the Italian impostor as if they were old friends.

By Christ, they couldn't catch him here! Gueldres thought frantically. He threw his deep blue sleeve over his face and ducked back into the alley, electrified by his own stupidity. He couldn't be found in company with the damned dwarf, weighed down with forged documents outside Furstenbein's lair!

The cunning dwarf had already slipped inside the wretched door, hanging precariously on its hinges.

'My Lord Vicomte! Hold, sir!' Bayard's melodious command flickered through his reeling brain. He ignored the imperious call, obsessed with intercepting the volatile dwarf. The little fiend could ruin all, just by being here! Gueldres could hear the dwarf's iron-shod shoes rattle up the staircase inside the shabby tenement. No time! No time! He tore the door back and ducked inside the mildewed hallway.

'Come back here you freak! You little shit, you slime-breathing toad!' Gueldres howled. 'You stole the wrong score you miserable frog! You cockeyed runt! You let Tarsi trick you!' he shrieked, taking the steep stairs six at a time despite the darkness. 'They're riding up the street now, you cockbuster, you filthy squinter! Where's the portmanteau, you fornicating whore's melt?' He reached the first landing and swung himself around the balustrade, craning his neck to peer towards the top of the leaning ruin.

Obolus was hanging over the banister, mischievously waving the black leather sack above his rusty head.

The poisonous reptile must have grown wings, flown to the landing to find his staring familiar. The tall stranger in the black gown had opened his door at the sudden commotion, a curved knife ready in his clenched fist, a large bundle tucked under his left arm. He peered down at the sawn-off fugitive and his apoplectic pursuer.

Gueldres gaped up the stairs as the dwarf ducked his head and ran between the tall stranger's legs, hurling himself into the man's dank room.

'Obolus? What, here?' It had to be Furstenbein, sick with terror and bewilderment at the fractured sequence of events. Gueldres knew how the impostor felt. He propelled himself up the stairs, drawing his dagger as he came. Furstenbein flung his package at him, the heavily-laden sack catching the Vicomte a glancing blow on his forehead. Gueldres staggered back, put his foot straight through a rotten board, and felt the bent nails rake his shins. He croaked in agony, dropping the dagger and holding on to the damp balustrade to save himself from falling further. The tall stranger ducked back inside his room and hurled the door closed.

Gueldres pulled at the rotten trap, tore at the broken boards screeching in fury. Two floors below, the side door was flung back, filling the drab hall with light. A couple of soldiers in papal livery peered into the back-street garret.

'Stay where you are, all of you!' the leading spearman called, hurrying up the stairs in clumsy haste. Gueldres yanked his leg free, ignoring the howling pain which shot up his thigh, spearing his groin. The nobleman went up the stairs on his hands and knees, nauseous with rage. He burst through another poorly-fastened door, and found himself in a filthy garret. A naked couple were lying on the ruckled bed, flushed with recent loveplay. Gueldres ignored their squawkings, limping over to the hanging shutters.

'Where the 'ell d'you think you are?' the male cried, grasping the bedclothes over his limp genitals. Gueldres grabbed at the man's discarded cloak and tore the shutters open. The woman – a red–headed whore with pendulous white breasts, threw back her head and screamed, attracting the pursuing soldiery straight to the invaded boudoir.

'He went out on the balcony! He's got my cloak!' the man bawled, jumping to his feet and following the soldiers towards the streaming window.

'What's the world coming to, if you can't have a peaceful fuck on a Sunday morning?' he demanded, jumping into his baggy braies.

The soldiers crashed through the swinging shutters, big men in weighty mail stamping and crashing about on the balcony overlooking the packed main street. The limping fugitive had prised himself over the dividing wall and burst into the shack door.

'This way!'

The spearmen were halfway over the frail wall when the entire structure came away from the wall in an explosion of rust and powdered stone. The ancient balcony fell into the Via Sant'Anselmo, depositing the shocked soldiers in a dusty heap.

Gueldres cowered in the darkness, holding his hands to his bleeding legs and listening to the havoc breaking around him.

Where was that damned dwarf?

Beside the Via Sant'Orso,
Aosta

Alberto Tarsi could hardly believe his own eyes. The Bastard Gueldres slinking off down an alley like a common footpad – in front of a dozen witnesses! The swine must have lost his mind, he thought hotly, tugging at his horse's reins to bring the tired beast around.

'Gueldres!'

Bayard grabbed at his ornate bridle, wrenched the horse back around before Tarsi could spur after the guiltily-fleeing Vicomte.

'Seigneur Tarsi, you will remain where you are,' the chevalier instructed, furious Gueldres had already ignored his order to halt.

The Italian cursed, fist clenched about the hilt of his sword. Having kept his word and surrendered to his parole, Bayard had in return allowed Tarsi to retain his dignity – and his arms – for the short ride to Aosta. Briconet had fought a stubborn rearguard action against Bayard's dangerous clemency, loudly insisting his life would be forfeit if the accused was allowed his sword. But Bayard – who insisted on giving every individual the opportunity of emulating his own blameless behaviour – had curtly overruled him, assuring the papal legate Tarsi would not harm him.

Tarsi felt a reckless urge to brush the chevalier's restraining hand away and spur down the alley after his bitter rival, cut him down to size once and for all. But Bayard's long-suffering frown stayed his hand. He jabbed his finger after the fugitive.

'Didn't you see him, running off like a pickpocket?' Tarsi spluttered.

'I saw him Seigneur, but we have not come here to brawl in back-lanes,' Bayard replied, his voice level despite the furious glint in his eyes.

'Then let me go my Lord!' Eldritch cried, urging his own mount alongside his chief. 'God knows he has wronged us both!'

'You?'

'I swear I'll bring him back unharmed,' the captain vowed in his schoolbook French.

Eldritch was trembling with anticipation, willing the chevalier to make up his mind. Bayard seemed to look straight through him, studying the dreary frontage of the hovel for clues to this deadly conundrum. He turned to the waiting spearmen, papal troops who had been sent ahead to open a passage through the Sunday-morning throng.

'Sergeant take your men down the alley. Make sure nobody gets out of the rear of the buildings,' he instructed. 'You, sirs, will remain with me.'

Eldritch fidgeted like a leashed falcon, anxiously awaiting Bayard's word. Surely he must be able to hear the frantic shouts from within the ruin, the sudden thumps and alarming screeches. Somebody was singing at the top of their voice, a screeching falsetto which stiffened the hairs on the back of his neck.

'This way sir, follow that shouting! Mind your backs for the Inquisition!' some wag called from the eyeball-popping crush behind them. Eldritch swivelled in his saddle, watched the boisterous populace divide like a shabby sea around Briconet. The inquisitor was wearing a white cloak and black hood of the Dominicans and riding beneath his own dreaded banners. The Hound of Christ was crossing himself and intoning prayers, one eye on the hooting and hissing crowd.

But none dared hold the inquisitor's dead-eye glare.

'Briconet,' Bayard called, watching him kick his way through the hostile mob straddled across a grey ass. The inquisitor had hurried up from his place at the rear of the column – hitherto unwilling to ride within a hundred paces of his sworn enemy Tarsi in case Bayard's childish trust proved misplaced.

'I want you here to see this,' Bayard said haughtily. 'The Bastard Gueldres himself has just taken refuge in that building! Perhaps you can provide an explanation for such an extraordinary flight?'

Briconet frowned, deeply alarmed by the unforseen development. He had been expecting to try, convict and execute Tarsi and his English bandits for conspiracy to rob and murder. Now it seemed the doubtful Bayard had found more red herrings to divert attention from their common goal.

'If it was indeed my Lord the Vicomte, running off in the manner you suggest, then I am sure he had ample reason for absenting himself,' Briconet simpered, even more alarmed by the chevalier's fiercely accusing glance than he was by the hostile crowd.

'It was him, God damn you,' Eldritch snarled, turning his horse in a threatening circle about the pale agent.

'My Lord Chevalier, I am sure there is a simple . . .' Briconet's angry retort was drowned out by the shriek of ill-oiled hinges as the shutters were thrown open on the long balcony above their heads. The rickety platform ran the length of the tenement, overlooking the refuse-littered alley to their right. A crouching figure in a black gown peered over the rusty iron railings. Eldritch stood up in his stirrups to point the fugitive out to the bewildered soldiers clambering over the adjoining balcony.

'There he goes!'

The pursuing troops crashed about on the platform, peering up and down like travelling players performing some crude farce. They turned after the fugitive, who had hopped over the partition and was tearing at the closed shutters of the adjoining apartment. The crowd in the alley below watched in thrilled fascination as the overloaded balcony tipped to one side, tumbling the soldiers back against the crumbling wall. In another blink the entire platform had come away, tearing great mouthfuls of plaster from the damp brickwork. The soldiers poised below covered their heads as mouldy bricks and rotten timbers collapsed about them, shrieking gendarmes and papal spearmen knocked sideways by the avalanche. The guards were swallowed up by a cloud of stone dust which boiled out of the alley and swirled around the astonished officers.

Bayard's horse reared. Tarsi hung on to his mount's mane as it plunged into a wall, whinnying in alarm.

Eldritch cursed. The fools were going to let Gueldres get away with their dismal clowning!

He made up his mind, drove his own bucking horse straight at the reeling hovel before the chevalier could stop him. His leg scraped against a window sill. He reached up blindly, locked his fingers about the crumbling base of one of the surviving balconies and swung himself up. The old iron grated in protest as he let his frightened horse slip from between his legs and bolt free into a mob of violently-coughing spearmen. The terrified animal knocked them aside, adding to the fearful havoc in the main street. Eldritch hauled himself up over the rotten sill, his face pressed into the wrought iron railings. He kicked out and felt the structure tip alarmingly, creaking and moaning on its ancient fittings. Eldritch knew the damned balcony wouldn't bear his weight much longer. He held his breath and heaved himself up and over the rotting obstacle.

Julius Furstenbein couldn't clear the terrifying vision from his mind. He had only caught a glimpse of Gueldres' face as he lurked on the landing – but the wild mask would haunt him for the last panic-stricken minutes of his existence.

Before he could blink little Obolus had darted between his outstretched legs and broken the awful spell – yodelling with terror as if all the fiends of hell were after him. The sudden movement had sent the spy fleeing back indoors.

He clapped the door shut, laid hold of the dresser which stood beside his unmade bed and hauled it over to bar the door. The dresser shrieked over the bare boards, grating his already-frayed nerves.

What was Obolus doing here?

He leaned the clumsy piece against the door and peered over his shoulder at the dwarf.

'Where's Tarsi? Has he sent you on ahead?' he cried. Obolus, as usual, seemed lost in his own turbulent world, dancing on his shadow like some demented hare. The last Furstenbein had heard, Obolus had been going to France with Mistress Angelica and that dog's breakfast Ambolini! There was a loud crash and a furious curse from the stairs. Furstenbein jumped, clenched his fingers about the kitchen knife.

'Open the shutters, call out the guard!' Furstenbein bawled. He would rather explain his presence to the glowering Aostan authorities than run the risk of being shut in with that mad bastard of a Vicomte! He crossed the room in a blink, stepping around the drooling dwarf.

'Fire, foes, awake!' he cried, tugging at the shutters desperate with terror. He dropped the knife, laid both hands about the latches and yanked with all his might.

Obolus stopped dancing, cupped his hand about his gold-ringed ear. 'Coming master!' he trilled.

Furstenbein wrenched at the shutters once more, the assaulted hinges pulling out of the woodwork in a flutter of damp sawdust and grit. Just then the dwarf strode after him, retrieved the dropped knife from the floorboards and plunged the eight-inch blade into the base of his spine. Furstenbein arched in agony, still clinging on to the creaking shutters.

Obolus hung on, working the honed steel between the Fleming's vertebrae as if he was opening a shellfish. Furstenbein gasped as the blade grated on his backbone. He staggered, his dying weight finally dragging the shutters open . . .

And bringing him face to face with his nemesis – Gueldres.

The fugitive had been crouching on the balcony, trying to force the shutters inward just as the maddened spy had been trying to wrestle them open.

'You?' Furstenbein gasped, his mouth moving sideways. Gueldres growled like a cornered wolf, propelled himself straight at the dying man. The two of them rolled back into the room, the Fleming screaming in torment as the blade bit deeper into his spine.

Gueldres rolled aside, springing to his feet in an instant. Furstenbein blinked back tears of humiliated pain, watched the dwarf back away from his horribly-bent body. For a moment Obolus seemed to tower above him, his tightly-muscled legs stretching the faded fabric of his hose.

'You!' he croaked, his dying mind lurching from shock to anger.

'You the spy!' he managed, before the words stopped in his throat and the dark room swallowed him up.

'I stuck him, I stuck him, I stuck hiiiiiiiim!' Obolus warbled. 'I killed him all for yoooooou!' he added, eyeing the exits and backing away from the panting intruder.

Gueldres took a painful step forward and clutched the little man by the shoulders of his colourful silk tunic.

'I killed him for you master!' Obolus repeated, unusually alarmed by the Vicomte's mad-eyed stare.

'You've done worse than that, you've knotted the noose about my neck, you fornicating toad-skin!' Gueldres screeched, yanking the protesting dwarf from his feet.

The jester squirmed, beating his fists against the Vicomte's chest. One wild blow connected, tearing a great rent in Gueldres' gown. The taller man staggered back, momentarily disconcerted by the dwarf's ferocious defence. He held him out at arm's length, stared in his grotesquely-distorted face.

'Ah, that it's come to this, my little Grecian coin,' Gueldres snarled in mock sympathy, trying to work his hand higher to lock his fingers about the little brute's neck. He didn't have one, that was the trouble!

Obolus kicked and scratched, jaws snapping as he swung in mid-air. He twisted about, reached up Gueldres' outstretched arm and clawed the taut skin. Gueldres yelped, releasing the biting bundle. Obolus collapsed on top of him, jabbing at his kidneys as the tall man fell awkwardly on his side.

Gueldres gasped with pain, kicked the dwarf away with a grunt of anger.

Obolus knew there was no way out. No chance of appeasing his deranged master now. He was trapped in this foul room, the ante-chamber to hell itself.

In that terrible, interminable moment, he stumbled over his senses, wandered from the shadow world he had inhabited into the pitiless bright light of day. He used up one or two of his last moments in serene reflection, realising the cackling harpies which had raced and rebounded about his head had finally found a way out, whistled out of his hairy ears like bats out after dark.

He gave a slow hiss like a boiling kettle, momentarily aware of all he had done, of all the monstrous atrocities he had committed. The lies, the throttlings, the petty hurts and dreadful betrayals.

He turned and hurled himself towards the balcony, partially blocked by the roughly-handled shutters. Obolus threw one leg over the battered hurdle, trying to force his way out of the shambles. Gueldres smiled, bent down and boosted Furstenbein's travelling chest over the floorboards. The heavy box crunched against the woodwork, pinning the wrecked shutters across the exit.

'Ho, ho, ho, lost your voice Obolus?' Gueldres snarled. 'I'm afraid I'm going to be forced to terminate our little arrangement,' he cried, watching the little man beat his legs as he tried to boost himself over the obstacle.

Gueldres swallowed hard, fought to control his breathing. It had all gone horribly wrong, but all was not lost. Not yet at any rate. As long as he had a tongue in his head he might yet be able to squirm his way out of this godforsaken mess.

Obolus gave up, slipped back down the trapped shutters.

Gueldres had taken out his wolf's-head dagger and was weaving the blade in front of his face as if he was trying to charm the deadliest cobra.

'You might have noticed, I'm not at all happy with the score you stole.' Gueldres intoned. 'I worked hard for that, thinking it all through. It hadn't occurred to me you'd been taken in by Tarsi.'

Gueldres knew he couldn't leave any witnesses to muddy the waters, to remember their lost allegiance before it was too late. He tilted his head, amused and appalled by the sudden crescendos of noise from the alley below. He knew there was no way out of this dump, not with half of Bayard's crusaders playing with themselves in the streets below. He would have to go quietly.

But Obolus wouldn't be going with him – not this time.

'You've been a handy spy. A small coin worth its weight in gold, eh? Many's the time you've helped me pull the wool over that oaf Tarsi's eyes. But all good things must come to an end, my friend,' he said sadly.

Obolus eyed him as if mesmerised by his soothing commentary.

Gueldres pounced, closing his left fist in Obolus' curly hair and lifting him from the ground. He thrust with all his mad-might, the dagger juddering under the dwarf's chin, impaling him against the battered doorframe. The skewered spy kicked feebly, feet barely brushing the floorboards. His blood ran this way and that over the shutters, red trails playing snakes and ladders up and down the peeling slats.

Gueldres looked around the room, quickly found what he was looking for. A bucket of small coal, pitiful pieces which looked as if they had been picked from some slag heap. He threw the fragments into the fireplace then walked to Furstenbein's table and lifted his rusty oil lamp. He shook it, listened to the satisfying slurp. Gueldres knew he would not have very long now.

The killer strode back to the grate and poured the contents of the lamp over the ashes, bringing them to instant, fiery life. He picked up the portmanteau the dwarf had discarded, in two minds now whether he should destroy it at all. It could be a double-edged sword if it fell into the wrong hands, but then again he could always claim he had caught *Furstenbein* attempting to burn the incriminating contents!

That might make some kind of sense, when he had had time to think it through properly. But there was no time now.

He built up the fire with the few bits of kindling the Fleming had left by the grate and tugged the portmanteau open, idly selecting a few sheets of their carefully-counterfeited correspondence.

'Ah, you did a fine job on these letters Obolus. It grieves me to see it all go up in smoke.' He tore the heavy vellum into strips and fed it into the fire.

There was a sudden shriek as the large dresser scraped across the floorboards behind him, alerting Gueldres to the fact that the door was being forced open at last.

He stepped across the bloody room to meet the intruder. The dresser creaked back on two legs and toppled over with a worm-ridden crash. The door fell open and Eldritch leapt over the threshold, sword in fist. Gueldres drew his dagger.

'Ah, look who it is. Captain Cunny-cheat come for his orders,' Gueldres smirked. Eldritch was breathing hard, his dark eyes everywhere.

'Give it up Geldray, I've orders not to harm you. Bayard knows what you've done; he knows all of it.'

'Bayard? That buffoon? He doesn't know his holy arse from his elbow. You've backed the wrong horse again, Eldritch!' he observed. The Englishman stepped carefully over the broken door panels, rounded the overturned dresser. The point of his sword flickered back and forth, tasting the blood-tang in the dust-choked air.

'I would love to oblige you, Eldritch. Another time, maybe.' Gueldres opened his arms. 'You can see I'm unarmed.'

'No matter. I'm to bring you to Bayard, alive. But if you were to fall down the stairs and break your neck . . . you won't see me shedding tears at your funeral,' Eldritch snarled. His darting eyes came to rest on the dwarf, hanging like a bloody puppet against the clutter by the window. The Vicomte watched his dark eyes flick back to him.

'You've shut his mouth for him, eh? I don't imagine the dwarf gave you much trouble, a fabulous swordsman like yourself.'

Gueldres chuckled.

'Oh come now Eldritch, you and I are peas from the same pod, if you will excuse the coarse expression. It's what you wanted, what you craved, isn't it? All this swordplay, the plotting? You knew what you wanted when you tried to trick your master and me back at Guisnes.'

Eldritch licked his lips.

'Get back against the wall where Bayard can see you. I don't want to face the temptation of pushing you down the staircase!'

Eldritch glanced sideways. The fire was burning merrily, a case of papers splayed beside the grate. He had been trying to burn the evidence!

More troops were hurrying up the stairs now, beating a path through the piled rubble and on up the smashed steps, finding their way through the fog of stonedust. The whole building seemed in imminent danger of collapsing over its rotten foundations. Eldritch menaced Gueldres with his sword, bent down to kick a sheaf of burning documents away from the grate. A pack of spearmen kicked their way through the demolished doorway. More were forcing their way in from the balcony. Gueldres babbled at them in their native tongue, calmly making his way towards the door. The spearmen levelled their weapons and backed away, giving him room.

Eldritch emptied the last of the documents from the case and used the heavy leather portmanteau to try and smother the flames so he could rescue the scorched evidence from the ashes.

Bayard stalked into the room a few moments later.

The chevalier looked from the crouching Englishman to the serenely-smiling Vicomte, not sure what he was seeing.

'My Lord Chevalier. Words cannot express how happy I am to see you,' Gueldres said calmly, as if Bayard had arrived in the middle of a delicately-poised game of tennis rather than a madhouse of burning, blood and murder.

Beside the Via Sant'Orso, Aosta

The Chevalier Bayard's first thought as he stepped into the garret was that Eldritch – that disobedient hound of an Englishman – had either fallen down in a dead faint or lost his mind. The captain had sunk to his knees by the fireplace, his long arms extended towards the grate like some heathen at prayer.

'Captain Eldritch,' Bayard called. 'What devilry is this?'

He glanced at the dwarf impaled on the shutters, at Furstenbein's body sprawled in its dark lagoon. A gored knife lay on the waxy boards beside him, surrounded by its own circlet of blood.

Eldritch was choking over the fire, tugging smouldering documents from the grate and beating the flames from the corners. A black leather portmanteau had been flung on the fire, the stiff folds curling as the trapped heat beneath warped the old hide. Bayard bent down and grabbed the corner of the satchel and tugged it away from the blaze.

'It appears Tarsi's spies have fallen out amongst themselves,' Gueldres observed calmly. 'Eldritch, the Fleming there, the dwarf Obolus. Everybody knows they are Tarsi's creatures,' he said with a shrug. More troops had crowded into the room, weapons ready. They jostled one another for a peep at the rumoured piggeries within, hung back in horror when they discovered their comrades had not exaggerated the carnage.

'Liar! He was trying to burn these papers when I burst ir

346

on him!' Eldritch snarled, sitting back on his haunches with the last smoking fragments.

'Me? You are mistaken sir. You have the sword, not I. He burst in and found the portmanteau, and menaced me while *he* tried to burn the evidence!' Gueldres accused. 'By all means take a look at the papers for yourself, my Lord, and decide who stood to gain from their destruction.'

'You forged these papers, serpent!'

'Enough!' Bayard cried. 'My Lord Vicomte. I regret that, in the circumstances, I must also place you under arrest.'

Geuldres looked pained.

'I understand how things might look and your concern to see justice done. In the circumstances, you have little choice,' he said smoothly. 'I can only look forward to clearing the name Eldritch and his master Tarsi have been pleased to besmirch!'

Bayard, weary with the bloody horrors he had uncovered, ignored his confident challenge.

'You will remain under house arrest until these matters can be properly investigated,' Bayard intoned, glancing down at Eldritch's sudden movement. The captain scrambled to his feet and hurried towards the ghastly puppet hanging from the shutters.

'He said something!' Eldritch cried.

'Nonsense, you snatched my dagger and stabbed the dwarf to implicate me!' Gueldres cried, furiously intent on confusing the immaculate chevalier. 'Watch him, Bayard, he's trying to finish him!'

'He's trying to say something!' Eldritch exclaimed, beckoning the chevalier to his side. Bayard strode across the room and leaned over the feebly-twitching figure. Eldritch reached under the dying dwarf's armpits to lift his body weight from the cruelly-stuck blade. He tilted his head, face to face with the sinister Obolus.

'What's he saying?'

'I can't hear with you shouting.'

Obolus raised his hand, curled his little index finger and

gestured weakly at Gueldres. The nobleman stood by, a nonchalant smile playing about the corners of his mouth as he watched their futile ministrations. Obolus repeated the gesture with his finger, pointed at Gueldres. He gasped something, spluttered blood and subsided with one last sigh, hanging on the deadly knife like a ham in a smoke-house.

'He's gone,' Bayard said.

'He said "a nella"?' Eldritch repeated.

'*Anello*, a ring,' Bayard explained. Eldritch looked up sharply.

'That's why he was doing this with his finger,' he copied the dwarf's gesture. 'He pointed at you, my Lord Vicomte,' Eldritch rasped.

Bayard nodded.

'Who can tell what he meant?' Gueldres asked. 'The death rattlings of a demented freak can hardly be considered as evidence! We're not in England now, Eldritch!'

Eldritch prised himself to his feet, his moist black eyes – stung by the smoke – flashing with sudden anger.

'I wager you can tell right enough,' he accused. Bayard laid a restraining hand on the Englishman's arm.

'You will have an opportunity to ask that question before a properly-constituted tribunal,' Bayard said levelly. 'You have my word this will be investigated.' Eldritch shook his head.

Briconet's belated arrival put a stop to their spiteful argument. He looked aghast at the dead dwarf, the peculiarly rigid body of the Fleming lying forgotten on the floor. Bayard silenced him with a glance.

'I would like a word with you sir, right away.' The papal legate narrowed his eyes as he tried to understand the slaughter.

'Wait!' Eldritch exclaimed. 'Now he's arrived, perhaps the Vicomte would like to explain what the dwarf meant by the ring.'

Briconet gave the captain a withering look, pretending he did not understand his outburst.

'I told you captain, you will get an opportunity to . . .'

'The little man,' Eldritch explained in halting French. 'Pointed at Gueldres and said "the ring". I wanted to know what you gentlemen think he meant by that.'

Bayard frowned. Briconet's agile mind was picking over possibilities, astonished at the Vicomte's appalling blundering. What was he thinking of, allowing himself to be taken in this wretched den, caught red-handed with a couple of corpses? Briconet thought it prudent to open some distance between him and the evilly-staring nobleman.

'Well, what have you to say to that, my Lord Vicomte?' he asked jauntily. Bayard narrowed his eyes as he followed the complex interplay. Gueldres smiled, trying to disguise the nervous tic which had developed at the creased corner of his mouth.

'You dare question me about the ramblings of the *lusus naturae*?' he inquired, his eyes black with threat. Briconet overlooked the warning glance.

'*Anello*. A ring, my Lord. His last words, pointing at Gueldres!' Eldritch repeated, exasperated by the papal legate's rapid French. 'He could have named his murderer; he could have named Gueldres. But he said "ring"!'

'Why don't you shut your filthy mouth, you stinking English peasant?' Gueldres snarled, turning his baleful glare on his principal prosecutor. Bayard bent down, lifted the charred portmanteau. He selected a sheaf of half-burned letters, quickly digested the carefully-transcribed contents. All the dispatches had been sealed with wax and stamped with the Tarsi signet ring – just like the bundle which had been so fortuitously rescued by Briconet's assistant. The chevalier closed his eyes, crucified by the very idea a gentleman could have stooped so low, counterfeiting evidence against his brother nobles.

'You have in your possession the Tarsi signet ring,' he accused, his voice drained of all emotion. Gueldres smarted.

'Tarsi's ring? Do you think he'd let me anywhere near it?' the Vicomte inquired, exasperated by their questions.

'Empty your purse Gueldres!' Eldritch snapped.

'Fuck you and your damned sisters! Aye, I recognised your name the moment Howath mentioned it! I heard your beloved Lillith's as popular a turn as ever, down on the dockside at Marseille!' he snarled back. Eldritch was stunned by the display of naked rage, electrified by the reference to his sister. Bayard gripped the younger man's shoulder, pulled him away from his grinning quarry.

'What did you say?' Eldritch choked.

'You heard! I'll look her up, next time I'm passing. She'd service the entire legion for a bronze pistareeni!' Bayard hurled the raving Englishman aside. Gueldres glanced over his shoulder as if he would risk leaping from the window. But there were as many soldiers in the rubble-strewn alley as there were pressing up the staircase. He racked his brain, wondering at the dwarf's deadly accusation. Had Obolus hung on to the damned thing, hidden it somewhere in here?

Gueldres went cold. His heart thumped. Good Christ alive, no!

'Get him out of my sight. I don't need to stand here and listen to some filthy *Transmarini* make unsubstantiated accusations about me!' Bayard threw the furious Englishman away with surprising force. Gueldres reached inside his torn coat as slyly as he could, and immediately closed his fingers about the ring. The ring Obolus had forced under his shirt as they struggled! His mind was reeling, crushed and lanced from a dozen directions at once. He was shocked – astounded he could have made so many appalling blunders – in one single day.

'He has a knife!' Briconet shrieked, mistaking his clumsy sleight of hand. Bayard swung round, his sword raised. Gueldres tore his hand free, cursing his own barely-believable stupidity. Tears of anguished fright stung his eyes. His mouth twitched with useless explanations, his razor-edged mind blunted by unfamiliar indecision. Bayard menaced him with the sword.

'Give it up, my Lord,' he breathed dangerously. 'Or on

my honour I'll cleave you in two, right now!' Gueldres grimaced, his features contorted. He withdrew his hand, turned his palm outward to reveal Tarsi's signet ring — stolen from Fabrizio back at the abbey and duly handed over to the author of the atrocity.

Briconet gasped with astonishment.

'I have a perfectly reasonable explanation. I would have shown you earlier, but the Englishman's . . .' Gueldres choked, his defiant voice trailing away into an anguished sob. Bayard picked the ring from the Vicomte's hand, passed it to Briconet.

'My ring!' Alberto Tarsi cried from the doorway. He hadn't been able to restrain himself a moment longer and had disobeyed Bayard's order to remain outside with the chattering spearmen.

For the first time in his entire life, the Bastard Gueldres lowered his head in defeat.

'What have you heard of my sister?' Eldritch demanded, trying to force his way past the stubborn chevalier.

Gueldres thrust his chin out defiantly.

'Wouldn't you like to know!'

The prisoner was bundled outside before he could be persuaded to elaborate. Eldritch stood in the midst of the blood and slaughter, his mind a battleground of conflicting emotions.

Anger won out, tottering over the pale corpses of love, hope and devotion. Anger at the swarthy Vicomte for hurling such diabolical poisons in his face, anger at Lillith, for betraying them all in the first place, and anger at himself, for not being able to control the furious turmoil of his mind.

Tarsi laid an encouraging hand on his shoulder.

'Men will say anything, accuse anyone, when they find themselves in such a pass,' he said awkwardly. 'Gueldres is the Godfather of Lies. I should know, my friend.'

'He's known something,' Eldritch replied softly. 'He's had something up his sleeve ever since we met in Guisnes. He was just biding his time, waiting for the right moment to cast his line.'

'Well it won't do him any good. He's cooked his goose, getting himself caught in this shambles! I'd like to see him talk his way out of this!'

Bayard was waiting in the doorway for them. He pursed his lips at Tarsi's optimistic assessment.

'The court will consider all relevant evidence,' he said stiffly.

Tarsi sighed in exasperation at the chevalier's unbending code of justice.

'Haven't you seen enough Bayard?'

'More than enough. But his innocence or guilt is no plainer to me than yours, Seigneur. Which is why we will proceed to trial. Now perhaps we can be on our way?'

Tarsi chuckled grimly, patted the dumbstruck captain on the back. Somewhere in the distance, the bells continued to clang the alarm.

Beside Mont Gilbert le Galliard, in the French Alps

Angelica had been woken by the strange girl's tears, her withering sobs rousing her, infinitely slowly, from her own miserable abyss. She had lain on the damp couch, still as death, her eyes fluttering as she tried to get her bearings.

Another of Briconet's tricks, surely.

The inquisitor had switched tactics, tried to fool her she was back in her own gaily-decorated chamber at Mont Galliard rather than lying on a straw pallet in the smoke-clogged ruins of the abbey. He must have gone to considerable expense, transporting her wall hangings and embroideries, her bulging wardrobes, all the way from the castle.

She ached all over, longing to stretch out, test her tingling limbs, but she dared not. If they saw her moving they would be back, back to begin their agonising inquiries all over again. Angelica closed her eyes tight shut, barricading her mind against the eruption of images which threatened to spill out of the darkness. The insinuating memory of the pain they had inflicted was even worse than the torture itself.

Instead, she listened. Eavesdropped on the whispering spies they had sent to watch over her restless sleep. Angelica could hear the strange girl's stifled sobs, whispered endearments she could not make out.

Of course! The girl was speaking English . . . imploring

her beloved to stand up? Straighten out? Courting couples in the dungeons of the Inquisition? She couldn't resist the temptation to open her right eye a notch, focus slowly on her favourite hanging, the eagle motif she had spent long hours stitching. She remembered serene evenings listening to her father, to Luca and Uncle Julius as they argued about war and politics beside the fire. A sunburst of candles illuminating her quiet needlework. Father had always scolded her when she tried to finish her embroidery by the flickering glimmer of a single candle. She would often fetch Constanzia to . . . Constanzia. Angelica remembered her that night in the abbey, the fiery-eyed maid framed in the doorway with the pitcher held above her head, ready to beat her skull in. The sudden, stomach-twisting confusion, the vile misunderstandings and accusations, the shouting and the bloodshed which had thrown a black sack around her mind and dragged her down into a terrible, never-to-be-forgotten abyss of pain and fright. Angelica tensed, her whole body stiffening like a pale corpse in a mausoleum. Surely they had heard her desperate cry? Surely they would be back to begin their examinations all over again?

The room was brightly lit, shafts of sunlight streaming through the open shutters. The bracing air had freshened the room, driven away the reek of old urine and terror-sweat. Bright clothing had been heaped over the couch, the gowns and petticoats she had discarded before the fateful trip to d'Eleron. The girl squatting beside the divan was rather taller and slimmer than she was, wearing one of Angelica's castoffs by the look of it. A copper-coloured ball gown she had grown out of the previous summer. Her father had picked it from her wardrobe to meet the deputation from Villefranco. By God, it seemed like a lifetime ago, but it could only have been a matter of weeks, Angelica thought wearily.

The girl's thick, dark hair cascaded over her face, obscuring her features from Angelica's awkward viewpoint. She appeared to be repairing holes in the divan's horsehair cover, running her hands over the brightly-coloured cushions.

354

Angelica raised her head a fraction and looked closer. She realised the unfamiliar fabric was wrapped tight about a pair of long legs, the bony, bare feet propped up on the armrest. The ankles were ringed with filth, long toes curled over like a falcon's talons. Angelica tried to prise herself higher, winced in agony as she shifted her hands.

The stranger sat up with a start, hands flying to her chest in surprise. She was strikingly attractive despite her evident grief, her sore eyes sunken in their sockets, smudged with nervous fatigue. By Heaven, she must look a hundred times worse, finding fault with strangers!

The girl wiped her eyes on her sleeve, talking quickly in English. She got up, gauntly tall, and sat down beside her, reaching out to lift her hands. Angelica realised the grey packages she had taken to be bundled underclothing were in fact attached to her arms. She sat bolt upright, horribly concerned, staring at the stained linen bandages. The girl was cooing, reassuring her in English, gently pushing her back into the damp depression in her mattress. Angelica thrust her shoulder forward, lifted the grubby swaddling, more alarmed than ever. The girl was shouting now, calling over her shoulder. An overweight nurse in a starched white bonnet hurried into the room, her skirts clutched before her. It was Sophia, her wet nurse, wrapping her fleshy pink arms about her wasted frame, crying out her name again and again.

'My girl, my girl returned to us! Thank the Lord!' she exclaimed, gently easing Angelica's bandaged hands back into her lap.

'Don't pull at your dressings, Gelli, you'll scar, and they're healing well enough, aye, given time.' The nurse was crying freely, great salt tears spangling Angelica's cheeks. Heal? In time? What had they done to her? What had they done to her hands?

And then she remembered. Dark images locked up in a black box in a corner of her brain spewed out in a filthy and confused stream, tumbling over one another as they flooded the vacant chambers of her mind.

Iron traps with rusty screws which squeaked like mice when they fastened them about her fingers. Flaming tapers, burning flesh. Slowly blossoming stains beneath her nails, complex apparatus stained with old, old blood. Her blood. Briconet had stripped to his stained undergarments to free his arms from his great heavy sleeves while he worked, sweat standing out on his furrowed brow. Souris had sweated worse, fetching and carrying, scraping a bucket beneath the armrests to catch the blood, his greasy face lit by the stubby candles . . .

She wailed, a hateful, bone-rattling growl torn from the deepest pits of her belly. Sophia was convinced it was the end, hanging on to her mistress' wasted frame as she bucked and quivered like a hooked eel, writhed in her dirty gown and damp bedclothes as if she was shedding skins of mortification.

'There girl, you're home, you're home,' Sophia reassured her, pressing the girl's limp body into her ample bosom, choking her anguished shrieks in the pendulous folds of her straining bodice. Home? Was it really Mont Galliard? Was she really in her old room, familiarly fragrant chamber?

Angelica subsided, looked up at the reassuringly flushed features of the nurse. 'Where's my father?' she asked at last, turning her head to stare at the concerned stranger. 'And who's she?'

Isolani had died that morning, his long, thin frame practically drained of blood, his exotically-tanned flesh wasted like parchment. Merron had barely left his side since the morning they had arrived, holding his ringleted head in her lap as the surgeon sawed the barb from the quarrel and removed the slick shaft. But the powerful missile had broken his collarbone, ripped through his muscles and drained his blood by the pint. Isolani hadn't recovered from the agonising operation, his cold grip becoming increasingly feeble as the short days drew on.

Tarsi had ordered the captain be taken care of alongside

his unconscious daughter, the string–bag creature Briconet had deposited on the causeway like so much trash.

The cursing soldier had hardly believed she could be alive, reduced to such skeletal stupidity by her ordeal. Eldritch had borne her back from the bridge, the swooning girl seeming barely as heavy as the sword he wore.

'They sat up with you, in your room here. Your father and my brother drank wine by the window, watching the camp there.'

Merron gestured at the fuming rubbish pits which littered the pass. The warcarts and wagons they had brought down from the north had been reduced to firewood, to be eagerly collected by acquisitive villagers from up and down the valley. All except the vast, black painted wagon which had housed the choir. The mobile treasure house Savvi's men had guarded so closely had been hauled down to Aosta – packed full of the very same choirboys who had been locked up inside it in the first place! They had screamed like lambs when they had realised how Bayard proposed transporting them. Her heart had gone out to the terrified boys as they were bundled back on board the nightmare wagon, placed under the questionable care of yet another set of leering soldiers.

Merron's French wasn't completely fluent, but they understood each other well enough to get by. Angelica had taken a dish of weak broth, allowed Sophia to give her a bath and gratefully changed her shift. Merron couldn't help staring at her hands, visualising the ruined fingers wrapped beneath the swaddling cloth. She gently laid her hand on the hateful bundles.

'The nurse was right. Give them time and they'll be as good as new.'

They wouldn't though, Merron thought quickly. She'd carry the scars of the Inquisition to her deathbed, and not just the livid pink puckers across her knuckles. Merron had listened in disbelieving horror as Angelica had told her story, from her hopeful arrival at the abbey to the terrifying attack.

'Why didn't they take us with them?' Angelica cried again, mortified to find her father had left her so soon.

'They went under guard. Your father had given up his freedom to earn your release,' Merron explained again.

'But I was there; I saw what happened at the abbey! Constanzia, it was my maid who betrayed us, betrayed us all! If they are to be tried, the court must be told exactly what I saw!'

Merron sat back in alarm, slim fingers tugging at her lower lip.

'But James . . . my brother, told me they would not let you testify at the trial, because they had released you back to your father in the meantime.'

Angelica could dimly recall the brother she referred to. A starkly-staring vision carrying her through a sea of mist as if she was a bag of blood-flecked feathers. Carrying her back to this shabby Camelot, Angelica thought fleetingly.

'They said your father would tell you what to say. He wanted you back so much, he agreed you would never be called as a witness,' Merron explained tearfully.

So Briconet's shrewdly brokered deal on the causeway had ensured her testimony would never be heard!

'That's why they kept the boy, Fabarazzo.'

'Fabrizio,' Angelica corrected quietly. At least he was still alive. She hated to think of him, lying on a pallet in a broken-down wagon as they carried him down to Aosta for the trial. It wasn't far – a day's ride at most – but Fabrizio had been grievously wounded. He had been too weak to face the inquisitor's questions, which was why they had concentrated all their hateful attentions on her. Angelica gritted her teeth, determined to lock the memories of her ghastly ordeal away.

'We can't stay here. Worrying and fretting about our loved ones. I refuse to simply sit and wait. You know who'll carry news of their execution? Gueldres. He's been waiting for this a long time. He's relishing every moment, bought himself a seat for their execution!'

Merron closed her eyes at the horrible prospect.

Angelica slumped back on her pillows, exhausted by her anger.

Merron worked her handkerchief between her fingers in anxiety.

'You can't travel,' she sniffed. 'Aosta's a long way.'

'Aosta's a day's ride,' Angelica insisted, crying freely. 'A day's ride to be by father's side if it should . . . if it should come to that.'

Merron sighed. *If* it should come to that?

'And I tell you this,' Angelica said, gripping Merron's hand with surprising force, 'I'll not let his death go unavenged.'

'We don't even know they'll be found guilty yet,' Merron protested, alarmed by the murderous glint in the girl's eye. 'From what James says the chevalier at least seems to believe them innocent.'

'Innocence? Guilt? What does it matter to fiends like Briconet? I was innocent, until Briconet took my fingers in his hands,' Angelica turned the linen bundles over in her lap, stared at the miserable bandages as if she could visualise the terrible hurts. 'He stroked my fingers like a lover, ran his hands over my knuckles as if he wanted . . . to make me confess. By the time . . . by the time he'd finished,' she said, her shrunken chest racked by sobs, 'I was ready to admit I had murdered Odo with my own hands.' Angelica slumped back, tears coursing down her sunken cheeks. 'I don't know what I told him, don't you see?'

Merron sat on the side of her cot, sickened by her new friend's pitiful despair. The righteous fire which blazed behind her eyes could never repair the terrible damage Briconet had inflicted on her frail body. She craved bloody revenge, but she wouldn't have had the strength to lift a paper knife, let alone a sword. The crying girl seemed to sink back into the bedclothes, a pale shadow on the rumpled sheets.

'They'll get more than they bargained for, if they try and burn him. If they think they're going to sit on their fine chairs and gawp while they murder my father!'

Merron freed her hand, laid the angry girl back against the pillow.

'Rest now. Try not to upset yourself, there's nothing more to be done.'

'There's plenty to be done!' Angelica cried.

'But we've hardly enough men here to provide an escort, let alone ride to their rescue! What can we do against Gueldres and the rest? You couldn't hurt a milk pudding, let alone raise your hands against a swordsman like Gueldres!'

'I don't mean to raise my hand. I mean to blow the fiends back to hell where they belong! We've enough powder here to raze Aosta to the ground, to bury it under the Alps.'

Merron shook her head at the girl's hopeless invention. Angelica propped herself up again, animated by her fierce revenge.

'I'll lie abed no longer. We'll find a way, you and I, to wipe the smiles from their faces.'

'No, no no a thousand times no. No in English, French and African, if you wish my dear, but no all the same!' Sophia exclaimed, hurling the sheets over her formidable forearm. Angelica was tottering beside the stripped bed, Merron helping her steady her fragile legs.

'I've slept enough,' Angelica growled, finding some reserve of energy from deep within her tortured core. 'I'll not sit here and wait for the Vicomte to come calling. He'll want more than the keys to Mont Galliard if they murder my father.'

Sophia crossed herself at the horrifying possibility.

'It's out of the question, Gelli, don't you see? I'll call the surgeon and he'll box your ears for you! You're as stubborn as your father, God save him, but you haven't his grit, girl! The journey will be the death of you, and he'll have nowt left on God's earth to remember him by!'

Merron thought for a moment the nurse's barbed common sense would persuade her where her own advice had failed. She seemed to faint away in her arms for a moment, before setting her teeth and fiddling with her shift.

'Hold your tongue!' she barked, surprisingly fierce. 'I'm mistress here now, not you! Fetch my gown, my mantle, and have whoever's in charge send a carriage round to the courtyard. We're not sitting here while they try my father for something he didn't do!'

Beside the Palazzo Salassi, Aosta

The grand hall of the palace was a draughty, timber-beamed barn. No more than an elaborate hunting lodge, to the refined tastes of the likes of Bayard and Runcini. The panelled hall was hung with tapestries – faded to the colour and consistency of a moth's wing. The bare walls between were studded with hunting trophies and imaginatively-arranged fans of crossed swords and boar spears. The fireplace, fully ten feet across, had been banked high, a battalion of sweating servants charged with stoking the blaze in an effort to keep the chills at bay. Not even the well-wrapped bodies of a hundred eager spectators and a fidgeting honour guard of papal troops could lift the debilitating cold.

The Count of Luningiana had ordered torches lit in every corner, brought out great iron stands weighed down with running candles. He had been mortified to hear the cardinal was still feeling the cold, and had sent for a thick, seal-fur rug to be brought up from his quarters.

Stroma had little else to do than fetch and carry for the legislators about to decide their futures. He had wished he could absent himself altogether, set off on a hunting trip into the nearby hills until the wretched trial had blown over – but his absence would only have drawn attention to his connections with Gueldres, tainted his already-stained reputation.

What had the Vicomte been thinking, getting himself

caught in the spy's lodging up to his neck in blood and bodies and God knows what else? He must have lost his grip – so humiliated by the fiasco at St Orso that he had acted without his customary guile.

All their complex plans set adrift because of that daft score!

Gueldres had finally woken up to the danger, filing counter-charges against Tarsi and accusing his assassin Eldritch of all manner of barbarities – but the ring, the bodies, those documents . . . Stroma dreaded to think where it might end.

The esteemed members of the tribunal had taken their places on a raised dais beside the fire, three wise men sitting uncomfortably behind a velvet-covered table. A tonsured clerk squatted at one end surrounded by a breastwork of ink pots and quill cases. The list of witnesses the prosecution intended to call filled several sheets by themselves, a mountain of neatly-ribboned paperwork which would keep them in kindling until the New Year!

The composition of the court had been agreed early in the proceedings, one of the only aspects of the case which hadn't sparked a flaming row between one set of advocates or another.

Bayard was there to represent the French king, on whose territory the atrocity under investigation had taken place. The chevalier was sitting in his rigid chair – right next to the blazing fire. He had been forced to endure the heat in order to allow his colleague Runcini adequate room to manoeuvre his vast, scarlet clad bulk. The chevalier had changed his notched armour for somewhat more manageable surcoat and a spotless white gown engraved with the crossed arms of his master's house. Every now and then he would lean forward and make a note, or compare the current testimony with a previously-rendered account.

Stroma scowled at his pious concentration. They had already heard the same story told a dozen different ways! The chevalier seemed to think he was Solomon re-incarnated, vigorously intent on keeping up with the constantly-fluctuating stream of lies each party swore was God's own truth.

The fool might just as well have tossed a coin to find the guilty party! Runcini reminded the count of an enormous, oily toad, squatting on his gilt-framed throne, his moist tongue licking back and forth as if he was trying to trap flies. The lugubrious cardinal was a mass of glowing meat, a rich, juicy joint barely restrained by his extravagantly-cut costume and the ornately-carved arms of his chair. The cardinal drummed his ring-encrusted fingers on the parchments in apparent boredom, scowling and huffing as yet more witnesses were called up before him. Stroma wasn't fooled by his bored bad manners. The cardinal was as sharp as a stiletto, and his deep-set, darting eyes were everywhere at once, weighing, calculating, anticipating each separate strand of the story.

Eustace di Magiore, Prefect of Saluzzo, completed the tribunal. He was an eminent lawyer with years of experience in the hopelessly-entangled affairs of northern Italy, as well as being a principal ambassador to Margaret of Savoy herself. If Bayard was there to represent Francis, Eustace, by implication, was there for the Emperor Elect. The two of them — lean as half-starved lurchers — would act as a counterbalance to the monolithic influence of the church — in the obscenely-bloated shape of Cardinal Runcini.

Stroma tugged at his beard, nerves frayed by his ally's dangerous plotting. His desperate gambles could see the pair of them hanged in place of Tarsi and that sneering crow Eldritch!

He had almost forgotten the business which had brought the cardinal north in the first place — his own long-awaited appeal regarding the road tolls. The case had been completely overshadowed, put back until the tribunal could rule on the murder of the esteemed abbot.

He had banked on buying Runcini's support — the cardinal's blessing was known to come cheap — but what good were road tolls if in the meantime he was found guilty of Gueldres' abominable plotting? There was little to be done other than sit tight and hope for the best. God knew Bayard couldn't be bought, not for all the gold in Italy.

The count glanced around the court, studying the bitterly-divided defendants. Their postures spoke volumes: contrasting signals not even the dullest courtier could have mistaken.

Gueldres was leaning back in his chair with his boots splayed as if he was waiting for Runcini to bend down and help him off with them. A sardonic smile picked at the corners of his mouth as he calmly weighed the evidence.

Tarsi, in contrast, was leaning forward with his elbows on his knees and his fleshy chin propped on his palms, fingers drumming against his jaw in acute agitation. He straightened up every few moments, glared about the courtroom and then hunched back down again, clearly as dubious as he was about the outcome of the trial.

And then there was Eldritch, his sour features blackening with resentment turning him from pale and distrusted foreigner into a swarthy, bloodthirsty Turk. He didn't seem aware his ferocious scowl would unnerve the court, help convince the righteous tribunal of his guilt.

Stroma brightened, wondering if he would look half as cocky when they tightened the noose about the rogue's stiff English neck.

What was that rat-scut of a count peering at now? Eldritch raised his chin, shot the diminutive nobleman a challenging glare. Stroma looked momentarily flustered and turned his attention back to the fire.

The Englishman was seething with frustration, desperately eager to settle this wretched business and be on his way. Gueldres' barbed jibes about his sister Lillith had snagged his heart, tugged his mind away from the impending ordeal before the cardinal. He knew he must clear his heart and mind, try and concentrate on this tissue of lie and half-lie which masqueraded as evidence. But every time he rediscovered the thread of their testimony the Vicomte's snarled allegation returned to haunt him, tickle him like a sleepy trout.

Did he *truly* know of Lillith's whereabouts?

Eldritch cursed under his breath. Here he was on trial for his life and yet he couldn't stop fretting about his sister. Would Lillith have put his welfare before her life?

Great God he didn't think so!

Events had moved devilishly fast since they had surrendered to their parole back at Mont Galliard. Fortune had spun him around like a dried pea beneath a trickster's cup, spilled what little wits he had brought with him over the sea. He was grimly aware he had overreached himself, playing these fiends at their own despicable games. He had been so intent on joining the wickedly sophisticated hunt that he had quite overlooked the quicksand into which the pack had led him. He knew he had to negotiate his own course if he was to survive the rapids, control the bobbing barrel of his fortunes as he and Tarsi hurtled towards the abyss.

It wasn't as if he could trust the Italian soldier of fortune any more than he could expect sympathy from the devilish Gueldres. Eldritch had caught his ally glancing his way, brows knotted as if he was trying to decide whether or not to cut him loose – blame the murderous misadventures entirely on his unruly understudy!

Well let him try! He'd strangle the swine in his own guts, if he thought to save his hide by incriminating James Eldritch!

Gueldres had been called to the stand first and by the time he had wound up his account a day and a half later even Eldritch had been half-convinced of his innocence. He had been taken in like the rest of them by the Vicomte's air of bewildered grief, snake-charmed by his peerless performance. Gueldres' all-too-plausible explanations would surely score heavily with the tribunal, Eldritch thought.

His crony Stroma certainly looked a good deal happier about their chances now his partner in crime had been given an opportunity to weave his magic. Gueldres had treated the court with dignified contempt, as if he had been personally insulted to have been called before the unworthy tribunal in the first place. He had remained calm, answering each question in carefully-modulated Italian, winning nods of approval all about the expectant courtroom.

Tarsi seemed determined to prove his innocence by demonstrating his complete contempt for such immaculate mannerisms. Called to the stand immediately after his great rival he had ranted and drooled like some lunatic numbskull, wagging his finger at the inquisitor as if bitterly regretting he had nothing deadlier to hand. He had shouted the prosecutor down, rudely ignored questions from the tribunal and even – God save their miserable souls – dared the court to do its worse!

Eldritch could feel the noose tightening about his neck. Gueldres caught his eye, raised his eyebrow a fraction of an inch in ironic salute.

Tarsi's self-righteous wrath had certainly made an impression – but hadn't resulted in the dire conclusion Eldritch had dreaded. The hounded father's angry accusations had silenced the gossips in the gallery and captured Bayard's attention from beginning to end. It was as if the sober-spirited chevalier could identify more readily with his fierce tantrums than he could with the suave Vicomte's calmly reasoned and masterful defence.

By the end of the day, Eldritch wouldn't have liked to have predicted who had got the better of it. And if the tribunal felt the same – if Runcini and his colleagues weren't able to make up their minds which of them was to blame for the atrocity – they might well be forced to rely on the evidence of the supporting cast . . .

Ambolini, Scaralatchi, the cook's apprentice!

Christ's bones, was his fate truly in their hands?

The clerk picked up his list of witnesses, noisily cleared his throat.

'The court calls James Eldritch, Captain of *Transmarini*.'

He noticed Bayard had sat up straight in his chair, as if anxiously anticipating what the Englishman had to say for himself.

★

Eldritch strode forward, acutely aware of the undergrowth of whispers which blossomed briefly about the arena. They had taken away his arms, forced him to leave his sword and dagger with the guards outside. He glanced at Tarsi, squatting in an oak enclosure to the right of the waiting court, bearded features black with barely-repressed rage. The wooden framework was studded with brass spearpoints to discourage the occupant from trying to climb out over the top. A squad of papal troops was seated on a bench next to him, just in case he contemplated any physical attacks on his rival – sitting in an identical enclosure nearer the fire.

He strode forward, skirting around Abandando Briconet and his overweight assistant who were seated at a small table at right angles to the tribunal. Briconet tensed as he swept by, as if he couldn't trust the Englishman to pass so close without attempting to throttle him. A nervous clerk was waiting at the end of the aisle, anxiously gesturing Eldritch forward. He walked up to the stand, bowed curtly at the assembled dignitaries and listened carefully as the clerk took him through his oath. Three more clerks carried their stools forward, taking up positions about the courtroom floor ready to translate the Englishman's testimony.

Their procedures were so completely foreign to him that Eldritch had no choice but to focus all his attention on their moist lips – too busy concentrating on their atrocious accents to worry about the possibly-fatal outcome of the case. The captain stood straight at the stand, tilting his head to listen to the clerk's babbling translations. He didn't mind the awkward delay – the momentary pauses gave him time to ponder his answers, look out for the traps Briconet was bound to set for him. Eldritch described the Ride's arrival in Guisnes and the first meeting with the ingratiating Vicomte. He told the court how his archers had humiliated their rival arquebusiers at the butts, how Gueldres had belittled the fearsome reputation of their longbows. He described the tensions, the sudden rivalries and ill-considered challenges. And the final, fateful game of dice in Gueldres' luxuriously-appointed quarters.

'So it is true that the Vicomte de Toinueill won the services of you and your colleagues through a simple game of chance?'

There was nothing simple about it, Eldritch thought guiltily. He nodded anyway.

'And so you began this alarming anabasis about France which you describe in your affidavit. Attacking any number of peaceful villages, on the orders of the Vicomte? Can this truly be so?'

The clerk translated the question as Eldritch studied the panel of judges, struck by the striking contrasts between them.

Bayard was studiously intent, head cocked to ensure he didn't miss a thing. Runcini had resumed his minute examination of his rings following one brief glance in Eldritch's direction. The third man, Magiore, staring straight through him as if he was a sheet of ice on a pond, his lips no more than a thin blue scar.

'And afterwards we impressed the menfolk into the Black Legion,' Eldritch agreed.

'The *Band Nere* we have heard so much about. Tell me captain, have you seen any of these troops here in Aosta, perhaps accompanying their alleged commander, the Vicomte?'

Eldritch admitted he hadn't.

'You say you marched the length of France in their company, but they disappeared like phantasms the moment you reached the Alps?'

'I did not say they disappeared. They marched on into Italy.'

'And then disappeared.'

'Savvi marched them off somewhere, I don't know where!' Eldritch snapped.

'Just so. Kindly continue with your story.'

'We had impressed at least three companies by the time we had reached Grenoble. Then we marched towards Mont Galliard, with the Chevalier's men at our heels.'

'You must have been highly alarmed to see them coming up to your rear?'

369

'Not particularly. Gueldres didn't seem concerned. I had no idea that we had been accused of the attack on the abbey.'

'What would you have done if you had been aware of the honourable Chevalier's suspicions?'

Eldritch thought hard, pondering the implications of Briconet's shrewd thrust.

'I would have attempted to meet the Chevalier in person and formally deny any involvement.'

'You wouldn't have taken refuge in the nearest available fortress?' Briconet inquired. Eldritch saw what he was getting at.

'My first concern was the welfare of my men. The warband, the women and children.'

'Admirable. In fact, you threw yourself into Mont Galliard almost the moment you arrived in the pass.'

'Not quite. Gueldres ordered me to attack the castle. I had no choice but to obey.'

'No choice? If you had any reluctance to come to blows you could have waited for the Chevalier's arrival, could you not?'

'I am a soldier, bound by a contract of indenture to serve the Vicomte for one year and one day. I had no choice.'

'So you launched your men at the castle, spotted my Lord Chevalier riding down the pass behind you and immediately settled your argument with Tarsi.'

'There was no argument with Tarsi. I had never met him, I had hardly even heard of him.'

'And all the correspondence seized in the pass, which suggests in fact you were in Tarsi's service from the first, has been forged, is that correct?'

'You have a counterfeit contract. I have the authentic document, signed by my former commander Lord Howath, and countersigned by Gueldres.'

'He says he never signed such a document.'

'Well that is exactly what he would say.'

'Let us assume for one moment you are telling the truth.'

'I am.'

'How is it the Vicomte would have been able to forge such a convincing contract of indenture for your services? The papers are almost identical, save for the names of the new commanders. Gueldres maintains Tarsi assumed control of your warband – through intermediaries – in Guisnes. You say Gueldres assumed command during a game of dice.'

'Gueldres had been shown copies of our company contracts. He had many spies about the camp.'

'The English practice is to cut the contract in two, is it not? One half going to the captain, the other to his commander.'

'It is. I have produced my half of my contract with Gueldres.'

'But he denies all knowledge of the other half,' Briconet pointed out.

'Of course. Just as I deny all knowledge of one half of a contract with Tarsi's name on it.'

The bored court seemed to lose interest, bewildered by Briconet's complex allegations. The inquisitor ignored the whispered opinions, went back to his table and picked through his notes.

Eldritch waited for him, glancing up at the blank-faced judges.

'Let us return for a moment to Grenoble. You have at least admitted you were there.'

'We were,' Eldritch agreed stiffly.

'And it was here that you say you first saw the black wagon at the centre of the conspiracy to kidnap the choir.'

'Gueldres ordered us to keep away from it. Any man who went near it was threatened by his thugs.'

'The Vicomte's thugs? Not Francesco Savvi's?'

'Francesco Savvi is Gueldres' locotenent,' Eldritch drawled.

The court erupted in whispers.

'I see. You thought the Vicomte had ordered you to keep away because he had loaded the wagon down with gold to pay his men.'

'It seemed the likeliest explanation.'

'When in actual fact the wagon contained a dozen choirboys, kidnapped at the Abbey d'Eleron?' Briconet inquired.

'I have already told you we never went anywhere near the abbey. We only discovered the choirboys after our arrival in the pass. From my admittedly brief studies of Seigneur Tarsi's maps, I concluded we were never less than sixty leagues from the scene of their abduction.'

His quiet confidence seemed to impress the rapt ranks of spectators, a frisson of conversation rippling towards the rear of the crowded hall.

'I don't imagine it would surprise you to learn the wagon in question had borne House Tarsi livery? Or that his household arms had been painted black?'

'No it would not. Tarsi's daughter travelled to the abbey in it. The Vicomte's troops stole it during the attack and then half-heartedly disguised it in a further bid to incriminate Tarsi.'

'When the Vicomte was hundreds of leagues to the north?'

'Aye, he was with us.'

Briconet winced at his mistake.

'Well you can't have it both ways, captain. Either he was with you in the north or he was raiding the abbey in the south!'

'He was with us in the north at the time of the attack, that much is true. But he has a long arm and many servants. I heard Gueldres and Savvi discussing the attack.'

'You need a translator here, but you were able to understand their private conversation well enough?' Briconet bit back.

'I understood something had gone wrong. Gueldres was very angry. Savvi was apologising for his mistakes.'

'Mistakes indeed. You possess a remarkable understanding of us foreigners, Captain Eldritch.'

'I'm learning fast,' Eldritch agreed. Several spectators in the front benches chuckled when his answer was translated by the stony-faced clerk. Briconet paused, refreshed himself with a drink of water.

Eldritch looked about the packed public benches, encountering several winks – some of them from females – a number of discreet smiles, and several surreptitious nods of encouragement.

The court seemed to think this *Transmarini* had endured the worst of the inquisitor's attacks. If he could stonewall an agent of the Inquisition, he must be telling the truth.

'You would have us believe all the documents which have been produced to this court, the correspondence between Seigneur Tarsi and yourself regarding the plan to attack the abbey, are all false? Crude forgeries, I think you described them as?'

'Crude indeed.' Eldritch looked across the hall, held Gueldres' gaze for a moment. 'I have a little Latin, but I am afraid I could not decipher whole pages of complex legal terminology. The Vicomte clearly over-estimated my learning.'

There was another sharp burst of conversation which Runcini silenced with an angry flick of his wrist.

'The documents are clearly counterfeits. The first I heard of these letters, letters I apparently could not understand but was willing to sign anyway, was when Seigneur Bayard's herald told me about them outside Mont Galliard. I denied any knowledge then, I utterly refute their authenticity now.'

Briconet listened to the Englishman's stubborn defence, his mouth pinched.

'Is it not possible they could have been translated for you, as our words are being translated now? Is it not conceivable you understood more of the letters than you admit?'

'I never saw the letters.'

Briconet climbed to his feet, placed his thin hands inside his voluminous sleeves.

'And yet weeks later, here in Aosta, when the Chevalier Bayard discovers you and the Vicomte in the lodgings of

373

the spy, Furstenbein, he catches you in the act of burning more of the said correspondence on the fire!' the inquisitor exclaimed.

'I hadn't realised the portmanteau contained more forgeries.' He paused, catching the cardinal's moist eye for a moment. 'All I intended was to stifle the flames, to stop Gueldres from destroying the documents.'

'And this dwarf you attempted to save, is he not the very same dwarf accused by your master Tarsi of being a traitor? Well?'

'Obolus was the traitor. But I didn't know it at the time. He was beyond my help either way.'

'You tried to help your master's bitterest enemy?' he asked, playing to the packed public galleries.

'I gave my word to the Chevalier that I would not harm anyone in the lodging house. I caught Gueldres burning the documents. He had already killed Furstenbein, and impaled the traitor Obolus.'

'You see the Vicomte claims in his evidence that he discovered *Furstenbein* trying to burn the documents. He and the dwarf had used the lodging as their hideout while they worked as Tarsi's spies in Aosta. The Vicomte further alleges that he had found the Tarsi signet ring on the floor, and placed it in his shirt for safe keeping. He was defending himself against Furstenbein when you burst in, accidentally killing Tarsi's spy with a sword thrust. You then forced the Vicomte to back away, and attempted to finish the job Furstenbein had begun.'

Briconet paused for breath. 'Which is how the Chevalier Bayard himself discovered you,' he ended neatly.

The crowd pulsed with excitement.

'You see, Captain Eldritch,' Briconet went on, 'the Vicomte's account is in every detail plausible as yours. But you are asking us to believe that you tried to rescue a traitor to your chosen house? The dwarf who Tarsi claims was responsible for admitting these mysterious killers into the abbey? I am at a loss to understand your evidence sir. Was he a traitor to the Tarsi family, or was he its most loyal

374

servant, desperately trying to complete his sinister assignment when my lord the Vicomte burst in on him?'

'He was a traitor! He betrayed Tarsi to Gueldres, he let the Black Band into the abbey, he tried to kill my sister outside Mont Galliard!' Eldritch cried, his earlier confidence evaporating as he tried to juggle Briconet's crossfire questions.

The court seemed poised on the edge of its seat, ready to decide one way or the other. He was acutely aware that one careless word, the tiniest inconsistency in his testimony, could swing the wavering verdict against him. He closed his eyes, determined to concentrate on one question at a time.

'Obolus was in the wagon with the choirboys; he had the forged documents with him in the pass.'

'The dwarf was responsible for all this?'

'Of course not, not all of it! He must have had a contact in the Chevalier's camp, to pass the damned things over!' he snarled.

The crowd gasped at his sudden loss of control. Briconet pursed his lips.

'And so you accuse the Chevalier Bayard himself?' he said *sotto voce*.

'I do not accuse the Chevalier!' Eldritch shouted. 'I accuse some crawling vermin within his camp. Somebody met the dwarf in the pass and handed him the documents which incriminated Seigneur Tarsi!'

Bayard spoke quickly to Runcini. The cardinal nodded, patted his rotund stomach.

'I think we'll call a halt for lunch, Monsieur Briconet. Much more of this and we'll be too starved to reach a verdict,' he said nasally, prising himself to his feet. His manservants fluttered out of the shadows where he had left them, attaching themselves to the white whale like rouged leeches. He allowed himself to be pampered, fretted over as if he was a sickly child.

Eldritch caught Bayard's eye, glad of the break but wondering why the chevalier had called the sudden adjournment. Perhaps he had had enough, as stuffed with lies and deceits as Runcini was with sweetmeats and sack. The captain knew in his heart the mournful knight was their only true friend in this rat-trap of a palace, their only real hope of salvation from the quicksand of accusations they faced.

Without him, they were dead men.

Tarsi strode past him, propelled by his halberd-wielding escort. The proud Italian showed his teeth, gave the Englishman a curt nod.

'No talking there!' Briconet called. 'I don't want them suggesting new ways to confound the court.'

The papal guards pushed the commander up the aisle towards the windowless wardrobe they had allocated Tarsi as a waiting room.

Eldritch took a seat, and waited for the hungry tribunal's return.

'Well my friends. What a web of deception we've been left to fathom,' Runcini observed, tearing a huge mouthful from the leg of pork he had been served for dinner. His hanging jowls were already slick with grease, his lips stuck with tiny pink fibres. The three of them had retired to Stroma's personal quarters, where they had been served what the cardinal had described as a timely and appetising snack.

The six-course repast – baked pike, roast pork, lobsters, a flank of venison and a barrel of steaming shellfish – had disgusted the down-to-earth chevalier, stolen what little appetite he had. The fussing servants had set enough food before the cardinal to keep the entire population of Aosta through the incoming winter.

Bayard despised gluttony, one of the several deadly sins which Runcini seemed pleased to ignore altogether.

That God's church should be served by such diabolical boors.

'I wouldn't trust either of them as far as I could throw a rhinoceros,' Runcini said through a mouthful of half-chewed meat. The chevalier pushed his platter away and wiped his mouth on his napkin, a peculiarly feminine gesture for a soldier, the watchful cardinal thought.

'What, Bayard, going already?'

'I believe it might be prudent to redirect Briconet a little. He seems to be straying from the point.'

'Really? I thought he was finally getting somewhere. That business about saving the dwarf! I've never heard such drivel! What sort of fool would risk his neck rescuing such a misbegotten creature?'

A man of God, for one, Bayard thought sourly.

'I don't like it, Bayard. English pirates making sport on our soil. I'm surprised you French can't see the dangers of employing such rogues. But then again, you let the Swiss fight your battles, and they're the worst rascals of the lot!'

'Perhaps the French are thinking of bringing over more *Transmarini*?' the hitherto-silent Prefect Magiore observed. 'Is it possible the Swiss have upped their prices too high for your King?'

'My advice to the king would be to do away with all such scum, let Frenchmen fight her battles for her,' Bayard growled. The last thing he needed was to quarrel with the prefect, who would naturally be championing the cause of his ultimate master, the Emperor Elect Charles V.

The cardinal sighed, returned his wandering attention to his meal. Bayard was right about one thing – the trial had dragged on too long already. In reality, Runcini didn't give a fig which argumentative buffoon had been to blame for the massacre at the abbey. The Dominicans could look after themselves well enough, and the papacy had enough on its plate without becoming embroiled in more of these hopeless northern intrigues. Their thirst for revenge might actually put a little fire in their bellies – God knows the Vatican would need the Inquisition, if it was to deal with the recent and very worrying outbreak of heresy in Germany.

The cardinal watched the chevalier push back his chair, bow his head curtly but coldly and stalk out of the chamber.

'Was it something I said?' Magiore asked innocently. Runcini shrugged, making his multiple chins wobble.

'Where's the wine? Damn that Stroma, he's always been a miserably mean host!' he called, waving his under-nourished serving boy forward. He lifted his fat palm under the table and ran it up the boy's thigh.

A nice, likely-looking lad.

Bayard intercepted the chief prosecutor in the dimly-lit passage leading towards the north wing of the palazzo. He caught the inquisitor by the sleeve, holding him back while Stroma and several of his companions sauntered off towards the count's private quarters.

'I've heard enough Briconet,' the chevalier said tersely. 'Eldritch is telling the truth.'

The inquisitor gave the knight a wincing smile.

'My Lord Bayard, whilst I have always entertained the greatest respect for your sense of justice, I feel your judge-ment in these matters has been somewhat . . .'

'He's innocent. He was nowhere near the abbey at the time of the attack. All you have is Tarsi's wagon, and only a fool would sport his own household livery in a massacre such as this. Tarsi may be many things, but he is no fool.'

'Tarsi's arms had been deliberately painted out,' Briconet objected.

'They might just as easily have been torn off and disposed of long before the wagon's role was discovered. They were clearly left on to incriminate him.'

Briconet shook his head in frustration at the chevalier's reasoning.

'If Eldritch had transported the choir, he would surely have had the sense to use an unmarked wagon – any old hay wain would have been better than his alleged master's per-sonal carriage.'

'He was merely obeying Tarsi's instructions . . . there were no other carts available to carry the choir away.'

'There were a number of other vehicles in the abbey stables which would have sufficed in its place. I know because I took the trouble to look. Did the agent of the Holy Inquisition examine the stables?'

Briconet bristled at the jibe.

'Of course! A few unkempt dog carts . . .'

'And the abbot's personal carriage. It would have done just as well to carry those poor boys. No Briconet. In blacking the wagon they blackened Tarsi.'

'The evidence would suggest . . .'

'The evidence, Briconet, suggests to me those documents were forged, and Gueldres had Tarsi's signet ring!'

'We cannot be sure of that.'

'I had my suspicions of those papers back in the pass. Now I am sure. Eldritch is as innocent of the attack on the abbey as I am myself.'

Briconet's quick eyes flicked over the chevalier's stern features. He would not be persuaded otherwise, and continual stonewalling would only drive the self-righteous fool further into his corner.

'My Lord. I urge you to consider the case as a whole. If I release Eldritch I am indirectly accepting the documents were falsified.'

Bayard nodded. 'Precisely.'

'But if we accept they are forgeries, then logically, Tarsi is innocent also.'

'Indeed.'

Briconet scowled.

'My Lord. We have not heard all the evidence of the case, and here you are suggesting . . .'

'I am suggesting nothing. I am *instructing* you to proceed no further against Eldritch. I think it's time to call Ambolini to the stand.'

'Ambolini? I thought we had agreed he should be left to the end?'

'This is the end. If he dies, Tarsi will have nobody to give his version of what he was hoping to achieve at the abbey. This is the only point of Tarsi's defence I doubt. I want to hear Ambolini's story, while God grants him the chance to give it.'

Briconet frowned, desperately anxious at the chevalier's unwarranted intrusion. He had no right to lecture a papal legate, an agent of the Inquisition, on how to prosecute a case!

'I would have thought it was in all our interests if I press ahead against Eldritch. He looks set to lash out at any . . .'

'Enough is enough, Briconet,' Bayard said sternly. 'Unless you want me to take the investigation into other, less savoury aspects of this case.'

'I don't know what you mean, Seigneur,' Briconet prevaricated.

'Just this: If you insist on muddying the waters any further I will be obliged to call my own witnesses.'

'Your own witnesses, my lord? Ambolini is not . . .'

'Your assistant Souris for one. I would like to question him in person, in detail, as to how it was he came on those documents. I've always found it a little intriguing, that the fattest man in the camp should have been the most nimble on his feet, that night in the pass.'

Briconet swallowed.

Of course he had known all along that Souris was one of Gueldres' creatures. He was a handy go-between, giving the Inquisition access to social circles agents such as himself could never frequent. But Souris was ridiculously transparent. It wouldn't take Bayard long to fetch it out of him on the witness stand – or elsewhere.

If Souris was forced to reveal all – as he knew he would be – his own role in the filthy business might be viewed in an entirely unfortunate light. The Holy Inquisition, surrounded as it was by heretics and enemies, could not afford to incur the wrath of the French King, the Empire and the Vatican – one at a time, perhaps, but not all at once.

If he was implicated in some filthy inter-household plot, the long-term effects for his office – and for the Inquisition as a whole – could be devastating.

'I will give your suggestion immediate thought.'

'Ensure you do. Kindly excuse me for a moment, I need some air.'

Beside the Palazzo Salassi, Aosta

Briconet found his treacherous clerk back in his quarters just off the north wing, cheerfully devouring a plate of chicken and rice. The clerk looked up in surprise, dabbing his lips with his napkin as he sprang to his feet. He had assumed his master would be off quaffing wine with Stroma, toasting the imminent success of the prosecution's case. Eldritch couldn't last much longer. He had tied himself in knots trying to evade Briconet's relentless cross-examination. And when Eldritch's feeble explanations failed, he'd take Tarsi's entire defence down with him.

The papal legate closed the door quietly, waving the clerk back to his meal. The hawkish inquisitor placed his bundle of documents on the table and sat down with a sigh. Souris nodded encouragingly.

'You had him going, sir, at the end,' his roly-poly assistant observed, helping himself to another spoonful of risotto. Give Stroma his due, he certainly kept a decent table.

'Of course, the translators saved him, slowing down your questions, blunting your attack to some extent, if you will forgive me for saying so.'

'He seemed to slip between ignorance and understanding at the drop of a hat,' Briconet said stiffly. 'Very convenient for him.'

'But you broke him in the end. I knew you would. Why

if it hadn't been for Bayard interrupting things for lunch, we might have wrapped things up by early afternoon.'

Briconet slid the plate over the table and tore himself a strip of fresh Aostan bread. He munched it for a few moments while Souris wiped his plate clean with his portion, greedily devouring the last sopping morsel.

'Bayard's getting tired of the trial. He's the only one who has ever paid any real attention anyway. Now even the shining chevalier has asked me to cut things short.'

Souris raised his hairy eyebrows.

'Cut things short? He's convinced of Tarsi's guilt then?'

'He's convinced of Gueldres' guilt,' Briconet corrected with a shrug, 'and I must confess, after all we've heard, I believe he may be right. These documents,' he tapped the ribboned bundle in front of him, 'aren't convincing anybody. Gueldres has been gilding the lily. The moment you look beyond the seal it is plain to see they are, as Eldritch says, crude copies of his original indentures. And only an imbecile would allow himself to be caught with the signet ring on his person, the very same ring used to seal the forgeries.' Briconet looked up sharply, caught a look of astonished dismay pass over his clerk's features. Souris modified the look in a moment, smiled weakly.

'Worse than that, he seems to think we were involved in the forgery in some way, or at the very least that we conspired to use them against Tarsi.'

'An outrageous fabrication,' Souris spluttered. 'Why would we have done such a thing?'

'In a crude attempt to re-establish the Gueldres clan's hold over a key region of northern Italy and southern France,' Briconet said casually. He waited a moment, the fat clerk holding his breath at the dreadful possibilities. 'The highly-corruptible Vicomte would make a useful puppet, in a troubled region.' He flicked his wrist. 'Well that's what this cretin Bayard thinks, at any rate.'

Souris deflated a little.

'Rid . . . quite ridiculous,' Souris stammered.

'That's what I said. But he wants you on the witness

stand anyway, to clear up that business about finding the package in the pass.'

Souris could not disguise his horror.

'The Chevalier imagines some inconsequential inconsistencies in your account, how you managed to get the bundle off this damned dwarf. It shouldn't take long to put his mind at rest, eh?'

Souris saw all in a moment. He hadn't been Gueldres' principal spy in Avignon for a dozen years without developing a sixth sense for threats or danger. He pressed his fleshy lips together, waited for his master to speak.

'You fool,' Briconet said quietly. 'You think I didn't know what you were up to? Gueldres has had you in his pouch for years. What he never realised was that I held him, in my pouch,' Briconet said crisply, shaking his head in contempt at his cowering clerk's lack of foresight.

'I overlooked your idiocies just so long as the Vicomte's objectives coincided broadly with our own. But he's gone too far this time. He's guilty, and he'll try and drag us all down with him, if we're not careful.' Souris lowered his head, his tonsured scalp gleaming pink.

'I am truly sorry for my weaknesses my Lord,' Souris said piously. He knew the one thing Briconet would not forgive was any attempt to insult his intelligence with any denial. 'I can of course assure you that at no time did my occasional activities on behalf of the Vicomte compromise my role as your assistant, or the work of the Holy . . .'

'Stop grovelling you puke-worm!' Briconet snarled. 'You've compromised us right enough this time! Do you imagine I wasn't fully aware of your dealings with Gueldres, you spotted toad!' he exclaimed, reddening. 'I would have had you chopped in pieces and fed to the hounds if your childish treachery had ever run contrary to my will! We have been cultivating Gueldres for years, as a handy if somewhat overzealous servant of God. But he's stuck his nose out too far, and Bayard means to chop it off.'

Souris quailed at the inquisitor's barely-controlled fury.

'He's got cold feet about the whole business, now he's

convinced we're in with Gueldres up to our necks.'

'But why would he allow the trial against Tarsi and this *Transmarini* to proceed so far?' Souris inquired, hideously bewildered by the trap he had walked right in to.

'Because he's cautious. Bayard wanted to make doubly sure his initial reaction was correct. He wanted to convince his head as well as his damned heart. Cah! The swine would try the patience of a saint, and God knows I am no saint!'

It was true the paths of righteousness demanded an occasional detour, if God was to be effectively served in this harsh, heathen world. Nobody could ever suggest Briconet had been anything but an effective instrument of God's will.

'Don't shite your shirt just yet. He's given us a lifeline; I mean to take it. I'll finish with that damned viper Eldritch before he loses his temper and attacks someone. I mean to call Ambolini before it's too late.'

'He is terribly sick, my Lord. One can barely understand what he is saying.'

'I don't care if he pegs out. He's the only one left who can give Tarsi's version of the attack on the abbey. Bayard isn't going to let an innocent man be hung, drawn and quartered for a crime he did not commit. God help us. If the pretty boy doesn't appease Runcini, I don't know who will.'

Eldritch had been staring glumly at the hangings around the walls, recognising the faces of his own family in the faded stitching. Was Lillith really whoring her way along the Marseille waterfront, just as Gueldres had maintained? Had she been killed in some back alley cat-fight? Had she married herself off to some fantastically wealthy duke and reared a brood of unruly children at the other ends of the earth?

Who would say? Apart from Gueldres. Eldritch had caught the Vicomte's eye several times, turned away from his sardonic smile, his ironically courteous salutes across the court.

He had known something from the first day in Guisnes.

Gueldres had looked up at the mention of his name as if it had rung some vague memory. Eldritch wasn't a common name, certainly not in the circles the Vicomte was used to moving in. Maybe he had met her, somewhere on his travels about Europe. The question was, how would he ever find out? Gueldres wouldn't relent, not even if he ended up on the scaffold. He'd see Eldritch eat his own liver before he told him of her whereabouts.

The grim truth was gnawing at his mind as he sat in the well of the court, waiting for the tribunal to return. He glanced up, distracted by the movement by the door. Two newcomers had caused a quiet commotion, squeezing their way along the back row towards a vacant bench. He rose from his seat as he recognised his sister's fiery hair, and a moment later realised the frail patient she was helping was none other than Tarsi's tortured daughter. His heart leapt, to think the two of them might have arrived in the nick of time to hear the tribunal pronounce sentence against them. He peered over the crowding heads, waving his hand towards the momentarily-glimpsed girls. The nervous guards sprang up like Jack-in-the-boxes, halberds ready.

Eldritch raised his hand, caught Merron's attention before he was thrust back in to his seat. She turned, waved back at her long-lost brother. The girl beside her had collapsed into a chair as if she could go no further, the dreadful bundles about her hands eloquent testimony to her own trials.

By Christ, Angelica had endured a sight worse than he had this morning. The captain steeled himself, tried to control the rampaging furies which see-sawed through his tense frame. How he longed to attack these fiends with cold steel, split their lying heads and hack their pointing fingers from their grasping hands!

And all the while Gueldres was smirking and chuckling to himself, enjoying the dangerous game as if it was some harmless piece of mummery, a mystery play to amuse these boorish, backwater citizens. The gaudily-attired women were the worst. They appeared to have been drawn to the trial as if it was some monstrous bear-baiting, a dog–fight to the death.

They were itching to see blood. His blood.

His idle inspection of the packed gallery was brought to an abrupt end by the return of the tribunal, presumably well fed and refreshed. The cardinal lumbered into his place at the centre of the dais, Bayard and Magiore resuming their seats at either end of the table. Briconet returned with his pale clerk. He looked as if he had eaten something which had disagreed with him, his cadaverous features paler than usual.

'My Lords, the prosecution is satisfied with Captain Eldritch's explanations as to his conduct, and does not wish to examine his testimony any further. We will proceed by calling the chorister, Fabrizio Ambolini to the stand.'

There was instant uproar around the improvised court-room. The packed public benches erupted in surprise at the unexpected clemency, an undergrowth of whispers and exclamations Runcini could only extinguish by repeatedly rapping his knuckes on the table.

'*Silence!*'

Eldritch didn't need a translator to comprehend the cardinal's furious shouts.

Gueldres was out of his seat in a moment, gripping the brass spearpoints projecting up in front of him. Eldritch sat still, wondering if Briconet had made some mistake, over-looked his lean presence after over-imbibing at lunch. A papal guard tapped him on the shoulder and jerked his thumb towards the back of the court. Runcini seemed to be taking an interest at last, looking up eagerly as the clerks echoed Fabrizio's name.

Eldritch got to his feet, glanced briefly at Gueldres. The papal guards had gestured the furious Vicomte to sit down. His advocate, a fabulously expensive Florentine, had bent over the bars to urge his client to remain calm. Eldritch couldn't understand the whispered Italian, but the look of blind hatred on Gueldres' face spoke for itself.

★

Fabrizio was carried into the court on a litter, his taut skin a shade lighter than the soiled linen on which he lay. His dark, ringleted hair made a stark contrast to his ghastly features, a curly black halo about his head. He had been propped up on a pillow, both hands folded over his heavily-bandaged torso.

The word around the court was that he was not expected to live. Some said he had been forced to such acts of depravity that his soul had given up and flown out of his corrupted body. Other gossips maintained he was suffering Herod's disease, that his abused insides were being slowly consumed by maggots. Either way, Ambolini did not look long for this world.

Angelica almost swooned when she realised it was him, a stick of bone on a beach, bleached white by time and tides. He tried to smile as they carried him down the aisle, his eyes like pots of liquorice in their sunken sockets. The distraught girl held her wounded hands to her chest, wept like a child as he was carried down towards the waiting tribunal. Merron grasped her, held the sobbing girl tight as they carried the boy off towards the well of the court.

The great, bear-backed man several rows ahead suffered no such restraint. He exploded out of his chair, knocking several rapt burghers flying as he threw himself towards his beloved assistant.

'FAVVY! What have they done to you?' Scaralatchi shrieked, his immense coat of many colours flapping as he jostled and barged his way towards the astonished bearers.

'Get back there!' the sergeant at arms bawled, alarmed by the block of lard bearing down on him, a look of murderous rage etched into his ripe features.

'Resume your seat or you'll be locked in the cells!'

The sergeant, an old campaigner long since grown used to the gentler opportunities of Aosta, menaced the man with his halberd.

Scaralatchi struck the blade away as if he was swatting a fly, ignoring the splash of scarlet across his palm. He back-handed the staggering sergeant over a gawping ancient, threw himself down beside the fearfully grinning youth.

'Favvy, what have they done to you, my boy, my life!' the distraught composer shrieked, snatching up the boy's cold hand in his bloodstained paw. The dripping wound splattered over the boy's white mantle. Cesar threw his head at the boy's shoulder, just as the guards leapt forward with their halberds. The broadleafed blades were poised at Scaralatchi's exposed throat, ready to lop the great bald head from his trunk.

Runcini hammered the table as the discomfited sergeant prised himself to his feet.

'Sergeant, bring that man forward!' Bayard yelled from the dais.

In the event, they had to prod and push the fat composer along the aisle, pausing now and again to drag the boy along with him. Not even the red-faced sergeant's cruellest punches could shift the wallowing composer away from his dying catamite. The packed public benches were agog. Some imagined the demented monster was the boy's father. Others, shrewder, told their shocked neighbours the truth. That this was the notorious excommunicant Scaralatchi, who had stolen the boy away from his scarlet counterpart. There, look! Cardinal Amerigo Runcini himself.

The crowd hushed, trembling with excitement. Angelica sobbed onto Merron's shoulders, her cruelly-abused hands throbbing in her lap as she shared Scaralatchi's agony.

The guards managed to prise the fat man aside long enough to set the litter down before the dais. Scaralatchi fell to his knees beside the feeble youth. Runcini stared at the top of that hatefully familiar head, the tufts of jet black hair he remembered so well. His broad features creased in disgust, lips peeling away from his teeth.

'Cesar Scaralatchi, you are right to abase yourself before this court.'

The composer looked up, his fat fingers entwined about Fabrizio's slender-boned hand.

'The youth Ambolini is called to the witness stand,' Briconet shrieked, outraged by the notorious excommunicant's mad-eyed zeal. 'You were not called, Scaralatchi. You will resume your seat and pray God forgives your filthy abominations!'

'I pray to God I can do one thing before you snuff me out, you snivelling worm-shite!'

Fabrizio mumbled, clawed weakly at the big man's shift in a bid to hold the furious heavyweight back. Scaralatchi rose to his feet, the boy's hand dropping away from his like a fallen branch.

'You have held the boy away from his loved ones, away from his family, away from me! You have tried to keep me away with your laws and your leech-lawyering, close my mouth with your threats and connivances! Even my own master Tarsi has urged me to hold my peace. But I will not stand by and see this boy tortured further, picked over like a reeking corpse by the vultures of the Inquisition!'

'You go too far! Heretic! Guards, remove this offal from our presence!' Briconet screamed. The guards took a fearful step closer.

'He can tell you nothing you haven't heard elsewhere!' Scaralatchi roared, drowning out the inquisitor's falsetto shrieks. 'What will he tell you, my lords, that I cannot? We sent him to d'Eleron, Tarsi and I. We charged him with persuading old Odo that a filthy excommunicant, a miserable sinner like me, had actually repented at last, and sought permission to grovel before him, before you all! Well I will grovel now, if it pleases you.'

Scaralatchi bowed ironically and threw himself flat. He writhed on the floor beside Ambolini's litter, the astonished courtroom watching aghast as he heaved and bucked.

'Devilry! Drag the demon from our midst, before he infects us all with his filth!' Briconet bawled. 'Close your eyes good people, that you will not have to witness his dreadful possession!'

'I abase myself before you, my cardinal!' Scaralatchi bawled. 'I beg forgiveness for my sins, of which God knows there are many,' he cried, curling and jerking on the cold marble floor, foaming at the mouth as if he was throwing a fit.

'Out! Unclean spirit!'

'Hear my evidence and let the boy go! I beg you, Amerigo,' he rolled to his knees, hanging his sweating head before the cardinal's scowling presence. 'I beg you from the bottom of my heart, let the boy die in peace!'

Runcini glanced around the court, the shocked faces of the citizens, the outrage glare of the court officials – all waiting for him to say something. He paused for a moment, relishing the centre stage, the opportunity to take total control of so many flailing destinies. To play God over these scampering flocks.

'Cesar Scaralatchi, you are excommunicate,' he cried, his rich voice ringing out over the tumult. 'You have no business here!'

'My Lord Cardinal,' Scaralatchi abased himself before the scarlet figure, magnificently profiled on the dais above him. 'I beg you one favour. Hear my evidence.'

'Evidence? You weren't there!' Briconet screamed, driven out of his wits by the composer's desperate imprecations. He scuttled forward to place his frail carcase between the composer and the cardinal.

'Hear my score, the full score which was stolen from this boy, from Tarsi's innocent daughter!'

'We've heard your damned score, you traitor!' Stroma shouted from his chair behind Gueldres. 'The unfinished score you sold to the Vicomte for a dozen silver pieces!'

'The score is the key, Amerigo,' Scaralatchi sobbed, his vast bulk visibly deflating before the cardinal like a fatty roast turned slow on the spit. 'Hear the score and decide for yourself who lies, Gueldres or Tarsi!'

'What nonsense are you suggesting! That the court should adjourn to listen to your diseased ramblings? I would rather impale myself than endure a moment of your ghastly witching songs!' Briconet accused, striding forward to urge the dumbstruck soldiers into action.

'Halt! What have you to say of this score? The deranged racket I was forced to endure at St Orso? If that is the best you can do, Cesar,' Runcini grinned evilly, 'then you are indeed past your best. You are better off dead.'

Scaralatchi turned his bloody palms up, his broad, coarse features suffused with tears as he implored the cardinal to show mercy.

'You have only heard the half of it, please God grant you the chance to hear it all, as it was written.'

'You sold it to me before it was finished?' Gueldres roared, appalled at the hideous farce being played out before him.

'Silence!'

'Let the d'Eleron choir sing out once more. Unshackle their hearts and allow them to sing God's praises as I intended!' Scaralatchi pleaded.

'Blasphemer!' Briconet gasped, his voice strangled by his furious terror.

'I'm going to puke, much more of this,' Gueldres snarled, fists clenched about the brass bars of his shrinking cage.

'Let the boys sing once more, I beg you!' Scaralatchi moaned, writhing beside the mortified Fabrizio. A thin stream of blood had leaked from the side of the boy's mouth as he had tried to sit up, as he had reached out for the crazed musician.

'Let the choirs sing out in glory to God!'

Beside the Palazzo Salassi, Aosta

There were tears in his eyes bigger than the fattest pearls, as he hurled open the ante-room door and strode towards the weary girl. The burly knight threw his arms wide, grappled her to him. Tarsi grasped the back of her head, the tangled curls she still hadn't had time to brush free. He pressed her pale face into his mantle, breathed her in.

'Gelli, Gelli . . . What are you doing here? I thought I told you to rest, regain your strength at Mont Galliard?'

'You are my strength,' Angelica said simply.

Eldritch stood beside the door, awkward in the face of such unrestrained emotion. Tarsi was crying and clucking like an old milkmaid over a basket of pups, emasculated by worry.

He felt a pang of . . . what, anger? Contempt? Envy? His chest whistled like a hollow gourd, long emptied of love the likes of theirs. His lips peeled from his teeth. He frowned, stitched them back together again in something approaching a smile of encouragement for Merron.

'James!'

His sister released her grip on Angelica's thin arm and came bounding over to fling her arms about him. Her hazel eyes were flashing, leaking tears of joy. Eldritch closed his arms about her slim waist, gave the crying girl a reassuring hug.

'Thank God it's over!' Merron exclaimed, wiping her

red nose on the back of her sleeve. Eldritch looked over her shoulder, caught Tarsi's eye as he finally tore himself free of his frail flesh and blood. Angelica looked paler than she had been on the causeway, her remarkably resilient constitution ruined by her ordeal beneath Briconet's probing knives and smouldering tapers. The gruff soldier remembered her ghastly trials, folded her back into the chair. Angelica sat back gratefully, a weak smile playing about her pinched features.

'Not quite over,' he growled. 'We're not out of the woods yet. But please God Runcini will be convinced of our innocence once and for all, the moment he hears the score presented the way Scaralatchi intended it.'

Briconet had used the last of his rapidly-evaporating authority to insist Scaralatchi be lodged away from the rest of the guests – for his own, and everybody else's safety. He had argued that the composer – demented by his own perverted grief – might lay hands on himself or others, while the balance of his mind was so clearly disturbed. Bayard had reluctantly agreed he should be detained in the cells beneath the south wing, while arrangements were put in hand to perform his mystical mass before the cardinal. Briconet had retired to his quarters to think, while the fuming Gueldres had been escorted back to his own quarters and confined under guard. His advocate had been locked in with him to repair his defence now that the case against Tarsi had so crucially faltered.

Angelica took a deep breath, her moist eyes wandering about the room. 'I thought I loved him,' she said hoarsely. Her father winced, his large mouth pulled in all directions in the midst of his bristling beard. He clenched her shoulder, appalled by her wasted bone structure. She had always been such a headstrong, athletic girl . . .

'Fabrizio, I mean,' she explained haltingly.

Tarsi frowned.

'There there now. Try not to upset yourself any further. Bayard's sent his surgeons to attend him, they did a remarkable job on you, my girl,' he said, his words of encouragement ringing hollow.

Angelica didn't appear to be listening. She was staring into the middle distance now, straight through Eldritch's nervously-churning belly.

'He was so handsome, so clever with his . . .'

'I really don't think you need to go upsetting yourself all over again, my dear,' her father said stiffly, glancing over his shoulder at the equally uncomfortable Eldritch.

'But I didn't know what love was, until I saw poor Cesar in the courtroom.'

'Yes well, he was obviously upset; we all were,' Tarsi growled, looking about the bare chamber for something to distract her attention. Stroma had provided a pitcher and bowl, and fresh linen. He clicked his fingers at Merron, nodded towards the washstand.

'I think you'll feel better after you've freshened up. I've waited so long to see you safe again, another hour or so won't be any trouble, eh Eldritch?'

'No trouble my Lord,' Eldritch said heavily.

Angelica gave a tiny smile.

'He loved Fabrizio more than I. He would have gladly given his life, right in front of us, if it would have saved him.'

Tarsi was breathing deeply, patting his daughter's back as if she was a favourite cannon.

'Quite so. Just as I would have died for you, or Eldritch here would have . . .'

'Just as Miguel died for me,' Merron said tersely, taking a sideways glance at her glowering brother. Eldritch caught her eye, looked away. This was no time to fling that in his face.

'Now I think we've all had enough excitement for one day,' Tarsi said briskly, eager to abandon the boudoir. 'You need your rest, girl, and Merron here will keep you company.' He lifted her hand, squeezed it within his own hairy palms.

'You cannot imagine how glad I am, to have you back,' he said, his voice raw with emotion. 'Remind me never to send you on dangerous errands again.' He bowed his head, lips compressed, and backed out of the room. Eldritch followed at a discreet distance.

Merron wafted across the room to prepare her new friend's toilet. Angelica sat back with a sigh, watched the tall girl pour the water into the basin, drape a towel over her slim arm.

'A few weeks ago Constanzia would have done that for me,' she said dreamily. 'But she's gone now. Uncle Julius, little Obolus, good old Luca with his booming voice, and my handsome Fabrizio . . .' her voice cracked like a frozen pond. 'All dead now.' She buried her face in her hatefully-bandaged arms, and wept so hard Merron couldn't understand what she was saying. She crouched down beside her, squeezing her arm down the back of the chair and about the girl's painfully thin waist.

'He's not dead yet my sweet, there's still hope for him, hope for all of us.'

'Here's a little advice for you Eldritch. If you marry, and God grants you children, have the daughters sent away to the biggest, strongest castle in the world. The Crak de Chevaliers, the crusader stronghold in Syria ought to do it. Have them bricked up in the highest tower, and gather the biggest army of the bravest knights the world has ever seen to guard them.'

Eldritch swallowed, appalled by Tarsi's unfettered grief. Tears rolled down his sun-scorched cheeks and lost themselves in the forest of his beard. He ran his gauntlet across his red nose, sobbing.

'They are sent from the heavens to warm your heart, sing you into the waking sleep of old age, and yet they dig themselves into your flesh like angel-faced weevils, ready to eat you all up inside.'

'God grant her a full recovery,' Eldritch said. Tarsi glanced around at him, shook his head in amusement.

'You're a funny crew, you English. Brave enough in battle, but so afraid of your own feelings! You've been through all I have in these last days, seen your own flesh and blood chased like game and shot at with arrows and quarrels and God knows what other disasters, and yet you fear a few tears will do you worse harm!' He wiped his finger along his eye socket, held the wet pad up in front of the stern-faced Englishman.

'They say, as a race, we are rather more subdued than our brothers in the south,' Eldritch said coldly, unwilling to allow himself such a frivolous display of emotion. 'But just because I do not cry, does not mean I do not feel.'

Tarsi shrugged, considered the captain's stern response.

'Well said, my friend. Now let us go and find out what joys Briconet and Bayard have prepared for us. I could eat a horse.'

Eldritch followed the burly Italian down the passage towards the main hall of the palazzo, his weary mind bombarded with images of his lost sister. Tarsi's avuncular accusation had reminded him sharply of his own worries, his own grief-shattered family.

Although the crowds had been packed off out of the main gate, the palazzo was still busy. Clerks and courtiers hurried about the long passages on missions of their own. Cooks and servants and men at arms came and went. Papal guards had been positioned down every gloomily-lit corridor to keep the rival parties at arm's length. Bayard's elite gendarmes had been stationed about the main palace on full alert, swords drawn in case of trouble.

The guards narrowed their eyes as the two men approached, but held their halberds well out of their way.

'I wonder where they've got that bastard Gueldres,' Tarsi wondered aloud.

'Maybe they've locked him in a cell with your friend Scaralatchi,' Eldritch remarked.

'Gueldres locked up with our Cesar, puking with grief over his lost love? I'd almost feel sorry for the lousy bastard,' Tarsi replied in an undertone.

The pair of them turned the corner and arrived in the broad, candlelit lobby outside the main banqueting hall.

The walls were hung with some of Stroma's finest paintings and tapestries, every corner and alcove cluttered up with classic busts or *objets d'art*.

Tarsi looked around, nothing that the majority of the pieces seemed to be poorly sculpted reproductions. Typical of that slime-breathing, money-raking reptile Stroma. The main doors swung open and Bayard strode out of the hall, the count in question hurrying at his heels. The pair of them stopped short when they recognised the recently-released prisoners. Stroma glanced over his shoulder, made sure his own guards were paying attention. Bayard possessed no such fears. He acknowledged Tarsi with a brief nod.

'I would remind you, Seigneur, that you are not to leave the precincts of the palazzo,' he said curtly. Tarsi chuckled.

'I wouldn't dream of it, my Lord Bayard. I have no intention of turning my back on my accusers, even at this late stage in the proceedings.'

Stroma bristled.

'We were only doing our duty, Tarsi. You would have done the same if my name had been stamped on those documents, I am sure of that,' he said icily. Bayard held up his hand.

'We have been discussing arrangements for the performance of Signor Scaralatchi's requiem. Cardinal Runcini has indicated he is to leave for the Vatican at the end of the week at the latest, which doesn't leave us very much time to prepare.'

'Your evidence against Gueldres?' Tarsi prompted.

'Runcini's heard enough of it to last him a lifetime, whoever sponsored the wretched thing,' Stroma butted in. 'It won't matter how much more of it your man Scaralatchi has come up with.' He ignored Bayard's restraining hand, took a step closer to his ancient rival. 'I shouldn't rely on him snatching your chestnuts from the fire! If you want my opinion, you're in just as deeply as you ever were!'

'My Lord Count! I have already warned you against outbursts such as these!' Bayard exclaimed.

Tarsi ignored him.

'We'll have to wait and see. He's agreed to listen to it, that's all that matters.'

Stroma was disconcerted by Tarsi's boundless confidence.

But the dwarf had stolen the score from the abbey, snatched it from under Ambolini's nose! Had Gueldres been so utterly duped? The choirmaster, Bembo, had warned there had been something amiss with the wretched score, but he had never questioned its authenticity. Stroma wasn't an aficionado of choral music, but Scaralatchi's precious requiem had sounded to him as if it was being sung backwards. He failed to see how Tarsi was going to convince Runcini it was anything other than a discordant, free-form improvisation.

Bayard seemed satisfied with Stroma's stubborn silence.

'As I said, gentlemen, you will kindly confine your walks to the grounds of the Palazzo Salassi.'

Tarsi bowed.

'Of course my Lord. We were only intending to stretch our legs. We will not be more than a few moments, given the rather cramped nature of the courtyard here,' he said innocently.

Stroma paled, his hand dropping automatically to the hilt of his dagger. Insulted in his own castle! Damn Tarsi to the uttermost pit of hell. But Tarsi and Eldritch had remained unarmed, and striking defenceless men, even scoundrels such as these, would rob him of his honour.

'Then I bid you goodnight, gentlemen,' Bayard said.

The tired chevalier waited until the feuding warlords had stalked off to opposite ends of the palazzo. He waved his senior captains forward.

'I don't trust either of them, or Gueldres. I fear there may be mischief done this night,' he explained quietly. 'I want double the guards on Tarsi and this Englishman. If either of them makes any move towards Stroma's quarters, or to the cells, or anywhere else for that matter, I will be informed forthwith.'

'It shall be done, my Lord.'

Constantin Muhlberg had ridden three horses into the dust, galloping across the broad Lombard plain like a black fiend from hell. He had taken the main roads rather than the backwater tracks the legion would have followed, making good time riding through the long, dark night. Endless belts of rice and wheat stretched in all directions, and the few peasants he spotted quickly hid themselves away. He had finally caught up with the slow-moving warband thirty-five miles to the south-west of Aosta, over halfway to their secret destination: Villefranco.

Muhlberg cursed to think he would be the one to report the promising operation had been cancelled. God knew the unsuspecting Duke wouldn't have known what had hit him.

If they had been allowed to continue according to Gueldres' original plan, the legion would have arrived on the Duke's doorstep long before his hopelessly inefficient spy network could warn him of their approach. His tiny army would scatter the moment they heard the legion's abominable warcry, '*Hut, dich, baur ich komm!*', and poor old Lodovico would have been unceremoniously toppled from the chess table of European politics.

The vacuum would have been filled by their paymasters the French, whose ambitious king Francis would have extended his influence over the Maritime Alps and tightened his grip on the tottering House of Savoy.

It would have been what the mercenary chieftains called a Good War. Casualties would have been light and there would have been rich plunder for the troops lucky enough to be involved. War could sometimes be a neat, simple and relatively painless business — so long as your opponent hadn't gone to the trouble of hiring himself some landsknechts of his own, or worse, a pack of those generally-despised Swiss.

But Muhlberg's news would throw the entire, carefully-orchestrated scheme into ruin.

★

The lantern-jawed corporal barked the passwords and spurred past the alerted guards, riding the flagging stallion straight towards Savvi's black and gold battle tent. Savvi had come bounding out to see what the commotion was, grabbing Muhlberg's horse as his dusty understudy levered himself out of the saddle.

'Good Christ in irons, what is it now?' Savvi asked, alarmed by the corporal's panic-stricken arrival.

'Gueldres . . . got caught with the ring. The little shit's done in . . . he's been charged with the massacre . . .'

'Whoa lad, slow down! Gueldres is dead?' Savvi demanded, shaking the corporal by his long arm.

'Obolus is dead. Tarsi's off the hook and Gueldres is in prison. They know he ordered the attack on the abbey,' Muhlberg gasped.

Savvi closed his eyes in horror. By God, if Gueldres had been arrested the authorities wouldn't take long to work out the *Band Nere*'s involvement in the whole sorry affair.

'You slack-bladdered mollusc! What did you think you were doing, butchering a gang of limpwrist monks? I told you this would happen!'

'It was Obolus as told us,' Muhlberg protested. 'Seems he and the master had a falling out . . .'

'Falling out?'

'Briconet's charged him with conspiracy.'

'Shit!'

Gueldres was a tough customer, but he wouldn't stand up to prolonged torture at the hands of the Inquisition any better than the next man. The canny soldier tugged his red beard, pondering his options. They would have to drop this jaunt for sure. Get out of Italy, bloody quick. A dash for the coast or double-time to the nearest Alpine pass. Turn about and march all the way back to Mont Galliard? But if Gueldres started singing . . .

'Hang on a moment. You say Gueldres and Tarsi are in Aosta?'

'But Tarsi's been pardoned, something about the damned score. It seems Obolus took the wrong bit, or the choir tried to sing it upside down or some such ballocks.'

Savvi was nodding his head. 'And Bayard, Briconet, they're still in Aosta?' Muhlberg nodded. The locotenent grinned.

'So who's in charge at Mont Galliard?'

Muhlberg frowned, wiped the dust from his eyes.

'Last I heard, Tarsi's horse of a daughter, a few companies of arse-wipe powder monkeys and those grunt-fucker English.'

Savvi chuckled, wiped his beard.

'Who haven't been paid in a week or two, and wouldn't get a penny if their master Tarsi was to get the chop.'

'I just told you, they reckon Tarsi'll get away with it.'

'But the men he's left behind in Mont Galliard – they don't know that. We've still got a few chests of coin to pay this shower, we could ride up there and trick the buggers into handing it over.'

Muhlberg's sloped brow furrowed in concentration.

'What, and then use it as collateral to buy Gueldres' freedom?'

Savvi smirked.

'If they think he ordered the massacre at the abbey, he'll be in hell before we could get back to Mont Galliard. No my friend, I think it's time we reviewed our indentures.'

Muhlberg shook his head, completely bewildered. Savvi sighed.

'We leg it back up there, lure those fornicating Spanish out with the promise of a tun of gold, and move in for ourselves. You and me Muhlie, what d'you say?'

The corporal pondered the locotenent's suggestion.

'Leave Gueldres to stew in his own juice, you mean?'

Savvi shrugged.

'He wouldn't have given us a second thought, you know that. We can barricade ourselves in for the winter: by the time the snows melt everybody'll have forgotten all about it and we'll end up in sole control of the pass. You and I will share the road revenues, pay off Margaret and her bloody crew, and put our feet up for once.'

Muhlberg grinned.

'Seigneur Francesco Savvi, Knight of Savoy, and his locotenent, Constantin Muhlberg.'

'We've done his dirty work long enough. What d'you say?'

'How long do you think it'll take us to leg it back there?'

Angelica had fallen into a troubled sleep, her face concealed by an outflung arm, still wrapped up in swathes of bandages. Merron listened to her breathing, the soft snorts and mumbled sentences giving way to more restful snores. It must have been well past midnight before she had finally subsided. She extracted herself from the girl's loose embrace and sat up on the edge of the cot, her hands and feet tingling with cramps. She was tired and hungry, and the cold water she had gulped earlier had gone straight to her bladder. She took up the rushlight from the dresser and tiptoed to the door. She looked up and down the passage, noticed the inquisitive papal guard peer out at her from his candlelit alcove. The man was balancing a plate of bread and dried fruit on his mail-clad knee.

'*Pissoir?*' she asked. The guard grinned, displaying a mouthful of half-chewed bread. He jerked his thumb along the passage and said something in Italian Merron couldn't catch. She gathered up her skirts and made her way along the panelled corridor, glancing at the faded paintings and waxy tapestries. The water closet was on her right, a small, bare chamber looking over the palazzo gardens. She tugged the thick velvet curtain across the doorway and strode toward the stone throne. The floor was dressed marble and her bare feet were frozen. She lifted the velvet-padded lid, saw her rushlight reflected on the water, twenty feet below. The stream ran out of the back of the palace, losing itself in a maze of fishponds and vegetable gardens which formed a highly productive moat about the north walls. Merron lifted her skirts and squatted down.

The intruder detached himself from the shadowed alcove to her left, crossed the floor in a single bound and clamped his hand about her mouth before she had a chance to scream. Merron fought back, but the black-clad impostor was fiercely strong. He twisted her head savagely, silenced her in his iron-fisted grip. Merron was horribly aware she had wet herself in fright. She felt the hot liquid soak into her petticoats. The fiend was wearing a black scarf, pulled up about his mouth. She didn't recognise him.

'Keep still you silly bitch, or I'll throttle you here and stuff you down the boggard!' his English was heavily accented. Merron, terrified by his swift strength, couldn't tell whether he was French or Italian.

'Don't worry, I'm not here to hurt you. I have come with a message for your brother.' Merron's eyes bulged over his clasping fingers. He jerked her head away from his face, whispered in her ear.

'We would have gone straight to him, but Bayard's watching us all like hawks. That's why we thought of you, *mia cara*,' he crooned, kissing her softly on her taut cheek. Merron flinched as she felt his breath through the scarf. 'Now listen carefully.'

Beside the Church of St Orso, Aosta

'He'll be here,' Tarsi growled, peering down the passage after his absent captain. Stroma raised his chin suspiciously. Bayard frowned.

'I gave word nobody was to leave the palazzo,' he said.

Tarsi nodded.

'He has not left the grounds, my Lord. I think the food here has been so plentiful, so rich and varied, that it has quite turned his stomach,' he said archly.

Stroma simmered.

'If I'd had my way you'd have been given a bucket of slops from the . . .'

Bayard closed his eyes at their continual quarrelling, holding his hand up for silence.

'Here he is now,' Tarsi called, watching the captain stride out of the shadows, buckling his belt as he walked. He'd get to the bottom of his absence later, damn him.

'Captain Eldritch. Are you fit to accompany us, or would you prefer to remain in the palazzo?' Bayard inquired.

'Under guard,' Stroma added. Eldritch smiled shortly.

'I am afraid I must have over-indulged myself with the snails. We don't take our food with quite so much garlic back at home.' Bayard could well imagine. He remembered the campaign back in 1513, when they had found more English dead from the bloody flux than force of French arms. The fools had pigged themselves on all sorts of exotic foodstuffs, only to sicken and die on the march.

'Cardinal Runcini and Monsieur Briconet have proceeded to the church in their coach. You and Seigneur Tarsi will accompany us.'

'And what of our friend Gueldres?' Eldritch asked.

'Don't you worry about him. He'll be there, same as you,' Stroma snapped, impatient to get the musical ordeal over with. He was dreading the return to St Orso – another excruciating hour of sermons followed by a repeat performance of the dreadful anthem. His widely-reported sponsorship of the score had already made him a laughing stock in Aosta – any further humiliations would drag his name down for years to come.

He had at least managed to convince Briconet and Bayard that he had only been talked into presenting the piece against his better judgement. They seemed to have accepted his flimsy explanation – either that or they were too busy frying bigger fish to worry about his own insignificant role in the sorry performance.

'Scaralatchi and Gueldres have been escorted to the church, under guard,' Bayard reported, leading the way down the steps towards the main door. They ran a gauntlet of papal guards and fully-armed gendarmes. Their horses were stamping in the courtyard, steaming in the early morning chill. Eldritch took one last look at the elaborate façade of Stroma's palace and hoisted himself into the saddle. He hadn't been to church for months. His last confession had been taken in the chapel at Gateshead, shortly before they had embarked on the *Snow Pola* for the voyage down the coast.

It seemed to Eldritch a lifetime ago.

Stroma reined back, brought his horse alongside the immaculate chevalier's as they trotted down the Via Sant'Orso towards the gothic church. Bayard had dressed himself in his spotless surcoat and flowing crusader gown, his colours picked out in gold leaf on his breast and horse bard. He wore his sword at his side, and a squire rode at his shoulder bearing his proudly-snapping banner. Another score of his monastic brothers in arms rode just behind, their lances streaming with colourful pennants. Stroma had buckled on a small dagger and left his colours back at the palace. He didn't want to draw any raucous attention from the bad-tempered crowd, not in front of the knights. Tarsi and Eldritch – who had remained on parole until the outstanding charges were decided one way or the other – rode without arms a little way ahead. Where they could keep an eye on the buggers.

'I've made some inquiries about his unexplained absence. I'm told he spent half the night in the boggard, the other in his own sister's quarters,' Stroma reported, nodding at the tall Englishman's back.

'She has attended upon Mistress Tarsi since they left Mont Galliard. I am not surprised to hear they sought each other's company.'

Stroma shook his head.

'Thick as thieves, they are.'

'Captain Eldritch was instructed to remain within the precints of your palace. It appears he did so.'

Stroma bit his lip. The rogue was hardly likely to have risked his parole at this late stage, he thought sourly. His new master Tarsi was boundingly confident the requiem would prove their innocence beyond the last shadow of a doubt – why should his new captain rock the boat now?

'Aye, he did so all right. In his sister's bed, I warrant.'

Bayard sighed.

'Unless you have several independent eyewitness reports to that effect, I suggest you keep such theories to yourself.'

Stroma grunted.

'Look at them my Lord. They mock us. I have already listened to Scaralatchi's mass. It's not fit to whistle to sheep-dogs, let alone present before such distinguished guests as the cardinal and your own good self.'

'That remains to be seen,' Bayard said coldly, clicking his spurs against his horse's flank to accelerate away from the suspicious count.

★

'Where did you get to? They were looking high and low for you!' Tarsi snarled under his breath. Eldritch rode on, staring straight ahead.

'I went to see my sister. We haven't talked properly since we left your pass.'

'She was supposed to be watching Angelica! Couldn't you have talked in her chamber?'

'It was a private conversation. About the captain of arquebusiers, Isolani, if you must know. He died back at Mont Galliard.'

Tarsi frowned.

'I'm sorry to hear that.'

'He died saving her life. I had argued with her regarding his intentions. I thought they were dishonourable; it appears they were not,' Eldritch said coldly, turning his head to glare at the red-faced soldier. 'My sister is very precious to me.'

Tarsi nodded, exasperated by the enigmatic Englisman's frosty disposition.

'I can see that. But you were missed this morning.'

'I sent word I was ill. I am here now.'

The teeming crowds which had turned out with such enthusiasm to greet the cardinal the previous Sunday had remained indoors or gone about their usual business. The few traders and townsfolk who were abroad hardly gave the subdued procession a second look as it passed in a series of fits and starts down the Via Sant'Orso. Stroma hadn't bothered distributing any alms for the repeat performance. The whole sorry episode had already cost him a pretty penny, and he couldn't afford to waste any more money trying to whip up a welcome for the reputedly out-of-sorts cardinal.

Runcini wasn't the only one eager to complete his business and get out of there. Stroma himself planned to retire to his hunting lodge in the hills, the moment his ungrateful visitors had departed. Maybe in a month or two his fellow citizens would have forgotten all about his ill-advised entanglement with the arts.

The cold winds blowing down from the mountains had driven most Aostans away off the main road and into the noisome side streets. Hawkers plied their wares down the alleys and lanes, or took cover in the doorways of the quiet inns and stores.

Most of them would have missed the cardinal's hectic arrival. Runcini had retreated into the shadowy corners of his sedan, the leather window flaps firmly fastened. His toiling bearers sweated despite the bitter cold, lugging the obese cardinal along at an uncomfortable jog-trot. They had been forced to run on the spot at several narrow intersections, waiting for the vanguard of mitre-wearing bishops to negotiate diverse carts and wagons. The bloody tenement block which had come within an ace of collapsing the previous Sunday had been boarded over and shored up with rickety scaffolding while the town engineers decided whether to knock it down or try and buttress the leaning building.

Despite the awkward obstacles, Runcini's bearers completed the half-mile journey in ten minutes. Sunday's elaborate progress had taken three times as long.

The cardinal's second visit to St Orso might have attracted far fewer spectators, but Bayard had decided against reducing his escort. As well as the full complement of footsore papal troops, Bayard had laid on several hundred spearmen to guard the procession, and lined the approaches to the church with hundreds more well-wrapped crossbowmen. He had detailed his officers to take up positions overlooking the street, at the highest windows of the surrounding buildings and in the slim spire of St Orso itself.

Three score of his own gendarmes had been lucky enough to be drawn duties inside the warm church, standing shoulder to shoulder either side of the ornate nave. Bayard was leaving nothing to chance. Both Gueldres and Tarsi could be expected to call upon any number of spies and agents to engineer some mischievous intervention – should it become necessary to do so. He didn't imagine the truculent Stroma would be beyond some kind of demonstration on the Vicomte's behalf, especially if his old ally Gueldres was — as widely anticipated — convicted of the conspiracy he had so fiendishly attempted to blame on Tarsi. Briconet hadn't missed an opportunity of reminding the chevalier just how convincing that evidence had been.

'Even the agents of the Inquisition make mistakes, my dear Chevalier,' he had confessed, somewhat shamefaced by his abrupt change of heart. 'I think you would admit the *prima facie* evidence against Seigneur Tarsi did appear to be damning.'

'Damning, yes. Worthy of proper investigation, certainly. But I can only hope, my dear sir, that you have learnt a valuable lesson about jumping to conclusions, before the full facts have been taken into consideration. A prudent man might have taken Mistress Tarsi at her word, rather than subjected her to agonising tortures. I find it inconceivable she could have been capable of the crimes you forced her to acknowledge.'

Briconet had bowed his head — cursing Bayard's pious soul to the uttermost pit of hell. How dare this virgin swordsman lecture him on jurisprudence? What did he know of the real world, the world of men agents like Briconet had been called upon to regulate?

'A valuable lesson for us all,' he had mumbled through clenched teeth.

Bayard had snorted his agreement. As far as he was concerned, the only man to emerge from the sorry affair with any kind of a reputation intact was Eldritch.

An Englishman!

The cardinal ducked out of the sedan chair with all the grace of a back-street tax collector, lowering his fleshy head and hurrying up the steps of the church of St Orso as if the cold winds were piercing his very soul. The unruly gusts blew his scarlet hat off, the leather fronds hanging from the brim tangling his sparse grey hair. He held on to his headgear and disappeared under the great rusticated doorway. A flock of attendants closed about him as he strode down the vestibule towards the slowly filling nave.

The cardinal was in a filthy mood, not least through having to pander to Bayard's mystic flights of fancy. Runcini was an easy-going tyrant, and wasn't used to having courses of action mapped out for him by interfering Frenchmen. To add insult to injury, Bayard had taken up the cause of one of his most bitterly-detested rivals – Cesar Scaralatchi! How he detested that ape-faced cretin, that foul-mouthed, heretical drunkard. Scaralatchi had thumbed his nose at the cardinal in the past, stolen a heart which had rightly been his. He had soiled one of the finest choirboys Runcini had ever seen, robbed the elite Vatican choir of its very soul. Ambolini's gorgeous voice had brought tears to his eyes, reduced the most blood-drunk soldier to womanly weeping. Runcini had sneaked into the choir's quarters to eavesdrop on their rehearsals. He had peeked through spyholes at the perfectly-formed youth as he ran through the complex chants and responses, rounding on his little colleagues if they could not keep up. Scaralatchi had robbed him of that exquisite pleasure, filled that perfectly-profiled head with filth and nastiness. Fabrizio's classical, olive-skinned features had reminded him of the bust of the charioteer from Delphi. His boyish laugh had shimmered and tinkled down his spine, made his toes curl in his slippers. Scaralatchi had infected him with his own vile view of the world. A few weeks of his malignant influence and Fabrizio had been braying like a horse, snorting and coughing, farting and belching like some up-country bumpkin wriggling his hairy arse behind the Forum. He had turned milk and honey to maggots and offal, left his own mortuary-house tang on the boy's palate.

Runcini had been physically sick when he realised how Scaralatchi had ruined his little choirboy. But this Bayard had turned Scaralatchi's inevitable excommunication to his own advantage, demanding that the obese composer be given an opportunity to redeem his lost soul.

Scaralatchi, repentant? Runcini could have choked with laughter at that ridiculous prospect, and yet the stony-faced chevalier seemed to believe his unlikely claim, arguing that

410

the wretch had earned his right to a second chance – to be absolved of all his previous errors.

Bayard had strenuously supported Tarsi's defence, insisting that this new score, this *meisterwerk*, would prove Scaralatchi's repentance as well as its sponsor's innocence.

The damned chevalier had manoeuvred him into a corner. He could hardly deny the scoundrel the right to be readmitted to the Holy Church. Scaralatchi had been declared *toleratus*, after all. The door should never be closed if there was a possibility of rehabilitation. The rosy-complexioned cardinal sat down with a grunt, his vast belly squirting with sour juices. His bishops settled themselves on the benches about him, like sand martins finding a comfortable roost. He stared at the graphic altarpiece, the ghastly triptych painted by some lunatic German. The dreadful images suited his foul mood, playing on his mind while the soldiers Bayard had insisted should accompany him clattered and crashed down the aisle, taking their places in the packed pews. What was the damned fool expecting, an invasion of barbarians?

The choirboys who had cried with shame at their own doomed efforts the previous Sunday were determined to banish that foul memory, singing out as if their very lives were forfeit. Father Bembo took them through their usual programme, their plainsong filling the church with celestial waterfalls. The Latin phrases and soaring responses rang around the gothic church. The soothing litany calmed Runcini's nerves. He began to study the choirboys, their pale throats taut as they reached for the higher notes, hairless chins lowered as they struggled to find the rumbling bass voices.

Runcini didn't see Gueldres arrive, closely guarded by half a dozen gendarmes. The scowling warlord crossed himself and took his seat, pointedly refusing to look at the gawping nobles who had turned out in force to witness the final act of this utterly compelling trial – the sensational twist which would see the accuser become the accused.

Briconet and his nervously-staring clerk filed into the church and took their places behind Runcini. Briconet muttered a greeting which the bad-tempered cardinal acknowledged with an irritated flick of his wrist.

Bayard led the last party down the aisle. Just as he drew abreast of the murderously-glaring Vicomte, the immaculate knight collapsed on his face. Gueldres started, wondering for a moment if Eldritch had stabbed the bastard chevalier in the back. He levered himself out of his pew, craned his neck over the panels.

No such luck.

The pious Bayard had simply thrown himself on his face, abasing himself before the ghastly altar. He remained there for several moments, while Tarsi and Eldritch crossed themselves and looked awkward. Tarsi raised his chin in contempt as he caught the Vicomte's darting eye. Eldritch stared straight ahead.

The chevalier picked himself up and took his place in the front row, on the opposite side of the aisle from the cardinal. The church was filling up now, filling with curious people and sublime sounds one could almost touch. It seemed as if the twelfth-century church was humming to itself, the ancient brickwork breathing softly.

Runcini had refused to look around, concentrating all his bad-tempered attention on Bembo's wonderful choirboys. Scaralatchi waddled down the aisle, prodded by a tone-deaf escort of peasant spearmen. The greasy rogue hadn't shaved, his flashing eyes were ringed with fatigue. He sat down two rows back from the chevalier, his bored guards shuffling in beside him.

Runcini sensed his foul presence, peeked over his shoulder and caught his eye. He held his gaze for a moment and then looked away. The Bishop of Aosta glided towards the altar to begin the service.

Runcini noticed Father Bembo peer around, and wondered what had caught his eye. The cardinal looked over his shoulder once more, frowned in bewilderment. What nonsense was this? What lurid spectacle was Scaralatchi planning to inflict on his captive audience? The church came alive with gossip and whispers, a restless seething like a distantly-heard sea.

A second choir was making its way down the aisle, led by a nervous, curly-haired cupid with rosy cheeks. He wore a rather grubby gown, clearly borrowed from somebody several sizes bigger than him. Runcini watched the newcomers file past the front row and line up in the open nave at right angles to the dreadful triptych. They faced the St Orso choir as if they were about to perform some pagan dance, or perhaps take part in some form of archery contest. The buzz of whispers died down. Everybody was on the edge of their seats.

Two choirs? What madness was this? Father Bembo nodded at the newcomers. They turned their music over.

It was Scaralatchi's mad masterpiece. A glorious leap of inspired imagination.

He had got the idea back in Novara, listening to the intertwined songs of the mockingbirds. One of them, trapped by a steel noose in an olive tree, had sung its little heart out, challenging its rival to greater and greater efforts. Scaralatchi had been struck by the sudden thought, the obvious solution to his overelaborate creations. He had written choral pieces so spectacularly complex that one choir would never have been up to the task of singing them. It had taken him the best part of twenty-five years to come up with the answer.

To use two choirs, one set of voices weaving in and out of the other, the choruses and responses ringing back and forth like the mockingbirds' enchanting song.

Gueldres had no great love of choral music, but he saw Scaralatchi's device in a blink – anguished moments before the bewildered cardinal finally realised what Scaralatchi had done.

He had been destroyed.

Gueldres cringed at his own stupidity, to think he had trusted his worthless servants, allowed them to embark on such a harebrained scheme. That sawn-off freak Obolus hadn't stolen an unfinished score, he had only snatched the half of it! The St Orso choir had only been given one portion of the complete work; it was no wonder they had turned it into a cat's chorus. Their criminally-fanciful plans had been blown away like leaves in a thunderstorm, a daisy chain of vague assumptions which had unstitched itself the moment they had tried it on. It was too enormous, too terrible to contemplate.

The Vicomte couldn't help it. He chuckled, shaking his head in wonder at the appalling extent of his disastrous blunders. It was that or weep like some lovelorn maid, and he would be damned if he would give Tarsi and the others the pleasure of seeing him cower at the prospect of his imminent ruin.

Tarsi leaned forward and peered along the pews, watching the rival's dark features crease up in barely-controlled mirth. The score would surely seal his doom, and yet he sat there laughing! Tarsi bristled in outrage. The bastard ought to be tugging his own eyes out in fury by now! The Vicomte had cheated him of his triumph, sitting in his pew hooting and sobbing as the wonderful score soared about their heads. The superb verses bounded and rebounded about the nave, echoed through the stone bones of the church as if the power of song would lift it from its foundations, transport the trembling structure straight to heaven.

The choirs seemed to sense the excitement, relishing the ground-breaking innovation, the sheer majesty of their creation. The congregation's response boosted their confidence and the eager boys flung their whole hearts into the magical work. Their throats were stretched, their chests ached, their bellies creased with cramps as they sought and found powers they hadn't guessed they possessed. They countered each resonant verse with sudden fanfares of notes, tremendous climaxes with soaring descants, high Cs which seemed to pulse and shimmer like fireworks, lighting up the gorgeous frescoes which had been so lovingly painted about the walls and vaulted ceilings. The beautifully-sustained choruses seemed likely to shatter the stained glass windows with their brilliant intensity.

The audience was stunned into silence.

Not even the dullest spearman from the hills could have failed to have been moved by Scaralatchi's masterpiece. Aostan burghers wept with joy. Hard-hearted sergeants sat transfixed, mouths agape.

Bayard was ecstatic, his limbs tingling, brain reeling at the soaring beauty of this creation. He looked around at fat Scaralatchi – that venomous heap of trash meat – as if he could not quite believe him capable of creating such a masterpiece.

God truly moved in mysterious ways.

The choirs stopped singing, the glorious echo of their voices dissolving into the rarefied air. The mesmerised congregation leapt to their feet, clapping and cheering in exultation before they remembered they were in the house of God. Runcini was unaware of their dilemma. He clapped his fat pink hands in glee, beaming over his shoulder at the suddenly bashful audience. They joined in once again with renewed vigour, raising the roof in their excitement.

Nobody had ever heard such a stunning piece of music. The innovative use of the double choir would be a talking point for years, and they had been privileged to hear it first.

'Bravo, Bembo, bravo!' Runcini cried. The cardinal spotted Scaralatchi, squatting in his pew like some moustachioed bandit from the hills. He paused, hands raised in mid-air. It was almost inconceivable such a beast had given birth to such bewitching beauty! Runcini caught that black eye, strove against its owner's demented glare for long moments. He started clapping again, nodded briefly, and turned his head.

Tarsi was bursting with excitement, tears streaming down his weather-ravaged face.

He reacted to Runcini's tiny acknowledgement as if the cardinal had hung flags all over the church, proclaimed his innocence from the tallest tower! An almost imperceptible nod of his chins, and Runcini had simultaneously pardoned his old rival, acknowledged his flawed genius and released his master from the very real threat of an agonising execution.

'Saved! Thank the Lord for Scaralatchi!' Tarsi exclaimed, clapping his sullen protégé on the back.

Eldritch had been unusually subdued throughout the breathtaking performance. He hardly seemed to register the score's elemental magnificence, unaware of its significance to their defence.

Their possession of the authentic score turned all Gueldres' evidence on its head, rubbished his carefully counterfeited correspondence. Not even the fanatically forgiving Chevalier could overlook such calculated villainy. Tarsi elbowed the scowling captain in the ribs.

'What's the matter with you? Don't you realise we're off the hook?'

Eldritch shrugged, hardly bothering to listen to the excited Italian over the tremendous tumult in the church. He watched as Bayard walked forward and held a brief discussion with the cardinal. Runcini nodded, squeezing between the packed pews in his haste to personally congratulate the beaming choristers. He patted their heads and pinched cheeks, clapped the nervously grinning Bembo on the back as if he had written the bloody score himself.

In the meantime, Bayard had turned on his heel and strode back to Tarsi. He looked as sober-minded as ever, despite the uplifting effects of the superbly-snug mass.

'Seigneur Tarsi. The court will reconvene after luncheon, to formally dismiss the charges laid out against you and yours. But in the meantime, you are free to come and go as you please. I offer you my unreserved apologies that you have been put to this terrible ordeal.'

Tarsi sighed.

'I accept your apologies, my Lord Chevalier,' he said, 'and I thank you from the bottom of my heart for having the faith to believe my explanations. Without you to listen to our case, I fear we would have been food for the crows by now.'

Bayard accepted the compliment with a curt nod, and strode over towards Gueldres. The prisoner was slumped in his pew, all laughed out.

Tarsi caught his eye, allowed himself a wry smile of satisfaction. One of the guards prodded the surly Vicomte to his feet, and Bayard followed him down the aisle and out into the bright, wintry sunshine.

'He did a very good impression of taking the charges seriously, for somebody who was convinced of our innocence,' the Italian observed tartly. Eldritch remained as impassive as ever. Briconet swept along the aisle with all the dignity he could muster.

'Gentlemen. Allow me to be the first to congratulate you on your new-found freedom. I can only regret we all went through such pain, before we found God's truth, here in His own house,' he said piously.

Tarsi smiled dangerously.

'Some of us went through more pain than others, my dear Briconet. I can only hope my daughter found her ordeal as uplifting as you so obviously did.'

Briconet looked edgy, fearing for a moment Tarsi might strike him dead on the spot.

'As I told you on the causeway, Seigneur, I am empowered to seek out the truth by whatever means comes to hand.'

'By whatever pain comes to hand, in Angelica's case,' Tarsi croaked. Briconet swallowed.

'The evidence . . . at the time . . . pointed to her involvement. I would not have varied my approach one iota, if it had been Gueldres' daughter who had stood accused; even if it had been my own.'

Tarsi seemed to deflate inside his fur mantle, revolted to his core by the obsequious inquisitor.

'No, I don't suppose you would have. But one word of warning, my dear sir. I advise you to find another route home to France. Le Col Galliard is a dangerous place this time of year, what with rock falls, ice floes and so on. One could so easily break one's neck, if one wasn't very careful.'

Briconet took the hint. He nodded, smiled wanly and hurried on, his clerk clinging to his robe as if he feared being abandoned to the vengeful barbarian.

Tarsi glanced at his morose captain. Eldritch hadn't paid much attention to their ill-tempered debate.

'Am I missing something Eldritch? Is there something you wish to get off your chest?'

The Englishman frowned, shook his head.

'The trial. It's been a strain for us all,' he said limply.

'Well it's all over now. Time to look ahead. Look at Runcini there, pawing those children. He seems pleased as punch with his score. We have earned ourselves a valuable ally, my friend, for the struggles to come. What about you, what will you do now?'

Eldritch thought for a moment.

'That remains to be seen,' he said coldly.

Tarsi opened his mouth but decided against speaking his mind.

With Gueldres about to be convicted of heinous conspiracy, his contract of indentures with Eldritch and the warband would be null and void. Tarsi had thought about inviting the Englishman to remain at Mont Galliard, to incorporate his men into his own command. Maybe he had misread the captain's intentions all along?

These *Transmarini* were queer fish for sure.

'Let us go,' he said, leading the way down the aisle.

Beside the Via Sant'Anselmo, Aosta

The blizzard which struck the town that afternoon took the last of the leaves from the trees, rattled the bared branches along the deserted avenues. The white-clad outriders of winter had driven most Aostans indoors, and hastened the cardinal's departure preparations. Well-wrapped officers went to and fro in the snowy courtyard, supervising the loading of the huge, gaudily-painted wagons. Runcini's elaborate household was eager to leave. The rag-tag camp outside the walls had already been struck, several companies of militia sent on ahead to prepare and repair the road to Rome, to flush out the teeming bandits Runcini was convinced were about to descend on them. Tarsi watched the preparations from the balcony, enjoying the icy tang of the wind on his face. He had pulled on his trusty mantle to keep out the biting cold, taking in great lungfuls of air as if he was an indentured slave recently released from long years of stifling servitude. He could hardly wait to get back to Mont Galliard, but he wasn't leaving until he'd watched Gueldres hang.

The toiling bearers completed loading another wain, impatiently waving the driver off to join the waiting caravan on the far side of the courtyard. The wagon left deep ruts in the crisp snow. Spearmen picked their way across the drifts, heads bent against the lashing winds. The soldiers raised their heads just long enough to pity the frozen workmen busy about the scaffold on the far side of the courtyard.

The sinister shape was rising from the trampled snow, casting a shadow over the piled lumber and coiled hemp they had fetched out to complete the formidable platform.

Tarsi hugged himself, stamping his feet to boost his stalled circulation. He was in two minds about wandering over and lending the red-checked carpenters a hand. The artisans had been hired in Aosta. Some of them had been busy setting up the complex scaffolding around the leaning tenement block on the corner, but they had jumped at the chance to earn a few extra pennies in the rather less exposed courtyard of the Palazzo Salassi. They were trying to warm themselves by working harder, getting the wretched contract finished in double-quick time.

Everything about the execution had been rushed through, age-old custom and practice turned on its head by the orders from up top. Finish the job quickly, cut any corners you can. Runcini had packed his bags and was itching to leave. They said the Fat Salamander was pining for the luxurious warmth of the Vatican.

The workmen had taken the foreman at his word. They hacked and sawed and banged and hammered, the grim scaffold sprouting out of the snow like the deck of a ship-wrecked galleon rising from the deep. They laboured, they missed meal-breaks and gulped at hot soup and spiced wine. The scaffold was nearing completion.

Tarsi watched them, warmed by their work.

Gueldres would be carried up to the scaffold in a straw-filled cart, like the common criminal he was. If he had been able to bribe his jailers, he might have been allowed to wear a padded jerkin under his stained shirt. He needn't worry about catching a chill where he was going, but his frozen shivering might be taken for cowardice, and the punctilious Vicomte wouldn't want that.

He would pause on the step, maybe look up at the gallows while the drummers beat the tattoo, saluting his death. He would be shoved forward with a soft curse, and begin to climb the ladder. Having ascended the nail-studded platform, he would press another coin into the hooded executioner's gloved fist. A generous tip for doing a good, clean job.

And what a job, Tarsi thought, rubbing his hands beneath his mantle. Gueldres would be hung up by his neck and half choked to death. A moment or two before he had finished kicking they would cut the rogue down and split him up the middle with a great, crescent-shaped blade. His torso would be opened from groin to throat, two men standing either side of his chained body, getting a grip on his exposed ribs as if they were struggling to open the rusty jaws of some deadly mantrap. Next they would use their long, razor-edged blades to disembowel their victim, holding the slick, steaming coils above their heads while the desperate prisoner stared at them through a fine red mist of his own blood. His pulsing organs — trailing from the gaping cavity like ribbons at a fair — would then be burnt over a brazier before the swooning victim was finally torn in quarters, his limbs wrenched apart by the pitiless chains manacled about his wrists and ankles.

Tarsi licked his cracked lips, delighting in every gruesome detail of the punishment to come. He would stand down in the snowy courtyard and watch Gueldres' execution just as Gueldres would have watched his if things had gone amiss.

A platoon of pikemen hurried through the gate and disappeared towards the stables, their long spears frosted from their march. They were followed by a squad of Bayard's gendarmes, kicking up flurries of snow as they cantered up to the main gate.

'I won't watch. Not even after all he's done to us.'

Tarsi glanced down at his daughter, her face paler than the snow which lay an inch thick along the balcony rail.

'I wouldn't want you to. Execution is never a pretty spectacle, in Aosta or elsewhere.' He shivered a little, opened the shutters and shooed the girl back indoors, lifting his fur-clad arms about her frail frame. Tarsi propelled the girl back towards the roaring fire, closed the shutters and leaned back against the frame as if he could single-handedly defeat the whispers of winter.

Merron strode towards her sickly charge, tugging her back towards her seat by the fire, scolding her gently.

'The girl's right, Gelli, you must rest!'

'I've had plenty of rest! I want to see Fabrizio!'

Despite the misgivings of Bayard's surgeons, the chorister had not perished from his dreadful stomach wound. The knife had cut through bands of muscle but had miraculously missed his vital organs. The youth had been reduced to a stick-like shadow of his former self, but the fevers which had raged through his slender frame had abated, and the surprised surgeon had dared to predict a full recovery.

Angelica said it was a miracle. The youth was resting in his quarters along the passage, being fussed over by Sophia. Angelica was still too weak to care for her lover in person.

And a good job too, Tarsi thought sourly. Marrying her off to a superannuated choirboy wasn't the match he had set his heart on. He looked up, wondering for a moment if the English captain might make a better partner for the headstrong girl. He seemed stern enough to endure Angelica's frightful tantrums. Honest, well-educated and with reasonably good prospects from his chosen profession. From the little Tarsi had seen of him, Eldritch was a fine, thinking soldier. He could use him in the days to come, re-establishing his hold over the valley he had kept away from so long.

He had been vague about his family and origins, but it was clear the Eldritch clan had been minor gentry, rich merchants back in England. And who was Tarsi to pick and choose over a partner for his daughter? He had been born in a filthy sheepfold in the mountains. All the money his family counted had been earned the hard way, by fire and sword and long campaigns in foreign lands. Eldritch would make a good enough son-in-law, he thought.

The captain was stalking up and down by the door, completely unaware of Tarsi's wondering glance. He had seemed distracted for days now, unable to concentrate since their escapades at St Orso.

★

Runcini had been obscenely eager to finish his business in Aosta and get back to the pleasures of Rome. Perhaps the possibility of being snowbound in the cold northern plains hadn't appealed to his warm, wine-loving nature. Maybe the cardinal hadn't relished the thought of spending the winter in the company of that whining, avaricious serpent Stroma. He had gone about what was left of the complex case with unusual zeal, accelerating through the outstanding matters at a single sitting.

Clerks and lawyers who had counted on at least another month of fee-swelling legal wrangling found themselves summoned to a resumed hearing in which the rejuvenated cardinal summarised heaps of evidence in a few brisk sentences, swallowing the bewildered advocates whole in his haste to get away.

Gueldres' Florentine lawyer, Umo Di Borgese, rose to his feet and appealed for time to reformulate the Vicomte's defence – in the light of the recent suspicions which had unfortunately fallen on him. He was about to launch into a long legal argument when Runcini cut him short, breezily informing the lawyer he had been given ample time to prepare his case. The Vicomte's obnoxious attempts to incriminate his colleague Tarsi for the ghastly massacre at the Abbey d'Eleron had been established beyond reasonable doubt. The authenticity of Tarsi's score had demolished the Vicomte's case, and as far as he and his learned colleagues were concerned, there was little more to be said. Umo had opened and closed his mouth. Bayard hadn't even blinked as the cardinal announced that the court would proceed directly to sentencing.

Tarsi had watched Gueldres turn pale, his supernatural reserve wearing thin at last. He had clutched at Borgese's sleeve, hissed last-minute instructions while the baffled advocate tried to listen to Runcini's summary judgement.

That the accused, Abelard, Vicomte d'Toinueill, had conspired with others to kidnap the choir of the Abbey d'Eleron, killing the abbot and divers monks and soldiers in the process. Further, that he had conspired with others to incriminate Seigneur Alberto Tarsi for his own monstrous crimes, counterfeiting divers documents to support his dastardly accusations.

Runcini hadn't finished. Alberto Tarsi, Angelica Tarsi, James Eldritch and all members of their respective households were free to go with the court's humblest apologies for the hideous inconvenience. In a terse afterword, Runcini announced that the excommunicant Scaralatchi was hereby absolved of all previous errors, and was to be readmitted to the Holy Church. Stroma's bid to divert the road tolls from the Aosta valley into his own coffers was curtly refused.

All that remained was to see Gueldres hang.

The bell in the north tower was clanging eerily, the lonely echo rebounding across the snow-strewn courtyard. The sudden clatter of horses brought Eldritch to the window. He wiped himself a spyhole in the jewelled condensation and peered down into the yard.

'Bayard's back.'

Tarsi looked up from his seat beside the fire. He had thrown his arm about his sleeping daughter, delighting in the simple contact. He had made a note to spare more time for her in future. Away from the bloody battles and deadly intrigues he had subjected her to. By God, they had hardly had a moment to themselves since Angelica's unexpected arrival earlier that week.

The Englishman seemed unaccustomed to such wasteful lounging about. He hadn't stopped pacing the room, furiously intent on his own family speculations. His sister seemed to have been blessed with a somewhat warmer nature, charmingly pleased to wait on them hand and foot, practising her French and Italian pronunciations as she fussed over the obviously-devoted Angelica. She had a slim figure and a bright eye, and her ready wit quite tickled old Tarsi.

But it was as much as the surly captain could do to acknowledge his lively sibling's existence.

Angelica stirred at the sudden clanging. She had fallen asleep on her father's shoulder, with the attentive Merron dozing at her feet. The tall girl sat up, stretching like a cat in the ferocious heat.

'What is it?' she yawned.

Eldritch strode to the door, strapping on his sword and pulling his cloak from the settle. Tarsi manoeuvred himself free and hurried after the lean captain, wondering what the scowling *Transmarini* had a bee in his bonnet about now.

The two of them found the newly-arrived and comically red-faced chevalier in the main hall, issuing new instructions to the blinking guards. There seemed to be more of Bayard's people in the palazzo than Stroma's. They had heard the count had taken himself off to his own quarters, deeply dismayed by the court's perfunctory dismissal of his case and refusing to see anybody.

Bayard looked up as the discomfited Tarsi hurried down the hall, tugging his mantle about his shoulders against the winds blowing in the open doors.

'What is it? Where's the alarm?' the Italian asked, watching the chevalier's officers hurry about their new assignments. Boots clattered in the stone passage. Shouts echoed about the warren of rooms along the north wing.

'We've had word Gueldres' forces are on the move to the north. His Locotenent Savvi has the best part of a thousand men and they would appear to be heading in this direction,' Bayard reported laconically, his broad features set. Tarsi slapped his hand about his sword hilt in delight.

'Champion!' he cried. 'All this law-jaw's not for the likes of us. What say you, Bayard, will you join forces with us and march out to meet the bastard?'

The chevalier shook his head.

'The majority of the papal forces have already set off for the Vatican. I do not intend to seek a confrontation at this moment.'

Tarsi waved his fist in agitation.

'We don't need some half-arsed militia to meet that

425

scum! I've two hundred and fifty of my men at Mont Galliard, and Eldritch here has about the same. They can be here in under a day!'

Bayard picked at his eyebrow as if bewildered by the Italian's lust for battle.

'The Black Legion is on the road to the north of us. We would have to fight our way through to meet your reinforcements.'

'His landsknechts won't stand up to your gendarmes!' Tarsi insisted. He elbowed the thoughtful Englishman in the ribs.

'And what about you? At least a score of your bowmen escorted Angelica down from Mont Galliard. Then there are those Scots men you captured in the valley, Bayard. They've been freed now. More than enough to kick the shit out of those black-arsed bandits!' Bayard frowned.

'I have not come here for a battle, Seigneur. If Savvi is on his way, he can only be interested in releasing his master.'

Tarsi tensed.

'You don't mean to hand the swine over?' he asked, alarmed.

'Only over my dead body,' Bayard said coldly. 'Gueldres is to be executed at dawn. But I believe he might be safer in the Torre Bramafam, on the south wall.'

The formidable bastion was considerably smaller than the palazzo, but its round walls and squat design made it a far handier place to defend. Tarsi nodded.

'Well then. Your gendarmes can man the fortress; we'll defend the north wall and gate. If Savvi wants him he'll have to fight his way past us,' the Italian vowed, his blood up.

Bayard seemed unimpressed with his strategy.

'I do not trust Stroma. He has more men within the walls than we do. I would suggest we stay together, until Gueldres is dead.'

Tarsi nodded anxiously, rubbing the hairy knuckles of his right hand into his broad palm.

'Aye. Maybe you're right. Only a fool would divide his

forces. We'd best move them out now.'

'I have already given orders to that effect. They are bringing the prisoner up now.'

Francesco Savvi hadn't intended to cause such a stir in Aosta. The fiery-tempered commander was intent on getting his tired, hungry and bitterly cold legion to Mont Galliard as soon as possible. He had double-marched his grumbling troops towards the north-east, lashing the stragglers with a bull whip, urging the weary sergeants to greater efforts. They took no rest; they set no scouts. They loped like a black-clad wolf pack, retracing their somewhat gentler-paced route south.

They didn't see the well-wrapped stradiots, hidden in a wood above the road, but the alarmed scouts certainly saw them. They had galloped back to Aosta with their news, convinced the grim legion was marching in their direction. If they had waited an hour longer, they would have seen the famished band swing to the north, heading for the snow-capped Alpine passes rather than the old Roman town.

Francesco Savvi was in charge now. For all he cared, Gueldres could rot in hell. Where he belonged.

'Come on Muhlie, get those sacks moving! They'll have been warned it's all gone wrong, if we don't get there bloody quick!'

'You want to get there any quicker, you should have got us some bloody horses,' Muhlberg answered under his breath.

Beside the Via Sant' Anselmo,
Aosta

Tarsi had left Eldritch to supervise the evacuation of their household, ensuring that Angelica and his sister, the wounded Fabrizio and his attendants were safely packed away in the by now notorious black wagon. Scaralatchi had climbed up on the running board next to Eldritch's hulking sergeant at arms. He had borrowed a large battleaxe from Stroma's armoury, and looked ready to take on all comers. Sergeant Hobby had grimaced as the composer had made himself comfortable beside him, tugging his multicoloured coat about his bulk.

'Ye mind what yer about, with that great lunker,' Hobby had advised. Scaralatchi had grunted.

Eldritch had ordered Hacker, Elver and Teague into the back, to make sure the nervous passengers would be safe from over-familiar spectators. They squatted beside the back door, bows to hand and arrow bags placed in their laps in case of trouble. Eldritch had ordered the rest of his mounted bowmen, along with Kerr's particularly surly moss-troopers, to escort the giant wain.

The reivers had been captured in the valley after the abortive attack on Mont Galliard. They had been kept in close captivity ever since, gawped at by their Italian captors as if they had arrived from another world. The furious Scots had only been released once the charges against Tarsi and Eldritch had been officially dropped.

The bow-legged bandit's hot temper had not been improved by the fearful captivity, and he had treated his captain's arrogant orders with withering contempt.

'Glad to see ye've not lost your charm, being away so long,' he'd sneered. 'I have nae had the chance, to thank ye for all your efforts on our behalf,' the Scot called to his detested captain's back.

Eldritch paused.

'Clearly ye left no stone unturned, in your haste to see me and mine freed,' Kerr accused.

'Think nothing of it.' Kerr had strode after the long-legged Englishman, reached up to tap him on the shoulder.

'Ye did not even come down to see our case for yesen!' the Scot growled, his voice strangled with irritation.

'I'd heard Bayard was looking after you. We were in no better state ourselves, I assure you.'

'Och, I'll wager ye were a sight better looked after than us! You were dolled up fine and dandy in yon hoose, while me and mine were locked in the fockin' cellars like slaves, man!'

'I knew Bayard would treat the rank and file properly. I did no more for my men than I did for yours.'

'Aye, that I can believe,' Kerr complained. Eldritch waited a moment, nodded at the waiting wagon.

'The contract with Gueldres is null and void. Technically, we're all Howath's men again. But you've made a good chief scout, and you can keep your title if that's what you're worried about.'

'Oh really? I'll try and stop the tears of gratitude coursin' down ma cheeks! Ye mean we've got rid o'one waster for the auld bloat? Pardon me if I don't dance a wee jig!' Kerr had spluttered.

'You're out now Sandy, that's what matters. And you're under orders to Howath. When he's not here, you answer to me,' Eldritch said coldly. Kerr simmered with anger, looked up at the burly Italian squatting on his horse while his underlings argued.

Eldritch darted forward, grabbed the surly Scotsman by his scruff and adopted his fiercest border brogue.

'Ye ken throw as many fits as ye like, man, but if ye din't de as yer bid ye'll be pissin' when ye cannae whistle next to Geldray!' Eldritch snarled, depositing the furious gnome back in the snow. The Scot shook himself off, glowering with rage.

'One day, Eldritch!'

'Aye Sandy. Now get about your business! We're a long way from home, no more than bluddy bandits in their eyes. We'll either stick together as a company of men, properly contracted to one of their own, or we'll run around like headless pullets, and be hounded down like rats in a barn. D'y ken me now Sandy?'

The reiver chief tugged his plaid straight, clenched his dirty fists. He stomped off towards his son, waiting anxiously on a borrowed horse. He threw himself up into the saddle and squatted there, steaming with rage.

Eldritch walked back to his horse, swung himself up with careless grace. Tarsi raised his eyebrows.

'Your men cannot be said to love you,' he said, amused by the arrogant Englishman's discomfiture.

'He'll be fine, so long as we've a common threat. The moment we're in the clear, he and I'll have words.'

'I don't doubt,' Tarsi had sighed, waving the waiting column forward.

'Damn those snails. I told you they were off,' Eldritch complained, easing his hand under his doublet to massage his belly. They were riding down the main avenue towards the fortress, the hastily-assembled warband packed in behind them. The jangling caravan had made good time down the deserted street, the snow trampled hard beneath their feet.

The bewildered Aostans peeped out of their windows at the hurrying troops, their banners and pennants pursued by a wicked Alpine wind. Chunks of snow slid from the pitched rooftops and exploded about the head of some half-frozen spearman, causing instant hilarity among his comrades. Bayard's fanatical gendarmes looked almost invisible against the drifts, the occasional beard or waxed moustache the only clue to their existence against the virginal backdrops.

Gueldres had been dragged up from his cell in the palazzo, his cloak thrown about his shoulders. His arms had been bound behind his back. He was leaning forward, bouncing uncomfortably in the saddle. His features were creased with terror, his white teeth clenched. The chevalier himself rode at the back of the column with a rearguard of crossbowmen, watching for any movements in the snow-clogged streets behind them. He hadn't seen Stroma. The wiry count had apparently taken to his bed, refusing to have anything to do with his unwelcome guests. Runcini, alarmed at Bayard's grim intelligence, had already taken to his sedan, and would by now be safely ensconced in the rather more formidable bastion near the cathedral. They would be safe enough, once Gueldres had been executed.

Tarsi glanced at his lean captain, his long face contorted with pain.

'Are you sure your Scots friend's barbs haven't hit home?' he asked archly. Eldritch grimaced.

'I've not felt well for days.' Tarsi could well believe that. The Englishman had seemed deeply unsettled despite the favourable conclusion of the trial. Perhaps he wasn't the iron-bound warrior he imagined himself to be.

'Ah, it's no good. I'm going to have to get to a boggard,' Eldritch moaned.

'Here? Ye'd best tap someone up. We've a fair ride to this damned tower.' The procession had turned off the Via Sant'Anselmo into the Via Sant'Orso, heading for the re-mains of the Roman wall on the southern outskirts of the old town. Eldritch looked up at the familiar tenement block on the corner, nodded glumly.

'The alley'll do. I'm not fussy where I shite.'

Tarsi nodded, spurred his horse on as Eldritch peeled away, held his horse against a hovel wall as the massive Tarsi wagon rolled by.

Hobby peered down at him from the running board.

'Anything up?'

'I've got the trots. Damned rich food.'

'I've never tasted such muck. Why have they always got to spread everything in garlic? Makes your . . .' the wagon rolled by in a flurry of snow taking the grumbling sergeant with it. Hacker was peering out of the back like an armoured owl. Kerr raised his chin and looked the other way as he led his reivers after the great wain.

Eldritch dismounted, walked the horse towards the alley. The tenement next door was festooned with planking, hung with ropes. The bloody hovel where Gueldres had stabbed Tarsi's spying dwarf. Eldritch glanced up at the unlikely structure. Flimsy poles supported a cat's cradle of knotted hemp, balanced narrow walkways girdled the decrepit structure. He tied the horse off to a beam and ducked under the overhanging planks, fiddling with his belt.

Gueldres gritted his teeth, his famished limbs aching as he tried to brace himself more comfortably in the saddle. He raised his head, ears raw with cold, his long nose running. The vanguard of the perilously-extended column had already turned down the Via Sant'Orso, the broad avenue narrowing about the leaning tenement where his grandiose schemes had gone so disastrously awry. The damned hovel was laced with ropes and wires. Ratlines wound about a shipwrecked galleon.

The flimsy scaffolding hung out over the street. Piles of rotten timber and mouldy masonry dug from the innards of the ruin had narrowed the highway even further.

Tarsi's black wagon negotiated the bottleneck, a squad of riders packing in behind the slow-moving vehicle. They wore rich green and rust-coloured blankets; their hair was as wild and red as the mountain fox. Eldritch's stinking Scotsmen, freed from their dreary prison. Gueldres tensed, worked his wrists against the leather bands. His horse was being led by a young knight, his innocent face blue with cold. His hands were trembling in his lap.

They approached the looming tenement, the gendarmes

in front reducing their front, riding two by two to get past the obstacle. They rode past the alley. Gueldres turned his head, spotted a cloaked rider waiting in the lane.

An alert sentinel ensuring the Aostan peasants who eked out a living in the filthy side street kept their distance as the great Bayard retreated into the fortress, he presumed. Wrongly.

The white-robed guard rubbed his hands, took a better grip on his red reins.

A horse whinnied just behind them. The knight glanced over his shoulder at the sudden commotion. The horse leapt out of the alley, its cloaked rider holding on grimly as the powerful stallion reared up on its hind legs. The gendarmes cursed as the beast bucked and reared into their prancing mounts, forcing two of the knights aside.

'Get a grip on him!'

'Hang on!'

'Look out!'

The scaffolding yawned sideways, as if pulled by an invisible string. The whole sorry structure seemed to hang in space for a moment before collapsing in a series of bangs and snaps. A portion of the newly-buttressed wall came away in a shower of loose bricks. The gendarmes looked aghast, covered their heads. The rogue rider ducked down over his horse's mane, dodging the sudden clatter, still trying to control his furiously-rearing mount.

Gueldres kicked out with all his might, his boot catching the startled guard's horse just under the ear. The alarmed beast lost its footing on the treacherously-packed snow, the young knight sprawling forward with a cry of alarm. The Vicomte squeezed his thighs about his horse's belly, leaned to his left. The frightened animal leapt in front of its staggering neighbour, dragging the shouting gendarme clean out of the saddle. The leather leading rein whipped free. Gueldres ducked his head under a swinging plank and urged the horse to its left. He hung on grimly as the horse found its footing, breasted a snowdrift and clattered along the alley.

433

The riders in front were milling uselessly, compressed by the falling scaffolding towards the far side of the road. One gendarme was lying in the snow, picking himself up with a curse.

The rogue rider bent down as his frantic stallion leapt over the prostrate knight and burst through the snowdrift after the fleeing Vicomte.

'After him!' the rider cried. The puzzled gendarmes mastered their horses, turning them in snorting circles in the sudden snowstorm. The wrecked scaffolding had brought down a ton of loose snow from the roof, the icy crystals dancing in the rarefield air.

'*Attendez!*' one of the sergeants bawled. The tightly-packed knights were forced forward, some of them being taken beyond the alley by the sheer force of those coming up from the cross-road behind them. Bayard was stuck in the middle of the press, hardly able to move his legs in the logjam of shouting gendarmes. The toppled scaffolding had blocked off one alley, and spewed planks and poles into the street. A fearsome cavalry trap which snarled half the column in a moment.

'Let me through! Get after him you dolts!' Bayard yelled, yanking off his gauntlets to rain blows on his confused knights.

'Don't let Gueldres get away!'

The litter-strewn alley came to a dead end just as Gueldres knew it would. Snow had drifted into the narrow brick canyon, formed a pillow against the dirty masonry which divided the side street from the wastelands beyond. Gueldres clamped his thighs and brought the frightened horse to a halt. He was panting as hard as the steaming horse, swivelling in the saddle to look over his shoulder.

Eldritch galloped down the alley after him, his dark cloak billowing out behind him. The Englishman tugged his reins, bringing the skidding horse to a halt. He was out of the saddle before the horse had stopped moving, reaching up to grab the panting Vicomte by his bunched cloak.

Eldritch heaved the rogue from the saddle, slammed the lighter man up against the wall of the hovel.

'I got your damned message, you scheming turd! You'd best sing out where she is, or by Christ I'll let those bastards cut you down!' he snarled, spittle flying from his blue lips.

'Over the wall Eldritch, get me over the wall and I'll tell you, I swear!'

'Now, you poxed whoreson!'

'Over the wall, you prick!' Gueldres snarled back. 'Faustilio's cut the bricks out, look. We can climb!'

Eldritch glanced at the sheer wall. It was ten feet high, built between the closely-packed tenements to divide the streets from the littered ground beyond. Gueldres knew the broken scrub fell away towards a broad ditch, the chattering course of a stream, a shallow tributary of the River Buthier. Eldritch heard the angry trumpeting behind them, knew they would have only precious seconds left.

'Tell me now!'

'Kill me now! I'll tell you all you want to know, over the wall!'

Gueldres had heard of Lillith Eldritch long before he had ever known of her brother's scowling existence. The raven-maned beauty had landed at Marseille a few years before, on the arm of some drivelling idiot of a sea captain. But the ambitious whore had soon bored of her shambling beau. She had set her sights considerably higher than some mean townhouse on the bustling, thief-ridden waterfront.

She had happened to meet a swarthy, meticulously-appointed nobleman at − ironically enough − a cockfight. The long-nosed dandy had an intelligent face, a caustic wit and a small fortune in winnings. He was Claude, Duc du Milhaud. The old Duc Gueldres' sister's son. None other than the Vicomte's crafty cousin.

In truth, Gueldres had not seen the notorious waster for years, but his dalliance with the English beauty was well known throughout their widely-dispersed family.

'She's in Marseille.'

'So you said! Where?'

A crossbow bolt clattered down the brickwork, skittered into the snow at their feet. A squad of soldiers had already forced their way through the wrecked scaffolding, opened a way for their cursing brothers at arms.

'Over the wall!' Gueldres choked. Eldritch cursed, let him down. He wrenched him around and slashed his bonds with his knife. Gueldres worked his bruised wrists. The crossbowmen were running down the alley after them. One fired as he came, the wicked bolt hitting Eldritch's horse. It whinnied in pain, its rearing hooves almost braining the cowering fugitives. Gueldres barged past the panting captain and ran his hands over the wall.

Umo de Borgese had been well worth his exorbitant fee. As well as representing him to the best of his ability before that damned court, Borgese had placed his own efficient assistants at Gueldres' disposal.

Faustilio, his Portuguese bodyguard, had planned the majority of the escape. But Faustilio wouldn't have been able to get him away from the fanatical clutches of Bayard's gendarmes.

Gueldres had been forced to rely on Eldritch for that, using his knowledge of the rogue's cock-hungry sister as bait. Faustilio had carried his message, managing to corner Eldritch's charming younger sister on the boggard back at Stroma's palace. Evidently Merron had succeeded in persuading her brother to go along with Gueldres' offer. Lend a hand in his escape in return for the whereabouts of the long-lost Lillith.

Faustilio had scoured the streets, searching out the best escape route. He had loosened the bricks in the dead-end wall, turned the insurmountable obstacle into a handy barricade.

Gueldres went up the wall like a monkey, clawing unseen handholds in the rough surface. Eldritch looked around, horrified to see so many crossbowmen hurrying after them. Bolts clattered against the bricks and scored the old mortar, but the terrified horses were prancing and rearing, spoiling their aim. Eldritch held his breath and scrambled up the brickwork, throwing his long leg over the wall as another brace of bolts whistled overhead. He leapt down into the snowy drift next to the frantic Vicomte. Gueldres was up and running in a moment, his cloak flapping. Eldritch prised himself to his feet, spat out a mouthful of snow and loped after him. The shouts on the far side of the wall diminished as they sprinted over the ugly wasteland, slid down the ditch on their backsides. They splashed into the half-frozen stream, the rocks and rubbish which littered its course capped with perfect mushrooms of snow. Eldritch caught the Vicomte by his shoulder, dragged him back.

'Where is she?'

'She's a courtesan, she lives . . .' Eldritch's furious back-hander sent Gueldres spinning. He lost his balance and sat down in the stream, the freezing water saturating his clothing.

'God damn you, she's no more than a common whore! She left her sailor friend the moment they stepped ashore!'

Eldritch felt the bitter truth of it slide into his guts like a red hot poker. Left her sailor friend . . . it sounded all too familiar for his wild-willed sister.

'Where?' Gueldres got to his feet, his cloak weighed down with water.

'We've got a while to run yet. We're not safe.'

'Where?'

'We follow the stream, right back to the palazzo. There are fishponds and garden plots on the north wall. Faustilio will be waiting with fresh horses. When you get me to him, I'll tell you the rest.'

'Tell me now!'

'You'll cut me down the moment I open my mouth!'

'And you'll ride off without a word!'

'You'll have to trust me, my friend!'

'God damn you!'

The fugitives scrambled and fell, splashed and sprinted

down the streambed. The little river was swallowed up by a great Roman culvert, which channelled the flow back towards the rearing hovels on the northern side of the town. The tunnel was lined with algae and running with rats. Gueldres went ahead, bent double. The stench was appalling. The tunnel was running with foul water. The chill gnawed at their bones.

They emerged in another stretch of wasteground, outcrops of turf dotting the stinking slurry field. They waded up the bank, hauled themselves up into a tangle of tree roots. An old, abandoned olive grove crowned the miserable bluffs. They loped between the gnarled trunks, leapt ancient and long-dry irrigation channels, choked with snow now. A bank of tall reeds hid them from the walls of the palazzo. There was no sign of any pursuit. Eldritch cleaved a way through the thick reeds, hauling the panting Vicomte along with him. They crossed a path and hid in the undergrowth, catching their breath. They could see the walls of Stroma's palace to their right, the bulkily-coated guards wandering about the towers. Stroma's banner hung limply on its pole. The ground about the north tower was covered in snow, but it still squelched underfoot. Stroma's predecessors had dug a broad moat, and supplemented the watery defences with an acre and more of neatly-dug fishponds.

Gueldres pointed. The path led around the pond to a tangle of old huts, where the hardworking Aostan peasants kept their gardening tools. The fertile land about the ponds had been pressed into service as allotments. Rice, corn, cabbage and other staples grew well in the wet ground. The fields had been abandoned for the winter, twisted canes and bolted crops disfiguring the landscape like the skeletal remains of a ghostly army.

'There are the sheds. Faustilio will be there,' Gueldres hissed. He rose, hurried along the snowy track towards the huts. They were half-smothered in brambles and besieged by nettles. Eldritch tensed, watched a plume of vapour rise from the outbuildings and disperse into the cold air.

A cloaked figure emerged from the nearest shed, sword drawn. Eldritch didn't recognise him, but he looked a well-balanced, handy fighter. The rogue's dark features reminded him of the pirates he had fought in the wilder days of his youth.

'It's all right. It's Faustilio.'

'All right for you!' Eldritch suddenly threw his arm about Geuldres' neck. He held his blade against the nobleman's taut throat.

'I told you he'd be here!' Gueldres gasped.

'Tell him to drop that cleaver!'

'Do it!'

Faustilio shrugged, laid his sword against the shed.

'This is it, my friend. Faustilio has brought horses.'

'How many?'

'Two. I didn't imagine you'd be coming with us.'

'I've been chasing you. If you give me precise details of my sister's whereabouts, I'll say you overpowered me and got away. If you do not, I cut your throat, stick your friend here, and claim the reward for catching you.'

Gueldres tensed. Faustilio inched towards his sword.

'She's with a cousin of mine. The Duc du Milhaud. Believe me Eldritch. I'm no happier than you are, but they are two of a kind, as you say.'

'The Duke du Milhaud?'

'He has a castle on the outskirts of the city, some minor estates in Flanders. He's not a favourite of the family,' Gueldres explained patiently.

'How do I know you haven't just made that up?'

'I've never seen your sister myself. But I have heard she has dark hair and black eyes. All reports I have heard particularly mention her eyes. Like Merron's, always darting about, eh? She is taller than your youngest sister though, perhaps, a little more buxom?'

It was Eldritch's turn to tense. The secondhand description was too accurate to be mere hearsay, the product of desperate invention.

'I'll find him,' he breathed.

'Good. He owes me money. You can clip off your commission for collecting it.' Eldritch pushed the chuckling wretch away, but kept his blade nocked against the rogue's throat. Gueldres glanced sideways at the panting captain.

'Is that it? You'll let me go, with Faustilio here?'

'Not before you make your escape a little more convincing.'

'What do you mean?'

'I didn't let you go without a fight. Your ape jumped out behind me.'

'You want Faustilio to knock you out?' Gueldres exclaimed.

'Don't imagine you'll brain me here and ride off into the sunset. I told Merron exactly what I planned. If they find me here with a dagger in my back, she'll tell Tarsi all. How you tricked me out here with tales of my sister, turned my head to treachery. He knows what I think of her: he'll believe her. Tarsi's got a soft spot for her.'

'I can well believe it,' Gueldres replied, standing still as Eldritch menaced him with the blade.

'If anything were to happen to me, she wouldn't rest until you were tracked down.'

'We're wasting time Eldritch. What do you want me to do, blacken your eye?'

'We must convince Tarsi you left me for dead.'

'A stomach wound?' the Vicomte asked ghoulishly.

'A cut to the face will do. Here.'

Eldritch held out his own dagger, keeping his sword against the rogue's throat. This would be the trickiest moment of the entire escape, but he could think of no other way of convincing the suspicious Tarsi he had tried his best to apprehend his enemy. The confusion back in the alley could be easily explained. The fallen scaffolding an act of God, the bewildered gendarmes might have misinterpreted what they had seen in the swirling snowfall. He was convinced he'd get away with his bizarre deception.

Gueldres took the dagger, weighed it in his palm.

'Why not let us ride off, and then slash yourself?'

'Tarsi's seen enough knife wounds. Any fool can tell which way a blow's come, if it was self-inflicted.'

'I hadn't realised quite how scientific you could be, my friend.'

'You can stow that "friend" stuff Gueldres. As far as I'm concerned you're just another piece of French shit. Now raise the point, put it below my left ear. If you try and kill me, I'll slit your throat and we'll die together.'

Gueldres smiled, his eyes glistening with fiendish anticipation.

'You've thought this out very carefully. What if I were to jump first, cut your throat before you could move?'

'You won't risk it. Not with a blade notched at your windpipe. One jerk,' Eldritch pressed the blade deeper, cutting into Gueldres' neck releasing a trickle of blood, 'and you'd be choking on your own lifeblood.'

'Well, you've convinced me,' Gueldres said briskly. He raised the knife slowly, held it below the Englishman's ear as instructed. They held their breath, steaming statues locked in a deadly embrace. Gueldres raked the dagger down Eldritch's face, opening his cheek like a ripe peach. The steaming blood splashed on the trampled snow. Eldritch felt the pain as a dull ache in his frozen face. He could feel the blood soaking his shirt collar. Gueldres held the knife away.

'Step back. Slowly.' Gueldres did so, weighing the knife in his palm. The blade gleamed.

Eldritch took a step backwards, raised his fingers to his face.

'A scar to remember me by,' Gueldres mused. 'As I will remember you, my friend.' He backed off towards the Portuguese bodyguard, who had by now retrieved his sword.

'Another time, Gueldres.'

'Give my regards to your sisters. Both of them.'

Faustilio led a pair of large-boned bays out of the woodshed. The animals snorted in the cold air.

A trumpet was blowing somewhere in the distance. Faustilio covered Gueldres while the weary Vicomte mounted his horse. Eldritch backed away. The riders spurred off in a flurry of snow and earth, left Eldritch standing forlorn by the broken-down sheds. Eldritch examined his fingers, slick with his own blood.

The bell in the north tower of the palazzo clanged mournfully. He looked up over the stiffly-ranked reeds, saw the stick figures clustered on the walls.

From that distance, they wouldn't have been able to tell what had passed between him and the fugitive Vicomte.

He watched the riders disappear over the wasteland, presumably heading for some prearranged rendezvous. An open gate, a carelessly-maintained stretch of wall which might be pulled down.

Eldritch trudged back along the track, anxiously fingering his wound. He paused, knelt down by one of the ponds, and stared at his reflection. Christ Jesus, the rogue had sliced his cheek right open!

Eldritch gazed at his own frightened eyes for a long time.

And that was how Tarsi found him, long moments later.